In the shadow of
Lady Jane

Edward Charles has been a university lecturer, a management consultant and a City and international businessman. He lives in Devon, where he writes, paints and tends his vineyards.

Also by Edward Charles in the Richard Stocker series

DAUGHTERS OF THE DOGE

EDWARD CHARLES

In the shadow of Lady Jane

A NOVEL OF TUDOR ENGLAND

MACMILLAN NEW WRITING

First published 2006 by Macmillan New Writing

First published in paperback by Pan 2007
an imprint of Macmillan Publishers Ltd
Pan Macmillan, 20 New Wharf Road, London N1 9RR
Associated companies throughout the world
www.panmacmillan.com

ISBN 978-0-330-45189-5

9 8 7 6 5 4

A CIP catalogue record for this book is available from
the British Library.

Typeset by Heronwood Press
Printed and bound by Mackays of Chatham plc, Chatham, Kent

Visit **www.panmacmillan.com** to read more about all our books and to buy them.
You will also find features, author interviews and news of any author events, and you
can sign up for e-newsletters so that you're always first to hear about our new releases.

This book is dedicated to Sian and Anna,
who are steadily building the future,
whilst I am fossicking around in the past

❧ CHAPTER 1 ❧

10th April 1551 – Shute House, Devon

Looking back, it was probably the most important day of my life, the day which would change everything, but at the time, soaked to the skin and shivering as I was, it didn't feel like it.

It had started so well. Everyone in Shute House and right across the estate was up early and looking forward to getting a glimpse of the Lord of the Manor, Lord Henry Grey, his fearsome wife Lady Frances, and his three daughters, Lady Jane, Lady Catherine, and Lady Mary.

Like everyone else, I had dressed in my best clothes and was in my allotted place in the Great Hall an hour before the party was expected to arrive. Then, at the last minute, came word that the cattle had broken loose and were in the yard – right where the Grey family were due to make their arrival. In a minute, the servants were panicking and, as Under-Steward, it fell to me to correct the situation – and immediately.

We soon had the cattle driven out from the yard and back to the fields where they belonged, but as we walked back toward the house, the heavens opened and by the time we got there, running as fast as we could, we were all soaked. There was no time to change clothes and in any event, as I was already wearing my best clothes, I had nothing suitable to change into, so the only thing to do was sit beside the huge fire in the kitchen and hope I dried out before the Grey family arrived.

It was not to be.

For the last three weeks, since we had heard that the Lord of the Manor was coming to visit his estate, there had been talk of nothing else, and considerable apprehension, for a visit by the Lord signalled change, and in these difficult times most of us in the valley assumed this would be change for the worse. Life here in Devon was quieter than it was said to be up-country, and that was how most of my friends and neighbours liked it. The death of King Henry VIII and his succession by the boy king Edward had thrown much of the country into turmoil and now the whole community feared that the arrival of the Lord from his distant lands would shatter the peace of our ordered, and by most people's standards, comfortable existence.

But I took a different view. I saw the visit as a challenge and as an opportunity to better myself, and that was why it was so disappointing to be here, wet, in the kitchen, instead of being prepared and in the entrance hall, ready to make a good impression.

Suddenly, there was a tense flurry of activity amongst the cooks and servants, and the party swept into the room. John Deyman (the steward and my immediate master) came last, speaking rapidly as he entered, his nervousness clear to everybody.

As expected, Lord Henry and Lady Frances, known more formally by their titles of Marquess and Marchioness of Dorset, listened attentively, eyes alert, missing nothing. This was their first visit to Shute, their only estate in Devon. As it was a long and difficult journey from their main home of Bradgate Park in Leicestershire, we guessed it would be some time before they visited again.

"And this, my Lord, is said to be the largest fireplace in England; larger even than the Great Fireplace at Hampton Court."

The whole family stood and admired the twenty-two-foot-wide fireplace. Then, slowly, one by one, their eyes moved to the corner of the inglenook and looked at me. I tried not to cower in the corner but put a brave face on it, and looked back at them, trying to appear more confident than I felt.

2

It was the three sisters who attracted my attention the most. They could not have been more varied in appearance. The tallest, and by far the prettiest, was as handsome a girl as I had ever seen. She looked older than her reported fourteen years, with a straight back, red-gold hair falling down a long neck to shapely shoulders, and the healthy glow of someone who has lived her life comfortably, and in the fresh air of the country. She was richly dressed, with a tight, embroidered stomacher making it impossible to be unaware of her developing figure. There was no doubt; this girl was, indeed, beautiful by anyone's standards.

She seemed disinterested in the formal proceedings, and, as John Deyman continued his inventory, her eyes remained on me, appearing to take in every aspect of my discomfort. She smiled, her long eyelashes lifting slowly to reveal soft hazel eyes. They reminded me of the golden brown cattle I had seen once on a fishing trip to the island of Jersey, but there was nothing of the cow about her look. Her gaze was long, confident, and penetrating, as if she were examining a peach before deciding whether to eat it or not. I was that peach, and it made me feel disturbed, yet strangely excited. I thought about standing up, but her eyes moved on; it appeared I had been dismissed. So that was Lady Jane Grey. She was beautiful, fascinating, but also, in a strange way, disconcerting; in short, quite a challenge altogether.

Relieved that the family's eyes had moved on, I took the opportunity to look at the other two sisters. The next was smaller, more petite and reserved, with red hair, very pale skin and freckles on her nose and cheeks. This must be Lady Catherine, I thought. She looked younger than Lady Jane, but perhaps not the three years younger that we had been told. Her manner was quite different from that of her sister; her gown was plain black velvet with little decoration, whilst her face, almond-shaped with high cheekbones, had a nervous, haunted look, totally lacking the vivacious self-confidence of her elder sister. As John Deyman continued his nervous description, her large brown eyes swept the room quickly, and before I could avert my gaze, she, too, caught my eye and held it.

3

Once more I felt uncomfortable; for this sister seemed to be looking at me disdainfully, as if I were a troublesome irritant in her life, but when I held her glance in return, and looked directly at her, she quickly looked away. Somehow I took an immediate dislike to her; she looked cold, withdrawn and self-consciously pious; much less fun than her sister. I could see that she carried a leather-bound book and seemed to hold it before her, almost as a shield, as, once again, she listened dutifully to John Deyman, who, regaining his confidence, continued to describe the items on his inventory.

"The kitchens are well equipped my Lord, and can comfortably provide a feast for over a hundred guests if called upon to do so. In your grandfather's day, the First Marquess and Lady Cicely would entertain grandly here, especially at Christmas and after the harvest. On Saturday you will see the proof of the pudding, for we have, as you instructed me in your message, invited the leading members of the community here to dinner."

Lord Henry Grey, the present Marquess of Dorset, nodded his understanding. He did not look very excited at the prospect; indeed it did not look as if he had any intention of entertaining regularly here, and why should he? Bradgate Park was known to be one of the great Park estates of middle England and on a far grander scale than Shute. Still, it was nice that during his stay here he intended to meet some of the local people and to offer them his hospitality.

Safe now from their attention, I looked round for the third sister. This must be Mary. She was different again. Whereas her older sisters were already beautiful young women, each in their different ways, she was not only much younger, but diminutive and deformed. It was hard to tell her age. It was said she was six, but she looked smaller than that, dwarf-like, with a hunched back and a pronounced limp. At the same time, her face was older than a child's – already more like an adult, with no softness and no innocence visible at all.

Quietly, I watched her standing in the corner, the firelight flickering across her face, and, for the third time, I felt uncomfortable. She wasn't like a normal child; there was something sinister in her manner as she looked round the room with black eyes. They reminded me of a raven, hopping round the yard, beady eyes missing nothing, as she surveyed the room from beneath heavy, lowered brows. I wondered what had caused her deformity; if she had been ill, or had been injured earlier in life. If so, she must have recovered well, for she did not appear to be in pain, and clearly had not missed a single thing which had taken place since the party had entered the room, including her older sister's look in my direction.

"And who is the handsome young man steaming himself dry in our kitchen? It seems that supreme fireplaces breed stalwart occupants."

I was shaken from my daydreaming by the booming voice of Lady Frances Grey. Confused, I looked up to see that John Deyman had stepped back from his address, and all eyes were now on me.

There was no escape. This was the moment I had planned for; my opportunity to make a good impression on his Lordship and his family and perhaps better myself in the process. Again, I thought of standing, but something told me not to, and instead I cleared my throat and leaned forward beside the fire.

"I am Richard Stocker my Lady, son of John Stocker of Shute. My father is a free-holding gentleman, and farms over near Northleigh." I nodded toward the window, feeling more confident now that I had started talking.

"My elder brother, John, lives and farms up the Umborne valley, toward Wilmington. Since John will also inherit my father's farm in due course, I came here three years ago, looking for a position, and have been in charge of the Park and farms for the last two years. Last year I was appointed Under-Steward."

Lady Frances's look was so penetrating that I ran out of words and paused, looking at her, waiting for her lead to continue.

"Well Under-Steward, tell me – why are you sitting there, soaking wet?"

By her manner, she might have been talking to her spaniel. I looked across to John Deyman, who shook his head imperceptibly and gave a small frown. It was clear he did not want me to admit to the mess with the cattle.

I said the first thing I could think of. "A storm came across the valley as I was coming back from the horses my Lady." Without thinking, I brushed the raindrops from my sleeve into the fire, which hissed its response. "It's only a bit of damp. I'll soon dry here by the fire if it please you my Lady"

Lady Frances grunted, moving closer to me, so close I could smell her perfume.

"Young man – can you read?"

This was the opportunity I had been waiting for.

"Yes my Lady, and write, both in English and in Latin. Colyton has a very good parish school and my mother made me attend from a young age."

She tipped her head, to catch the reflected firelight and examined me like a good judge of horseflesh, about to buy a horse. She was an imposing woman, nearly as tall as me – little short of my six feet in height, large-framed and confident, with a voice to match. Once more she leaned close, and again I could smell the heavy scent of her perfume. Looking deep into my eyes, as if to convey an inner message, she grabbed my leg, high on the thigh, then squeezed it hard. I dared not speak, but stared into her searching eyes.

She smiled at me and without turning, called to her husband, laughing. "He's got the thighs of a horseman." Then, to me, and speaking under her breath, she added, "And the sausage of a countryman, I'll wager." At the same time she squeezed my leg again, this time a little higher, and more gently.

I looked across the room to see how his lordship was reacting, then back to her. I was aroused, nervous and confused, but already she seemed to have forgotten me. She stood back, carefully avoiding the stone arch above the fireplace as she did so, and turned to John Deyman, the mood changing in an instant.

"Do we hunt this country, Steward?"

John Deyman stiffened, as all attention was once again focused on him. Carefully, he tried to regain his composure. "When we

6

get the opportunity my Lady, yes we do, both with the bow and the falcon."

"Excellent. Then we shall have some sport. Organize the best hunting you can for tomorrow morning. I have ridden at cart's pace for too long on the journey down here and need some proper exercise." She walked over to the window and looked down the valley toward Colyton.

"Are those our deer parks I see down there?"

He was more confident now. "No my Lady, those are the parks of Colcombe Castle, which was owned by the Marquess of Exeter, Henry Courtenay, until his execution. They were escheated by the Crown and sold to the merchants of Colyton six years ago. Your estate spreads over the hill behind us, toward Dalwood, and up the Umborne valley to the right."

"Sold off to the merchants eh? King Hal was always short of money." It was the first time Lord Henry had spoken, but Lady Frances cut him short. She looked briefly at her husband, who avoided her look, and turned her attention back to me.

"Is your Colyton a rich town young man?"

I answered proudly. "Aye Lady, third or fourth in Devon they say. The wool trade does us well in these parts."

She nodded. "Very well." Her interest in business matters seemed to have waned as rapidly as it had arisen. Casually, she addressed the room, clearly confident that all were listening and hanging on her every word.

"Right! Let's to work. Never mind the neighbours, it's hunting we are discussing. Come on Richard, you and the Steward rouse yourselves and show us some action. I expect the two of you can muster up everything we shall need. I will use a full longbow – none of your silly little cut-down bows for women. Full-sized, do you hear?"

She turned to her daughters.

"Catherine, I assume you and Mary will ride out with us?"

"Of course, Mother, nothing would stop me."

I looked across the room, confused, for the reply came from the sister I had assumed to be Lady Jane.

The matter was immediately resolved, for Lady Frances continued, now clearly addressing the smaller and quieter of the two elder sisters.

"What about you Jane? Surely you can leave your books for a morning? The Devon air will do you good."

The smaller, more pious sister smiled quietly. "Thank you mother but you know I do not enjoy the chase. I should prefer to read in the garden. It looks beautiful, and I can get all the Devon air I need there. I shall enjoy the view. Perhaps, God willing, I will be able to watch you hunt the valley from the garden path."

Lady Frances shrugged dismissively. "Do as you please. You normally do."

She turned to Lord Henry. "We seem to have planted a weed in our garden. I suppose all this education will pay off one day. Come Henry, let's complete this inspection and let the cooks get to work. I could eat a bullock."

The group swept out of the room, and I was left pondering my faulty identification of the sisters. The Grey family were every bit as forthright as their reputation, and failing to recognize which sister was which was not a very auspicious start. But first I had to get my clothes dry. I would need them in the morning, if I was to join in the hunt – and with Lady Catherine riding out, I would not miss it for the world.

❧ CHAPTER 2 ❧

18th April 1551 – Shute House

I looked around the crowded room. Already the buzz of conversation was deafening. This was going to be a dinner to remember – for all of us.

It was seven days since the Grey family had arrived at Shute, and thanks be to God, the hunting had been a success. The whole of March had been wet and the beginning of April no better, but now, at mid-month, the mornings were clear and bright and, if you could keep out of the keen wind, it was quite warm. John Deyman and I had been run off our feet, ensuring that the family enjoyed the best sport the estate could offer, and so far we had been lucky.

Although Lady Frances's hope for wild boar had once again been disappointed, the deer had run particularly well this morning, and she had shot a large stag unaided, returning to Shute House in good spirits. As usual, Catherine and Mary had stayed up with the hunt all morning and as they dismounted their horses in the yard, both had been talking at the same time, and glowing with fresh air and excitement. I ran forward to warn the cooks.

The girls had still been talking when they trooped into the Great Hall a few minutes ago. We had known for days that today's dinner was to be a large and formal affair. The Dorsets had sent messages to John Deyman even before they had arrived that they regularly kept open house at Bradgate Park, entertaining up to 200 of their neighbours and the merchants of nearby Leicester, and would expect to do the same at least once while they were visiting their Devon estate. As a result, he had immediately prepared a suggested guest list, and as soon as it was approved, had issued it with as much dispatch as he could. Now, a week later, we were here. The centre table in the hall was crowded with the local dignitaries. Everyone wanted to be close to the high table, where the family sat, and I had finally found a space at the far end, between two freehold farmers, friends of my father, from across the valley.

I was as excited as my neighbours around me. The visit of the Lord of the manor was seen by everyone in the valley and the area beyond as a significant event, and the more important in our case, as, with a distant Lord of the manor, it happened only rarely. Just to be spoken to by Lord Henry Grey, Marquess of Dorset, was honour enough, but to be invited to join the family at dinner was very special – something I knew would be talked about for months afterwards.

My father was as excited as any and had pushed his way into a prime space close to the high table, where he was deep in conversation with two wool merchants from Colyton and a ship owner from Lyme Regis, who called himself Merchant Blackmore. Nobody knew his first name and none dared ask him, for he was a huge man with a black beard, and his temper was said to be fearsome. None the less, it appeared he had heard about the event and managed to wheedle himself an invitation.

The table was already full and the food was beginning to arrive, when I noticed a latecomer slipping quietly into the room, and trying to find himself a space. It was Thomas Marwood, from Blamphayne, in the Coly valley; the immediate neighbour of my father's farm. Dr Marwood was a physician, who had learned his medicine at Padua in Italy a few years before, and who now practiced in Honiton, about six miles away, over the hill. As always, I was pleased to see him, and making a space beside me, beckoned him to sit down.

"Well Richard. We are indeed in exalted company today. How goes your arm these days?"

I lifted my left arm as far as the crush around us would allow. "It is well Thomas, thank you. Totally healed and with no weakness."

I had broken the arm in two places when a falling beam in my father's barn had landed on me during building work. I was only eleven years old at the time and the break had been bad, made worse by a gaping wound from oak splinters. My mother had worried herself sick. She was sure I would lose the arm, or worse, but Dr Marwood, who had not long then returned from Padua, had cleaned and sewn the wound with Woundwort and splinted the arm with hazel sticks. Thanks to his ministrations, I had made a total recovery, and I and my family were forever grateful to our skilful neighbour.

"Glad to hear it boy. I hear you are hunting with the royals these days?"

I looked at him sideways. "Hardly Thomas, but I was allowed to ride with his Lordship and his family yesterday and today – except Lady Jane that is; she does not hunt with us."

Thomas looked along the smoky room to the diminutive pale figure on the high table. "Ah yes. I have heard a great deal about our Lady Jane. I have it on good authority she is one of the brightest stars in the country; nearly as learned as his Majesty King Edward. They say she reads and writes Latin, Greek, Italian and French indeed, and is an accomplished musician to boot."

I followed his eyes and watched Lady Jane pecking delicately at her food. I nodded. "I have not heard her speak any of those languages, but she does always have a book in her hand and keeps herself to herself." Instinctively, my eyes strayed further down the table. "Her sister Catherine is beautiful don't you think?" I tried not to sound too interested, but I must have failed, for Thomas grinned at me before turning back toward the high table.

He followed my gaze and for a few moments studied Lady Catherine as she chatted animatedly with all around her. He smiled at me conspiratorially. "Indeed. A real beauty." His look became more serious as he said, very pointedly, "Two beauties, and born of a powerful family with royal connections. No doubt they will both be traded in the marriage market before too long."

I must have looked disappointed, for he quickly changed the subject. "Where is the third sister?"

I tried to point as unobtrusively as possible with the end of my knife. "There sir. At the end of the table. The – er – the very small one."

Dr Marwood nodded. "Ah yes, the dwarf?" He watched carefully for a few moments, taking in the mannerisms of his subject and the way those around her responded to her obvious affliction. After some time, he nodded, quietly, as if making a decision, and turned back toward me.

"An interesting case. Why, I wonder, did the Good Lord bring that malady upon her? All the brains gone into the first and the beauty into the second perhaps? Nothing left for the third." He leaned over, carefully cupping his hand round his mouth and, beckoning me to lean close, whispered, "I have a theory it's to do with in-breeding. Too much undiluted Tudor

11

blood. You get the same problem with sheep and cattle, but don't say so out loud or we'll be flogged or worse." He winked.

I stared at him, not for the first time, shocked at his candour. Ever since I had known him, he had been an inspiration. Full of ideas, many original, or so it seemed to me, and some of them appearing to border on the heretical, although he was, as we all were in the valley, a devout Catholic. On long winter nights before my move to Shute House, I had loved to walk down the valley to Blamphayne and sit with him, listening to his thoughts about medicine, life, and the world in general. What courage it must have taken to leave Devon and travel all the way to Italy to learn medicine. Since my arm had been mended and I had come to Shute, I had had little opportunity to see my friend, and it was good to be sitting next to him again.

The feast began to arrive; it was like nothing I had ever seen before and would have fed my family for months. Nor, judging by their reactions, had any of the Colyton merchants seen anything like it either.

First there was soup, thick and hearty, made with proper meat stock, not like the thin stuff we normally ate. Next came the turbots. I knew these were fresh from Axemouth, as I had been to get them myself. These were followed by chickens, geese and mutton – all fresh from the home farm, with sundry vegetables gathered from all over the valley and some even from Exeter market.

Finally, this was topped by apple pies and a vast choice of French cheeses, which John Deyman had had sent over from Lyme. Perhaps that was how Merchant Blackmore had found his way into our throng; the cheeses must have come over from France, together with the wines and brandy, in one of his boats. What I could not understand was how John Deyman had managed to find apples in such good condition in April; I knew that those we had stored in the house had run out or gone bad soon after Christmas. But find them he had, and the pie was sweet and good.

The French wines and brandy kept flowing, and our neighbours kept accepting it. Not much came free to any of us these days and, as one of the Colyton merchants said to me, as he burped his way through enough food and wine for half-a-dozen men, it would be churlish to reject hospitality so carefully planned and so lavishly presented.

The afternoon wore on, the guests relaxed and the atmosphere grew increasingly merry. But throughout it all, everyone's eyes remained on the high table. The Marquess and his Lady did not seem in the slightest put off by everyone watching them – I suppose they were used to it – and ate heartily and toasted their guests liberally. I noticed that Jane ate little and drank even less, but the family seemed not to notice. She seemed remote from the other members of the family, and I could only assume it was because she was excluded from discussing the pleasures of the hunt, not having taken part.

Catherine, on the other hand, seemed to be right in the middle of things, and really enjoying herself. I watched her bright eyes in the flickering light of the rush lamps, as the afternoon wore on, and on a number of occasions she seemed to look down the table and notice me at the far end. The next time she looked at me I smiled. Perhaps it was my imagination, but she seemed to smile back as she looked at me, and her eyes held mine for a moment, as if she was trying to send me a message.

Again, I looked up at the high table, and again she seemed to be looking at me. What were those looks meant to convey? I had noticed that she had ridden quite close to me for most of the morning, but apart from a few seemingly accidental moments when she had brushed against me as we squeezed though narrow gaps in the trees, nothing specific had passed between us, and we had barely spoken.

As I watched, I saw her say something to her father, who looked down the room at me, and turned to the steward behind, who immediately signalled to me to approach. What had she said? What had I done wrong? Nervously, I clambered from my tight position on the long bench and approached the high table.

Lord Henry looked at me. "Master Richard?" I nodded.

"Lady Catherine here has a question for you." He turned to his daughter, who spoke immediately, looking at me intently with those huge eyes. "Are we a long way from the sea here, Master Richard?"

I was about to reply, but Lord Henry frowned at her. "The sea, girl? What interest do you have in the sea?"

"Father, I am nearly old enough to be married, and I have never even seen the sea." She turned back to me, smiling her lovely open smile and, as my knees weakened, spoke directly to me.

"Father says Bradgate Park is almost the belly-button of England; it's as far from the sea as it is possible to be in any direction, and for that reason, I have never seen it. I would love to see the sea. They say it smells of salt? I don't understand that, for salt does not smell of anything, does it?"

I was surprised. I had been born only three miles from the seaport of Colyford and not more than five miles from the open sea at Axemouth, and had often joined boats fishing in the bay and sometimes sailed as far as the Channel Islands. Once, I had been allowed to join the crew of a trading vessel, carrying kersey cloth and Honiton lace from Colyford to Antwerp. The sea was as familiar to me as the fields, hedges and rivers. How could anyone have lived in England and never have seen it? I tried to concentrate as the whole family gave me their full attention, and I was aware that the noise in the room had suddenly reduced to a murmur as everyone tried to hear what I was being asked, and what my reply would be.

As soon as I started to speak, I felt more confident.

"The sea is very close Lady Catherine. If you rode with me to the top of Shute Hill – here, at the back of the house, I could show it to you. It is indeed salty – you may even be able to smell it from the hilltop if the wind is in the right direction. With permission I could even take you right to the water's edge and you could walk in the sea in your bare feet." I looked carefully at Lord Henry as I said it, afraid that I had over-stepped the mark. He didn't respond, but looked at Lady Catherine.

"May I ride with Master Richard to see the sea, Father?" she asked animatedly. As she spoke, I noticed a change of expression pass fleetingly over young Lady Mary's face. What did it signify? There was something strange about the diminutive figure opposite me; as if she was in the family but not of it, a member but not a participant. Yet as I waited for Lord Henry to reply, I realized that the youngest daughter took full advantage of being overlooked (in both senses); those raven eyes were watching again, capturing and considering every piece of conversation which passed above her head. She made me feel uncomfortable.

"I will not have you ride out alone."

Lady Frances, had made her announcement in a loud voice. She seemed fully aware that the eyes of the room were on her, and now all ears awaited the remainder of her reply. "It is not seemly."

Catherine began to protest, but her mother, leaning across to her close in front of me, continued in a lowered tone. "Perhaps you and Master Richard may ride to the sea tomorrow morning Catherine, so long as both your sisters accompany you, but we will not decide it here. We shall discuss this later." Her eyes lifted and she signalled me to return to my place at the lower table. It was clear who made the decisions in the Grey household, and it was not Lord Henry.

As I turned to return to my place, my heart sank. It seemed unlikely that the prim Lady Jane could ride a horse at all, and my chance of a private conversation with Catherine would be severely limited if Raven-eyes was watching us every second.

I was stepping down from the high table when Lady Jane continued the conversation. I paused and looked back. She appeared to be speaking to me.

"I should very much like to join you Master Richard, but as your invited guest, not on sufferance, as my sister's chaperone." I looked at her in surprise. It was the first time she had acknowledged my existence, let alone spoken to me. I bowed my head, in acceptance, hoping I was doing the right thing.

"Enough. It is agreed, you will all go tomorrow. We can discuss the details later." Lady Frances hissed her decision to the family, Mary's participation seemingly being taken for granted without anyone waiting for her reply. Lord Henry sat back impassively, and I made a hasty retreat to my place at the other end of the room. The mistress had spoken and ours was to obey – including, it seemed, her husband.

❧   ❧

Later that evening, when the guests had departed, I received a message confirming that the journey to the sea would take place the following morning and that I should make the necessary arrangements. I was told we should leave early, as we must be back in time for late family dinner at two o'clock.

I immediately went down to the stables and began preparing the horses for the morning. I was pleased we would be able to have an early start, for the wind often blew offshore for the first few hours of the day, and given a bit of luck, that should allow us to reach Axemouth and to return safely, before tomorrow's likely showers.

I was helping the under groom brush Matilda, Lady Jane's palfrey (Jane had told me she was called Matilda because she was 'a saint among saints') but she was not living up to her name. Her docility was being sorely tested by Jack, my stallion, who was blowing hard and biting his crib in the next stall. I grinned to myself; if Matilda was coming into season, the girls might have more of an education tomorrow than they had bargained for.

"Your stallion seems to have taken a fancy to Mattie. Jane may be doubly mounted in the morning if you let him have his way. That will dent her equanimity."

I turned, to see little Lady Mary, sitting on an upturned bucket, swinging her little legs and looking at me closely with those black eyes. There was something strange about this child. She seemed to have an understanding of the adult world that belied her age. I smiled back, carefully, not daring to trust her one inch. "I have prepared your pony Lady Mary. I assume you will be joining us in the morning?"

"You too," she replied. "Everyone assumes. No one ever asks

me. Ignore the dwarf. She doesn't count. I know I'm only six and I will never be as tall as Cat, but I am not stupid. I am a whole person and I see and feel and understand everything."

I was taken aback, and had not been prepared for such a sharp a response. "I apologize if I presumed my Lady. It was necessary to prepare the horses for an early start, and I did ask you as soon as an opportunity arose."

Mary stood up and, carefully avoiding the palfrey's hind legs, walked over toward me, and touched my arm. She smiled – the first time I had seen her do so.

"Indeed you did and you stand un-rebuked. Can we be friends? You will soon see that ours is no ordinary family. Jane, Cat and I are Tudors, descended direct from King Henry VII in three generations on my mother's side. Mother says that her bloodline gives us special abilities and special responsibilities. Jane has most of both. She is extremely clever – some say more so than our cousin Princess Elizabeth (although Elizabeth is older) – and being the eldest of us, Jane has most of the responsibilities."

I was confused. "How old is Lady Jane? She looks younger than Lady Catherine?"

Mary laughed. "I know. To start with you got them muddled up didn't you? I noticed. Everybody makes that mistake, because Cat is taller and looks older. Jane will be fourteen in October but Cat is only eleven. She is a very advanced eleven though." The last phrase was accompanied by a raising of the black eyebrows and a knowing look well beyond her years.

"Lady Catherine said at dinner she was nearly of marriage-able age."

"Quite so. I told you it was different for us. I expect you will wait till you are nearly twenty or so, and have a steady income, before getting married. Mother says most ordinary men do. Our marriages – well, perhaps not mine, but certainly Jane's and Cat's – will be arranged for us, within the next two or three years, in pursuit of power and money, and we will have little gainsay in the matter. So if you had the same thoughts for Cat that your stallion seems to have for Mattie, you can forget them."

17

I could not believe my ears and felt myself reddening in embarrassment at being caught out by a mere child. "I had no such thoughts."

Mary smirked. "Perhaps not, or not yet, but listen to me now, and remember what I said. Cat is reckless and a flirt. She has her eye on you, I can tell. Jane says she is a terrible tease but in the end, be assured, she will obey our parents and marry according to their wishes."

I found myself accepting her words and nodding in agreement, but deep down I was confused. Was Mary right? Was Lady Catherine – a lady of royal blood – interested in me? For someone so young, Mary certainly seemed to know what was going on. Perhaps because of her affliction, her sisters did not see her as a threat, or as a competitor, and therefore felt able to confide in her.

Seemingly satisfied with the effect of her words, Mary rose to leave, stroking Mattie's flank as she passed. Mattie rolled her eyes and stamped a foot. In the next stall, Jack snorted in response. As if by accident, Mary brushed against my leg as she left the stall. She turned and looked up at me.

"I wouldn't give up if I were you. She might take pleasure in the odd adventure before that day comes. You never know!"

Before I could respond, she had left the stable, scattering the chickens in the yard as she went.

❧ CHAPTER 3 ❧

19th April 1551 – Axe Valley, Devon

Dawn had not long broken when we clattered out of the courtyard of Shute House, rounded St Michael's Church, and began to climb the hill. We rode into low, almost freezing cloud, which swirled around us, so that the horses' manes and our own hair stood out like spiders' webs after a frost.

Mary and Jane were quiet. Mary was still rubbing the sleep from her eyes, but Jane seeming to radiate the contained calm of a nun as we climbed away from the house and her parents' influence. Catherine rode beside me, her eyes at the same time seeming sleepy and watchful. Like a waking bride? I thought, my mind running in all directions every time she looked at me.

"What is the sea like, Richard? Is it a torrent, wild and frightening? How far does it extend?"

Here was my chance to appear knowledgeable.

"It extends as far as the eye can see – to the very horizon and more again. If you sail upon it in a ship you can lose all sight of land and have to navigate by dead reckoning with a compass, or by using the stars. Sometimes, when the wind blows fiercely, it makes huge waves, taller than two men, which crash upon the shore. But on calm days it is like a sighing lake, ebbing and flowing twice every day, so that beaches appear and disappear and harbours empty and fill."

"Why does it do that?"

I shrugged my shoulders, for in truth I was not so sure myself. "Some say it is God's will, but the fishermen say the tide follows the moon. Certainly the tides vary in height as the moon waxes and wanes. You can see it every month."

At that very moment we topped the shoulder of the hill and a view began to open below us and to our right. As we cleared the trees, a final puff of wind lifted the clouds from around us, the sun broke through, and, as if a window had just been opened, a splendid view was spread before us. I had seen it so many times, but it never ceased to please me.

Below lay the Axe valley, with Colyford in the neck of the estuary and Axemouth village beside the marshes at the left side of the water. Beyond, the sea itself sparkled in the sunshine and we stopped our horses and took in the view, the sisters uttering gasps of utter amazement.

"Come, let's ride down and touch it," cried Mary, standing as high in her stirrups as she could.

"Lead on then," I replied, "the path is even, but a little muddy after the rain. Take your time, Lady Mary."

Excitedly, Mary led us down toward the river valley, Jane

riding close behind her. For a moment I paused as they cantered ahead, then, as I went to kick Jack forward to follow, Catherine put a hand on my arm.

"Hold on a minute Richard. I have a stone in my boot. Can you lift me down?"

I turned Jack back into the clearing, dismounted, and tied his reins to a branch. As I reached up to Catherine, she lifted her leg over the pommel of the saddle and began to slide down toward me. I still don't know what happened next, but as Catherine slid toward me, her gown must have got stuck on the saddle pommel. I tried to hold her, but she kept sliding. Suddenly my hands were beneath her gown and under her arms, whilst she was naked before me, with nothing to cover her modesty between the top of her riding boots and the gown, which was now completely over her head.

I didn't know where to look or what to do and started to release her, but as I began to let go, she called out from within the gown. "Don't let go now Richard, I will suffocate. Release this damned dress from the saddle pommel before I choke to death."

At that moment the problem solved itself, as, with a loud ripping sound, the gown gave way and deposited the two of us on the forest floor. I found myself lying on my back, with Catherine on top of me, our bodies held tight together, but her face still hidden from me by the gown, which had now fallen over my face. She made no attempt to get off me, but lay panting, as I reached up and pulled the heavy material down until I could see her face. I thought she might have been embarrassed, or even frightened, but I could not have been more wrong. Her face was flushed with excitement as, deftly, she smoothed the gown over me, leaving my face visible, but my body and my hands, most certainly within.

"Damn. That wasn't meant to happen," she giggled, as she lay panting above me, her face closer to mine than it had ever been. She looked deep into my eyes, confident and conspiratorial. "Well sir, what will you do with me now, for I fear I am totally at your command?" As she said it she moved her hips against me and I, in return instinctively held her in the small of her back, and pulled her toward me.

I could smell her sweet breath as she moved against me. She kissed me once, then again, more hungrily, and I pulled her even closer and kissed her back. I began to stroke her body and immediately felt her respond. She was not the first girl I had held like this and I knew, excitedly, that she was going to let me have her. I began to roll her onto her back, but as we turned, and she arched her back in expectation, something − I don't know what − made me check.

She felt my change and stiffened in response. "What is it?"

I began to pull back. This was what I had dreamed about last night, but now, with the dream becoming reality, I knew what we were doing was wrong, and suddenly I was frightened. This was the first time I had held − actually touched in the flesh − a lady of quality, and the experience made my fingers burn.

I tried to release her, but she clung to my shoulder, pushing her hips forward again, in invitation. "No. Don't stop! Not yet. Hold me a little longer Richard. Touch me. Touch me here." She took my hand and brought it between her legs.

It was no good. The mood had broken, and instinctively, I pulled away from her.

Her mood changed in an instant. She pulled her head back and glared at me, sullenly. The voice that had been eager and inviting seconds ago was now cold and angry. "What's wrong? Am I not attractive? Not woman enough for you?"

My mind was in a turmoil. This was not how it was supposed to be. The dream was turning into a nightmare. Slowly, uncertainly, I tried to kiss her, but her lips were cold and hard. I tried to explain.

"Yes of course you are Catherine. You are a beautiful woman, you know you are. But this is not the way it's meant to be." Quietly I let go of her and eased the dress back into position around her body, as comfortably as the large rip would allow. She stopped fighting and relaxed, then lay against me for another moment, looking hard into my eyes as if trying to make a decision. In return, I looked deep into her eyes, with all the sincerity I could convey.

"May the Lord save us, what is all this? I seem to have been cast in the role of chaperone after all?"

We looked up. A few yards away, Lady Jane sat on her palfrey, looking down at us.

In an instant, Catherine tried to make small of it. "Ho sister. I had a stone in my boot and Richard helped me retrieve it."

Lady Jane sneered at the inadequacy of the excuse. "Was it necessary for him to climb inside the boot to do so, and with you still wearing it?" She turned her horse. "Come Mary, our sister seems to be literally in good hands. By all accounts we must continue our ride in solitude."

Frightened for my life, for the sisters were of the royal blood and what I had just been found doing was a hanging offence, I turned to Catherine.

"What do we do now?"

"Why remount of course. What else is there to do? It seems I have lost the urge and you have lost the opportunity."

"But Lady Jane?"

"Oh don't worry about her. She may be pious and a cold fish as far as men are concerned, but she has her reasons and she won't say anything. She is, after all, my beloved sister and although we differ in many respects, we have a pact to hold together as a way of getting through this difficult life."

I helped her to her feet and brushed down the gown as best I could, then helped her back into the saddle and remounted myself. We rode down the lane in silence, Catherine looking at me with the same look I had seen at dinner.

I followed her down the steep lane toward the sea, watching her back sway in response to her horse and wondering what she was really like. That she would make an exciting lover there was no doubt, but would she make a loving and steadfast wife? Her moods seemed to change so fast that it was hard to understand who the real Catherine was, but underneath the apprehension which remained with me as we rode, I knew I wanted to remain close to her and to try to find the real Catherine – and, if she would let me, to show her the real me.

We caught up with the others at the bottom of the hill, and no more was said about what had (or had not) taken place in the clearing. The rains of the previous weeks were still draining from the sodden land as we skirted Whitford village and crossed the ford toward Musbury. Now we turned seaward again, following the left bank of the river as it widened toward its estuary. By the time we reached Colyford, the tide had begun to fall, although the few craft which were tied up downriver still floated on the muddy estuary water.

Catherine's mood seemed to have changed again; she had grown unusually quiet, and kept looking at me with *that* look, whilst Mary seemed to have adopted her invisible role. I was, therefore, relieved that Jane let her horse fall into step alongside me and began to make polite conversation as we continued, riding in the shade of Boshill, through Axmouth village, before finally reaching the stony beach below Haven Cliff.

To my great surprise, away from her parents, Jane was completely different. She relaxed, and even sang in a high, clear voice, as our horses rounded the cliff corner and, for the first time that early morning, felt the full force of the sun on our faces.

Thank goodness, the combination of the sun, Jane's singing, and final arrival at the sea, seemed to lift Catherine's spirits and she dismounted by herself (more expertly this time) at the top of the steep shingle beach. The horses did not like the shifting shingle, so I tethered them to the stunted trees, and Catherine and Mary walked together, down to the beach on foot.

Catherine looked back at me, smiling again. It appeared I had been forgiven. "I cannot believe how wonderful this is," she called as she sat down carefully on the stony beach. She looked out to sea, and as she did so, a fishing boat left the mouth of the estuary and set out into the bay. She waved to the fishermen, who appeared surprised at the unusual adornment on their beach, and waved their hats in reply. Catherine watched them sail out of the estuary, making good time in a freshening morning breeze, then turned back and waved to Jane and myself, sitting at the top of the beach.

Sitting quietly beside me, Jane also seemed surprised and overcome. "The sea is simply enormous; much bigger than I would ever have believed. And the waves … I am spellbound."

I smiled. I, too, was spellbound, but not with the Axemouth beach or the sea beyond. My spell was now gingerly paddling into the water, trying to hold her gown clear of the waves and gasping for breath as each one brought another flood of cold water around her ankles.

As I leaned back on my elbows, watching Catherine and Mary giggling at the water's edge, I tried to sum up my thoughts. Apart from my failure to respond to Catherine's advances, the day seemed a success; the early start had been worthwhile and the sea beyond their expectations. One thought kept coming back to me. Despite Catherine's confidence, I was still afraid that one of them would mention the affair in the woods when they returned. But looking at the two sisters as they ventured out into deeper water, only to retreat again, shrieking with laughter as the next wave came, and at Jane, sitting calmly beside me, her eyes closed, absorbing the warmth of the morning sun and apparently lost in the sound of the waves, my brief encounter with Catherine seemed to have been forgotten already.

Yet *I* could not forget. I could still feel the eager warmth of her as she arched her back and pressed against me. Yes I had rolled in the hay with my fair share of lusty farm-girls (most of them, it had to be admitted, a good deal larger than Catherine) and, encouraged by harvest cider, made love rather clumsily to a few of them. But this morning was different. Catherine was different. I could still feel the tension in her body as she held me, the urgency of her look just before she had kissed me. And I could also remember, with a vividness which made my stomach ache, the look of hurt rejection on her face as I changed my mind and turned away.

I had acted instinctively, and in doing so, had not considered how she would respond. My first thought afterward had been that she would be relieved that things had not got out of hand – that I had not taken advantage of an unlucky accident (if that is what it was). Then I had thought she would cry – though whether from embarrassment or rejection, I could not be sure.

But she had done neither of these things. Instead she had regained her self-control, withdrawn, and looked at me with a cool calculation that, as I remembered it now, still discomforted me.

For an instant I had feared she might seek revenge. If she did, I knew I was finished. A charge of misconduct with any girl was a serious matter, never mind an under-aged lady of royal blood. And if the allegation were brought by the Marquis and Marchioness of Dorset, I would surely hang.

"Come Jane, come Richard. Join us. But beware – the water is freezing." Catherine was waving to us.

I looked at Jane, inviting her to join me with her sisters, but she declined, smiling. "I am very comfortable here Richard. Please join my sisters. I shall be alright."

Without removing my long riding boots, I walked down the beach to the water's edge and smiled at the two sisters, who, now screaming with laughter, had begun to throw seawater at each other. I looked at Catherine, still unsure what the outcome of our intimacy might be, but hopeful that there might be a positive one. She caught my glance and looked back. For a fleeting moment she was serious, holding my eyes with an expression which I could not interpret, but which nevertheless made my insides turn upside down.

The moment passed and Catherine looked across the river mouth, and along the beach to the small fishing village of Seaton. She pointed. "Look! What are those? They shine so brightly in the sunshine."

Jane and I followed her gaze as Mary, ending her game, climbed from the water onto dry stones and looked to see what had attracted Catherine's attention. At least I could sound knowledgeable here on my own doorstep.

"Those are the sea-cliffs at Beer. A hundred feet of chalk-stone. There is a quarry behind the hill where, since Roman times, men have cut stone for houses – and fireplaces ..." Suddenly my words drifted away as I looked beyond Beer and realized the size of the approaching storm. The clouds were purple-black and, it was evident, held a veritable deluge within them. It did not look good. These April storms could hit our valley suddenly and with a frightening ferocity. Now I was more worried than I had been at any time that morning.

"Quickly Ladies, we must return. Look at that storm approaching."

As the two younger sisters donned their riding boots and made for the horses, I helped Lady Jane into the saddle and looked again at the approaching storm. It was even worse than I had first thought; a storm of truly enormous proportions. Already it had covered the hills inland from Beer, which had completely disappeared under its drenching. I could feel the wind growing second by second, and soon it would be upon us.

It was going to be a hard ride home. After a long wet winter and all the recent rains as well, the ground could not absorb any more water; there was only one way for it to go – into the rivers – and we had to ford the biggest of them to get back to Shute. There were two fording points across the river, at Whitford, where we had crossed before, and at Colyford, which was lower down the river and therefore potentially deeper, but nearer. It might be safer to cross at Colyford, before the river rose too high. It was a gamble, but whichever I chose, one thing was certain: it was going to be an uncomfortable ride before we got home.

≫   ≪

It was amazing how quickly the change in the weather changed the mood of our little party. There was no laughter, and no conversation, as we clattered through Axemouth village and rode upstream alongside the rapidly rising river, heading for Colyford. The wind and rain hit us as we were fully exposed on the treeless banks of the river estuary. Even though I knew the way like the back of my hand, I found it almost impossible to follow the track, for we had to ride direct into the wind, which was now funnelling down the valley with increasing force.

Breathless, and soaked to the skin, we finally reached the ford. The water was flowing fast and rising rapidly. I had to make a decision, and quickly. It would be impossible to take the long way round and in any event there was no shelter on this side of the river. There was no alternative; we had to cross this ford and cross it immediately.

Staring at the rushing, muddy water, the sisters looked apprehensive, and I was concerned they would refuse to cross until it was too late. Finally, I decided to lead them across one at a time. Jack was steady in water and could be relied upon to pick a safe route through the flood, which by now was as deep as a man's waist and flowing frighteningly fast – without a horse it was already impassable.

Mary looked nervous and I decided to take her first. Her New Forest Pony, Rufus, was the smallest, and even at this stage it would be difficult. If the water rose any more she would not be able to keep her footing and I did not want to think about little Mary trying to control a frightened, swimming horse.

Trying to look more confident than I felt, I took the pony's rein in my left hand and led her into the river. The water was now up to Jack's belly and making a powerful wave against his right side. As a result, there was a shallow eddy hard against his left side; if the pony could be held there it would be protected from the full strength of the current. The ploy worked and the little pony, with Mary clinging to her reins and mane, passed without a stumble to the other side.

I led Mary and her pony into the lee of a stone wall which offered some limited shelter, and then returned for Jane, whose horse was standing nervously at the water's edge. Again the ploy was successful and Jane was quickly taking what shelter she could find beside the wall with Mary.

Once more I retraced my steps, but as I crossed the river for the fourth time, I realized the water had already become nearly a foot deeper than it had been for the first crossing. I shouted to Catherine to hold on tight, for this time the horses might lose their footing and have to swim the deepest channel.

"I'm alright Richard. Let's go and get this nightmare over." Her raised voice was barely audible above the shriek of the wind.

Once more I used the size and strength of Jack's body to create a lee shelter which gave Catherine's smaller horse a chance of keeping its feet. We were nearly across when a sudden squall of wind hit us. Even though it was heavy with rainwater, Catherine's torn gown billowed as the wind got underneath it and her horse immediately panicked. It plunged for the opposite shore and Catherine, unsighted by the billowing clothing, lost her seat. In seconds she was in the water, already yards downstream of me, and moving away rapidly.

There was only one thing to do. Catherine's horse had made it to the bank and was walking toward the other horses. It would be alright there. I had to save Catherine using Jack. Looking downstream, I remembered the long bend 100 yards below. Jack and I had to make for the sandbank on the inside of the bend. With luck we could catch her there. I wheeled Jack and regained the riverbank, kicked him into a gallop and blinded by the lashing rain, covered the field in seconds. A low hedge separated us from the bank nearest the bend in the river. God knows how he could see it in the wind and rain, but Jack took it in one blind leap, landed on the muddy bank, slipped, then regained his footing, and together we slithered to a halt beside the rushing water.

The sandbank was covered by water, but we plunged in, just as Catherine appeared round the corner. Taking a chance, I took Jack as deep as I dared and, leaning from the saddle grabbed the hood of Catherine's gown, as she swept past. I reined back with my left hand and squeezed hard against Jack's legs. "Back, Jack! Back, I say."

Jack heaved himself back into the shallow water and onto the stony slope where, on quieter days, the cattle would walk down to the river to drink. As soon as the water was shallow enough, I slid from the saddle and dragged Catherine to me, frantically pulling the sodden clothing from her face. She was ashen. For a moment I was sure she was dead. Then to my relief, she coughed and spat violently.

"God that water tastes foul." She looked up at me. "Oh Richard. Thank God! I thought I was finished!"

I was shaking with relief. "Are you alright Catherine?"

"Get me home Richard. I am soaked and freezing. Please get me home."

I lifted her and carried her in my arms back to the shivering horses and her relieved sisters. With Jane's help I lifted her into the saddle, and despite her cold and exhaustion she found a way to smile at me. All she could whisper was "Thank you, Richard – thank you."

☙   ❧

It was a sorry party, indeed, that sloshed into the courtyard of Shute House a long hour later. Lady Frances was at the door and took command, drawing her daughters into the house and shouting for blankets, brandy, and hot drinks.

She turned to me as I stood, drenched, holding the reins of four equally drenched horses. "Away with you, young man. You have done damage enough. See to the horses. It's all you are good for."

Almost gratefully, I led the horses into the stables. I hadn't expected her thanks.

❧ CHAPTER 4 ❧

20th April 1551 – Shute House

The rain finally cleared by mid-morning of the following day. I had been up early and, as usual, doing my rounds of the horses. The grooms could normally be trusted to look after the working horses day by day, but I liked to check every animal at least once a week. John Deyman had also decided that while the

Marquess, his wife and daughters remained at Shute, I should look after their horses personally. Hoping this would give me an opportunity to speak to Catherine, I had accepted. So far the plan seemed to be working, although it had led me into deep water in more senses than one.

I checked the horses carefully. Jane's Matilda, Mary's Rufus, and Catherine's Dobby, did not seem any the worse for their excitements of the previous day, but Jack seemed to have cut his leg quite badly – perhaps as he was backing out of the river – and I spent some time cleaning and poulticing the wound with mashed herbs before completing my rounds.

It was mid-day, shortly before dinnertime, and I was checking the feed supplies in the main house stables, when Will, a young servant found me. "What is it, Will?" I asked, as the diminutive boy rushed wide-eyed into the stable.

"Master Richard, you are wanted at once in the Great Hall. His Lordship and their Ladyships are all present and await you urgently. The Steward is also present. It looks very serious. What has happened Master Richard? I have been told to find you on pain of death."

I smiled at him, cuffed his head in as friendly a manner as I could muster, but inside my guts were turning over.

"Don't worry, Will. All is well. Just some administration I am sure. The family lead busy lives and there is always much to be done. I will wash my hands and attend at once. Tell them I am coming forthwith."

Will looked relieved and rushed red-faced out of the door and across the courtyard to the Great Hall opposite. I went to the horse trough and washed my hands and face. Which of yesterday's events was to be the cause of my punishment (for surely punishment was the certain outcome of this inquisition)? As I dried my face on the tail of my shirt, I prayed that the lesser crime – of subjecting the daughters to risk by leading them into a flooded river – was the indictment. Had any of the three girls mentioned the dalliance with Catherine? Had their mother noticed the ripped gown, and if so how had it been explained?

30

As I reached the entrance to the Great Hall I stopped, looked at the rapidly-clearing sky and took a deep breath of fresh Devon air. Was this to be my last day of freedom? Might I be a condemned man before the sun went down this evening? I shuddered, took one more deep breath, and walked into the Great Hall.

෭ ෴

"Master Richard Stocker," announced the steward as I entered the hall. The great table had not yet been laid for dinner and the whole family sat opposite me, cold as a line of judges.

"Come forward Master Stocker and stand before us."

The faces in front of me were grim, not least that of Henry Grey, Marquess of Dorset, Lord of the Manor of Shute and diverse other estates, as he addressed me. This did not bode well.

Although themselves seated, they did not invite me to sit – there was not even a chair or a bench on my side of the table. I stood before them, droplets of water from the horse-trough dripping from my fringe where, in my hurry, I had not dried it fully after the quick wash outside.

Lady Frances leaned forward. "Perhaps we should address you as Master Dog-Fish, for you seem to have an equal affinity for water as you do for our daughters here. What say you to these events of yesterday? For I declare I have not heard the like of it for many a long year."

As I entered the room I had been trying to think what I would say, but I was immediately wrong-footed by these remarks. Clearly I was being indicted and should do my best to defend myself. But defend against what charge? Not knowing what was being held against me, what reply should I give? If I defended against the wrong charge, I might raise issues which none of the sisters had (as yet) informed their parents about, and in so doing, make matters worse for them and for myself. I tried to stall.

"My Lady, I tried to do my duty as I saw it."

Henry Grey began to reply, "What was your duty ..." but Lady Frances was in full flow and waved him down.

"Your duty, sirrah! Bringing me back a daughter with clothing torn asunder and after subjecting her to such experience she cannot speak of it?"

She was standing now and, being a big woman, matching my six feet eye-for-eye across the table.

Inwardly, I began to shake. It was, after all, to be the greater indictment. I tried to speak, but my head was spinning with confusion and I could not find the words.

"I ... er ... that is, my Lady ..."

Lady Frances put her hands on her hips and addressed the room, as a politician making a speech to a captive audience.

"Is this our learned gentleman, who reads and writes in English and Latin? It appears he has lost the power of speech in both."

I did not know which way to turn. I looked along the table for some sign, some small indication of support. Lord Henry Grey shifted uncomfortably and looked into the middle distance. It seemed he was used to his wife's ranting and had learned not to interrupt her when in full flow. Lady Jane looked down passively at the table, her hands in her lap. Her face was unusually pale and she made no attempt to speak. At the end of the table, Mary's raven eyes scanned the room as she silently absorbed everything that was happening. Catherine refused to look at me. I was lost.

What should I do? Should I confess and ask their forgiveness and understanding? Admit to intimate knowledge of their young daughter in the presence of her sisters? Acknowledge that having almost seduced the one, I had nearly drowned all three? For a moment there was total silence in the near-empty hall as Lady Frances and I eyed each other across the table.

The silence was deafening. I began to feel sick. I started to go dizzy and took a number of deep breaths to steady myself.

"Mother, stop it! I beg you! Enough! We have teased him enough. The joke is out of hand!"

In an instant the mood in the room changed.

Henry Grey leaned back and laughed aloud. Catherine

32

giggled and put her hand over her mouth in mock-manners, her eyes bright and wide open. The paleness left Jane's face and she flushed heavily, cheeks now bright red, clearly embarrassed by the unfairness of the family's jest.

Mary alone remained expressionless at the end of the table. Lady Frances, having had her moment's fun, guffawed and slapped her thigh, laughing until she choked and had to take a draft of ale, brought quickly by a confused John Deyman, before she could speak again.

"Father, rescue this poor man at once, for I declare I shall have to visit the privy if you don't," called Catherine, still bright-faced.

Totally confused, I looked at Lord Henry and prayed for his rescue.

"I am sorry young man, but you must let us take our fun when we can. In truth, I called you here to thank you. My daughters have explained how you led them by safe ways to the sea and showed them the wonder of it, for which they, and we, thank you. Indeed so telling was their description of the white cliffs beyond, I should want to see them myself before shortly we return to Bradgate.

"All are agreed that it was you who saw the danger of the approaching storm long before they appreciated its significance, and insisted they return forthwith. I know my daughters sir; to draw them away from a new-found pleasure is an achievement indeed.

"In particular, however, Jane has expressed the care with which you used yourself and your horse to lead her and Mary to safety beyond the flooded river when that was the only available way to shelter. And our dear Catherine has told us she owes you her life, her very life, with her shredded gown the proof of how you dragged her from the torrent at risk to your own life, and without which action on your part she would surely have drowned."

The three sisters nodded in compliance, their sideways glances to each other giving the first indication that they had agreed their story in advance, and managed its telling to their parents with the guile which their upbringing had taught them.

"Come, Richard, let me embrace you with thanks."

Lady Frances had walked round the table and now enfolded me in her ample bosom. She held me there, calling "Thanks, thrice times thanks" to the open room, whilst my vain attempts to draw breath ensured that I would not forget for some time the heavy scent and glowing warmth of her generous cleavage.

કે જ

Minutes later, I staggered into the courtyard, reeling from my experience.

I had met clever negotiators before – merchants and market men who did not indicate whether they were to buy or sell before determining the price being struck; poachers who could talk their way out of a sticky corner with the landlord's deer hidden in a hedge not ten feet away; and on long winter evenings, Dr Marwood had often engaged me in philosophical debate, wriggling around an argument and reappearing on the other side, without ever appearing to have changed position – but this family was different: their guile was of another order. Even now they had not declared the outcome of the matter, but had told me to return at ten o'clock the following morning to complete the conversation.

It was all very strange. Like pursuing a wounded boar in thick undergrowth – frightening and exciting at once, so that time seemed to move in slow motion, and you remembered every second afterwards.

And what had his Lordship said about shortly returning to Bradgate? One thing was certain, I would not sleep tonight.

⁊ Chapter 5 ᔐ

22nd April 1551 – Shute House

"Sit you down Richard," invited Lord Henry as we met in the family's private rooms the following morning. "What made you of yesterday's play?"

"I was most confused and, until the outcome, much vexed my Lord. I did not understand the joke and thought I had done serious wrong."

"How were you so self-indicted? What sins have you not confessed?"

This time, I saw the signs better: I was being played with, a fish about to take a bait, and must avoid ensnaring myself on unseen hooks.

"None Master. I took my guidance only from the tone of address."

Lord Henry smiled. "Good. You have learned. The game was not without purpose, for I have a proposition to make to you and it was necessary to test your responses. There is a bigger world out there and, I believe, a place for you in it. But beware; it is no country village, surrounded by family friends. This is national politics and all must proceed with caution."

"I think I understand my Lord. I realize I have much to learn, but I wish to improve my lot and the world beckons me, even if there are risks."

"Then let's to business. Would you be willing to leave Shute, to leave Devon, if the right opportunity arose?"

"Yes my Lord. As the second son, and with an elder brother who makes the very oxen look frail, I need to find a place for myself outside the farm and household. That is what brought me here and I do not see this place as the end of the journey."

"Well said Richard. In that case let us proceed. We owe you a debt of gratitude for your recent protection of our precious daughters. I am minded to offer you an appointment at Bradgate Park. You have potential and our estates here at Shute are but small beer. Bradgate Park is ten times larger or more, and we have other estates nearby in Leicestershire, at Groby and Ansty for example, which add to our responsibilities there. My wife and I believe you are wasted here, and have decided to offer you a post at Bradgate for your advancement. The post is Second Master of Horse – a significant promotion if you take the sizes of the estates into account, for surely the second carp in a large lake exceeds in girth and consumption the largest in a small pond."

My heart jumped excitedly. I would be near to Catherine and ... who knows? Besides, it was an opportunity for real advancement.

"Thank you indeed my Lord. I can confirm here and now that I would be pleased to accept your kind offer. When would this happen?"

"We plan to depart next week – on Tuesday. You shall travel with us and learn our ways as we go. With this continuing rain, the journey will be slow, I suspect."

"I shall be ready my Lord. With your permission I shall ride to see my father and mother at Stocker's Farm and take my farewell of them. Likewise my brother John and his new wife Joan and my father's neighbour Dr Marwood, at Blamphayne."

"Of course. Visit them and take your farewells, for who knows, you may be away from here for a long time if you use the opportunity well. Dr Marwood – is that the physician we met here the day of the dinner?"

"The same sir, and much respected in these parts. He has been a mentor to me and I would not want to leave without his blessing."

We were shaking hands to confirm the agreement when Lady Frances came into the room.

"Is it done Henry? Has Richard accepted?"

I turned to her excited. "Indeed my Lady, this last minute. I understand that I will travel with you to Leicestershire next week."

Lady Frances continued to look at her husband, as if I had not spoken. Irritated at my stupidity, I realized that I had spoken out of turn and that she had addressed her question to her husband, not to me.

"Was it as we discussed?" she asked Lord Henry, continuing where she had left off.

Lord Henry nodded in affirmation. "Yes my dear. Second Master of Horse."

"And Adrian?"

"As agreed my dear, Adrian will become Master of Horse. I have sent him a letter to that effect by messenger."

She smiled in evident satisfaction. I looked from one to the other, trying to fathom out their relationship, and wondering how far Lord Henry's offer had been designed by her.

Now, finally, she acknowledged my presence. "Excellent. You will enjoy Bradgate and perchance ..." there was an almost imperceptible pause "... we will enjoy you. Our Master of Horse is Adrian Stokes, from whom you will take your daily instruction. You will find him fair but firm." She looked across at her husband and nodded meaningfully. "Very firm."

Henry Grey gave her a strange, almost sad look, but did not respond.

❧ Chapter 6 ❧

End April 1551 – Stocker's Farm, Devon

At mid-morning on the Saturday, I set off for the short ride across the valley to say farewell to my parents.

As I rode Jack through Colyton I met first one, then another, old friend from my schooldays, and stopped to tell them of my opportunity. The town seemed to get busier every day. Devonshire kersies had been acquiring celebrity and were an important article of commerce to Europe, the Mediterranean, and as far as the Levant. Those finished in Colyton were considered amongst the finest of cloth.

Turning the corner of the square, I met Joan Kettle, the

baker's wife. She looked at me proudly, for she had known me since I was a baby.

"My, Richard, how you have grown. You must be six feet if you are an inch. Quite the ladies' man now. You've got your lovely golden hair to thank for that. All the girls like a tall hand-some man with blond hair. Stands to reason."

Her husband Jack Kettle came out of the bakery to see who she was talking to. He was short, and bald, except for a small ton-sure of short dark hair, which made him look like a monk.

"Morning Master Richard. Are you trying to steal my wife again? Don't encourage her. She's bad enough already. Get on with you woman." He spanked her bottom as she pushed past him into the bakery, howling with laughter, the narrow door barely wide enough for them to pass each other.

Turning past the Common, I could see that the dyers and fullers had been hard at work, for there were six racks of freshly dyed cloth drying neatly, and I could hear the thump and grind of the watermills upstream along the Coly toward Puddlebridge, and my route home. Just as I was leaving the town, I bumped into three of the feofees – the local businessmen who had mort-gaged the town from Henry VIII for the enormous sum of £1,000. It did not seem to have impoverished them. John Buckland, wool merchant, John Byrde, a silk and serge maker, and my father's old friend John Maunder, who manufactured cloth just along the river, all looked positively comfortable.

"You are looking very pleased with yourselves gentlemen," I called, as I dismounted and shook hands.

"Indeed Master Richard, we are, for we were just celebrating the first full year of exporting our best kersies direct from Exeter, and cutting out those thieves of middle-men in London."

"Will you join us in a celebration?" called John Buckland, who had managed to collar much of the trade in raw cloth from Exeter to Colyton, as well as the return traffic in finished and dyed cloth, bound for export. His pack ponies were always to be seen on the Exeter road, fully laden, whether climbing up the hill or down it.

"Thank you kindly John, and John, and John (I nodded acknowledgement to each as I spoke) but I must get to my father's place before dinner or I will never hear the end of it."

"Oh dear! Mother's boy as ever was, Richard. Suit yourself," they chided, and turned into the tavern as I remounted.

                                          ❧ ❧

It was gone noon by the time I passed the turning at Blamphayne Cross and rounded the familiar white cob walls of Stocker's Farm. Kate, my younger sister, was feeding the hens as I dismounted, and ran into the house in excitement.

"Richard's here! Mother! Father! Richard's here!"

As always, I was welcomed warmly, not least by Tic, the sheepdog, who never seemed to get any older, and I sat back comfortably in my old place at the kitchen table as my mother fussed and grumbled. "You should have told me you were coming. I could have prepared more food."

The comfortable familiarity of my old place at the table, my father's special brew of strong ale, and the smell of my mother's home cooking, did not make my news any easier to impart, but I explained it as carefully as I could and by the end of the meal they had started to run out of questions.

"Promise me Richard you will keep to your studies. You must have learning these days to advance. Promise me you will work at your reading and writing."

"I will Mother. I shall be amongst educated people at Bradgate. People who speak Latin, French, Italian, and Greek."

"Italian and Greek! What's the world coming to? Well I suppose you know what's best. We have done the best we can for you all – haven't us Father?"

My father nodded. He was proud of his sons, had worked hard on our behalf and we knew it. But it was our mother who had harried us into maintaining our education. For years John and I had both walked the two and a half miles into Colyton in time for school and walked the same distance back in the evening. It had continued for years until the family could afford a spare riding horse, which we shared for the journey. I remembered how we would let him loose in old Widow Hardwick's field by the Chantry Bridge just as school started and have to catch him up in the evening before we could ride him home again. Sometimes we would double up, me riding behind John, but more commonly we would go ride and tie, taking it in turns to ride and to walk. We did have one rule between us – whoever was riding carried the bag with the books and our dinner.

Thoughts of my brother flooding back, I called over to my father. "How is brother John? I haven't seen him since the wedding. Has he settled at Nyther Halsted?"

"Aye," said my father, "he says there's a lot of work to do though. Widow Matilda had tried hard with it, but struggled to keep on top since her husband died. How long ago was that now Mother?"

"Seven years," she called from the washhouse, "summer 1544 he died, God rest his soul. A good man."

"Aye indeed," agreed my father, lost in thought. "John Gye." He shook his head in memory. "A good man, John – always straight and to the point. Honest, good to do business with. He made a good drop of cider too." He sat for a moment, nodding to himself at the memory of an old friend.

I nodded my agreement. Old age. It comes to all of us. I had noticed changes in my parents these last few years. Since brother John and I had left home, their conversation had changed. When I was a boy, they were always looking forward; now I noticed that they had started to look back. At least they hadn't got like my grandfather: in his last years he reckoned the country had "gone to the dogs, not like the good old days when King Hal first came to the throne."

Oh well, I sighed to myself, *I expect it will come to us all one day*.

"I thought I'd ride over and see John and Joan tomorrow, before I go back."

"Oh yes," said my mother, "you must say farewell to John. By the time you see him next, God willing, Joan will have a young 'un to show you." She raised her voice "Looking forward to being a grandfather, aren't you Father?"

Father grunted non-committally and took another swig of his strong ale. "Just so long as young 'un's healthy, that's all. Talking of healthy, Thomas Marwood should be home this weekend if you wants to see him. Still comes home to Blamphayne once a week does Thomas, even though he is building a big house in Honiton. Says he prefers the air in this valley."

I put a restraining hand on Kate, who was feeling left out of the conversation, and trying to show me her new puppy. "Then I will go down and see him this afternoon, if that's alright with you. And I shall go over to John and Joan in the morning, and ride direct back to Shute from there, on the old Axminster Road."

"God bless us," cried his mother. "You have only just arrived and you are talking about leaving."

"I know, Mother, but you know me. What was it you used to say when I was younger? That I was 'half flea and half spaniel'. Nothing's changed. Now, I've got to get on."

Mother flapped her hands in the air in resignation and turned back to the fire.

"Leave me exhausted you do. You and John. Both as bad as each other." She half turned toward my father. "Innum Father? Both as bad?"

Father put down his ale and wiped his mouth on the back of his hand. "Reckon so." He turned back to me. "Listen here, flea. If you'me got so much energy you can help me awhile. I've got a stock-gate needs hanging and it's work for two men. Everyone else is busy. Old Arthur is down the bottom field with Robert Shawe and young Tommy is gathering the sheep up on Watchcombe Moor."

"Arthur? Do you mean old Arthur Blewett? Is he still working for you Father? How old is he now?"

"Who? Arthur? I suppose he must be seventy-summat. Still one of the best workers I got is Arthur. Nobody can lay a hedge like Arthur. Tight as a drake's arse and twice as waterproof is his hedges."

"Father! Language! I heard that. I do not want this boy learning bad language in this house. One of these days Richard will become a proper gentleman and your bad language won't help him then." The voice emerged from the washhouse.

Father winked at me and lifted his head. "Sorry Mother, slip of the tongue."

I laughed. Nothing had changed. I stood and smiled at my father. "I'll go down and see them when we've hung that gate. I haven't seen the boys for ages. Come on then Dad, let's be at it before it's dark."

❧ ❧

We had just got the gate swinging evenly and almost to our satisfaction, when the puppy ran into the field, followed by a gasping Kate.

"Richard! Richard! The Doctor's coming down the Honiton lane. I can see him."

I looked at my father, who nodded his dismissal. The gate would do like that. I washed my hands in the trough, and, wiping them on my breeches, picked up my jerkin and walked into the lane.

Dr Marwood arrived, as always, beaming. He dismounted, blowing hard as he did so. "Well, Richard. Well met indeed."

I could not resist the urge to tease him. "Good Doctor! How fare you then? By the tightness of your jerkin the physical business must prosper. I swear you have put on weight since I saw you only last week."

Thomas Marwood looked at himself. He was short – not much over five feet – and stocky, in fact typical Devon farming stock. "Cheeky puppy! No so. The wind is cold upon Widworthy Hill and I have taken to wearing two shirts as a precaution. I'll swear I am as fit as you are."

He waved to my father, who was still swinging the gate, unsure if it would do after all.

"Come Richard. If your father can spare you, join me at Blamphayne and we'll take a bottle of wine together over supper."

We walked down the lane together, laughing and talking, Dr Marwood leading his horse by a loose rein, for he knew his own way from here.

        ❧   ❧

It was approaching dark as we pushed back our chairs and sighed. I had described my promotion and the rescue from the river, although I had omitted the earlier events with Catherine. Nevertheless, her name had come up in the conversation so frequently that my friend had no illusions about one of my motivations for accepting the move to Bradgate. He lifted the empty wine bottle and looked across the fireplace.

"Special occasion. Shall I open another?"

It was a temptation. I did not want the moment to come to an end, but finally I shook my head. "No Thomas, best not. I am over to my brother's in the morning and you must give your family your full attention, for I know they miss you when you are in Honiton."

Marwood dropped the bottle gently into the basket of logs at the fireside. "They will join me in the summer. I am building a house in Honiton – at the top of the High Street, where the Axminster road begins to climb the hill. We will make our family home there and it will also be my place of medicine."

He nodded to himself, smiling gently. "It's a satisfying trade, medicine. I have never regretted it. It was 1540 and I was already much older than you are now – twenty-eight, in fact – when I set out to Padua. It was an adventure, I tell you, for I had no Italian, although my Latin was good and sufficed, thanks to our good school in Colyton. Now here I am, eleven years later and getting set in my ways. Sometimes I wish I were your age again, setting out on life's adventure. How are your parents taking your news?"

I considered his question, for in truth I had been more preoccupied by my own challenges ahead than by the effect my departure would have on my parents.

"They say all the right things, but deep inside I can see they are worried. Neither of them has ever travelled further than Exeter or Taunton."

It was getting late and I stood to leave. Thomas put a hand on my shoulder.

"It is always harder for those who remain behind. You have the world in front of you. New people. New places. New experiences. But they cannot see any of that. They only see their loss in your departure."

To my surprise, I realized that his comments had irritated me. My great opportunity had come and with luck and hard work, might change my life forever. What did he expect me to do – give up the opportunity just because my parents had not been offered, and accepted, similar challenges? "But I cannot do anything about that," I blurted out, my anger clear.

Thomas, as always, remained calm, and as he showed me to the door, patted my shoulder again. "No indeed. It is ever thus, the order of things. You are a grown man now and have your life to lead. Neither I nor your parents would want to hold you back in any way. But be aware, for they will worry, as all parents do."

෭ ෯

The next day I left my brother's farm near Wilmington and followed the old road toward Axminster. As I skirted the valley side, I looked at the fulling mills spread along the Umborne Brook, which provided them with a reliable supply of fast water for a full twelve months of the year.

The cloth business was booming and there were more mills every time I came this way. I had counted five in the two miles before I reached Easy Bridge and turned up the hill toward Shute House. How long, I wondered, would it be before I rode this path again? Which would prosper more, these mills or my own faltering progress through life? Only time would tell. Yes, part of me was afraid. But the rest of me was excited, keen to move on – to success, to fortune, to – who knew what?

I was not short of advice, indeed they had all given me advice. My father, never one to make a fuss, more inclined to get on and do things than talk about them, had taken my hand and held it hard as he was leaving. "Just you remember Richard, they are only people, however learned or high born. Don't be over-awed by them. Don't be afraid of nuthin' or nobody."

My mother had hidden away in the washhouse at the back of the farm, leaving the men to "talk men's talk" as she put it, but when I had gone to find her, she had held both my hands in hers and repeated her message: "Don't neglect your learning, it's the ladder to success."

Finally, Thomas Marwood had seen me off at the gate to Blamphayne Farm with his own words of wisdom. "Remember Richard, you are going into a very different world from the one you know. One of your great strengths is your honesty and courage. You have developed those mainly because you have been successful at what you have done and been treated fairly by those in the valley who have in turn been treated fairly by you. But out there you may find it different; men with a lot to gain or a lot to lose will resort to any tactics they can get away with. Be aware you will not always be dealing with honourable men; you will be misled, cheated, lied to and probably threatened over the next few years. Promise me one thing – whatever they do to you, do not change your inner nature, Richard – that would be folly. Trying to turn yourself into a different person will lead to unhappiness, for you will be living a lie. Truth will always win in the long run."

But there was one question that none of them had been able to advise me on – the question I kept asking myself, only to put it aside. Did Catherine play a part in my future? She was so young in years – too young for me to have taken seriously under normal circumstances. I would not have looked at a village girl her age – even one as well developed as she was. Common sense told me she was far too young for me. But common sense did not work. Common sense did not apply. For Catherine had a maturity I had not met in any young person before the Grey sisters; she was a woman, and although five years younger than I was, probably three years ahead of me in understanding the ways of the world I was about to inhabit.

"Like mother, like daughter," people in Colyton often said. Would Catherine finish up like Lady Frances? Would she rebuke and dominate her man, as her mother seemed to?

Whatever special skills she had – a worldliness, an understanding of how things are, of people and motivations, of risks and dangers, of politics – I knew I certainly did not share them. It was something that I envied, but which at the same time disturbed me. One thing was certain, it was the stuff of the world I was about to enter.

As I turned into the gate of Shute House, I twisted in the saddle and took one last private look at the valley which had held my childhood and which I knew so well.

Only time would tell. In the meantime I had a lot to learn.

❧ CHAPTER 7 ❧

1st May 1551 – Bradgate Park, Leicestershire

Dear Father, Mother and Sister,

I have arrived safely in what I can only describe as the palace of Bradgate Park. The Park is very extensive – much bigger than the deer parks in our valley – and the house is simply enormous and made like a palace, with three storeys, brick facing in patterns called diamonds and diapers, and huge white stone windows, many of them filled with glass, so that even in winter you can see out and over the parkland.

We had a long and eventful journey.

We took the pilgrim roads from Taunton, past Glastonbury and Wells, climbing high into the Mendip Hills to Cheddar, where we visited many water mills beside the fast-flowing river. Lord Henry has such a mill here on the estate and he was insistent that we visited these examples, to observe the latest ideas.

From there to Bristol, where Lady Frances insisted that we took boat, which we did – right up the River Severn to Tewkesbury, that part of the journey taking us two days, but restful after the riding through thick mud for days before that.

Thence cross country again, staying for a night at Warwick Castle, where we were joined by John Aylmer, a jovial man from Norfolk and tutor to the ladies. I hope I can call him my friend, for he is a man of great kindness and learning and I have taken great pleasure in the conversations I have had with him.

We arrived here at Bradgate Park late last night and I have been allowed pen and paper in order to write you this letter, which will be brought by the same messenger who will carry letters from Lord Henry and Lady Frances to those people they wish to thank for their recent visit.

I hope this letter finds you all well, and will write again as soon as the opportunity arises. I do not know when the next messenger will be coming to Devon – most of the messengers seem to travel to the Court, in London, so my next letter may eventually find its way to you through that great city. I hope one day to visit it, but at present have much to learn and understand here at Bradgate.

Signed this 1st May 1551 at Bradgate Park,

Your loving son,
Richard

☙ CHAPTER 8 ❧

Early May 1551 – Bradgate Park

There was a clatter of stones as I reined Jack to a halt at the top of the knoll and turned to look down at the house I was learning to think of as home.

It had all turned out so differently from what I had expected, although, in truth, I was not sure what I had expected. In one way I was disappointed. The land in the Park at Bradgate was much rockier and sparser than I had assumed. I had thought it would all be rich, fertile farming country, like that I had left behind in east Devon. Yet much of this was forest and scrub, with heather and rocks where the tree cover was thinnest.

But as my new friend, Zachary the Parker, had pointed out, that had always been the way things were done in this part of the Groby manor. Since the days of the Ferrers family in the thirteen hundreds, the good lowland was farmed by the tenants and the forest and heathland were used for hunting. It *was* good hunting country to be sure – I had never seen so many red and fallow deer.

I looked down at the huge and impressive house. This certainly had not been a disappointment. It faced south – down the slope and away from me as I sat on the knoll – and was far, far bigger than any I had seen before. I had been told the house was 200 feet wide and the main building thirty feet deep, and it certainly looked it from where I was sitting. At either end were wings, each forty feet deep and stretching sixty feet away from the main façade, forming a letter 'E', with a foreshortened middle section, leaving a huge courtyard to greet new arrivals in front of the imposing main door.

The main construction was of red brick, laid with intricate diamond patterning, and cornered with pale grey granite, which also formed the windows and door surrounds. There were three towers – to the northwest, southwest and southeast corners – each rising four storeys tall, with the body of the building itself a full three storeys, with large, imposing windows.

The little river Lyn ran across the front of the house (the far side from where I sat now), whilst below me there were gardens and a sizeable pond. I could see clearly from my elevated position how someone had made a dam in the river, high above the house, and led the water by a leat, to a position above the back of the house, where it fed the fish ponds, the fresh water supply to the house, and the drains. There was so much water that it was also diverted to a mill attached to the side of the house, where a big water wheel was turning, powering the grinding wheels within, whose rumbling noise reached me even now, as I sat on the hillside.

It was only after visiting the mill with Adrian that I had fully appreciated Lord Henry's interest in the mills at Colyton, and the reason we had all been diverted to Cheddar in the course of our long journey to Bradgate. It was all very impressive. Yet at the same time, something was missing. I wondered, looking at what was now my new home, and which (I had been told) accommodated 200 people, how I could feel so lonely. I thought back over the two weeks since my first arrival here.

I had hardly seen Lady Catherine, who had returned to her studies and to play with her pet animals; and only once had had an opportunity to talk to Lady Mary, when she had generously offered to show me the parterres in the garden, an offer I had yet to take up.

Lady Jane was immersed in her studies with John Aylmer, and apart from one or two meals, which the family had taken publicly in the Great Hall, I had not seen her since our arrival. For the same reason, I had not had the hoped-for opportunity to get to know John Aylmer, who had made such a good impression on me when we had first met.

Most of my time over the last two weeks had been spent with Adrian Stokes. That relationship, at least, was working well. Adrian was eighteen years old – only two years older than I was – and like me, and John Aylmer years before us, had come to the house as a servant, with hopes of personal improvement. At our first meeting, I had thought Adrian was an imposing personality. He was even taller than me – well over six feet – slim and muscular. His face was elongated, with a long, rather hooked nose and very large brown eyes, which looked direct and unblinking at you whilst you spoke – unnerving until you got used to it. Thank goodness he also had his imperfections. His hair was dark and worn short, so that his ears, which were somewhat large, appeared to stick out. Adrian appeared to be conscious of this, and although he was not lacking in self-confidence, that uncertainty prevented him from appearing too self-important.

We had got on well from the first minute. Both of us loved horses and we rode equally competitively and equally well. Both of us hunted with dogs and the bow, both loved hawking, and we even shared pleasure in the gentle art of fishing. Adrian had ridden with me the two miles to Groby Pool, famous for its good fishing for hundreds of years, and we had made plans to visit it again with rods, as soon as our duties allowed.

On my first day at Bradgate, Adrian had introduced me to the Park by riding the length of the pale – a tall wooden fence, carefully constructed on top of a mound, with a ditch beside, on the inner side, to prevent the deer from escaping. It was an impressive piece of work, and kept in good repair by the parkers.

We had met Zachary Parker mending one of the gates on the road to Newton Linford, the nearest village, and he had invited us back to his house for supper. I was surprised to see that the house, although inside the pale, was additionally protected with a moat and heavily barred doors and windows. Zack had made light of it, explaining that in his grandfather's and father's days there had been a lot of resentment about the razing to the ground of the old Bradgate village, when Thomas Grey (the elder) had extended the original deer park and doubled its size. No one would dare take action against the Lord of the manor, but venison was a valuable commodity, and the parker was considered a fair target.

"Ain't so bad these days though," said Zack over supper, "which is just as well, as I wouldn't want my children growing up in fear. We wuz born to this, see – Parkers by name and parkers by nature, this five generations. Reckon the job came first and the name followed. What about you Richard? What's your family name?"

I could see the line of conversation immediately.

"Stocker."

Zack's eyes perked up at what was a clear opportunity for some fun.

"Cows then? Wuz you a stocker, then, before you come here? Have you progressed from cattle to horses?"

I laughed. "You're not too far off, Zack." I turned to Adrian, to complete the jest.

"And you Adrian? Stokes? Were your ancestors charcoal burners in the past?"

Adrian shook his head. "Not that I know of. My father's family were merchants."

Zack looked across the smoky room at him, a mischievous grin on his face. "We all knows the fire what Adrian stokes when he gets the chance, don't us Adrian?"

For the first time since I had met him, Adrian was wrong-footed. He reddened and closed off the discussion rapidly. "Don't you start mischief-making, now Zack. Richard and I have to get back to the house."

❧   ❧

My second day was wet, and with Lord Henry and Lady Frances away in Leicester for the whole day, Adrian suggested we use it to explore the house and to introduce me to the members of the household as we did so.

As Master and Second Master of Horse, our duties at Bradgate were confined to the parkland and stables, which were situated next to the main park gate, just across the river Lyn from the house. Adrian therefore asked the Steward if he could spare the time to conduct the tour of introduction in what was, after all, his domain.

The Steward, James Ulverscroft, seemed pleased at the recognition of his authority, yet at the same time uncertain of my real interest. I didn't know why, but he seemed suspicious of my presence, fearful that I was trying to usurp some of his power.

"The house is large Master Richard, and we have many people here. What would you prefer – to walk round quickly, or to see us in our full detail – warts and all?"

It was clear to me that to ask for a quick tour would be churlish, and would express my lack of true interest in the areas under James's command, so I gave the politic reply. As a result, we spent the whole morning moving slowly through the house, with James pausing in each room to explain its features and function and to point out the few items of furniture we encountered along the way. He also introduced me to the more senior members of the household and explained their functions, although I seemed to have developed a capacity for forgetting names and positions the instant they were announced.

By the time we gathered in the Servants' Hall for dinner (the family being absent) we had only completed the ground floor and cellars beneath, but my head was already spinning with new information and new names. In the west wing, the kitchen and bakery were similar to, if much bigger than, those at Shute, and I took some pride in noting that nowhere was there a fireplace to match that back home. But the Servants' Hall and Great Hall were on a scale I had never seen before and could never even have imagined.

James accompanied me to the east wing, which contained the family's private quarters, comprising the chapel, summer parlour, winter parlour and a second, smaller, private kitchen, situated close to the base of the southwest tower. Here, to my pleasure and amusement, we bumped into John Aylmer. He was taking cake and mulled ale to Lady Jane, who had refused to travel with her parents. Instead she had been studying since very early that morning in her rooms above. He seemed busy and preoccupied. I immediately decided it was not the right opportunity to renew the conversation about helping me with my studies, and chose instead to wait for a more suitable occasion.

The summer and winter parlours were clearly the rooms where Lord Henry and Lady Frances spent most of their time when not hunting. The rooms were cluttered with various items of hunting equipment but I noted with some surprise a distinct absence of books. I had understood that the Greys were well known as a learned family, but the source of their learning certainly did not lie here in their private rooms.

Between the two parlours, and overlooking the terrace, was a small, sunny music room, with two lutes, a harp and a cithern. Here we found Catherine and Mary at their music studies, playing a traditional song about exchanging kisses – although how seriously they were studying was in question, as they were accompanied by two spaniel puppies, a bird in a cage, and a pet monkey chained to a stand. They greeted me civilly enough, but in the presence of Adrian and the Steward it was soon clear that this was a formal visit and our party quickly passed on.

As we entered the chapel, I was expecting an ornate interior such as those I was used to at home, but to my surprise, this chapel was very plain. James Ulverscroft explained in hushed tones that, despite the Chaplain's continuing efforts, his Lordship and her Ladyship used the chapel only lightly; the most frequent users were the Chaplain, Dr James Haddon, Lady Jane and John Aylmer. Their preference, implied Ulverscroft diplomatically, was for the less ornate, Reformist style, and between them they had quietly made their influence felt over the past few years.

We paused to pray for a moment. Kneeling in this simple, quiet room, I could almost feel Jane's presence and understand how she, in her dislike of the noisy, active, unsubtle ways of her parents, would find solace, peace and strength here, as she did upstairs with her books. I remembered my mother's final words to me – not to neglect my studies – and I resolved, as soon as the opportunity arose, to ask John Aylmer to help me. Since I had first felt the influence of this family a short time ago so much seemed to have happened, and in the process life seemed to have become much more complicated.

Adrian was busy in the afternoon, after dinner, and James and I completed our tour without him. In the Greys' absence, James gave me a hurried – almost furtive – view of the family's private rooms on the upper floors above the chapel and parlours of the east wing, being careful in the process not to interrupt Lady Jane at her studies.

Later we returned to the west wing, where we wandered, more comfortably, around the officers' and servants' quarters, stopping more frequently now, for John to introduce me to my new colleagues.

Finally, nearing suppertime, I returned to my own room, where I fell upon the bed, exhausted. The last thing I remembered was the smell of cooking meat and fresh bread wafting up from the kitchens below.

A week later, looking down on it all from Jack's saddle, as we paused on the hillside above the house, I remembered lying in that room, thinking, *If those smells are typical, I shall wake from this bed early every morning.* So far, my prediction had proved correct. I took one more look across the valley at the Park and the house that had so quickly become my life and my home. Jack was beginning to become restless, but I could not bring myself to ride back into that affray quite yet. I needed to think. I patted the stallion's neck, and wondered where it would all lead, and how the strange, huge, frightening, but at the same time exciting, world which this family inhabited, would influence my life.

Was there, I wondered, anything, or any chance of anything, between me and Lady Catherine? I knew I was unable to think about her without my insides churning and my mind making instant jumps from what was sensible, likely, and reasonable to what was possible, even if it was the stuff of dreams. Did she feel the same – or indeed anything, for me? It was impossible for me to tell. I had held her, she had asked me to do more, but did that mean anything? Or was I like the monkey in the music room – just another pet, to be chained to a stand, and used for amusement until the mood changed?

And what of the diminutive Lady Mary? I could not make her out. Common sense said she was a child – only six years old, and unable to comprehend, let alone explain to me, this world of the Grey family. Yet everything she said rang true. Perhaps her circumstances had made her, in her own way, as unusual as her sisters. They were both grown up beyond their years, and with them as examples, perhaps sharing their secret thoughts with her as with no one else, she did have access to a deeper understanding. Then again, perhaps she, too, was manipulating me, using me for her own ends. But what could those ends be? There was so much I didn't understand.

My thoughts turned to Adrian Stokes, who had welcomed me openly enough and who could not have been more diligent in introducing me to the places and people of Groby Manor in general and Bradgate Park in particular. Would our relationship continue? Would I be able to perform my duties to the standard of Adrian's expectations? It was hard following someone into a job while that person was still present. Do it poorly and you let them down. Do it merely adequately and they are disappointed. But excel, do the job better than they had in their time, and you threaten their position, showing that they could have done better. Why was life so complicated?

What of the Steward, James Ulverscroft? He was hard to read, a bit of a cold fish, James, with his lists and his pen. Yet he had welcomed me well enough, shown me round, even given me a glimpse of the family's private quarters. Had I made a fool of myself with James? I had found it so hard to think of sensible questions to ask as we had gone from room to room, and I had forgotten half the names of those I had met along the way. Later, of course, I had thought of a thousand things I could have asked, but by then it was too late.

As if aware of my worries, Jack began to blow and stamp the ground and my mind was diverted as I calmed him down. I looked down at the house again, unwilling to ride down the hill and rejoin all the activity there until I had marshalled my thoughts. As Jack quietened, I began to think about Lord Henry and Lady Frances. Why was Lady Frances so offhand with her husband? Most women I knew were subservient to their husband, for surely he was Master of the House. Lady Frances acted differently. Perhaps that was because (as she never missed an opportunity to remind people) she was of royal blood, as were her daughters. But even if she had her reasons, why did Lord Henry let her get away with it?

And what was behind their strange relationship with their daughter, Lady Jane? Why did they hound her so relentlessly? In the limited time I had known them, she had appeared to be a model daughter and a faultless student. John Aylmer had said as much, yet they never missed an opportunity to diminish her, to criticize her, or to find fault. It was so unfair, especially as they did not seem to treat Lady Catherine or Lady Mary in the same way.

None of it made any sense. It was as if my mind had started to run off in its own directions, directions I did not seem able to control. I began to wonder, for example, why Lady Jane occupied my thoughts so frequently. It was Catherine I had set my heart on, and Jane was nothing like Catherine. She was not nearly as beautiful, and nothing like as easy to talk to. Nor did she like any of the things that I liked. She appeared to me to be, as her mother had said, weak – at least in a physical sense. She was also inaccessible, bookish, and remote. Then why had I felt such a glow of pleasure when, at our first meeting, John Aylmer had praised her so strongly? I certainly did not love her as (perhaps) I loved Catherine. But there was something, some special quality that, despite her bookish aloofness, made her both vulnerable and interesting, and I knew I wanted to know her better, and be her friend, if she would let me.

Reluctantly, for I seemed to have made no progress with my worries, I turned Jack's head toward the house and began to ride home. Why were there always so many questions and so few answers?

ঙ CHAPTER 9 ৬

Mid-May 1551 – Bradgate Park

The long wet winter had dragged into a longer and wetter spring and everyone was depressed. Hunting had been difficult in the muddy conditions and the fresh food which by now should have been enlivening the tables had hardly appeared, so late was the season.

Then, in the middle of May, the pattern broke and spring and summer arrived together. By the third week of May, the Park was transformed with young green growth, and everyone's spirits had lifted.

By now I had become familiar with the rules of the house – stated and unstated – and as a result, when my duties and Adrian's demands permitted, I was able to enjoy the Park and those parts of the house where servants and officers were permitted, without fear of reproach.

Unlike the vegetable garden behind the house, one place that was clearly off bounds was the formal garden. This stood on the east side of the house, immediately below the terrace, which linked it to the family quarters. Here the land fell away gently into the Lyn valley below, and to compensate for this, a huge stone wall had been built all round the garden, with gateways and bridges leading outward, north to the pond, and east, across the Park to Cropston.

With the exception of the gardeners themselves, who were expected to do the majority of their work early in the morning, and to vacate the garden if any member of the family appeared, access to the garden was limited to the family and their guests.

I had noted the garden from the window of the music room on my first conducted tour of the house, but had never had an opportunity to enter it until this particular morning.

I had been returning from Groby and approaching the house across the bridge over the Lyn when I saw someone waving to me from the top of the garden wall.

I rode over toward the wall and stopped Jack at its base. Jack was seventeen-and-a-half hands and I was six feet tall, but still the top of the wall was well above my head. This delighted Lady Mary, who had climbed onto the top of the wall from the raised walkway within, and now sat, legs dangling, two feet above me.

"Ho Richard! I can see the top of your head!" she giggled. "I have never seen that before. How strange it looks."

I bowed in the saddle and saluted her. Although she was only a child, and diminished by her affliction, in recent weeks I had grown used to her strange looks and manner and now felt kindly toward her. She had never had a cross word for me, and she *was* a very useful source of information.

"Good morning my Lady Mary. What a beautiful morning. How warm the sun is. I have just ridden from Groby and have felt a warmth I have not felt since last summer, back home in Devon."

Mary frowned. "Are you saying my family has shown you no warmth since you joined our household? That is a rebuke indeed!"

I looked up at her, uncertain. They could be so sharp this Grey family. One false word and you could be in trouble. To my relief she clambered from her perch on top of the wall to the walkway behind it and proceeded to jump up and down in delight.

> Richard came a-riding
> He made a loose remark
> Richard came a-riding
> And heard a Lady bark.

I bowed low at her song and gave her my best smile. "Well versed indeed, my Lady. I am outclassed in height, in wit and in song."

She clapped her hands. "Pretty talk Richard. They will make a courtier of you yet. You deserve a reward. Pray come and join me up here in the garden, for today it is at its best."

I thanked her, rode Jack around the base of the wall until we reached the track to Cropston, tethered him to the hitching post, and walked over the small footbridge to the garden gate. There was a scrabbling noise behind, but the heavy iron-studded oak door refused to move.

"Can you open the door Richard? It's stuck."

I pushed open the iron gate and found her inside the garden, still skipping and singing her song, which she seemed rather proud of. A small spaniel puppy was running round her feet and she picked him up and cuddled him as I came through the gate.

My immediate impression on seeing the garden for the first time was the sense of order it imparted: the rectangle created by the walls was perfectly proportioned; the outer walls were stepped, creating a raised walkway all round, some two feet below the top of the wall, and four feet above the centre of the garden. It was a clever piece of design: it protected the interior from the wind, and gave clear views, not only over the interior of the garden, but also over the parkland beyond.

The centre of the garden was divided equally into four rectangles by raised paths two feet high, bordered by low, manicured boxwood hedges. Within the rectangles were parterres – sunken lawns, cut very short into intricate patterns, which immediately reminded me of Honiton lace, the earth between the patterns being dry and perfectly weed free.

"Do you like it?" asked Mary, proprietarily.

"It is amazing my Lady. I would not have believed a simple garden – for apart from its complex patterns, the number of different plants is few – could create such an atmosphere of calm."

She clapped her hands again, clearly delighted with this reply.

"Mr Aylmer says it resembles the ideals of the Reformist church, for it brings simplicity in the face of ostentation, and order out of chaos. Jane says this garden is a second chapel, for here you can be close to God and His words become clear to you, unjangled by the cacophony of life."

Not for the first time, I was aware of her ability to learn a phrase and repeat it verbatim. But behind the parrot copy was an idea that stuck in my head and would not go away. Order out of chaos was exactly what I had been seeking, and here, in this beautiful garden, simplicity seemed to be the key.

Now, perhaps, I could understand why Lady Jane and John Aylmer dressed so plainly compared with those around them. If my life was complicated, Jane's must be a thousand times so. She was subject to so many pressures, so much torment. Perhaps her way of handling it was, like retreating into this garden, to withdraw into the ordered framework of her books and the simple truths of her religion. Perhaps the garden could bring me answers too. I looked around for inspiration.

As I turned and studied its ordered perfection, Mary looked at me. "It has reached you too, hasn't it? The garden? Just then you seemed so deep in thought. Was it my sister you were thinking about?"

I looked at her, startled. How had she known I was thinking of Lady Jane?

I looked up, my mind still on Jane and her troubles. "Yes I was. How did you know?"

There was a strange, secretive look on her face and she turned away from me as she spoke, as if catching my eye would break the moment.

"Because she keeps thinking about you. She told me so." She turned to see the effect of her words.

I looked at her, almost beyond words.

"She does?"

"Of course she does. You must have noticed. Cat can't keep her eyes off you. She says she dreams of you. She keeps remembering when you took us to the sea – when you lifted her from her horse – in the woods. You do realize she made me loosen her gown and unlace her stomacher before we set out that morning don't you? I'm sure she's in love with you, but whatever you do, don't tell her I said so."

Now I was totally confused. If I had found order for a moment, it had been replaced by total chaos now. I couldn't think straight; I needed time. She was looking straight at me now, those black eyes penetrating. To gather my thoughts, I began walking round the garden, seeing nothing, my brain in a whirl. I turned back, to find her following a respectful distance behind, clutching her puppy, as if aware of my torment.

"Catherine cares for me? Is it true? Can it be true?"

"Of course she does, but don't you see, that makes it worse, not better."

I was more confused. This didn't make sense. The girl didn't understand what she was talking about.

"How so? How can it be worse if I … and she …?"

Mary stroked the puppy's long ears. "He doesn't understand at all does he Floppy?"

She put the puppy down, and it sat and faced her, responding to the sound of its name. Mary reached up and took my hand, leading me to the steps up to the terrace below the music room. She turned and sat on the lowest step, her black eyes for the first time looking soft, without their customary inquisitive sharpness.

"Catherine likes you very much. Perhaps she even loves you; she has a very romantic nature. Who knows? You were the first one to … well, you know. But it's different here. In Devon you were a romance, an outsider, a dream, a passing fancy. But now we are back home, and you are here, with a position as a servant in our household, she has to return to reality. It's so difficult for all of us. We have so little freedom. We are prisoners of our situation."

Once again, I could hear the echo of someone else's words, but whose? Jane's or Catherine's?

My eye caught a flash of movement behind the window of the music room. Mary saw my glance. In an instant she stood, and began walking across the garden, leading me back toward the gate that I had entered only minutes before. Her voice was a conspiratorial whisper.

"You must be careful, and so must she."

❧   ❧

The moment had passed and the mood had been broken. Our conversation had been brought to an abrupt halt; there had been nothing left to say.

I had taken my leave and galloped Jack round the Park for an hour, trying to clear my head, to bring order again out of chaos. But the garden of my mind had been ploughed asunder, and order would not return.

❧ CHAPTER 10 ❧

Late May 1551– Groby, Leicestershire

One of the many questions flying around in my head received an answer a few days later. The weather had held. It was a quiet time in the hunting season, and the horses were all out on fresh grass. As a result, Adrian and I found the opportunity to take time off from our responsibilities and decided to ride over to Groby Pool to see what fish we could catch.

Fishing poles, with braided horsehair and catgut lines, were kept in the mill for use in the Bradgate pool, and we rode through the forest, carrying them upright on our stirrups, like lances. It was a perfect summer morning: cool after a dew-laden night, but with a clear sky and the promise of a hot, sunny day.

Adrian was in his usual high spirits and looking forward to a good day's sport, with no responsibilities to get in the way of enjoying himself. Usually, when we rode out together, we raced our horses as fast as we could, and competed with each other at jumping every obstacle we found in our path. This competition usually escalated from easy jumps to difficult ones, followed by the improbable, and inevitably the impossible.

Today our fishing rod 'lances' prevented such boisterous behaviour and we had to fall back on talking to each other as we rode.

"Well Richard. It must be nearly a month since I first saw your smiling face at Bradgate. You seem to have settled in very well, my workload has never been lighter and no member of the family has had reason to find fault with either of us. I congratulate you on an excellent start. Long may our success continue, for I feel we make a very capable team." I lifted my 'lance' in salute.

I was pleased and not a little relieved to hear this praise, for I had been unsure how Adrian viewed my efforts. I had certainly worked hard at it, getting to know and understand every aspect of the Groby Manor Estate, Bradgate Park, and the House.

"Thank you indeed Adrian. It is good to hear you say so, for in the early days I feared it might be otherwise."

Adrian seemed surprised at the remark, checked his horse, turned, and frowned.

"Otherwise? Why so? Did you hold your abilities in such low regard?"

"Indeed not. I was confident in my own abilities, but less sure how we would get on together. Since I had been appointed by Lord Henry in your absence, I thought you might see me as a usurper – as a threat to your position."

Adrian stopped his horse and looked at me hard.

"Did you see yourself as a usurper?"

I shook my head and held up my free hand, palm facing toward Adrian, as if in surrender.

"Absolutely not. I considered only your position."

For what seemed to be an eternity, my companion sat stock still in the saddle and looked at me. Then, slowly, he seemed to make up his mind, and kicked his horse forward once again.

"Thank you for your concern, but despite my congratulations just now, I have never considered you as a threat. Your appointment enabled my advancement – which Lord Henry had informed me about by letter before I met you."

We both kicked to a trot, as if to leave behind the awkward moment. We rode for five minutes in silence. Then Adrian began to speak, looking not at me but ahead, along the lane through the forest.

"I am ambitious, Richard. I did not come to Bradgate Park to be a junior servant, and I was not content even when I held the position you hold now. Once my father was a rich man, a successful merchant with wealthy customers in mother church, who paid good prices for his wares and did not quibble. But when the monasteries were closed, his business was ruined. He kept it going long enough to give me my education, but in the end it was too much. My mother died of grief and my father now lives in poverty."

I didn't know what to say. "Adrian I am so sorry. I didn't know."

He shrugged off the offered hand. "No reason you should. Not many people do. Lord Henry knows. He knew my father and respected him. This family has been my salvation. Through their kindness and generosity, a number of young men, including John Aylmer and myself, have been able to gain education, social standing and betterment in this world. Some wicked men say Lord Henry has too great a liking for young men, and only offers the hand of friendship for his own ends, but he has never made advances to me."

"Those are scurrilous accusations," I responded. "Who made them?"

"Lord Henry's enemies. Like everyone in a position of

power, especially those close to Court, the Greys have enemies. It does not help that Lady Frances treats fools like idiots and competitors like dogs, and in both she is usually right. I would recommend you not to incur her wrath if you want to save your plums. My advice would be to pay no heed to such rumours; judge people as you find them, listen to advice, but in the end, always draw your own conclusions. One thing to remember, Richard. This is a tough world, where a man has to look after himself. I plan to better myself and I don't care who I tread on to get there, so work with me and we'll get on fine, but stand in my way, and you will regret it."

It had become a difficult conversation and we both sank into an uncomfortable silence for the rest of the ride to Groby.

☙   ❧

The pool was deep and still, overhung by trees on two sides. The sun had warmed the water and caused the weeds to grow fast, so that they covered more than half the water's surface. Nevertheless, we were able to find two holes in the weeds in the shade of a large oak, but far enough away from it that we could lift our fishing poles without obstruction.

Adrian had instructed one of the stable boys to dig us a goodly quantity of small worms from the dung heap and these proved to be an effective bait. By the time the sun had moved round far enough for the shade of the oak to have been lost, we had caught a dozen fish between us, including a good sized carp and a pike which had grabbed a small roach as Adrian was pulling it in, and clung on with such ferocity that I had been able to jump into the shallow water and grab it, so that it, too, had finally been pulled onto the grass.

Having made enough commotion to frighten every fish in the lake, we decided to find another shady spot and retrieved our ale bottles from the tethered horses as we went.

"Pah, this ale is red hot!" shouted Adrian in disgust, for his ale bottle had been tied to his horse's saddle and his horse had found that standing in the sun provided respite from the flies.

"Try this." I had brought my ale in a stone flask that I had used for years, since being given it in Lyme. It was made of glazed pottery and round, with drilled ears through which a thong was threaded for carrying. I had been told it was called an 'owl' in that part of Dorset, and I knew from experience how good it was at keeping drinks cool during haymaking and other hot summer activities, including those which traditionally took place amongst the hay when the haymaking was over.

"That's better. Well done, Richard. Countryman's ways win again!" Adrian fell back in the dry grass under our new tree, to rest in the warmth of the early afternoon.

"Returning to this morning's conversation Richard," he called, without opening his eyes, "would you describe yourself as ambitious? Were you poor in childhood?"

This was an important and difficult question and one not to be answered in a hurry. I leaned on an elbow, took the blade of grass from my mouth and considered my reply.

"It was different for me. I was brought up on a farm. Apart from a few merchants in Colyton, the nearest town to where I was brought up, I suppose everybody in my part of the world could really be called 'poor' by the standards you were describing this morning. But we were all in the same situation together, we had enough to eat most of the time, except, perhaps early spring, when the winter stores started to run out, and the new crops were not yet ready, but even then everybody experienced it each year, so it was normal.

"Over the past fifty years the wool trade has made things better for Colyton people and I suppose it rubbed off on the farming community as well, so we all had a bit more than in the past. My neighbour and friend Dr Thomas Marwood says that all wealth is relative. He says the Great Lord who has been brought down from three great estates to only one feels he has lost everything, whilst the poor man with a dry roof over his head and a full belly, who used to be homeless and hungry, thinks his prayers have been answered."

Adrian opened his eyes in surprise. "We have a philosopher

in our midst. But does your philosophy make you ambitious?"

"I don't know. That is, I am not sure. My father brought me up to believe in hard work. He says that most farmers are given the farm they live on, and cannot change it, but every man should farm his land to the best of his ability. In my case I do want to make the most of life but I am still not sure of the direction. Thomas Marwood told me to remember that 'a thirst for knowledge is better than a hunger for power'. I think I agree with him on that – although, so far, I have little experience of either."

Adrian laughed. "A good jest Richard, but I am not sure I agree with you. I have observed power and lived amongst it. Power brings wealth. And wealth buys everything, including food, drink, knowledge and, some would have it, even eternal salvation."

I was unsure and avoided replying. Bradgate Park and the lives of the Grey family were evidence themselves for some of what I had said. Yet the division of the spoils was very uneven. Lord Henry and Lady Frances clearly used their power to create wealth and seemed to use that wealth in pursuit of even more power. Yet I had seen little evidence in my short time in this place that their hunger for power was in any way matched by a thirst for knowledge. And as for eternal salvation, I would prefer to hedge my bets.

But Lady Jane's attitude was the reverse. She seemed to have no desire for power and shunned ostentatious sartorial displays of wealth, preferring to dress simply. And there was no denying the extent of her thirst for knowledge. John Aylmer had summed it all up when we had first met at Warwick Castle. And as far as Adrian's final point was concerned, there was one thing I felt confident about; in the race for eternal salvation, Lady Jane was already three lengths ahead of everyone else.

The thought seemed to clear my head and I sat up abruptly, so that Adrian opened his eyes and sat also, fearing something was amiss.

"Thank you Adrian. You have answered something that was troubling me."

He jumped to his feet. "Now let's get back to work and catch some more fish. I'll wager you cannot repeat this morning's trick and catch one fish inside another a second time!"

Laughing, we returned to the waterside.

&ᴖ CHAPTER 11 ᴖ&

Early June 1551 – Bradgate Park

A week later, my thoughts went back to that fishing trip. I had been up to the top of Warren Hill – about a mile to the north of the house – with Zachary Parker. Zack had told me there were peregrine falcons nesting in the rocks near the top of the hill, and agreed to show me where the nest was. Although very familiar with hawking – I had been working with hawks for longer than I could remember – I had never had the opportunity to bring on a bird of my own. This brood was, according to Zack, about eight weeks old, already beginning to fly and just ready to be taken from the nest.

It had been a gamble. Rearing and training a young hawk was notoriously difficult; you had to give them all your attention for the first few days and most of the first few nights, and I had only been inclined to try by the fact that Lord Henry and Lady Frances had gone to visit Lady Frances's cousin, Princess Mary, at Audley End, in Essex, and would not be back for at least a week.

There was another risk with a peregrine; traditionally eagles and peregrines were reserved for royalty and I certainly did not have the status to own one of my own. However, I had thought that if I could get the bird flying to my hand, and obeying my commands, then I might be able to present it formally to Lady Frances (who, I thought, was royal enough to merit the breed) and continue to fly it on her behalf on hawking trips. It would be a good plan if it worked, for not only would it give me a chance to hawk with the family, but it would put me in Lady

Frances's good books. If I was ever to make any progress with Catherine, that was where I needed to be.

In the event, the whole scheme had come to nothing, for the birds had quit the nest as Zack and I climbed the rocks, and circled angrily around us until we gave up for the day and returned to our horses. We had agreed that the only answer was to creep up to the nest about dawn the following morning, and try to net one of the young as soon as the parents took their first flight of the day. To be honest, I did not have much faith in the plan, but Zack was such an enthusiast, and so persistent, that most of his schemes did seem to work, eventually.

Now I reined Jack back, as we reached the domestic fish-ponds and followed the fast-flowing leat, skirting the vegetable garden at the rear of the house. I was just about to clear the trees, remembering with satisfaction the fishing and the conversation Adrian and I had shared just a few days ago, when I was startled by a small figure stepping out from amongst the track-side bushes.

"Hello Richard," called Catherine nonchalantly. "I thought I recognized you riding down the hill just now. What took you to Warren Hill this early?"

"Lady Catherine! You surprised me." I threw back my riding cloak, for it had been cold when I set off early that morning, then dismounted and tied Jack to a branch.

I was excited at the opportunity of her company alone and my heart started beating faster. "Good morning my Lady, this is a pleasure."

"Please call me Catherine when we are alone."

She looked at me out of the corner of her eye. "Anyway, I am not your lady." She took a couple of paces away from me, turned, threw her head back and looked direct into my eyes.

"Yet."

My heart beat even faster. I became breathless. Eagerly, I walked toward her and took her hands in mine, pulling her toward me. She was fresh-washed; I could smell the soap and herb mixture she loved to use.

"Catherine!"

I put my arms round her and she did not resist. I kissed her and she responded, holding me tighter and opening her mouth, uncertainly at first, and then hungrily. I could feel the heat of her body as I pulled her closer, allowing my riding cloak to fall around her.

There was a sound of footsteps and laughter as two girl servants made their way from the pond to the vegetable garden gate, carrying a basket of fish between them. They saw us and turned away, discreetly. As the girls ran toward the house, we could hear them chattering and giggling together, animatedly.

She stepped back and looked at me, uncertain, her expression changing second by second. I reached forward, put my arm round her shoulder, drawing her back beneath my riding cloak. We stood close together, breathing each other's breath, clinging to the moment and not knowing whether the interruption had broken the spell or whether we could, or should, move forward again.

She began to speak into my chest, as if she dared not look at my face as she did so. She spoke quietly, uncertainly, so that I had to bend to hear what she was saying.

"Richard. Is it real – for you I mean? Am I to be more than just another one of your conquests?"

I stroked her hair and spoke into it, also afraid to make eye contact as I spoke.

"What conquests?"

Now she pulled away from me, tears running down her face.

"I know you are experienced, that you have had so many girls. They all fall at your feet. The servant girls look at you as you walk by, nudge each other, and go red in the face. I have seen them. You are tall, strong, handsome and – so desirable. You must have had your way with most of the girls on this estate if half the rumours are true."

I wiped the tears from her cheek with the back of my hand, kissed one eye, then the other, then her lips, and pulled her back into the protection of my cloak.

"You silly rabbit. You should know better than to believe tittle-tattle like that. I don't believe there are rumours as you say, and if there were, none of them would be true. I have not laid a hand on any girl, not even noticed another girl since the day you looked at me across the fireplace in Shute House. You must believe me, for it is God's truth."

She gave me a little punch in the chest. "Don't blaspheme, Richard." I knew it was not a rebuke; I could hear the relief in her voice. I hugged her close, then, slowly, not to break the moment again, brought her to arm's length and bent down so that my eyes were level with hers.

"Catherine. I love you. It's as simple as that. There are no other women in my world, just you."

She clung to me, shaking, sobbing like the child she still was when the mask slipped, snuffling against my jerkin.

"Oh Richard. What are we going to do? It is so difficult here for Jane, for Mary and for me. We are tied to a regime. Up early, morning prayers, breakfast, studies, dinner, more studies, supper, music studies and reading then bed and the whole cycle repeats itself. The only respite from this prison is that our gaoler, Mr Aylmer, is the kindest man you could wish. Without that, I think we should all have gone insane. Particularly Jane, for she bears the brunt of our parents' displeasure."

I stroked the back of her head gently. "I have seen them do it, but cannot understand why. For surely she, above all of you, is a model student?"

She looked up at me, wiped her eyes with her knuckles.

"That's the point. She has surpassed them, in deportment, in music, in ancient languages, and modern. But most of all, she has outgrown them in religion and philosophy. They feel stupid and clumsy in her presence and think she is laughing at them behind their backs. Their ambition is easy to see – it stands out like a beacon. They always wanted her to marry our cousin the King. That is what she has been shaped for since she was very young. But now she has attained all the necessary graces and her intellect matches that of King Edward and the Princess Elizabeth, they cannot deliver the contract. Thomas Seymour's promises came to nothing and my sister was sacrificed to that scheming lecher with his morning visits and disgusting exploring hands."

Something in what she had just said raised an echo of a previous conversation – who was it with – Mary perhaps. But now was not the moment to be talking about Lady Jane. Now I wanted to talk about Catherine – and me.

"What are their plans for you Catherine?"

"I don't know. They will marry me off, of course. Someone powerful, who can strengthen the trump card of my mother's royal connection and bring my family the further wealth and power they believe it deserves."

"Do you mean you could be told to marry just anyone? You have no choice?"

"The law says our views have to be taken into account, but the reality is that we must accept. We have two choices. Accept the easy way – quickly – or try to fight and finish up accepting the hard way, having it beaten into us."

All of my protective instincts were now at work.

"But that's disgraceful. Surely we can do something. Couldn't we get married in secret?"

Now she smiled the smile she used when explaining basic house rules to her puppy.

"The marriage would be annulled. Doctors would be brought in to testify I was still a virgin so that, in any event, the marriage had not been consummated, and you would disappear quietly within a week. *That's* the reality."

I felt the situation had suddenly reversed. A minute ago, it had been I who was the strong one, comforting her, now I did not know what to do, and she it was who took command. Now, for the first time since the Grey family had entered my life, I realized how all-pervading their influence was upon those around them.

I needed to get the conversation back to where it had been leading before I had asked about Jane. She hadn't actually said she loved me, only implied it by her apparent jealousy.

71

"Catherine?" I held her face in my hands. "Do you love me as I love you?"

The tears began to flow again, even faster this time. "Of course I do. But what are we to do? I cannot marry you. They would never allow it, and even if they did, the King would not allow it."

"The King? What has it to do with the King?"

She shook her head, and snorted, indicating that I had no idea of the workings of her world. This was not going well. I was becoming desperate. "We could become lovers in secret." As soon as I had said it I regretted the words.

"In secret? Have you ever tried to keep a secret in this household?"

Suddenly we heard the sound of an approaching horse. We pulled apart, Catherine wiping her red eyes as best she could, whilst I tried to look relaxed and informal.

"I must go Richard. We will think of something. Do not forget me." With that she was gone, slipping through a small gap in the bushes as the horse grew nearer and Adrian rode into view.

"Ho Richard! What are you doing down there? Collecting caterpillars?" His eyes scanned the scene, the tethered horse, and the footprints in the side of the track, the small gap in the hedge leading back to the house.

He waved me toward him, a friendly but serious smile on his face. "Come Richard. Ride with me for a while, for we need to talk."

I mounted and we rode together round the house and away from it, upstream along the river Lyn, until we reached the dam, which diverted some of the water into the leat. The water was running over the dam, making enough noise for our conversation not to be overheard accidentally.

"You are a good man Richard, but you have a lot to learn about life in this family. You are in love with Lady Catherine, and think you have a future together." I went to protest, but Adrian waved me down.

"Don't try to deny it. I have seen you look at her with calf-eyes. You are not the first and you won't be the last. Yours is not the first heart she has broken. She is beautiful, intelligent, a talented musician and in the royal line. She will make someone a good wife, Richard. But it won't be you, unless the world turns upside down."

Again, I went to reply, but Adrian had not finished.

"But that's not the real danger. The real danger lies in the fact that she looks at you the same way. I have seen it and so have some of the servants. So far, Lady Frances seems to have been too pre-occupied with her own thoughts to notice anything. But when she does, you are in deep trouble. Have a care Richard. Have a care. For her sake as well as your own."

He turned his horse and rode off, leaving me sitting astride Jack, by the side of the river, once again lost in thought.

❧ CHAPTER 12 ❦

Mid-June 1551– Bradgate Park

As the weeks went by, I slowly began to realize that the size of Bradgate Park had a large effect upon the way it worked as a community.

It seems stupid now, looking back, but this obvious fact only really dawned on me one evening, in mid-June. I was sitting alone in the servants' hall, in the quiet period when supper was over. The tables had already been cleared and scrubbed, but most of the servants – those who did not have the privilege of a separate (if shared) bedroom – had not yet returned with their bedding to prepare for sleep in the rushes on the floor.

I could have kicked myself when I realized the simplicity of the error I had made. I had assumed that daily life at Bradgate, although on a much larger scale, would be essentially the same as it had been at Shute. In reality the two places could hardly have been more different.

Shute had been one community. Although everyone, from the highest to the lowest, had an ordered place and knew what it was, everyone had shared the same space; we passed each other many times during the day and often spoke as we did so. Everyone knew everyone and most of the time we were aware of events around us.

In the temporary quiet of that evening, I finally realized two things: not only did Bradgate work as two separate communities – family and servants – but the building itself had been built that way, with the east wing planned from the very beginning as the family's private quarters. It was also clear, once I began to think about it more closely, that as time went by, that decision had been strengthened, for, as James Ulverscroft the Steward had explained to me as we made our original tour of the building, the private kitchens on the corner of the east wing had been added later (by Thomas Grey, 2nd Marquess, in the 1520s) and as a result, the family quarters were now self-sufficient from a day to day point of view. The fact was, the family was steadily (if quietly) withdrawing from ordinary people like me, and the household servants around me.

I also realized that that separation affected me directly, and in more ways than one. Not only did it keep me from talking to Lady Catherine as often as I would have liked (which was daily), but it was the reason I had been unable to continue my discussions with John Aylmer. I realized now that he had made the transition to the family circle, and as a result, had a room on the top floor of the east wing and ate with the family when they retreated to their quarters. Conversely, it seemed I had not, after all, become a true part of the Grey family circle, as I had hoped.

I was still trying to think of a way to overcome this problem when the man himself passed by the window, walking along the back of the house, toward the rear entrance. Quickly I jumped to my feet and ran through the doors into the Great Hall, just as John Aylmer entered from the rear of the house.

The family had, once again, withdrawn into the east wing, and there were no guests present in the house who might need to sleep there, so the Great Hall was empty as I cannoned into the room. John Aylmer seemed lost in thought as I entered the hall, but quickly broke into one of his friendly smiles as I nearly ran into him.

He spoke before I could gather my thoughts.

"Richard, just the man. I was thinking of you, as I took my evening stroll. I owe you an apology, for I agreed to meet with you again to discuss the continuation of your education. I trust that little has been lost, for your first few weeks here must have been education enough, I'll wager. Come, let us walk outside, for the evening air is cool. I have just been watching the swallows catching flying ants. There are hundreds of them above the vegetable garden this evening, for there is no appreciable wind."

I had to smile. The man had style, and for all his learning, still had retained the country knowledge of his Norfolk childhood.

"Well met, John. I was thinking of the same thing, and how the architecture of this great house has conspired to ensure we never meet."

John took my arm and we walked through the rear entrance and joined the path between the house and the vegetable garden. He waved his arm to signify the air around us.

"See how they swarm. And what a feast for the swallows."

I nodded, as enthusiastic as the man I hoped to call my friend. "Then we should visit the river, for I'll wager the trout will be as interested as the swallows in this gift from God."

We walked away from the house and joined the river just below the leat dam. Sure enough, the deep pool below the dam was alive with rising trout, which were gorging themselves on the flying ants as they fell onto the water. John sat on the leat wall and watched the activity. "Nature's wonder. Never ending, each season handing a gift to the next, as each human generation leaves something for those who follow."

He seemed happy, but I was in more sombre mood. "Quite so John, but just as some years are fat and some are lean, so the legacy left by some generations is more a burden and less a gift than that left by others."

He put a hand on my arm. "You are troubled Richard. What's wrong? At your age you should feel invincible."

I began to talk and as soon as I did so, it poured out from me.

"I am so confused John. I wake every morning full of energy and optimism, and want to fill the day to overflowing. Yet most evenings, as I fall asleep, I feel – well, not a sadness, that would be too strong a word – but a disappointment, at an opportunity missed, as if the day had been too short, or incomplete.

"Inside me is an appetite, but I do not know what for. Just before I left Devon, my friend and mentor, Dr Thomas Marwood, told me that a thirst for knowledge is more important than a hunger for power. I think I believe that. I dislike power. I dislike what it does to people, the unfairness it produces."

My companion looked over the water at the still-rising trout, but I knew he was still listening; he just needed time to think. Finally, he half-turned back toward me, a serious look on his face, but instead of facing me fully, he spoke to the river. "Remember Richard, that the pursuit of knowledge is at no other man's expense, but the pursuit of power is nearly always a competitive one and a rougher game by far."

A large trout was rising close under the bank opposite us. Unlike the splashy rises of the smaller fish, this old grandfather was sipping down the ants, almost without leaving rings on the surface. John Aylmer watched it for a while, then spoke again.

"Power can be benign. The power of God, the power of … a good king."

I looked at him. "You were going to say 'the power of the church', weren't you?"

At this, John Aylmer turned toward me. "For a young and declaredly confused man, you can sometimes be very perceptive, Richard. I did indeed swallow my words, for I wished to avoid getting into a dangerous political discussion. I was going to say that I believe the power of one church may be benign, but another may be malignant."

I nodded. "I am beginning to feel that too. I felt it in the parterre garden, which I visited with Lady Mary some time ago. She said you considered the garden brought 'simplicity in the face of ostentation and order out of chaos', as does the Reformist church. I think I believe that. Certainly deep inside I know I seek order out of chaos, but every time I gain some semblance of order in my life, a new piece of chaos seems to arrive."

"That's because, sometimes, we create our own chaos by the actions we take. Have you ever watched someone trying to row an over-laden boat against the flow in the middle of a fast river? The harder he tries, the bigger the bow-wave he creates, and the bigger the pressure from the bow-wave, the more he leans back and pushes harder. In the end he is exhausted and the strong current drags him back downstream."

The story rang so true; I remembered the problem well enough from my childhood on the estuary of the River Axe. "What is the answer, John?"

Again, he spoke to the river. "There is no one answer. There may be many; wait for the current to subside, re-trim the boat with less weight in the bow, sit forward not back, or perhaps take short strokes not long ones." Now, as if in emphasis, he turned and faced me.

"Or try rowing up the side of the river, nearer the bank, where the current is less strong."

I knew he was telling me something important. "What are you trying to tell me John?"

He turned his back on the river, and gave me his full attention. "I will not tell you how to live your life any more than I will the three Ladies in my care. I offer them life's choices and let them decide. So it is with you. Your Shute was like a small stream. Bradgate Park is a large river. But the Royal Court is a raging torrent. You are now standing on the edge of that torrent, although you may not realize it."

I thought for a moment before replying. Dare I mention her name? I decided John could be trusted.

"Do you mean Lady Catherine?"

Aylmer nodded. "Your regard for each other is clear and understandable. But you are fishing in someone else's stream Richard, and it's private fishing."

77

I clenched my fist, seething at the warning. How dare he! No one owned Catherine.

"Thank you John. I understand what you are saying, but some things in life cannot easily be determined by tactical considerations."

John Aylmer looked at me hard, his hand now on my arm. "Mistake me not Richard. This issue for you is not tactical. It is strategic, and you are no Machiavelli."

A cold shiver ran through me. It was unlike John to produce so pointed a threat.

"I know it John. I have much to learn and thank you for your direct and honest counsel."

We sat together, looking at the river. The evening had grown cooler, the ants had stopped swarming, and the trout had dropped back to their accustomed positions, closer to the rocks at the bottom of the river. The activity had ceased and it had become quiet.

"Will you help me quench my thirst for knowledge please John? If I am to draw my boat away from the main current and into the shallows, I shall have more time for contemplation."

John Aylmer roared with laughter and punched my arm in delight. "Well said sir! Well said indeed. For a moment I thought I had dampened your spirits."

❧   ❧

We went back into the house, found some ale, and took it outside again, then continued talking late into the night. We discussed what studies might be of benefit to me. My English, he said, both spoken and written, was good but my Latin would benefit from discussions in logic and debating. Since most of these tended to focus on religion and the scriptures – only Lady Jane had entered Plato's Republic – Aylmer himself would make time for me.

He also volunteered some time with Dr Harding, who would teach me another language. For some time, we debated which language it should be. Finally, remembering Dr Marwood's extended stay in Padua where he had trained as a Doctor, I chose Italian. Since this was rapidly becoming the leading language of international diplomacy (thanks more to the Venetians than Rome, as far as England was concerned) John Aylmer quickly agreed.

It was almost dark when we finally returned to the house. As we walked in the door, the sounds of the multitude preparing for bed reminded us that our privacy was coming to an end. Aylmer took my elbow and pulled me close to his whispering voice.

"Don't forget Richard. Row gently. Gently. And keep out of the main stream if you can."

෨ ෫

I lay in bed, thinking.

"If you can."

That did not sound like an instruction, but more of a dispensation with accompanying warning. As always when I lay in bed, I began to think of Catherine. Her last words to me had been "Do not forget me". I would never do that, could never do that.

Somehow we would find a way, but we would have to be discreet, and this place seemed to be designed to make it difficult.

෨ CHAPTER 13 ෫

Mid-June 1551 – Bradgate Park

I saw her the next day. She came to the stables, bold as brass, when we were at our busiest, asking for Dobby.

I saddled the palfrey for her and led it to the mounting block, to help her mount. She looked round, and for a moment we were alone, the stable boys and girls having magically found urgent business elsewhere.

"Richard, I must talk to you. Can you ride with me now?"

I found a horse already saddled and we rode together, away from the house and toward Ansty. As soon as an opportunity arose, she turned off the track and I followed her into a small clearing in the woods.

She did not dismount. It was clear that she was in a hurry.

"Quickly Richard, for I must be in Ansty to meet my parents and I am late already."

She turned the palfrey so she could lean closer to me from her saddle.

"I just wanted to tell you that I love you. I have decided that we cannot live our life in the shadow of tomorrow, but must make what we can of it, from day to day."

My mind was racing. She had said "our life" not "our lives".

"I will find a way, using our studies as a cover. I understand John Aylmer is to give you tuition in Latin and philosophy, and Dr Harding in Italian? That is good. I will try to get my father's agreement that John can teach you in the book room. That is within the family quarters on the east wing. Once our studies are progressing, he often leaves us to get on with them alone for some time. I expect the same will be true for you. That will be your opportunity to slip away. My bedroom is directly above it, with a small staircase nearby. Leave it to me ..."

She leaned over and kissed me, turned her horse, rode quickly through the branches to the Ansty track, and was gone, without a backward glance.

My heart was racing at the prospect of our being together, but somehow, I was not sure this plan was going to work.

                                    ❧   ❧

By the time I got back to the house, my heart had slowed, but my mind was still racing. What exactly had she meant by "living our life"? I also kept returning to the other question that appeared and reappeared in my mind – what had caused her to make this sudden announcement? There had been an urgency in her remarks that exceeded enthusiasm. I knew her well enough now to recognize her impetuous nature – that was part of her charm – but this was something more, as if she was afraid of something.

As I reached the stables I saw Mary hovering in the courtyard.

Instantly I could tell this was no accident. It was clear she had something to tell me and was dying to do so. I dismounted and turned toward her. Before I could say anything, she was talking.

"Richard, have you heard the news? Our sister Jane is betrothed! To Edward Seymour, Lord Hertford!" She rolled her eyes. Clearly the ladies of this household thought Lord Hertford was a real catch.

I had seen Hertford at the house on a few occasions. At first I had been unsure who he was, as Frances habitually called him 'son' and treated him as one of her own. Even now, I didn't know much more than that, as he had never spoken to me personally, but I understood he was very serious and well educated. I did remember seeing him deep in conversation with Jane as they strolled round the gardens together; perhaps this was one marriage which had been arranged in heaven as well as in the counting houses?

I beamed at Lady Mary and bent to speak to her more easily.

"That is good news is it not? Is Lady Jane pleased with the arrangement?"

"Oh yes. She is. She is delighted, for she and Edward share pleasure in study and in books. He is also very handsome and quite charming. I suppose it will be Catherine's turn next?"

Her eyes flicked toward me as she spoke. The remark had more than the effect she expected. I stood and stared at her. What did she mean? Surely not that I ... and Catherine ...?

Then with a crash it hit me. Catherine expected to be betrothed to someone else, and in the near future. Her urgency was driven by that expectation. It would have been inappropriate for her to be betrothed before Jane, but now Jane's future was arranged, they would be planning hers. That was what she had meant by 'make what we can of it, day to day'. She meant a temporary romance.

I waved to Mary and walked into the stables in a daze, returned the borrowed horse without thought and ran back to the house, the stairs and my room. For an hour the thoughts flooded into and out of my head. Slowly I realized that she was right, that our long-term futures were not to be together, but that, perhaps, for a short while, we might truly love each other.

❧ Chapter 14 ❧

Mid-June 1551 – Bradgate Park

"Look, like this."

Zachary Parker held the spoke-shave and pulled it lightly along the yew branch, from the centre, toward the end, which was deeply embedded in the leather apron around his waist. He turned the branch and repeated the action at the other end, then turned it again, occasionally hefting it in his hand at its centre, testing the point of balance.

Slowly the shape of the branch was transformed, and I could recognize the strong taper of an English longbow emerging from the wood beneath Zack's hands. It was fully six feet long and, after two hours of careful effort, had the smooth, even taper of a deer antler.

Carefully Zack cut notches into each end, then laid the bow carefully on his bench.

"There. That needs to dry out slowly now for three months before we can string it, otherwise half the power will be lost. Notice I don't fall into the trap of leaning it against the wall in the corner of the room? Distorts the bow, that do. Ruins it. No shortcuts in this job. Gotta be a proper job or nuthin'."

I looked at the finished bows, lying flat along dowel pegs in the cross beams of the little shed and marvelled at the craftsmanship on display.

"They are beautiful Zack. I never realized just how much went into making a good bow."

"Make a proper job. That's what my old man used to tell me when I was a young 'un. The good Lord gave us skills and He demands that we uses them to the best of us ability. I never had a bow snap. Never."

He eyed me mischievously.

"Seen a few fingers broke in the pullin' of 'em though!"

We both laughed.

"How you getting on with that Adrian then?"

I was not surprised. I had known Zack would return to that old theme. He always did.

"I have no complaints. Adrian has been good toward me, showed me round and made sure I met everyone I needed to know. Even you, you old rascal."

Zack laughed until he started to cough, then sat down wheezing.

"Just you make sure he doesn't lead you into bad ways, that's all."

"Bad ways, what bad ways would he lead me into then?"

Zack picked his teeth with a splinter, and then threw it on the fire.

"You know how a parker does his job do ee? Mainly by keeping quiet. You see everything if you keep quiet. Deer, badgers, foxes, poachers and young lovers in the woods. That's why they calls us nosey parkers, 'cos we keep us eyes and ears open."

"Which young lovers have you been spying on now then Zack?" I asked, not sure I wanted to hear the answer.

"Well I seen you more'n once — with that Lady Catherine. You want to be careful Master Richard. She's a real beauty that one, although still half a child, and many would be jealous. Tongues will wag if you're not careful and if the Master hears of it, you're finished."

I was concerned now, not for myself, but for Catherine.

"Whatever you do, don't say anything to Adrian," I said, urgently.

"Adrian? He's not your risk, he's up to his neck in it himself. No, you must be careful Lord Henry don't hear anything, or you are finished."

My immediate reaction was to relax. I knew full well the risk if Lord Henry got any inkling about me and Catherine. But what had Zack said about Adrian? "Up to his neck in it himself"? With whom? A shiver ran down my back. Not Catherine? Not with Adrian? Surely not.

I slipped the question out as nonchalantly as I could. "Adrian? What's he been up to then? You can tell me Zack. I shan't say a word — I dare not!"

Zack enjoyed his moment. He found another splinter and cleaned his teeth with it for a couple of minutes, until I thought I would burst with impatience. Finally, Zack cremated his latest toothpick, and grinned. He tapped the side of his nose as he spoke.

"Her Ladyship of course. Lady Frances. At it like hammer and tongs they are, whenever the opportunity arises. You would be amazed what happens when the hunt gets dispersed."

I could not believe it. "She's old enough to be his mother!"

Zack looked at me in mock amazement. "That's good, coming from you, and your head buried in the cradle of her second child!"

"But that's not the same. Our age difference is only five years. But she must be …"

"Doesn't seem to stop her, any road. And the expression on his face last time I saw them together did not look like disappointment."

A log from the fire shifted suddenly and Zack moved to prevent it falling into the hearth. His sly old eyes squinted across at me through the wood smoke.

"And if you didn't know about that, I reckon you must be blind, deaf and daft. You must be the last person in the household to realize it."

I sat back and picked up the flagon of cider that had been by my elbow throughout the conversation.

Well I'll be damned! I thought. *Adrian, the sly fox. And after all that advice he gave me.*

CHAPTER 15

Late June 1551 – Bradgate Park

A week later, the family held a large dinner, to which everyone from Bradgate to Leicester was invited. After hiding themselves away in their quarters for weeks, apparently deep in discussion, the deliberations that had preoccupied them, appeared to have been resolved. It had been announced that Lord Henry would shortly be leaving for Dorset House in London, but that the remainder of the family would remain here in Bradgate. After their enforced isolation, the Greys had clearly decided to make up for it, for the Great Hall was full to groaning.

It was an ostentatious show of wealth and power. The great and good of Leicestershire were present and every opportunity was taken to show how well the family were doing. In addition to the usual fare, rare birds, including peacocks, were placed on all tables and at the end of the meal I saw more strawberries than I had ever seen before, carried aloft by the cooks.

The high table was dressed in its finery, so that most of them were sweating in the summer warmth from the heavy brocades, sable collars, pearls, and other jewels. One diminutive figure stood out, as always. Jane was dressed in a plain dark blue velvet gown with a single pearl brooch hanging from a gold chain around her neck. Catherine had chosen the middle ground, and although well adorned and much more so than her sister, did not share the Christmas decoration of her parents.

I thought she looked agitated and tried to catch her eye, but there were over 200 people in the room and try as I could, I could not gain her attention, although she kept looking round the room as if looking for me. Eventually, in sheer frustration, I gave up the effort and concentrated on the excellent wines instead.

~ ~

There had been more than enough ale, wine and good French brandy present and all, including me, had consumed their share.

In due course, I had to excuse myself and make my way to the privy behind the servants' quarters, for the nearest facilities already had an uncomfortable queue outside them.

As I pushed though the crowd, I was suddenly aware of Catherine, at my elbow. She pushed a note into my hand and whispered.

"Richard. Hide this now, but read it later. I had to write to you. I am so sorry my love."

I tried to catch her. I hadn't spoken to her for over a week, but before I could gather my wits, she was gone, and I was carried forward by the uncomfortable line of over-indulged diners.

෨ ෪

Finally, I got back to my room and flung myself on the bed, head reeling and stomach uncomfortably full. I pulled the letter from my doublet pocket and held it up to the candlelight to read.

I immediately recognized her neat, even handwriting.

Richard, my love,

My heart is breaking, and I cannot continue like this. It hurts me so to look at you every day, to pass near you, and yet to be unable to talk, let alone more.

Inside I want to be with you, to have you touch me, to have you love me. I have dreamed of this since shortly after we first met, and even before we went to the beach together, I wanted you to touch me. What happened that day was not fully an accident, for I had made certain preparations that modesty forbids me to explain more fully. How I now wish my plans had been more carefully laid, for I should have been your lover on that morning and you mine.

Since returning to this house we have danced a public galliard, bowing here, acknowledging there, but never allowed to touch fully as we would both wish. You know it was my remaining dream to know your love completely before I was irrevocably committed elsewhere, in a direction not of my own choosing. But mine is a hopeless dream. I am like my own pet monkey, believing I have freedom to move where I am bid, but chained, always chained to my stand. If I break

the rules, my chain will be jerked hard. I could take that discomfort for the joy of knowing you love me and feeling your
love just once, but the greater penalty would be for you, and
I cannot contemplate being the originator of your downfall.
If we persist, we will both end up getting hurt. I cannot
make my own decisions, and now that you have entered
my father's employ, it is clear, neither can you.

My love, we must stop this before it hurts us all.

Please be assured of my undying love.
Goodbye.

Ever Yours
Cat

I could not believe it. I read the letter three times and still I would
not accept the truth of the words I read there. What had happened?
It was less than two weeks since she had found me in the stables,
we had ridden together, and she had told me of her plan for us
both. Now, suddenly, oh so suddenly, she had ended it, and like this,
in writing. She was not even here to question, to ask why.

That was the clue to it. That was why she had written. She
could not do it face to face. Then, miserably, I realized that this was
not her decision. The monkey's chain had been jerked already.

Who had done it? Had Adrian told Lady Frances during one
of their trysts? Or had John Aylmer taken Catherine on one side
and told her to act like a lady, and to obey her parents? Next
time I saw John Aylmer I would find out.

❧ CHAPTER 16 ❧

Early July 1551 – Bradgate Park

John Aylmer had been as good as his word. Not only had he put
time aside himself to help me with my studies, and arranged for
Dr Harding to be available, but much more important, he had
obtained Lord Henry's blessing and support, together with his
agreement to release me from my duties three mornings a week

(and any other times I was not required) in order to pursue my studies.

Whether Catherine had influenced the decision I didn't know, but soon afterward John Aylmer invited me to take lessons, in the book-room or the schoolroom, whichever was not being used by the sisters at the time.

The rooms were next to each other, above the winter parlour and adjacent to the southwest tower, which Lady Jane had largely made her private retreat, for she no longer attempted to join the rest of the family in hunting or social pursuits outside the house. As the days went by, I became more comfortable walking through the middle floor of the east wing, and the family got used to my presence there, particularly Jane, who I seemed to meet at some stage in every visit. We soon began to have short, polite conversations, mainly on the subject of religion, and I found myself becoming fascinated by her confidence in what she called the true faith. When I listened to Lady Jane, it all seemed so clear, but away from her, the doubts and uncertainty crept back and I found myself in a morass of confusion and concern.

John Aylmer was a sensitive teacher and today opened our conversation by asking what was troubling me.

As soon as he offered me the opportunity, I blurted it all out and once started, I could not stop.

"John, I need your help, I am confused on the subject of religion and feel a strong need to understand more clearly. My conversations with Lady Jane have been few, and mainly short, but they have influenced me greatly. I have become much attracted by her idea of 'Order out of chaos'; to be able to understand with confidence life's purpose and how best we should live it, must be a wonderful support. But as to the choice between rival churches, and the true balance of the argument between them, then I am lost.

"Like most country people of my generation in the west of England, I was brought up as a Catholic. As a child, I was unaware of any alternative. There was one God, one parish church and one parish priest. Now I am confused by the arguments I hear around me, of one God but two churches."

Aylmer sat, his hands still in his lap, and gave me the calm smile of one who was once equally confused but who now has the comfort of having found the answer, and who believes in it with absolute faith. Quietly, over the next few hours, he explained the differences between the old and new churches and why, in his view and Lady Jane's, the new church had the right of it. He was, however, careful to warn me of the dangers of these thoughts, for this was not just a matter of religion, but of high politics.

"Let me try to help, for we are entering the fields both of God and of man. You will be aware that since the days of King Henry, this discussion is the stuff of politics, and therefore dangerous. This is not an easy subject, but I will try to spell it out for you as simply as I can."

He explained how King Henry had become Supreme Head of the Church of England and how the severance from Rome had created an opportunity to reform the practices of the church, to make it more accessible to the people. He took me through the arguments which had been addressed in the Act of Six Articles and the uprisings of 1549 which had followed its repeal by King Edward.

"I believe the country is moving in the right direction Richard. In March of last year, Archbishop Cranmer's Ordinal replaced the old Catholic Pontificale and last November the Council, in accordance with the order of the Archbishop of London, Nicholas Ridley, told the bishops to remove those altars which still remain and to replace them with communion tables.

"As far as clarity is concerned, I expect that in due course the Council will call for the publication of a second and revised Book of Common Prayer, which will clarify some of the present uncertainties, and will do so, I fervently hope and believe, within the Reformist framework. We are, after all, blessed with a Reformist King, one who knows his own mind and has the courage to follow his convictions."

During most of this exposition, he had stared into space, as if to focus his thoughts, but now he turned his eyes back to me and looked deeply into mine.

"Now, Richard, it is up to you. You must look deep inside yourself and seek the truth. I will give you any help I can, but I cannot tell you what to believe."

It was a lot more answer than I had ever hoped for or expected, and I was grateful.

      ☙   ❧

As I walked down the steep stairs after my lesson with John Aylmer, I was somehow aware that I had just experienced one of the significant moments in my life. Something made me want to slow down, to savour the moment, so that I would remember it with greater clarity in the future. I paused on the staircase and looked out of the small window at the garden below.

Something changed today, I thought. *In years to come I shall remember this day and appreciate its significance. For now, I wonder what that significance is.*

John Aylmer had not told me what to believe or what to do – indeed he had been careful to avoid doing either. Nor had I been suddenly converted to the Reformist cause. But nevertheless, something important had happened. I felt I had, in some manner, matured, as if I had moved on from my previous juvenile uncertainty to a new confidence. Not answers – I still had to find those – but now I felt more able to lead the search for them myself. Was this what growing up felt like?

Perhaps it was as simple as this.

I had at least found the questions. Now I had to find the answers, and I had a new confidence to undertake that task.

I believe it was a quieter, more thoughtful, Richard Stocker who took his place at supper in the Servants' Hall that evening.

2nd July 1551 – Bradgate Park, Leicestershire

It was three days later, just before seven o'clock on a beautiful July morning, and I was about to take a late breakfast, when a maid brought me a message.

"Her Ladyship says she wishes to see you right away sir. In her chamber, sir. She says to come immediately."

This was unusual in the extreme. I was not usually allowed on the top floor of the east wing (my lessons were taken on the floor below) and I had to follow the maid to avoid making a mistake and finding myself in the wrong room. The maid waved me into the room and departed hurriedly, looking a little embarrassed as she went.

"Come Richard. I have a duty for you to perform."

That, at least, was not unusual, for most conversations with Lady Frances Grey centred around the duties she wanted others to perform on her behalf. She was standing at the window, looking out across the river Lyn to the parkland and the open valley between them and Cropston village. She spoke without turning.

"Please remove your boots Richard; you will dirty my rug, and it cost a fortune."

Feeling out of place with the rugs and hangings in this rich room, I removed my boots and stood, uncertainly, in my stockinged feet. Although the room was unfamiliar, something did seem out of place. Here in her private day room, she was wearing a velvet cloak. Not unusual in the winter, but unexpected of a sunny July morning. Now, for the first time, she turned and looked at me, a long, almost anticipatory stare. Without taking her eyes from mine, she reached up to the clasp and undid it, holding the cloak together with her right hand.

"I knew the first time I saw you in Devon we would one day meet like this."

With a gesture, she released the cloak, which fell to the floor, revealing her nakedness beneath. She kicked the cloak away from her bare feet and walked toward me.

"What do you think?" she asked as I looked at her, silhouetted against the window, the morning light shining on her shoulders and making her hair glow, like a halo in a religious painting.

What could I say? She was a Tudor, the Lady of the House, wife of my powerful employer and a powerful woman in her own right. She was also naked before me, and very much a woman. Although now thirty-four years old, and having had five children, three of whom had survived, she still had a fine figure. She was tall – taller than her husband – her breasts had remained firm, and her stomach flat, with the muscle tone of someone who, as I knew well, rides every day, sometimes for hours.

"Come, Richard. You have me at an advantage. Remove your shirt and breeches and let's be on equal terms. Fear not, we are private here; my husband and his whoring brothers have gone carousing together in Leicester Town and will not be back this three days, as I know from experience."

With thumping heart I removed my breeches and stockings, and began to pull the shirt over my head. She was touching me before I had released it, running her hands down my back and over my buttocks, like a judge at a horse fair. She stepped back and I waited, naked and still, in full view of the window, while she decided. Finally she took my hand. "You'll do. Come. Into my bedroom. We will be comfortable there."

She led me into the bedroom and pulled me to her hungrily, this time holding me hard against her, so that I could feel the warmth of her body along the whole length of my own. Slowly, still kissing me, she began to push, edging me backwards, until the edge of the bed pressed against the back of my legs, and she eased me onto it. She lay heavily on top of me, her breath hot and sweet, her body warm and heavy with perfume. This lady had not just arisen from her bed. She had prepared carefully for this. She straddled me, smiling a secretive smile.

"Do you know what today is, Richard? It is the 2nd of July. In two weeks time it will be the 16th – St Francis's Day, and also my birthday. And where do you think my husband will be on my birthday? He will be attending his Majesty's investiture at Hampton Court and I am not invited. So, as my husband seems to have forgotten my birthday, I have decided to give myself an early present. You, Richard, will be my birthday present to myself."

This was a new experience, one that I had not been prepared for. I was excited but nervous, enflamed but afraid. Somehow I felt more like a sacrificial lamb than a birthday gift. I was not sure what I should do. Part of me wanted to respond, but her dominance had also made me feel like a little boy, with my mother washing behind my ears. I drew himself back against the bedhead, but she pursued me and straddled me again. Despite my increasing awareness of the effect of her warm body close against me, my reluctance must have showed and, with her hands on my chest, she pushed herself away from me, sitting upright across me, her eyes blazing.

"What's the matter Richard? Am I not attractive? Not woman enough for you?"

I stared back at her, shamelessly kneeling astride me, her every part exposed to my view.

"Am I not attractive? Not woman enough for you?"

They were exactly the same words Catherine had used three months before. How many times since then had I laid in bed, early in the morning, thinking of Catherine, and heard those very words ringing in my ears?

But Catherine had been supplicant, generous, wanting to give herself to me. Her mother was the opposite; taunting, greedy, demanding, wanting to take me for herself, as she always did.

In an instant my mood changed. I hated her for it. I hated the effect she had on those around her. I hated the way she saw Catherine as a possession, to be trained and traded like a lap dog. I hated the way she ignored poor Mary, arranging her life without once asking what *she* wanted, what *her* view was. I hated the way she bullied her husband, shouted at him, and interrupted him in front of others. For sure, he was a weak man, indecisive, shallow, and, as this morning's departure had shown, easily led, but there was no need to treat him quite so badly.

But most of all, I realized to my surprise, I hated her for what she was doing to Lady Jane; her pointless, unfair, and endless chastisement. Jane – honest, talented, studious Jane, who only wanted to please, but could do no right in her mother's (and therefore her father's) eyes. Jane who had never, to my knowledge, ever said anything bad about anyone, who, after years of chastisement, had disappeared like a snail into her protective shell of books, studies, and, as I was beginning to become aware, the ideas of the new Reformist Church.

I was brought back to the present by Lady Frances's strident voice, demanding as always.

"Come sir! How dare you? I did not drag you into my bed to watch you dream. You will do your duty by me when I demand it. If I say 'take me' I mean 'take me' and I mean now."

So I took her. I took her as I had never taken any girl of my own age. I grabbed her wrists and turned her on her back, her very strength suddenly a challenge. I crushed her lips with mine, and, for the first time feeling powerful and in command of the situation, entered her and rode her like an unbroken horse, until, finally, her head went back, her mouth opened in silent moan, her back arched, and her whole body shook with release.

When it was done, I lay beside her, our shoulders touching; yet feeling a thousand miles away from her. She had wanted lust and I had given it to her, simply that, no less, no more. But beneath the excuses I regretted what had happened. I had bedded Catherine's mother and I felt unclean.

She was silent now, still, for the first time since she had led me into the room. For a moment I thought that I had exhausted her. But as I turned to look at her, I saw something in her expression I had not seen before. She had relaxed. She had stopped fighting. She was, just for a moment, at peace. And in her peace, she was beautiful.

She rolled toward me and put her head on my chest. Instinctively, and for my own comfort as much as hers, I brought my arm round her and found I was stroking her hair. A tear slipped slowly from the corner of her eye and I felt it trickling down my chest. She began to speak, quietly, in a voice I had not heard before.

"Oh Richard, you must think I am such a wicked woman. A shrew, so froward. But you have no idea. I am a Tudor, my mother Mary sister to King Henry VIII and daughter of Henry Tudor and Elizabeth of York. I cannot be as other women. The Tudor line must be preserved and strengthened. Why do you think we ride our Jane so hard? She is destined to marry King Edward – they were made for each other, and together they will strengthen the line. But royal responsibilities are great. She will be on show at all times, and must learn to take life's burdens without regard for herself.

"Most of the time I have to bear this burden alone. You have no idea how hard it is, how lonely I am. My husband is a lightweight, a bantam cock, a wastrel, with no sense of responsibility, poor political judgement and precious little talent for making or preserving money. I have carried him since our marriage, and I will do so steadfastly until one or other of us is taken from this place."

She half-rose and leaned on my chest, looking at me hard, wanting to be sure I understood, needing to convince me.

"This is my destiny, my role in life and my responsibility, and I *will not* break my promise to my parents. I will make something of this family. We shall have our place in history, even if I die in the attempt! And now, just when there is an opportunity to influence important people and events at the King's investiture, I cannot be there to make sure he does it properly."

She lay back silently for a few moments. The mood had passed, her anger dissipated. The quiet girl returned. She took my hand and brought it, almost shyly, between her legs.

"Again Richard. For you this time."

Somehow, I felt that this was a special moment, taken outside our normal lives, with different rules and different obligations. This time, despite everything, I took her more gently, and with a different understanding.

❧ Chapter 18 ❧

Early July 1551 – Bradgate Park

"Richard, I have some news for you." I looked up at my new tutor John Aylmer.

To begin with, my lessons with Aylmer had been very difficult, but now I would not miss them for the world, as John had a natural gift as a teacher, and over the last few weeks I had learned so much. He was, however, full of surprises; it seemed to be part of his technique to keep the student awake and interested, and I found myself wondering what he had in store this time. Surely he could not know about me and Lady Frances?

"Lady Jane has asked me to invite you to join her in a discussion on Christian Virtues."

Appreciating the opportunity that had been put my way, I had made great efforts with my studies. My Latin had improved steadily, and according to John, my progress with early attempts at Italian suggested I might have a natural aptitude for languages. Nevertheless, the prospect of a face-to-face intellectual discussion with Lady Jane was not something anyone took lightly, and the subject matter did sound rather serious. I was half minded to try to get out of it, but, at the same time, Lady Jane of all people might help me find some of those answers I was searching for.

❧   ❧

As I climbed the stairs, I was feeling quite nervous. Although I had seen her many times, passing through the house and (less frequently) the garden, and spoken to her on quite a few occasions, this was to be our first formal, private discussion. Jane was, of course, a long way ahead of me (and, it seemed, the rest of the country) in her studies, and I felt quite intimidated at the prospect of being alone with her. Deep down, I was afraid I would not be up to the subject and would make a fool of myself.

When I joined her in the schoolroom, however, I began to feel a little better. Not only was Jane two years younger than me, she was a full twelve inches shorter, so that she had to look up at me as I entered the room. These two factors alone might have been enough to allay my fears had we been riding, hunting, or even fishing, but this was literally her home ground and some of my apprehension remained. However, she welcomed me with such charm and kindness that all fears of humiliation disappeared and I accepted the offered cakes and wine with deep relief.

Jane took the lead, as I had expected (and hoped) she would. After so many years as the student, she seemed to be enjoying her new role as tutor, gently coaxing me into Latin and reverting to English only when I became completely tongue-tied.

Then, when things seemed to be going really well, she threw me completely.

"Mr Aylmer has told me of your sincere mission."

For a moment, I stared at her blankly. My Latin translation sometimes let me down and I was unsure what my 'sincere mission' was, or whether I had mistranslated it.

She was so kind. Undisturbed by my lack of response, she tried again, this time in English.

"I believe Mr Aylmer has been helping you in your quest to find the true way to God. I am confident that his sincerity and clarity of explanation will be of great benefit to you, as, over the years, it has been to me."

I was relieved and intrigued; relieved that I had translated her Latin successfully and intrigued that John Aylmer must have been discussing my poor beginner's search for basic truths with someone whose faith and religious knowledge were so advanced.

I looked at her helplessly, feeing inadequate and not knowing where to start.

"Yes, my Lady, I am indeed looking for the truth and John Aylmer has been a great help and an inspiration. May I ask you a very personal question my Lady? How are you able to have such an absolute and confident faith, for I must admit I am struggling with my conscience and have been for some time?"

To my relief, she did not take umbrage at my impertinence, but answered me straightforwardly and without talking down to me. She explained that she had been reading extensively, and thinking deeply about the subject since she was very young. She referred to the influence of those who had helped her: her nurse Mrs Ellen, Dr Harding, who had been her first tutor, and especially Queen Katherine, during their time together at Chelsea and Hanworth. I noted that she did not make reference to her later time with Katherine Parr at Seymour Place (after the Queen's marriage to Sir Thomas Seymour), and I wondered if there was some truth behind the veiled suggestions which Lady Mary had made to me two months before.

Most of Lady Jane's praise was, however, reserved for John Aylmer, who, she said, was not only an inspiration in his own right, but had introduced her to many learned men, including Roger Ascham, and (by correspondence) John Sturm in Strasbourg and Henry Bullinger in Zurich. It was, she explained, the latter who had, in the event, caused today's meeting to have taken place.

As I sat in the book-room, morning sunlight streaming through the window, listening to Jane speaking quietly, I became aware of something I had never noticed before. When she spoke of those who had nurtured her education and helped mould her faith, Jane seemed to float off into another world, unrelated to Bradgate or her family. It was as if she had two lives; the one she had been born into, and the one she had created for herself, perhaps for her own protection.

She was so unlike her sister in this respect. Although shy by nature, Catherine was always in this world, eyes flashing, aware of the impact she was making. Even when I had seen her studying or practising her music, Catherine was playing to the crowd; she never seemed to lose herself as Jane appeared to do now.

"Mr Bullinger is a very special case in point. He recently and with great kindness, sent to my father a copy of his most excellent treatise, entitled 'Of Christian Perfection'. Since my father is away in London on Council business at the moment, I have written to Mr Bullinger and thanked him. During the last week, I have read the book most carefully. Knowing that my father is not expected to return in the near future, and even if he did, would be unlikely to read this treatise, I thought of you. Rather than taking upon myself the responsibility for translating and interpreting this most excellent work, I thought you might like to borrow it and read it for yourself. Mr Aylmer assured me your Latin is more than sufficient to absorb this work, a judgement which I fully support after our conversation this morning.

"You have, I know, been looking for the true path to God and to eternal salvation. I think it is likely that this work will serve as a most excellent map to guide you in your search. I ask only two things of you. First I ask that you look after the book with great care, for I value it most highly. Second, please promise me that, having absorbed its contents, you will return to discuss it with me."

I could not believe my ears. Gratefully, I thanked her profusely for her kindness in thinking of me. I was grateful for the generosity of the offer, and especially appreciated the implied compliment – that I would be able to follow the Latin and understand the ideas expressed.

I agreed to guard the treatise with my life and confirmed that I looked forward to our next discussion, finally admitting that I did so with more confidence than I had approached this first one.

Jane laughed at that.

"Am I such a source of trepidation that you feared to join me in discussion? Is the stallion afraid of the foal?"

I had been long enough with this family now to recognize the opening gambit of a courtiers' word game. "Not so, my Lady, but perhaps the kestrel would do well to take lessons from the wise owl when searching for game in the dark."

I seemed to have got it right, for she was still laughing as I descended the stairs, carrying the book, and feeling far more self-confident than when I had climbed them earlier that day.

❧ CHAPTER 19 ❧

Early July 1551 – Bradgate Park

The long wet winter had given way to a very hot dry summer. First the crops had failed through lack of water, and then, recently, there had been news of a recurrence of the much-feared sweating sickness. This time, they said it was really bad. There had not been an outbreak like this since 1520; the disease was raging across the south of England, and thousands were dying.

They said it was a frightening disease, which struck without mercy and without warning. A strong man could sit down to dinner and fully enjoy a hearty meal and be dead before supper-time. Nobody knew what caused it and there was no known cure. All you could do was isolate yourself at home as best you could and hope it didn't come your way. Those with long memories said it normally disappeared once the cooler weather arrived in the autumn, but that was two or three months away and meanwhile the bodies were piling up.

Then, early one morning, messengers had arrived and called for Lady Frances. She was in the Great Hall when they arrived. Such was their hurry, they ran to her and blurted out their message there in the hall, in front of a number of the servants, including Adrian and me. I had never seen her Ladyship looking frightened before, but she certainly did now. She went as white as a sheet, put her hands to her mouth and moaned aloud.

Only a month before, Lady Frances had visited her close friend, Catherine Willoughby, in a house she was renting in Kingston, near Cambridge, where she could keep an eye on her beloved sons Henry and Charles, who were living and studying together at St John's College in Cambridge. The first news of the outbreak had reached them there and it was feared it would reach Cambridge within days. Lady Frances had been warned to return to Bradgate, whilst Lady Suffolk took her sons to Buckden. For weeks now, Lady Frances had been waiting for further news.

Now it had come, and it was the worst news possible. Henry

and Charles had died within two days of each other. Lady Suffolk, totally distraught, had retired back to her house at Grimsthorpe, unable to face the consequences, leaving her two sons' bodies buried in simple graves at Buckden.

For a whole day Lady Frances did virtually nothing. She ate little and did not ride. Her only activity was to pray in the chapel, and to walk quietly round the parterre garden, which, somehow, seemed to have gained a new significance in her time of grief.

On the second morning she asked Adrian to join her and I could see them, walking slowly and with heads bowed, along the river Lyn in front of the house. Whatever the outcome of their discussion, it seemed to galvanize her into action, for after dining privately in the east wing, she sent for me.

"You have, no doubt, heard our terrible news." It was a statement not a question, and I could only nod my confirmation. Everybody knew.

"I must ensure my husband is fully informed. He may not have received the news in London, for there are so many dying, and in Court they will be preoccupied with preparations for the King's investiture. Richard, I must ask you to ride to Dorset House, in London, tomorrow, at first light. Take Mark Cope with you."

She must have seen my face fall. If you needed a reliable companion for a difficult journey, Mark Cope was the last person you would choose. I had spent much of my time at Bradgate Park avoiding him.

Lady Frances responded immediately.

"Yes I know he's a rogue but he has visited our London house before, and knows the way. He can be your guide, but make sure you keep him on a tight rein, and don't let him see any of the money I give you. Take him and five others. Make sure you choose strong, reliable men, the people are starving and afraid and, although as dry as they will ever be, the roads are dangerous. Oh – and make sure you take spare horses and be choosy where you rest at night. I will write to my husband this afternoon and give you the letter after supper. Come to me then and I will also give you money for the journey."

As I left the room, Adrian came with me. I waited until we were out of earshot, and then pulled him to one side.

"God's teeth. I have never seen her as cut up as that."

Adrian agreed. "She has had a terrible shock. She loved her half-brothers and they her." He put an arm round my shoulder conspiratorially, looking right and left before he spoke again.

"But there's more to it than that. What you may not have realized is that Henry and Charles's death means that the Suffolk line passes by default to Lady Frances. It is essential that you make sure Lord Henry gets her letter. There is a power struggle taking place in the Privy Council, which Lord Henry is deeply involved in. In his concentration on other matters, he may have overlooked the significance of these deaths and the opportunity it offers him, even if he has received the news already.

"Have a care Richard. You are travelling into danger and in dangerous times. The family at home is a dangerous enough place, but Court is a viper's nest. My advice is to look and learn, and say as little as you can get away with. Don't try to be clever. The courtiers will always outsmart you – if necessary by changing languages to one you are not fluent in. How is your Court French?"

The expression on my face was reply enough.

☙ ❧

I was in serious mood as I mounted Jack at dawn the next morning to lead our little group of followers on the road to London. To travel the road to London alone, apart from servants, was challenge enough. To do so in the middle of the worst harvest for years and following price rises and riots across the country the previous two years was another. But to be riding through an epidemic of the sweating sickness, carrying news that could transform the fortunes of what was already one of England's great families, was an added responsibility.

Yet it was none of these risks or dangers that filled my thoughts as I set off that morning. It was the prospect of seeing London.

⤳ CHAPTER 20 ⋞

Early July 1551 — Outskirts of London

I had thought I was prepared for London. In the past, I had visited Exeter, Bristol and (once, very briefly) Antwerp, but nothing had prepared me for London.

We had been riding hard for four days. As we rode south, down the long Middlesex hills from Barnet, I sensed something ahead of us, something new and extraordinary. The weather had been hot and dry during our journey, and we had taken to resting in the heat of the day, and riding late into the cool of the evening, before starting again very early every morning. So it was not long after dawn, with a chill early wind from the south, as we climbed upward from Cony Hatch, that I began to smell it. Finally we topped Muswell Hill and there it was, ahead of us, some ten miles distant.

We eased the tired horses to a halt and looked down into the saucer-shaped bowl of the Thames valley ahead of us. From here it looked as if the whole city was crammed into one great walled castle, which had been set on fire but was refusing to burst into flame. The whole area was covered in thick black smoke, rising high into the morning air and slowly drifting north, toward us.

Mark Cope looked and sniffed.

"That's coal smoke. They have burned most of the wood nearby and the price has gone sky-high, so now they bring coal from Newcastle by ship and burn that. It's much cheaper they say, but by God it stinks."

I agreed. It was disgusting.

Mark laughed. "Hides the stink of everything else though."

We took a swig of ale and ate some bread and meat pasties, still sitting in the saddle in order to make the most of the view. Then we started down the steep hill into Islington village and London itself.

⤳　⋞

"What did you say?"

Mark looked across at me and cupped his ear against the babble of noise in the street around us.

"I said do you know the way from here?" I shouted.

The place was a circus. The place was a madhouse. The place was a dung-heap. It was also the most exciting place I had ever tried to force my horse through. We were riding through Cheapside and it felt as if every merchant in Europe was trying to sell us something at the same time. There must have been well over a thousand stalls, spread the length of the wide street, on both sides. As well as the country fare, on stalls grouped around the towers along the way, carrying the names of Middlesex, Essex, Kent and so on, there were foreign traders, competing just as loudly, and in a variety of strange accents.

An old crone was selling tiny bread loaves, yelling her prices at us as we rode. "How much? A halfpenny for that measly loaf? You must be joking." The prices here were three times those in Colyton or in the villages round Bradgate.

"Yes, we continue this way until we get to the river, then it's a short ride to Whitehall and we're there," Mark finally yelled in reply to my earlier question.

The noise (and the smell) eased a little as we left the City at Ludgate and rode along the riverbank toward the palaces at Whitehall. It was well named: despite the ubiquitous black smoke, the walls of the palaces shone white from their fine stone facings. We were nearly there.

It was an exhilarated but very weary party which finally rode into the gates of Dorset House, with me demanding to be taken to his Lordship as a matter of urgency.

ื่อ   ี่

Lord Henry had just returned from a meeting of the Privy Council when I was shown into his private study. He took the letter and read it immediately. I pretended to look out of the window, but was watching him intently out of the corner of my eye as I did so. As he reached the second page of the letter, I noticed his eyes widen, just for a moment, but he regained his composure and his face was expressionless by the time he lowered the letter and turned toward me, standing quietly by the window.

"Judging by the date against my wife's signature, you have made good time. I thank you for that, as the contents of this letter have a special significance in today's troubled times. King Edward had already been informed of the death of his cousins and in turn kindly told me. Henry, Duke of Suffolk was one of my closest friends. However, this letter contains – um – aspects of the situation that had not been fully clear, and its arrival at this time is very helpful. Tell me, how is Lady Frances?"

"She is well in body sir – the sweating sickness had not reached Bradgate Park when I left, but it appears she has been brought low by the news from Cambridge."

"Indeed. She was very close to them both, Henry and Charles. As we all were. And my daughters?"

"They are well also my Lord. Bradgate is as safe a haven as they can have while this situation lasts."

Lord Henry put the letter on the table and looked toward me, his eyes glazed, apparently lost in thought. Abstractly, he rubbed his lower lip with the thumbnail of his left hand for a moment.

"Amen to that Richard. Now join your men downstairs and get something to eat. My steward will find lodgings for you all nearby. It's easier at the moment as so many members of the Parliament have fled London until the sickness abates, and the French ambassadors are being lodged at Richmond with their entourage. Please return here after breakfast tomorrow and I will tell you what our plans are."

❧   ❧

I was excited. It was early in the afternoon and I had the rest of the day to explore the city. I was very tired, but who knows, I might never see London again, so sleep could wait.

๛ CHAPTER 21 ๑

July 1551 – Dorset House, Whitehall

"Good morning Richard. I trust Edmund found you satisfactory lodgings and you didn't have to spend all of last night in the Bankside whorehouses?"

I grinned in reply. My master was not too far off the mark. Mark Cope and I had caroused a bit last night, but not to the extent that Lord Henry suggested. Mark had been keen to show off his knowledge of London and was all for taking a wherry across the river to the bathhouses for some entertainment. Perhaps it was as well that tiredness and a sense of duty had finally caught up with me, and I had talked Mark out of it. We had still had our share of fun though.

After four days travelling and a night in London, I understood why Lady Frances had called Mark a rogue. He knew every trick in the book. His motto was 'if the plague don't get you, the sweats will' and he planned to live every day as if it were his last. Mark was just twenty-one years old and reckoned he had already had more experiences in his life than his father had had in twice those years. Perhaps he was right. When you heard the numbers of people dying this summer, you did not feel inclined to make detailed plans for the long term future.

"I have a task for you Richard, which will require your careful attention," continued Lord Henry. "You will accompany me to Whitehall, where I shall be attending meetings of the Privy Council. I need you to carry my papers and to act as my personal messenger. I cannot trust any of my London staff. They are all the same. 'What's in it for me?' is the only question they ever ask, and one silver piece buys their loyalty overnight."

I tried to look alert, honest, reliable and studious.

"Go with Master Tucker here. He is my steward in this house."

Edmund nodded at me in acknowledgement. "We met last night my Lord."

Lord Henry continued. "Good. Well as I was saying, Edmund will find you some clothing, which will allow you to walk the corridors of Whitehall without attracting quite so much attention as your present country apparel. Be back here by twelve o'clock and I will explain things over dinner."

As we were leaving the room, Lord Henry called after us, with a wry smile.

"Make him look presentable Edmund."

Edmund Tucker threw back his head and replied in a low voice.

"Don't you worry My Lord, I shall turn our country boy into a dish fit for a Queen."

As I followed Edmund Tucker down the steep wooden stairs, I was still wondering quite what a 'dish fit for a Queen' was meant to refer to in these circumstances. I was still not sure about these rumours. Lord Henry seemed normal enough, but there was something unusually feminine about Edmund, and they seemed to share a secret somewhere between them. I could not put my finger on it, but there was something …

❧ ❧

Arriving back at dinner time, I was relieved that the chosen clothes, although well made and of good materials, were not too dandified. They did not seem to offend the King's new sumptuary laws, nor the Reformist principles to which I felt increasingly inclined, and I felt I could have stood before John Aylmer and Lady Jane without causing offence. There were no ruffs, no slashed sleeves, and no velvet breeches, like some I had seen on our journey through the city. Instead I was dressed almost entirely in smart black: black worsted breeches with black stockings and black leather ankle boots and, above, a black shirt covered with a black leather jerkin. I felt smart and important, but at the same time able to move comfortably.

Lord Henry looked at the result and nodded his approval. He angled his head toward his steward. "No visits to the fripperers then Edmund?"

Tucker pursed his lips and took a sharp intake of breath in mock-alarm.

"My Lord! We were sent out in search of formal day-wear, for the Parliament and Court."

With his left hand on his hip, and the forefinger of his right hand to his lips, he looked steadily at me, eyes moving from the top of my head to my feet and slowly back again. I felt distinctly uncomfortable at being the subject of so direct an inspection, and not just because I was wearing my unaccustomed new clothes. Finally Edmund's examination came to an end and his eyes rested on mine. Without taking his eyes away, and in a strangely husky, almost feminine voice, he continued to Lord Henry.

"My Lord, we can always shop again for the more – private – occasion, if you wish?"

Lord Henry laughed, a long and hearty guffaw. He and Edmund clearly knew each other well and enjoyed the banter of their wordplay. I started to relax, realizing this was another element of the Court game, which I would have to observe, and hopefully one day, learn.

&ea; &ea;

Dinner was a remarkably informal, but businesslike, affair. A good piece of cod, with fresh vegetables was followed by a capon, cooked with herbs and lemons, and wonderfully aromatic. Wine was offered but declined, and I noted his Lordship's nodded approval at my decision.

Lord Henry explained that the issues being addressed by the Privy Council were of the utmost importance. He demanded, and got from me, a firm vow of secrecy.

"The work you are about to undertake with me will involve you in carrying secret papers and in observing many things that you will be required to forget. You will no doubt overhear many pieces of conversation, and you must always forget them or, if unsure, report them to me. As a direct result of the failed policies of the former Protector, Somerset, we are in a state of partial war with France and with Scotland, and the poor finances of the country mean we must end them. Warwick has begun the process but the visit of the French ambassadors has been delayed since April by the outbreak of the sweating sickness. In place of the original St George's Day celebrations, the King now intends to use his investiture later this month – on St Francis's Day – as the basis for securing strengthened relations with the French."

At the mention of Lady Frances's birthday, I expected to see some glimmer of recognition that, for this year at least, he would be unable to celebrate the event with her, but there was no sign that the date registered with him at all. He was much too immersed in the affairs of Court.

"Each step of the way is delicate and we must tread carefully. Not every one of the Privy Council shares Warwick's conviction that the plan will succeed. Somerset, of course, is desperate to prevent Warwick getting the credit for overcoming the problems he created during the Protectorate. Underlying many of our deliberations are issues regarding the church and these continue to cause divisions between men. Wriothesley died last year, so he is out of the way, but be on your guard against Derby, Shrewsbury and Arundel, who still support Somerset, even after his fall from grace."

Lord Henry walked to the window, opened it, and looked out over the river Thames. Dusk was falling and the smell of the Lambeth Marshes opposite wafted damply into the room. He continued, speaking over his shoulder and still looking out over the Thames as the lights of a passing wherry approached the Privy Steps.

"Make no mistake Richard, the future well-being of our nation is at stake at the moment and we shall all have to make sacrifices to ensure its safe delivery."

As he spoke, I noticed that his manner, although informal, almost friendly, was very confident. Here, away from his wife, he seemed a different man. Perhaps Lady Frances's influence constrained him. She had described him as a lightweight, a wastrel, with poor political and business judgement. Yet here he stood, at the window of this fine house near Whitehall, at the very centre of power, apparently in command of the political situation, and clear and confident about his own role in it.

"We will need an early start tomorrow. With this latest and most virulent outbreak of the sweats here in London over the last few days, his Majesty has sensibly retired to Hampton Court and will receive the French ambassadors there. We must be at Hampton Court no later than eight o'clock, for the ambassadors meet the King at nine. We will leave at five o'clock. My private wherry will be waiting on the river steps at the back of the house here. Do you know where they are?"

I nodded my confirmation. Since arriving at Dorset House I had been shown round by Mark Cope and now knew my way around comfortably.

"Good. Then five o'clock it is. Edmund will arrange a basket of breakfast and we can eat it as the wherrymen row. The tide will be favourable, so we should have an easy journey."

As I was leaving, Lord Henry raised a hand. "Oh Richard?"

I paused, door in hand, looking back at the man who had suddenly grown in my estimation.

"Bring a warm cloak. It's cold and damp on the river in early morning, even in mid-summer."

❧ CHAPTER 22 ❧

14th July 1551 – Hampton Court

Despite having eaten as much of the contents of the breakfast basket as I dared without appearing greedy, I was still frozen and tired as the wherry eased against the great pier at Hampton Court. There was activity right across the river; three royal barges were pulling back into mid-water to make room for the later arrivals and wherries were ducking and diving for position everywhere.

The huge iron gates had already been drawn open, and were attended by pike-men in the royal uniform. I assisted Lord

Henry up the steps, still slippery with morning dew, and together we followed the path through the enormous gardens, lit either side by cresset lamps, six feet tall and spiked into the ground, with oiled rags burning in the cages at their tops. In front of us was Hampton Court, the great palace built by Cardinal Wolsey and later given to King Henry VIII. Its magnificence was beyond any imagining. As we approached beside a long rectangular lake, the low morning light shone on the red brick and white stone facings of the royal lodgings, and they were reflected perfectly in the ripple-free water. I had thought Bradgate Park impressive, but this was another order of magnitude and magnificence.

"This will give the Frenchmen food for thought when they arrive, eh?"

I agreed. "See how the morning light strikes the stonework around those enormous windows."

"That, my boy, is Beer stone, brought to London by ship from your part of Devon and then up the river by barges. It is the very finest. Nothing catches the light like it, not even the Charnwood granite we have at Bradgate. See how precisely the blocks have been cut and fitted one to the other and shaped around the windows; superb workmanship."

Lord Henry was clearly looking forward to the day. He was wearing his finest clothes, although I noted that he was not wearing quite as much jewellery and adornment as he had at the last dinner we had attended at Bradgate. He must have noticed my gaze, for as we walked into the palace courtyard he turned and in a conspiratorial voice said, "Doesn't do to over-adorn at Court, Richard; his Majesty is the shining light and we are merely his reflection. It would be a foolish man who outshone him."

We were close to the house now and I looked through the palace doors at the milling crowd of excited diplomats and noblemen, smiling to myself, as Lord Henry continued.

"Mind you, it would take some effort to outshine him, especially on a formal occasion like this. You wait and see."

I wondered whether I would get an opportunity to see the King in all his magnificence.

❧ ❧

The occasion exceeded my wildest dreams. We were by no means the first to arrive. There seemed to be hundreds of people present, great lords greeting each other formally, and their retainers following behind – some, like me, appearing wide-eyed at their first visit to this great palace.

At eight o'clock the crowd began to separate, some of the servants being sent back to the barges and wherries waiting at the great pier on the river, but the luckier ones being allowed to remain with the throng as it moved into the Great Hall. I looked at Lord Henry for instructions and was delighted when I was told to "Stay with me boy, you may be needed to carry messages."

The first thing I noticed on entering the Great Hall was the ceiling, which rose in three tiers of carved wood above the cream-coloured walls. It was lit by enormous windows, and framed a stained glass window at the far end of the room. As we moved forward into the room, I realized that the lower walls were covered with rich tapestries, now partly hidden by the milling crowd of excited men.

"Where is the King?" I whispered as we moved through the room toward the door at the other end.

"He is in the Presence Chamber of course. The King does not come to us. We go to the King." I must have looked excited, for Lord Henry continued with a disparaging look. "We who are invited, that is."

❧ ❧

"The Marquess of Dorset indeed. Well met sir, on this glorious day."

The speaker was middle aged, tall, dark, bearded in the Spanish style, and supremely confident. He was dressed all in black velvet, except for a white ruff around his throat and shirt cuffs. Lord Henry bowed low.

"Good morning to you my Lord Somerset. It is indeed a great and glorious day. Let us hope our French visitors think likewise."

Somerset agreed.

"I have the papers my Lord." Lord Henry signalled for me to step forward with the leather folder of papers, which I had been carrying so carefully ever since we left Dorset House. I reached forward with the folder, unsure whether to give it to Lord Henry or direct to Somerset. I looked from one to the other in uncertainty.

"Give it here boy."

I looked at Lord Henry for a response, a signal, but there was none. That was message enough.

Somerset held out his hand and I passed over the precious parcel, looking at the great man as I did so. As he took it, Somerset caught my eye and, just for an instance, seemed to be evaluating me. It was the deep, piercing look of an owl, and for that instant, I felt uncomfortable, as if my insides were visible.

Somerset took the parcel, nodded, and moved away. I eyed him carefully as he handed the papers to a secretary and moved on round the room. So this was Edward Seymour, Duke of Somerset and former Lord Protector, who, although deposed from that great title, still wielded enormous power – although if Lord Henry was to be believed, mainly for evil. I watched as Seymour worked his way round the room, touching an elbow here, patting a shoulder there, seemingly knowing everyone and always affable and smiling.

At nine o'clock there was a commotion in the next room and the French ambassadors arrived. Somerset greeted them in turn, and introduced them to the twelve nobles, including the Marquess of Dorset, who formed the welcoming party.

As they moved toward the Presence Chamber, I could see Somerset counting the numbers of people in each party. There were so many in the French party that it exceeded the thirteen English nobles and their immediate followers. This seemed to create a problem of protocol, for the King would be disadvantaged if the English were outnumbered, but it would be difficult at this late stage to reject any of the French party and in any event, it did not appear to be clear who held what precedence.

Somerset looked back, round the room, as the French and English groups disappeared through the door. He was looking right at me as my eyes scanned the room and we made eye contact. Suddenly Somerset seemed to make up his mind and with a slight jerk of his head, he signalled me to follow. Two others received the same signal and the three of us hurried to join the tail end of the party as it moved into the next room.

Lord Henry looked surprised as I entered the room and joined him at one side.

"Somerset signalled me to come through, perhaps to even up the numbers," I explained. Lord Henry inclined his head and whispered, "Keep out of the way then, over there, and do not speak once the King is in the room."

There was no mistaking when the King entered. He was announced by royal trumpeters, whose fanfare blasted the room so none could speak, resulting in total silence when the fanfare finished.

The King was preceded by a troop of the Yeomen of the Guard, their uniforms embroidered with the royal crown and the letter E. They looked almost like brothers, for they were all exactly the same height, and all had blonde hair. The last entered the room just as the last notes of the fanfare were dying away, and they stood at silent attention as the room waited. The King entered in theatrical silence, his soft slippers making no sound on the stone floor, as he mounted the dais and turned to face the room under the royal canopy. My first impression was of youth, for the King was not yet turned fifteen years old, and very pale and slim. But one look at the short auburn hair suggested this was not a man to be trifled with, and as his deep brown eyes slowly surveyed the room, all fell to their knees in silent obeisance.

King Edward stood for some time, surveying the kneeling figures below him, and allowing the scene to make its own statement about his position in relation to all others present. Then, half-turning, he seated himself on the throne behind him.

"The King is seated," announced the herald and the room rose to its feet.

I was now in a position to look at our monarch more closely, although I kept my head lowered for fear of catching the King's eye and his possible wrath. Any initial thoughts now evaporated. Young he might be, but this King could not be underestimated, for he created and maintained a dominating presence in a room full of seasoned nobles. His clothing made no acknowledgement of the King's well-known Reformist commitment, and was clearly designed to impress. Red, white and purple all made their presence felt and acted as a backdrop to pearls, rubies and diamonds, the whole effect rounded off with gold thread and ermine edging.

There was a further fanfare, and Somerset entered, leading the French ambassadors, who walked the length of the room toward the king's dais, the crowd in the room parting to give them access to the royal presence. Somerset introduced them in turn. The Maréchal de St André was followed by François de Rohan de Guyé and Sire de Vielleville, the French Ambassador. Each knelt and kissed the King's hand, then stepped back. The King now rose, and in clear, confident and fluent French, welcomed them.

"My Lords, you are welcome for three reasons – One, thus is confirmed in perpetuity a good peace between my brother of France and myself; Two, it enables me to meet the Grand Maréchal, whom I have so long wanted to see; and Three, that you all, being witness to the oath of loyalty I shall take toward your King, will remember how it will be kept – for I know that your lordships are so high in my favour that you can make me both love and hate you, as you will. *Vous soyez encore, M. le Maréchal, le mieux que très bien venu.*"

There was a murmur of approval throughout the room. It was an impressive start, and the formal proceedings which followed, including the presentation of letters from King Henry II of France, flowed as fluently as had the King's French. In what seemed no time at all, the ambassadors were leaving from this, the first of many planned meetings over the next weeks, to be escorted to their rooms, until dinnertime. As soon as they had left the room, the English lords knelt again, and the King rose, leaving the room as silently as he had entered it.

Lord Henry turned to me and winked.

"Not a bad show, eh?"

I admitted I was very impressed and was sure the French ambassadors had been as well.

"That's the way it's done at Court, Richard. Nothing is what it seems. Four weeks of preparation and everything flows as it should, and that includes the 'impromptu' speeches. Now go and find our wherry and tell the oarsman to wake up. I shall be along within the hour, but first I must talk with Somerset."

As I walked slowly back through the gardens to the Great Pier on the Thames, I reconsidered everything I had seen since we had left the jetty of Dorset House early that morning. I had not been able to draw any views about the French party, who had not really yet entered into the detail of their discussions. No doubt they would do so as the week progressed. But it had been a very impressive start. The King, who had stamped his presence on the occasion the moment he walked into the room and who, despite his youth, had dominated the occasion from beginning to end, had particularly impressed me. Where, I wondered, had he gained that self-confidence, and presence?

Then I remembered Lady Jane, who, I had been told by her mother, had for years been groomed to marry the King. Perhaps that was it, that was how it was done: training, preparation, rehearsal, for years and years, until the role was automatic and the necessary skills were honed to an almost casual fluency. Perhaps people like the King and Lady Jane *were* born to greatness, but by God, they also worked at it.

I thought about Lady Frances, lying next to me in bed and gritting her teeth with determination that her family should succeed. Her family had fought for power and gained it. Now she was not easily going to let it slip away. Perhaps they were all alike, the Greys, the Seymours, the Howards. Perhaps that was what differentiated them from the people I had known for most

116

of my life – their sheer desire to succeed – and the opportunity to do something about it.

At the moment, I was not sure I had either.

✾ CHAPTER 23 ✾

16th July 1551 – Hampton Court

It had been another early start, another cold, damp wherry from the Thames steps at Dorset House at dawn, and another landing at Hampton Court, this time for the King's investiture.

Last time I had landed here, I had been both excited and apprehensive. It was amazing what a difference a couple of days made. This time I felt exhilarated by the prospect of the King's investiture and just hoped I might wheedle myself a place from which I could see the ceremony unfold.

To the excitement was added anticipation. Our journey up the Thames had been more difficult this time, for the wind was downstream and the tide was starting against us, so that the wherrymen had had a difficult row and we passengers a wet and uncomfortable journey. But the journey had not been boring. As we splashed steadily upriver, Lord Henry had explained the latest scandal, which could easily wreck today's events.

"You remember de Guyé from the day before yesterday?"

I said I did, although I was not sure which of the Frenchmen was which.

"Well apparently he said he had been given a warning that he would be poisoned whilst in England, so he has had French food delivered to him by way of Boulogne and Dover, all the way to Richmond, where they are all now staying, and he refuses to eat English food at all."

This did not make sense. "Are the whole French party refusing to eat our food now?"

"No," replied Lord Henry, "that's the point, only de Guyé's people – the others are all eating their heads off."

Once again, I was confused. "Why would someone poison only one of them? It would not stop the diplomatic proceedings, would it? Perhaps it's personal?"

Lord Henry would have none of it. "Pah, the man is making a fool of himself. The French Court think they are a cut above us when it comes to civilization. I expect someone has pulled his leg about the meagre food in England and he has taken it all in. I was with them yesterday at Richmond, and they were arguing about it in my hearing, not realizing that my French is more than passably good. Neither de Vielleville nor Maréchal St André has received a similar warning. But de Guyé and his followers are adamant and all sticking to their imported diets."

"Won't the King be ... excuse me ..." Trying to keep dry under my cloak, I had been working my way through a generously large meat pie during this conversation and the combination of my Devon accent and the mouthful of food might have made my question less than clear " ... won't the King be upset by this snub against his hospitality?"

Lord Henry seemed quite unconscious of my crumbs falling about his feet.

"Quite possibly. He can get very upset on occasions, especially when he thinks his authority is at risk. That's when he does his impression of his father: standing with legs apart, he tucks his thumb into his belt, and tries to shout in a deep voice. Swears like a sailor on occasion. The trouble is, as you heard the day before yesterday, he hasn't got a man's voice yet and the effect is often to cause amusement. But if it happens, whatever you do, don't snigger or laugh, or you will be in real trouble. There is another problem, though, which is likely to be more significant."

As deep in the pie now as my ears would allow, I signalled my continuing interest by widening my eyes and nodding.

"Apparently de Guyé is very upset that he has been told to stop his chaplain from celebrating Mass in public during their stay. You are aware of the King's view of what form of worship is now appropriate, and he takes his views personally and seriously, as the Princess Mary knows all too well. If de Guyé takes a public stand on that issue, we really are likely to see fireworks. There is another side of the King, and that's the way to provoke it."

I was more excited than ever, and spent the rest of the journey in fierce anticipation of the events of the day.

જ ઉ

But if I had thought my previous visit had prepared me, I was sorely mistaken.

No expense had been spared. Now I knew why Lord Henry had insisted I carry aboard a huge waterproof canvas bag and had then entrusted me with a much smaller bag, which I clutched carefully to my chest for the whole of the journey up the river.

On arrival, I had been left in the entrance hall, nodding to people I had seen on the previous visit, and awaiting the return of my master, who had taken the bags and disappeared to a changing room. Now he returned, looking as resplendent as I had ever seen him and I was reminded of the advice about not overshadowing the King.

As we moved into the Great Hall, the issue became more pressing, for every English Earl, Duke and Marquess was present, and all were smothered in jewel-incrusted finery, whilst their personal servants hovered discreetly near them, dressed (as I was) in the latest of Court fashion for a person of their status.

The greater lords, including Dorset, now moved into the Presence Chamber and the servants crowded to the door, which (whether thoughtfully or carelessly) had been left open, to see and hear the proceedings.

Using my height to advantage, I peered above the crowd to see the King on his throne, raised on the dais at the other end of the room. I need not have worried on the King's behalf. I had never seen anyone – man or woman – so finely arrayed or looking so – well, beautiful. His youth was now an advantage, for he carried the diamond, ruby, pearl and emerald-incrusted garments as well as any woman, yet lost none of the dominance that reminded everyone present that he was the King, and all-powerful.

The three envoys, preceded by their gentlemen carrying the

robes and the Order of St Michael, entered the Presence Chamber. They were clearly impressed, for they stood for some time, looking around them. Meanwhile the King, totally aware of the dramatic effect of this moment of pure theatre, beamed his most generous smile at the assembled throng, as if to say "Welcome" to his guests and "Well done" to his nobles.

The King then proceeded into the chapel, walking between St André and de Guyé, where he received the communion alone. The French party looked on, the English lords behind them, with those servants who, like me, had dared to enter and cross the Presence Chamber, stretching to gain a view of the proceedings through the chapel doors.

The bible was presented to the King and he swore his oath of allegiance to the Holy Order of St Michael. He was then invested as a Knight of the Order by St André, who hung the Order, with its chain of scallop shells, around his neck. De Guyé then hung the robes around his shoulders, and a fanfare of trumpets and hautboys, followed by a roll of drums, signalled the ceremony had come to an end. With a spontaneous cheer, the French and English nobles began embracing each other, many of them in tears.

The King began to move toward the doors and this signalled a rapid retreat by the servants and gentlemen, allowing the King and the Nobles to process down the great staircase to the Banqueting Hall below. It was clear that the lesser persons present were not expected to follow, and we were quickly led by the back stairs, to a separate hall, where we dined together loudly.

Many of the English servants had been affected by the atmosphere of the recent events and tried to make conversation with their new 'friends' from France, but few had the language and hardly any of the French party spoke any English. Eventually, with a mixture of English, French, Latin and sign language, supported by copious quantities of wine, a rapport was achieved and we lesser mortals settled to our own rapprochement.

The banquet was followed by tilting. The division of the classes was maintained, and we servants found our own way to the tilting ground. I found a place hard against the rail and for the next two hours watched an impressive display of tilting at the buckler and at rings. The King did not take part (although one of the crowd told me he was probably the match for most of those participating), but his shouted encouragement to the competitors clearly showed his enthusiasm for the sport.

As the sun fell and the temperature began to drop, supper was served to the Lords as they sat, and musicians replaced the jousters. The event turned into a second joust, for the French had brought their own musicians and the players began to alternate, turning the evening into an impromptu musical competition.

For some time it appeared the French would have the better of it, for they were represented by trumpeters, a cornet player, flutes, shaums and sackbuts. Apparently seeing the balance of competition going against him, the King ordered up reinforcements from Hampton Court and Windsor Castle and within an hour the numbers of musicians present had almost doubled. King Edward had even summoned the choir of the Chapel Royal to add their voices to the proceedings and the end of the evening was accompanied by John Taverner's *Kyrie Le Roy*, drifting across the meadows and gardens of Hampton Court on a perfect summer's evening. The slow, interweaving voices seemed an appropriate ending to what had been a splendid occasion.

☙ ❧

As a summer dusk fell, the now-weary partygoers bade their farewells to each other and staggered back to the Great Pier, where the boats home to Richmond and London were waiting. I had seen Lord Henry weaving rather drunkenly toward the pier shouting "Dorset, Dorset" to the gaggle of wherrymen, and I ran to get there first. Luckily, the Marquess's wherrymen were up to the mark and were already pulling to the steps as we approached. Lord Henry was badly out of breath as I reached the wherry and he fell into the seat in the stern gratefully, as I bent to step aboard.

"Ah Richard." He flapped the back of his hand as if clearing a wasp from his suppertime fruit.

"Go back. Go back. I must have my bags and travelling clothes from this morning. You will find them in the side room beside the Great Hall. Hand this to the servant." He handed me an ivory peg engraved "Marquess of Dorset".

I looked at it. *That*, I thought, *is attention to detail.*

∽ ∽

It was nearly eleven o'clock when we finally pulled out from Hampton Court into the main flow of the river. A whole tide had come and gone during our revels and the latter part of the ebb was now flowing strongly with the current of the river. The wherrymen were rewarded for their fifteen-hour wait by an easy row home, gliding down the river in the growing dark, whilst Lord Henry snored gently in the stern, leaning against me and sharing my heavy cloak.

John and Dick Barley, the wherrymen, who were twin brothers, looked at each other in resignation.

"Alright for some ain't it?" muttered Dick.

I grinned back. They were being well paid.

I wondered how much, if anything, they understood of the great events they rowed the Marquess to and from. I looked from one to the other, as they rowed with the easy fluency of experts at their task. I had heard enough of their banter to know that they saw more than they admitted to, and had, in their own way, weighed up the various personalities in the family.

But there it ended. They saw, they heard, and they commented to each other, but they didn't ask why. They did not look deeper and question the bigger events which influenced Lord Henry and his wife and family; events to which the family were, in turn, responding.

That much I had learned already. As a young man in Shute, I had understood that the Steward, whilst ruling the roost from day to day, was not all-powerful, but was answerable to the Lord of the Manor. I had assumed, however, that the great Lord was himself all-powerful and wholly in command of his destiny. But my short time at Court had made it clear that this was untrue, for I had seen that the Lords were at all times deferential to the King, whose ancestors had probably been the source of their family's wealth, and who could, at a whim, take it away again.

More than this, however, I had begun to recognize that the King himself was, to a degree, controlled by larger events – the threat of war with other countries and the need for alliances, and the sort of power games we had just been witnessing.

Did no man feel free?

Perhaps the Barley brothers had got it right – row your boat, keep your trap shut and stay out of trouble.

❧ CHAPTER 24 ❧

19th July 1551 – Hampton Court and Windsor

"Good morning my Lord. Windsor is it today sir?" John Barley doffed his cap as Lord Henry and I climbed aboard the wherry once again at Dorset House. It was only hours since we had climbed out of the wherry last night. Nevertheless, the Barley brothers looked as wide awake and as ready to row as usual. *They must sleep the sleep of the just*, I thought.

"Yes please – John," replied Lord Henry uncertainly, for the brothers were so alike he found it difficult to tell them apart.

"Have the horses gone on ahead as I ordered?" I asked, very conscious that this was an area of my responsibility, and that, this being a hunting day, I had more to contribute than on the recent, more formal, occasions.

"They have sir, in the barge, last night sir, with all the hunting gear, as instructed," replied Dick Barley, knuckling his forehead. "Stable boy went with them and was told to stay all night. Stabled at Hampton Court they was to be, and ridden over to Windsor this morning at first light, to warm them up a bit."

"You are remarkably well informed, Dick," I replied. I had learned to tell the brothers apart by a nick in Dick's ear, sustained in a street fight in Bankside years ago, as he had proudly told me.

"Ha ha sir." Dick tapped the side of his nose with his fore-finger. "Stable boy's named Simon Barley isn't he? Our younger brother is Simon. Keep it in the family I says. Good lad is Simon. Good with horses."

"Can't row to save his life though," growled his brother John, watching Lord Henry, as he slipped and staggered against the side, nearly tipping the small craft in the process.

"Can't swim neither," agreed Dick, straight-faced.

                                       ॐ   ॰

Arriving by boat at Windsor Castle was even more intimidating than arriving at Hampton Court, which we had passed on the way upstream some time before. Windsor did not have the grandeur of Hampton Court, but its fortified structure and commanding position on the hill, high above the river, made it in some ways more imposing.

The horses were waiting for us by the river, but we did not ride up the steep path to the castle itself, as we were told the King and the ambassadors had remained at Hampton Court the previous night and were riding over this morning. Instead we followed the groom to the Great Park and awaited the King there.

He did not keep us waiting. The party arrived from Hampton Court in jovial mood. Gone was all the formality of the previous occasions. The Maréchal de St André arrived first with the King, clattering across the hard track from the castle and skidding to a halt in front of us.

"Beat you by one length," called the King, laughing breathlessly.

"Beaten indeed, your Majesty, and by superior horsemanship I vow," replied the Maréchal, chivalrously.

The carts carrying the dogs and the bows arrived with the rest of the party, and the huntsman and the King conferred on tactics. After some discussion it was agreed to draw the large wood opposite us with horses and dogs, while the bowmen, including the King, waited quietly hidden in a glade near the river – the natural escape route.

The ruse was successful; the dogs had not been in the wood for more than ten minutes when a dozen fallow deer, including two large bucks, trotted into the glade, looking back carefully but without great apparent concern. The does were in summer colouring of chestnut brown with white spots, but the larger of the bucks was almost white and the other, known as a menil, was pale brown and spotted. The bucks were in the course of growing new antlers, having shed their old ones at the end of May. Nevertheless their size and dominance singled them out from the does, as they walked confidently through the dappled light of the glade.

The arrows hit almost simultaneously, each in the crease behind the foreleg of their respective animals. Both bucks dropped dead on the spot, with hardly a shiver.

"Good shooting my Lords," called Lord Henry, as the King and the Maréchal stepped from their leafy hiding places at the edge of the glade.

The King was ecstatic.

"Did you see that, Dorset? I whispered to the Maréchal to take the white buck and I would take the menil. We whispered 'ready' and shot together. Was there ever such sport?"

"None indeed your Majesty," replied Lord Henry. "A truly magnificent example of controlled shooting and, if I may say so …" – he waited for effect, the King and Maréchal looking intently at him – "of partnership!"

The Maréchal beamed with pleasure and the King whooped with delight.

"Partnership indeed. Well said Dorset." He rattled off some rapid sentences to the Maréchal in French. Their effect seemed to please him for he slapped the King on the shoulder and shouted, "D'accord!" as they returned to their horses.

Lord Henry Grey, Marquess of Dorset, turned in the saddle to those seated around us who, by their passivity, clearly did not have the King's faculty with the French language.

"His Majesty has told the Maréchal that this signifies that the English longbow is now only to be used in partnership with our French allies."

There was nodding all round at this deeply appropriate commentary and glasses of the best French brandy were brought to celebrate.

"Let's course," called the King.

The dogs were let loose once again and as we followed, they began a steady trot across the valley bottom and up the opposing hill. They topped the hill and a large group of bucks broke cover and began to run downhill. As we chased them, the deer split into two groups and those following automatically did likewise. It was a long run, but nothing to Jack, who was clearly enjoying the chance to open his stride, and after two miles, I found myself close behind the King and the Maréchal, with the rest of the party wallowing some way behind.

We were riding flat out, with the King screaming encouragement to the Maréchal, when the King's horse hit a rabbit hole, dropped to its knees and tumbled heavily. The Maréchal and I skidded to a halt, fearing the King had been seriously injured, but although badly winded, he quickly rose to his feet, as I tried to help by putting an arm round him.

As the rest of the party joined us, the King leaned against me and thanked me for my help. The King's horse did not seem to have broken anything, but it was clear he would not carry anyone for the remainder of that day.

"Take my horse your Majesty," called Dorset and five others in unison, but the King would not hear of it. "No I shall ride one of my spare horses when it gets here. Until then I will rest and get my breath back. Dorset, I pray you take the Maréchal back to the others in the valley bottom and I shall join you there in a few minutes."

"As your Majesty pleases." Reluctantly he obeyed, and filed off slowly down the remaining hillside.

"What is your name good sir?" asked the King as I helped him to a nearby tree stump, to rest.

"Richard Stocker, your Majesty, late of Shute in Devon, but now Second Master of Horse to the Lord Henry Grey, Marquess of Dorset."

The King winced as his ribs signalled their bruises. "Second Master eh? Then Dorset's Master of Horse must be a rider indeed, for you have kept up with me all morning, as I remember."

"Thank you your Majesty. I love to ride and Jack here has carried me faithfully for a few years now and never put a foot wrong. The Master of Horse at Bradgate Park is Adrian Stokes. He is indeed a good horseman your Majesty."

"But not as good as you eh? What is your county of Devon like Richard? I have not yet had the opportunity to travel that far west. Wool country, as I understand it? And tin from the stanneries? And fishing?"

"There's little to add your Majesty. You have summed it up in a nutshell. Perhaps I should add the beauty of the countryside, the grass and ... the rain."

"Courtenay country wasn't it? – Devon?"

"Indeed, much of it still is, but my master holds the land near Shute."

"Shute you say. I do not believe I have heard of it. What's the nearest town and city to you there?"

"The nearest town is Colyton your Majesty and the nearest city Exeter."

"Colyton. That name rings a bell from my childhood. Did my father not sell that estate by enfeoffment to the citizens?"

Once again, I was impressed.

"That is right your Majesty, in 1546 it was, and a great event in the town."

"Ha. I was nine years old then, but still I remembered it. And Exeter – that was the source of trouble two years ago. There was a siege. Why was that? Lord Russell relieved Exeter after what? Six weeks?"

This was difficult ground – revolts were not easy things to discuss with a King. "Indeed your Majesty, after six weeks."

Luckily at that moment the servants arrived with one of the King's spare horses and he mounted with a sharp intake of breath. "Thank you, Master Stocker. I shall remember our meeting."

I remounted Jack and watched as the King rode slowly down the hill to rejoin the others. I patted my faithful companion's neck. "Well Jack, I spoke to the King and the King spoke to me. Mother will never believe it when I tell her."

જ ઉ

The rest of the day was an anti-climax. The hunting slowed dramatically after the King's accident and we soon returned to Windsor, where boats were taken to Hampton Court, the horses being left to follow on. Lord Henry told me to accompany our horses as far as Hampton Court and then to allow Simon Barley, the stable boy, to take them on to Dorset House, whilst I waited for him to finish his business at Hampton Court.

જ ઉ

It was another late finish. Lord Henry didn't appear until after supper and I roused the brothers for yet another wherry ride back to Whitehall. I was surprised how stiff the riding had made me, after only a couple of weeks of relative inactivity.

Luckily we caught the tide and drifted gently downstream, Lord Henry congratulating me on behaving well in front of the King, and re-telling how the day finally unfolded. He droned on, as I tried hard to keep my eyes open.

"We dined at Hampton Court, rather late and informally. It was excellent. The King was very relaxed and seemed to have recovered from his fall completely. After dinner the royal guard gave an exhibition of archery in the butts and the King and Maréchal shot again – at targets. Later the King played the lute for the ambassadors and they were entranced. He really has made an enormous impression on them."

I dozed in the wherry. *Yes, and on me* I thought.

"Richard!"

I shook myself awake. "Sorry, my Lord, I was thinking."

"I am sorry to drag you away from your royal friends, but tomorrow I need you to ride to Bradgate. I need my wife to join me here, for the political scene is warming up and her presence will be invaluable. I will draft a letter when we reach Dorset House. Is that horse of yours sound after hunting?"

"Yes my Lord. Jack is sound enough. I shall prepare myself for an early start."

❧ CHAPTER 25 ❧

Late July 1551 – The Road to Leicestershire

"What does the letter say? Let's open it. Come on Richard, let's open it."

Mark Cope had been niggling on at this theme since we had left Dorset House two days before.

Cart traffic on the roads had been light, for although the dry summer – the second in succession – had made travel easier (if dustier) it had also decimated the harvest, and with it the market trade which would normally have been busy at this time of year. The outbreak of the sweats had also deterred people from travelling, and although it now appeared to have subsided – certainly around London – no one was keen to venture out.

As a result, we had decided early in our journey to follow the old Roman road, by far the most direct route when it wasn't packed with carts and pack-horses, and in two days of steady riding had cleared Buckinghamshire and were well into Northamptonshire. We were riding through Towcester Hundred when Mark started again. "Come on Richard. If you won't open the damned letter, then let me have a go. It's easy, I've done it lots of times."

I was becoming angry. "I don't care if it's easy, it's wrong. This is a private letter from husband to wife and entrusted to me for safekeeping."

Mark was not to be deterred.

"Look. We are knocked around by our so-called masters like shuttlecock and battledore. They make all the decisions. They make all the rules. And what do we do? We follow along like sheep, never knowing what life has in store for us, and never able to protect ourselves or better ourselves in any way. All I ask is a chance to look at the letter and then re-seal it and put it back. No one will know and no one will be affected, except possibly you and me. At least we will know what's going on and which direction to face for our own protection."

The mental battering had been relentless. On and on since shortly after we had left London, Mark had maintained his theme. Finally, if only for peace and quiet, I agreed and pulled the leather letter case out of my jerkin.

Mark took the carefully sewn parcel and jumped from his horse. Pulling a little pointed dagger from his belt, he carefully teased open the stitching, careful not to break it. Then he extracted the letter and, sitting close under a hedge to protect himself from the wind, made a small fire with his flint and tinder.

"What are you doing Mark? You cannot burn it!" I shouted apprehensively.

"Don't you worry, Richard. I am just making a little fire to heat my knife, so we can re-melt the wax and re-seal the letter once we have read it. Now, read the letter out loud while I make sure we don't set the whole field alight. This stubble is as dry as tinder."

He handed the opened letter to me, and I took it as if the paper itself were on fire.

I began to read it, quietly, to myself.

My Dear Frances,

As I expected, events here in London are moving on apace. The negotiations with the French are continuing well. They have taken to the King and he to them, and Warwick predicts a complete agreement to our key terms before they leave at the end of the month.

With our back door protected, we can move forward with the great plan. Princess Mary will have no foreign support for the Catholic cause and can be safely put aside. The King is adamant he will marry a foreign princess who can deliver the money and alliances the country needs, so our original plan is probably finished. Instead I suggest and recommend we should use Jane to strengthen our ties to the Dudley family, for it is clear that Warwick is in the ascendancy and the final and eventual demise of Somerset only a matter of time. That being the case, Jane's betrothal to Hertford now offers no advantage and possible risks, and I suggest it can be quietly forgotten.

My position with Warwick continues to grow secure and he has pledged his support for the opportunity which you reminded me of in your letter, following the unhappy deaths of your half-brothers. This should be our next priority. I therefore request and suggest that you join me at Dorset House as soon as you can make suitable arrangements, but no later than the end of July, so that we may use your family connections in pursuit of our venture.

I hope that affairs at Bradgate remain in order and that you and our daughters are in good health. I pray the sweat has now receded, for there have been few cases here in London this last week, and that it has not breached beyond the pale of Bradgate Park.

I am sending this letter by Richard Stocker, whom I now deem to be fully reliable, and trust it reaches you safely. It would be my strong suggestion that you return to London with him, and allow Adrian Stokes to look after the Park whilst James Ulverscroft controls the house, for we may be in London for some time if our plans play out successfully. Our daughters will be safe in their hands, with John Aylmer at their side.

Your loving husband

Henry Grey

Mark had his fire going nicely and was gently warming the blade of his knife with it. "Well? What does the letter say?"

Reluctantly, I was about to hand the letter to Mark when something made me pause.

"You will have to read it to me, Richard, for I have little learning and cannot read."

Relieved, I took the letter back and began, very slowly, to read it aloud, editing it carefully as I went.

"My Dear Frances,

"As I expected, events here in London are moving on apace. The negotiations with the French are continuing well. They have taken to the King and he to them, and Warwick predicts a complete agreement to our key terms before they leave at the end of the month.

"The King is adamant he will marry a foreign princess who can deliver the money and alliances the country needs, so the strengthened relationship with France may have come at an opportune time.

"Warwick expressed his condolences at the loss of your half-brothers, sends you his kindest regards, and hopes you recover from the shock as soon as possible. I of course, agree with him. Your recovery should be our next priority my dear. I therefore request and suggest that you join me at Dorset House as soon as you can make suitable arrangements, but no later than the end of July, so that we may be together in this difficult time.

"I hope that affairs at Bradgate remain in order and that you and our daughters are in good health. I pray the sweat has now receded for there have been few cases here in London this last week and that it has not breached beyond the pale of Bradgate Park.

"I am sending this letter by Richard Stocker, and trust it reaches you safely. It would be my suggestion that you return to London with him, and allow Adrian Stokes to look after the Park whilst James Ulverscroft controls the house, for we may be in London for some time. Our daughters will be safe in their hands, with John Aylmer at their side.

"Your loving husband

"Henry Grey"

Mark sniffed. "Is that all it says? Hardly worth writing. Are you sure it says nothing else?"

I looked him clear in the eye and proffered the letter.

"Nothing. That's it. See for yourself."

Mark brushed my hand away, embarrassed.

132

"Come on, let's re-seal it. Fold it exactly as it was. Good. Now turn it over and put the corner of your shirt on it."

I did as he suggested, quickly realising how the deception was to be made. Mark applied his warm knife to the cloth and waited until the heat had transferred sufficiently to re-seal the letter. He turned the letter over. The seal had been re-attached to the paper, but the imprint of Lord Henry's signet ring in the sealing wax remained un-melted and still legible. Then he returned the letter to the leather pouch and, taking a bodkin from his saddle-bag, carefully re-stitched the leather binding until it looked as good as new.

"There! Nobody will ever know." Proudly he handed the pouch back to me, and I pushed it back inside my jerkin.

We mounted and rode on in silence for some hours, Mark seemingly satisfied that he had finally learned our master's secrets. But I was uncomfortable with the double-dishonesty which the situation had dragged me into. I had protected my master's main secrets, but it had, still, been a breach of faith and I wished I had been strong enough to withstand Mark's pressure, and not to have opened the letter in the first place.

❧   ❦

We had passed through Daventry and were approaching the hamlet of Ashby St Ledgers when we saw smoke. Kicking Jack forward, I rode into the village to find the bake house afire, the dry thatch burning like tinder, roaring in the light breeze. Men were running across the narrow lane to the duck pond, carrying buckets of water and returning for replenishment, but the water seemed to be making no impression.

As I pulled Jack to a halt and tied him to a tree a safe distance away, I saw a young woman, hair on fire, come running out of the building, screaming.

"My children. God help me, there are three children in there. Help me someone, help me."

I looked for assistance from Mark, but he had halted his horse well back from the flames and was clearly committed to remaining uninvolved. There was no time to spare. I grabbed the heavy horse blanket from its roll on the back of my saddle and ran into the pond, unrolling it as I went. I emerged soaking.

"Where are they?" I yelled to the distraught woman.

"Upstairs, at the back. The stairs are afire!" she screamed in reply.

I didn't wait for more details, there was not time. I didn't think of the danger. I simply acted. Throwing the heavy and soaking blanket over my head I ran into the door and up the burning stairs. There was a heavy door to my right and I pushed it open, running into the smoke-filled room and kicking the door shut behind me.

Three tiny children, dressed in rags, were cowering in the corner, coughing and crying. I picked up the smallest and shepherded the other two toward the tiny window. "We can't open it," said the boy, who could not have been more than five years old.

"Hang on," I shouted and, baby in arms, kicked the window out with the heel of my riding boot. The smoke in the room flooded out of the window and the door behind us, fanned by the increased draught, began to burn. I put my head out of the window. "Catch them!" I shouted to the men below, who were still desperately trying to quench the flames, and pushed the boy through the window. One of the men below caught him and retreated, making room for another. Now the girl, probably only three years old, was thrown down and caught.

The door was now fully alight and the heat in the room intense. The window was too small for me to climb through whilst holding the baby and the baby too small to throw. Holding the child against my chest, with the blanket round both of us, I sat on the windowsill, as far back as I dared, then rolled backwards. I felt the cool air in my lungs even before my back hit the ground. I waited for the pain but it did not come. Instead I was aware of a hairy snout investigating why someone had suddenly fallen into her sty.

Women lifted the baby from me. It was shaken and afraid, but breathing, and the mother came running round the end of the house to regain her. Two strong men lifted me out of the midden and helped me away from the house, for the thatch and roof trusses were now well alight and falling down all round. Almost as an afterthought, someone released the pig, which ran squealing from its sty, two small boys gleefully chasing it down the road.

They washed my shirt and jerkin in the stream and hung them on bushes to dry. They plied me with strong ale, fresh bread and good beef, each being delivered with slaps on the back by the person concerned.

"That was a true act of bravery, young man. I do not know how to thank you."

The speaker was the baker himself. He was white faced and covered in a paste of flour and water, but as happy as any man who has just lost his home could be.

"The children are all safe, thanks to you sir. My wife gives you her unending thanks. The stonework of the house, including the ovens, remains and we will rebuild it together. The whole village will help. We have our lives, our friends and a future. That's all we ask."

I sat by the village pond, looking at the blackened but smiling faces all round me. Everyone wanted to shake my hand and slap my back. These people had little, but what they had was mine to share and their response was overwhelming. I looked round for Mark Cope, and saw him holding our horses, well back from the crowd, the only person in the village not part of the celebration.

I waved Mark over. "Is there food for my companion?" I called, and more was brought. Mark took it gratefully, but his face expressed what he was surely feeling; isolation from these people, separation from this event in which he had taken no part.

❧   ❧

Little was said as we rode on from the hamlet into the evening sky. We were committed to getting home tonight, and time now had no meaning. As we crossed the border into Leicestershire and rode up through Lutterworth, there remained only ten miles to Groby and another two before we finally reached Bradgate Park. We would just ride steadily and try to get there by nightfall.

Some time later we crossed the Stour at Sutton Thorpe, hardly speaking. Whatever happened, I knew that Mark Cope and I would go our different ways. We could never be friends now. What had happened had placed a barrier between us. Nothing had been said by either of us; it was the unspoken words that echoed round in our heads as we rode on.

After the excitements of the early afternoon, I felt strangely sad and alone. My mind went back to my first arrival at Bradgate Park. How much seemed to have happened, and how I had changed since that fateful day when the Grey family had visited Shute House.

For a start, I was much more aware of the situation in the country. When I had lived in Devon, my world had largely been limited to my own valley, with occasional visits to Exeter. Now I had seen much of southern England and was very aware of the difficulties the country faced. Peace with France and the prospect of peace with Scotland were surely encouraging, but the land did not feel encouraged. The two bouts of sweating sickness, which had swept inland from Bristol, Poole and London, driven, it was said, by infection from French sailors, had decimated the country.

But underlying the mood of the countryside appeared to be a greater unhappiness.

There were few constants in people's lives: the seasons, the King and the value of money, and God and the Church. All seemed to be at risk.

The seasons had gone mad. Winters seemed wetter than ever, but then the last two successive summers had been so dry that the crops had died before they could be harvested and the price of bread had doubled.

Some of the blame for that might be laid at the Protector's door, for it was said he had debased the currency on more than one occasion. I could not believe that the King knew anything about that. Surely the King would not allow the coins which bore his face to have the proportion of silver to base metal reduced time and again, until a shilling would only do the work of a sixpence? It was simply too cynical. Or was it? There were those who believed the King was not really in control, but was being driven – initially by Somerset, the Lord Protector, and now by Warwick.

The final constant in people's lives that had become unstable and unpredictable was the Church. Since the latter part of King Henry's reign, the Church of England had begun to cut its own path, away from the Catholic Church and the Pope in Rome. King Edward's attempt to define a universal church through the Book of Common Prayer had resulted in further confusion. As I began to travel the country, I was aware of local factions, either for the Catholic Church or for Reform, and the Reformists seemed to be arguing amongst themselves as to just what the process of Reform was supposed to be creating. No wonder people were confused and frustrated.

As I rode along, occasionally throwing a glance at Mark Cope, who was riding next to me, expressionless, I wondered how much of this confusion was universal and how much was just inside my head. Over the last four months my life had turned upside down. In March I was living quietly and without expectations in Shute. Now at the end of July I had attended two great occasions and had spoken to the King.

I thought of all the new people I had met since the Grey family first set foot in Shute House. Lord Henry, who had seemed so weak in his wife's presence, but who seemed more than capable of handling the politics at court on his own account. Lady Frances, who dominated the family, but who had cried on my shoulder in her own bed. Lady Catherine, who had first caught my attention and who I thought I had loved, but about whom I realized with a jolt I had not thought at all during the last two weeks.

Against that, there was Lady Jane. When first we had met I had thought her cold, distant, opinionated, a weak flower who could not handle the rough and tumble of outside life and who wanted to live in isolation, wrapped up in her books and her religion. Strangely, just as I had not thought about Catherine during the last two weeks, I had thought about Jane a great deal, for she seemed to represent my main insight into the world of the King, the Tudors, and the nobility.

The thought came to me that Lady Jane and the King were in many respects very similar. Both were highly intelligent and their intelligence had been honed by extensive personal tuition and education. Both were self-driven and hard working. Both were isolated by their positions and appeared petulant and self-important, especially when matters turned to the Reformist views they appeared to share.

We rode on into the growing evening, the light starting to fade and the occasional bat beginning to hunt for moths along the swathe made by the road through the trees. Mark continued to ride in silence, apparently as aware of the invisible rift between us as I was.

It is strange how things turn out, I thought. *When this ride started I could not think for Mark's voice going on endlessly about the contents of this letter I am carrying, and now I can't get him to speak.*

I sat up in the saddle, with a start, patting the chest of my jerkin with my hand. "The letter! Where is it? I must have lost it"

In all the confusion of the fire, I had forgotten about it. They had stripped my clothes after the fall into the midden, and washed all except my breeches, which I had insisted on wearing. I looked at Mark in alarm.

For the first time since we had left Ashby St Ledgers, Mark grinned. He reached into his own jerkin and pulled out the leather wallet. "I wondered how long it would take you to remember it," he laughed. "It fell to the floor when they undid your jerkin. You were not really in a fit state to notice at the time."

Mark threw the wallet across to me and I caught it gratefully. For a parcel that had been immersed in a pond, dragged through a blazing house and sunk in a pig's midden, it seemed in reasonable condition.

"'Thank God Mark. For a moment, I thought it was lost."

Mark grinned again, looking happier now.

"I couldn't arrive back at Bradgate with you the only hero in the party could I?"

I laughed, and as I looked up, I saw the gates to Bradgate Park ahead of us, through the trees.

❧ CHAPTER 26 ❧

August 1551 – Bradgate Park

We clattered into the main courtyard of Bradgate Park in good spirits. I immediately asked the whereabouts of Lady Frances, as I had an important document to deliver personally. Running into the Great Hall, I encountered James Ulverscroft, looking pensive and serious.

"Have you seen her Ladyship, James?" I asked breathlessly.

Ulverscroft seemed more remote and offhand than usual. We were not great friends – I found him a cold fish and James seemed to view me as a provincial upstart, but we normally managed to get along acceptably well. This evening's performance certainly seemed to be at the cold end of the scale.

"If you have a communication for her Ladyship, it might be better if I took it, Master Stocker."

I was taken aback by this unaccustomed formality. I pointed to my own chest. "Richard Stocker! Remember me, James? My name is Richard, and I am under personal instruction from Lord Henry to hand this communication to her Ladyship and to no one else."

Ulverscroft seemed unimpressed but responded. "Very well, please follow me. Her Ladyship is in the Summer Parlour."

As we entered the room, she was looking out of the window, over the terrace to the garden beyond. She continued to look for some time, making it clear that this was her house and her room, and she would respond to my arrival as and when she wanted to.

I waited patiently. I had seen this play-acting before, and more recently by experienced practitioners of the royal court; there was only one thing to do – wait.

"I will speak to Master Stocker alone, James."

Ulverscroft bowed and retreated out of the room.

"I have an urgent letter from your husband my Lady," I began, but she cut me short.

"You may leave it there, on the table. I have a serious matter to discuss with you."

For a moment I wondered whether the serious matter involved taking my clothes off, as it had on a previous occasion. After three days hard riding, a rescue from a smoke-filled room and a fall into a midden, I didn't think I was at my most attractive at that moment.

Lady Frances picked up a book and held it up for me to see.

"Do you know what this is?"

I knew in an instant. "Yes, it's a treatise. 'Of Christian Perfection', by Henry Bullinger."

"Do you think this is a rare book? Valuable perhaps?"

"I am sure it is, my Lady, both of those things."

She banged the book down on the table with a loud crash. "Then can you explain why such a book, written in Latin, and presented to my husband by the author himself, was found hidden deep amongst your possessions in your personal chest?"

Four months ago, I would have been terrified. Now I took the question calmly.

"Indeed I can, my Lady, for the book was lent to me by Lady Jane, for my personal reading and advancement, on the recommendation, I think, of Mr Aylmer. I gave Lady Jane a personal commitment to look after the book with absolute care. When your husband sent me to London, my departure was so hurried there was no time to return it to Lady Jane, so I put it where it would be safe."

At that moment there was a gentle tap on the door and Lady Jane and John Aylmer entered the room.

"Mother, Mr Aylmer and I have finished our lessons for the

evening. I wondered if you would wish to join us in the music room?"

Lady Frances turned to her daughter. "Do you remember a book being sent to your father by Mr Bullinger in Zurich?"

Jane smiled broadly. "Indeed I do mother. Such a wonderful book, I read it three times, and then recommended it to Master Stocker. Did you benefit from it as much as I did Richard?"

Something made me refrain from replying.

"Where is the book now?" barked Lady Frances.

Jane's eyes swept the room rapidly. "Why mother, had it not been lying there on the table in front of you, I should confidently have told you that Richard had it in safe keeping, until he was ready to return it to me." She turned to me smiling graciously.

"I see you have already returned it, Richard, by which I conclude that you have now finished with it. Thank you for the prompt return. I shall consult with Mr Aylmer and consider what other books we could lend to you."

Lady Jane looked coldly at her mother and awaited the response. Lady Frances was clearly thrown by this outcome and blustered her way into retreat.

"Very well. On this occasion I seem to have been misinformed. I shall draw my own conclusions from that. Jane, please return this book to your father's personal library shelves where it belongs. Richard, you may go. I shall read the letter you have brought me and will inform you of any reply in the morning. Please come to me after breakfast."

        ❦ ❧

It took me half an hour to find my possessions. In my absence someone else had taken over my room, and my chest, containing all I possessed apart from riding tack, had been removed and stored. I decided to go down to the servants' hall and try to get some supper.

As I crossed the courtyard from the foot of the staircase, I heard a whistle.

"Psst. Richard. Over here." It was Lady Mary, standing in the shadows, looking more mischievous than ever.

"How are you Richard? What has been happening? What did you think of London, and Dorset House?"

I joined her in the shadows and for half an hour told her much of what had happened since I had been sent south. I spoke with pride about meeting the King and being spoken to by him, and about the fire in the bakery on our way home.

She wanted to know all the news and all the gossip, and I did my best, being infinitely more successful with the former than the latter. Finally I asked what had been happening at Bradgate.

"Oh not much. We have been carrying on with our lessons as usual. Mother had a huge row with Adrian Stokes two weeks ago. I could not catch what it was about, but it seemed to involve you because afterwards Adrian became very jealous of you and started finding fault in everything you had done. He was plotting with James Ulverscroft to have your things moved out of your room and there was something going on about a book, but I don't know what. Can you guess?"

I could guess all too well. With Lord Henry in London on her birthday Lady Frances may well have awarded herself another birthday present – this time Adrian. It would appear that somewhere along the way the truth of our earlier encounter may have got out and made Adrian jealous. That was a complication I could do without, for Adrian made a good friend, but would, most surely, make a bad enemy.

Mary had saved the best for last, as was her guileful manner.

"Oh by the way Richard, Catherine has been pining for you. She has been quite out of sorts since you went away. She asked me if I thought you were thinking of her. I assured her that you most certainly were – on a daily basis. I was right wasn't I?"

I crouched down conspiratorially, in order to whisper in her ear.

"Absolutely right. Not a day went by when I did not think of your sister."

She nodded triumphantly. "I knew it."

I did not have the heart to tell her she was thinking of the wrong sister.

There was something else, to do with Lady Mary herself. At some time in the recent past it had dawned on me that if she was such a good source of information to me, she was just as likely to be passing on what I told her to someone else. Sadly, I realized that the 'special relationship' between us probably did not always work to my advantage. It was much more likely that it worked to *her* advantage and that *she* was the one who traded in information, and decided who was told what. Furthermore, as I got to know my way around, and became privy to more information about the family and their intentions, the harsh reality was that my usefulness to Mary was probably increasing, whilst her usefulness to me was diminishing. I would be more circumspect in the future. What a hard little world I had found myself in.

ॐ CHAPTER 27 ॐ

September 1551 — Bradgate Park

It was a good breakfast. Fresh eggs and bacon from the home farm, with bread baked in the house and still warm. It made up in part for the poor night's sleep.

As my room was no longer available to me, I had been forced to sleep in the servants' hall, and the endless shuffling and coughing had kept me awake half the night; that and the recurrent thoughts about Adrian Stokes.

I was sure Adrian had been behind the loss of my room, with my possessions being thrown into a store-room, and the accusations about the book, but there was probably no way to prove it, and in any event, I would be leaving for London soon, so what did it really matter? Adrian could stay here at Bradgate and sweat.

I was feeling rather better when I reached Lady Frances in the summer parlour, but was surprised to see Adrian already in the room, and earnestly talking to her, when I entered.

"Ah, Richard. Just in time. I have decided to join my husband in London. I need a change and I am sure he could do with my company. The harvest, such as it is, is already gathered and there is nothing to hold me here."

"Shall I prepare our horses my Lady?"

Quickly I bit my lip. As I had said it, I realized that I was being presumptuous, and in danger of revealing information which I should not have.

"No, that won't be necessary Richard." There was something emphatic and final in the way she said it.

"Adrian will make all the arrangements. He will accompany me to Dorset House."

Adrian half turned toward me and smirked confidently. I was confused. This was not the arrangement I had been expecting. I hesitated further.

"But ..."

"But what Richard? I have told you, Adrian will accompany me and you can stay here. I shall leave you in charge of the Park and James Ulverscroft will look after the house. That is clear isn't it?"

My heart sank.

"Absolutely clear my Lady. Thank you for putting your trust in me to manage the Park."

She was brisk, methodical and distant.

"Good. Then if there are no more questions, Adrian and I will prepare for the journey. Thank you Richard. That will be all." She dismissed me with the back of her hand.

❧ ❦

I was still furious when I saw the party depart shortly after dinner. Neither Lady Frances nor Adrian had spoken to me again. I was rejected, cast aside, unimportant in their plans and, seemingly, already forgotten. How had this come about?

I understood clearly enough why Adrian was jealous and why he had taken his revenge. But what had I been able to do about it? I had not pursued Lady Frances, God forbid, for she could be a formidable monster when the mood took her. It was she who had entrapped me, and now, it seemed, she had decided to switch her favours back to Adrian.

"Don't let it upset you Richard. If you are to live in the grown world, you have to be prepared to take the knocks, and learn to recover from them. Besides, you really don't want to re-establish that relationship do you?"

I turned away from the window, to see John Aylmer standing in the doorway, still holding the door handle as he paused.

"Oh John. Come in."

I laughed to myself. "You are right, of course, but how did you know?"

"Come, Richard. In a place this size, everything is visible to him that bothers to look. It was well known that you had been propositioned by her Ladyship – the housemaid saw her do it, just as she had seen her with Adrian before you – and again since. Surely you realized that event alone would have made Adrian jealous, but when you were preferred by Lord Henry and allowed to attend the royal functions at Hampton Court, why everyone was jealous, and Adrian became positively resentful."

I shook my head. "I hadn't realized I was attracting so much attention."

John Aylmer laughed aloud. "For goodness sake Richard. You are six feet tall, with long blond hair and bright blue eyes. You run around saving people from fire and water and then dally with mother and daughter at the same time, and you expect people not to notice? I have seen oxen with more subtlety."

I was crestfallen. When put like that it didn't sound so good. And until last night, I had thought everything was going so well. Aylmer put as much of his arm round my shoulder as far the difference in our heights would allow, and led me to a bench beneath the window, where we could talk quietly.

"In the last six months you have grown up a great deal Richard. Much has happened to you, some that you initiated, but most of which was generated by others, others more powerful than you. Learn from these things and benefit from them. Do not distress yourself if occasionally you make mistakes. We all did – and we all still do. The important thing is to learn from your mistakes and to try not to make the same mistakes a second time."

He looked out of the window. For a moment he seemed far away, as if remembering something from the past.

"When we are young, time seems endless. The horizontal scale of life seems so long and so limitless that it doesn't matter, so we fritter it away, charging though life, trying to get to the next step of life's journey, whatever it might be, with precious little thought for the consequences and without pausing to enjoy it. We exaggerate the significance of the vertical scale, so that every experience is a triumph or a disaster. Day by day, we move from pinnacle of elation to deep slough of despond and back again.

"As we get older, we begin to recognize that the greatest single reality of life is death itself, that life is precious, and that occasionally, it is worth slowing the horses from a gallop to a walk, in order to get our breath back, to enjoy the view and to smell the flowers along the way. As we experience more of them, we realize that most of the mountains in our life are only hills and the sloughs simply shallow valleys whose far sides can usually be scaled with time and persistence."

He turned away from the window and looked straight at me. There was a directness in his gaze, which, as so often before, made me concentrate hard on the words he spoke.

"With time, life becomes less impetuous. We think more carefully about the likely consequences before we act, and although still making mistakes and learning from them, we try harder not to hurt other people in the process."

He looked at me carefully. What did he mean by that?

"Do you mean Lady Catherine?"

Aylmer smiled at me. It was a smile of understanding, not of criticism.

"Yes, in part. She is young and impressionable. Part of her knows she is born to a life of service to the families of which she is, and will always be, a part. At the moment she sees you as rep-

146

resenting something else – freedom, escape, romance and excitement. But you cannot offer her all of those things, for she was born to the position she occupies, and, being brutal about it Richard, you were not born to a position which allows you to change that."

I nodded my understanding. It was hard, but I knew deep down that it was true. Aylmer patted my hand and continued.

"But that does not mean you cannot offer her the hand of friendship and companionship, or, with your skill with horses, the occasional excitement."

It was the voice of reason, and it made sense. But it was incomplete.

"Does Catherine understand that?"

"No. Not yet, but she will, and you can help her to do so."

I looked out of the window. The dust from the recently departed travellers had hardly settled. It felt as if part of my childhood had departed with them. I stood and shook John Aylmer's hand, swallowing hard.

"Thank you John. You are a good friend and a thoughtful teacher. I shall remember your words and act upon them." I started to laugh. "Or at least, as often as I remember to do so."

We both laughed and walked together down the staircase and into the sunshine outside.

❧　❦

I had not long parted from John Aylmer when I saw James Ulverscroft coming toward me, walking rapidly. I could see no benefit in a conversation with the steward and started off in the other direction. However, to my surprise Ulverscroft called after me and ran to catch me up.

"Master Richard, I have come to apologise, for I now understand from Mr Aylmer and Lady Jane that I have been misled and that you have been falsely accused. Please accept my most humble apologies."

This was indeed a change of fortune and I was happy to respond in like manner.

"Thank you James. I am pleased to hear it said thus and so kindly, for last night I did indeed feel wrongly accused. Please tell me, who was the source of the accusation?"

Ulverscroft looked awkward and wrung his hands.

"Oh dear Richard. I would rather you did not ask me that question. Let us just say her Ladyship was already strongly influenced when I arrived on the scene and would hear no other counsel."

I did not need to hear any more. It was as I had thought; Adrian had been whispering in her ear and had got her to the point of anger where she would not listen to reason or even consult those, like Lady Jane and John Aylmer, who could have explained everything simply and truthfully.

"Allow me to make amends Richard, for if we are to work in partnership, you with the Park and me with the house, there can be no falling out amongst us. I have already given orders for your chest to be put back in your old room. If there is anything missing, please let me know."

I thanked him. This was an improvement, and removed one of the main concerns I had had since my revised responsibilities had been announced, for the prospect of co-existing with Ulverscroft under conditions of war had filled me with foreboding.

"I should be grateful for your assistance in one matter Richard."

What was coming now, I wondered. First came the sweetener, then the request. I raised an eyebrow and waited.

"The gardens; in particular the parterre garden? I wonder if we could agree that they form part of the Park, rather than the house? The gardeners are really park servants and would, I think, be more than happy to take their instruction from you."

This seemed a strange request to make at this time. Ulverscroft continued, grinning.

"Of course, if you were responsible for the garden, it would be necessary for you to inspect their work and that would entail your having the right to walk through the garden at any time, in order to do so."

I grinned. What a crafty little devil Ulverscroft could be, on occasions. However, I could play the same game.

"It is, of course, an additional responsibility James, but if you felt it would assist you and the family, I should, certainly, be willing to do my best. Perhaps you would inform the Ladies of our agreement. I should not like to surprise them unpleasantly by my unexpected presence in their garden."

ॐ   ॐ

It had been agreed and it had been done. After supper, I decided I should take my new responsibilities seriously and ensure that the garden had survived my first afternoon of responsibility. I was walking slowly in the evening light, looking carefully at the workmanship that went into this little haven of peace, when I heard light footsteps on the path behind me.

"Hello."

It was Catherine. We stood, looking at each other, she perhaps as aware as I was that we were overlooked by the house, and each of us uncertain what to do or say next.

"I have been made responsible for the garden. I was just checking everything was alright."

"Yes, so Mr Ulverscroft told us. And is it?"

"Is it what?"

"Alright. Is everything alright?"

I smiled and walked toward her. "It's better now you are here." Hesitantly, I reached toward her and, when she did not retreat from me, stroked her cheek with the back of my finger. "Are you alright?"

She nodded. A tear ran down her face. "How was London? And Hampton Court? I believe you saw the King?"

We sat on one of the seats at the end of the garden. For an hour I told her everything that had happened since I had last seen her, my journey, Dorset House, the ambassadors and the investiture, and my conversation with the King. I told her of the return journey, but underplayed the fire in the bakery. It made no difference, she had already heard it all from Mark Cope, and made me go through it all again, in minute detail.

When I had finished she stood up and took my hand.

"Come, let's walk awhile."

We walked round the garden, occasionally stopping to look over the wall at the river Lyn, or to watch the bats which had begun to perform their evening flights.

"What are we going to do?" she asked.

"We will be friends. We will tell each other what is going on in our lives. We will be truthful with each other and we will see what life brings. Our lives are largely driven by others, so we must enjoy each day as it comes and hope it turns out well for both of us."

She squeezed my hand, looked deep into my eyes, and smiled.

"That's what John Aylmer said to me, too."

❧   ❧

We were disturbed by a gentle and discreet cough. Catherine looked over her shoulder.

"Sister! Come join us, for we have nothing to hide and you have no need of discretion."

Lady Jane stepped gently down from the terrace and joined us.

"Richard, how lovely to have you back. We have all missed you."

I was not sure if she was genuine or teasing me, and pulled a face in reply. Catherine might genuinely have missed me, but I was not so sure about Jane. She answered my silent question by taking my arm and leading me toward the far end of the garden, turning to Catherine as she did so.

"May I steal him for a while Cat, or are you going to hog him all evening?"

In other circumstances Catherine might have been jealous, but I had noted that she trusted her sister and had no fear of competition from that direction.

"Steal away sister, for I must obey a call of nature." She looked at me in mock seriousness. "With both our parents away, I trust I can leave you in the dusk with my elder sister without her virtue being at risk?"

150

Jane reddened, then squeezed my hand as she replied to the rapidly retreating Catherine. "I should not be too confident Cat, for I do believe this man has grown both in stature and in manner since he left us for the King's Court. Perhaps he has learned the ways of courtly love and has a secret plan to carry me off into the forest, whilst singing me a madrigal."

Catherine hesitated, but nature's call appeared to win the argument, and she ran to the house, frowning slightly.

"Before we say anything else, Richard, I must apologise for the manner in which you were falsely accused on your return here."

I went to reply, but she lifted her hand toward me and continued.

"In case you have any doubt, let me say immediately that I know who was behind your accusation and I can guess why, although I should prefer to be spared the details; our mother's appetites are frequently an embarrassment to all of us. Catherine, of course, does not know why Adrian accused you and I am sure we both prefer she does not find out."

I looked at her in amazement. She knew about me and her mother – or enough to matter, but nevertheless she took it all so calmly. Somehow I felt I had to explain.

"It was not of my instigation."

She cut me short. "I do not want the details Richard. It is done and best forgotten. You were by no means the first and will assuredly not be the last either. Just try to make sure Catherine does not find out or work it out for herself. She would be distraught to think that you ... and our mother ... I have said more than enough."

I shared her concern.

"How did you ...?"

"The chambermaid. She has already been dismissed for not keeping her mouth shut. Hopefully the other servants are more discreet. Let us talk of other things. I believe you spoke to the King and he to you? How did you find him? Was he well and in good spirits?"

"Both, my Lady. I thought he was very impressive. He has a

presence in front of large crowds which marks him out and demands respect. Yet when he spoke to me he was kind, and friendly, as if he were my friend. I really liked him."

"What did you think of Hampton Court Palace?"

"Magnificent. There's no other word for it. I have never been anywhere like it. Even the French ambassadors seemed over-awed. The whole event was wonderfully organized. I saw Warwick and Somerset – powerful and impressive men. I would not like to cross either of them. The whole journey was a reve-lation and a great experience. I am only sorry I am not return-ing to London at this moment, with your mother's party."

She pulled back from me. "Is my company such a poor alter-native then? Are you so disappointed to be stuck here with Catherine, with me, and with little sister Mary? They will be so upset when I tell them, for we have all, for our different reasons, been looking forward to your return."

I groaned. I had done it again. When would I learn to be a diplomat and stop using the wrong words? "No, no, that's not what I am saying at all. It's wonderful to see you all again, for I too, had my separate reasons for wanting to see each of you again."

As I said it, I could see the trap I was tumbling into.

"Really? I am well aware of your special reason for wanting to see Cat, and no doubt you hope Mary will continue to be your confidante and source of information, but what, pray, is your special reason for wanting to see me again?"

I realized with a jolt that I had finally reached a moment that I had been thinking about for many weeks. In my head I had rehearsed what I would say if ever the opportunity arose to tell her how much I respected and regarded her. It had been so easy, lying in bed on dark nights, thinking what I would say and selecting the words, which expressed my thoughts clearly, with-out sounding like a gauche boy. Now the opportunity was here, what could I say? Sitting beside her, could I tell her the truth, or should I play the courtier and try to make clever word games, whilst hiding my inner feelings?

She tipped her head to one side, waiting for my reply, and

perhaps guessing at the turmoil going on in my head. "Well?"

"I would just like to be like you."

All the lying awake at night, all the word selection, all the rehearsal, they were all wasted as I blurted out the words.

Lady Jane looked at me, then at herself. "I think you would have difficulty getting into this dress."

I was exasperated, and she wasn't making it any easier. I took a deep breath.

"That's not what I meant, my Lady. What I meant to say was that I envy your intellect. That I would like to emulate your easy way with words, to articulate arguments with the clarity and fluency of language which you display every day, not just in English, but in French, in Italian, in Greek and Latin, and now I believe, in Hebrew as well. In short, I wish I had your education, your clarity of thought and the capacity for exposition which you demonstrate so clearly, on so many occasions."

"Richard!" She clapped her hands in clear delight. "What a pretty speech. John Aylmer could not have put it better himself.

Encouraged, and now in full flight, I went on.

"But more than that, my Lady, I admire the depth and certainty of your religious belief. I have listened to you and to John Aylmer. The King, it seems, has similar views — that was apparent from a number of things I heard him say while I was at Hampton Court."

I took her hand and she made no attempt to take it away.

"Please will you help me to find the true faith? To be between two churches is to be in neither, and that, I assure you, is a silent and lonely place."

She placed her free hand upon mine, as I continued to hold the other.

"Rarely have I heard a man speak in so genuine a fashion, and with such simple honesty. I respect the conviction of your search for the truth, and I shall do all I can to help you find it, Richard, as, I am sure, will John Aylmer. We will discover the truth together."

I felt a great sense of relief wash over me. Here, at last, was someone I could really talk to. Not since leaving Devon and my mentor Dr Marwood, had I been able to talk like this. Only now did I realize, despite all the experiences I had had since leaving home, how lonely I had been in this strange and sometimes frightening environment.

I gripped her hand hard. "Will you be my friend Jane?"

I relaxed my grip, realizing that in my concentration I was in danger of hurting her. I need not have worried, for she squeezed back. "Yes, if you will be mine."

"Ahem."

For the second time that evening, I was interrupted by a gentle and discreet cough, this time from Catherine.

"Well! I do believe if I had been away any longer, you two would have been betrothed upon my return. See how you hold hands and look so seriously into each other's eyes. Your noses are nearly touching."

Embarrassed at being caught out like this, I tried to let go of Jane's hand, but she held onto me.

"Catherine, you have a good man in Richard, and you should appreciate him, for he has many great qualities." She patted my hand, and then looked back at her sister. Quietly, Jane stood and placed my hand in Catherine's, then leaned over to her sister conspiratorially.

"He may be your secret lover, Cat, but I hope you do not mind if he is also my good friend."

With a squeak of delight, Catherine embraced both of us.

"I could not think of anything better."

* CHAPTER 28 *

September 1551 – Bradgate Park

Catherine and I lay in the long grass at the edge of Swithland Woods, looking down across the valley toward Bradgate Park. The last two weeks had been the happiest I had known since leaving Devon six months earlier.

Freed of her parents, with a (seemingly) understanding John

Aylmer and a now indulgent John Ulverscroft, Catherine, too, seemed happier than she had been for a long time and snuggled against me as I stroked her neck.

As always when we tethered the horses and found ourselves a quiet and secluded glade, I felt mixed emotions. The very nearness of her, the feel of her skin and the smell of her hair, made me want her desperately and I knew by the tenseness of her body when I held her that she felt the same. Yet something always held us back, with the result that we hovered on the edge of physicality, quivering with unfulfilled passion, but unable to satisfy it.

I looked down at the house, which had now become my home, and wondered where it would all end. Later today, no doubt, we would release our tension once again, by riding back at full gallop, racing each other over ditches and the smaller hedges, laughing as we went. But how long could we continue like this, tight as lute strings, and waiting, almost passively, for the future to unfold itself? Surely one day we would be lovers in the real sense. At the moment I felt it was her unwillingness to take the final step, which I honoured out of love and respect, which held both of us back. But what if, one day, she lay back and said 'take me'? Would I think twice? Would I consider the consequences or would I satisfy my own desires whilst leaving her with the moral responsibility? The truth was, I didn't know and, frustrated as I was, I felt a certain sense of relief that, so far, I had not been put to the test.

As if sensing my mood, Catherine rolled onto her back and looked up at me.

"Would you?"

"Would I what?"

"If I asked you to make love to me, here, now, in the grass. Would you?"

"I don't think I could stop myself."

"And afterwards. Would you regret it?"

I shook my head. Yet it was a difficult question, one which I had often asked himself, and which I could not truly answer.

"I don't know Cat. That's the truth. Not because I don't love you or want you. Not because you aren't beautiful. Not because we wouldn't enjoy it, but because ... well I suppose because there would be no going back and I would hate to put you in a situation you might later regret."

She rolled toward me and kissed me. "I cannot believe I would ever regret it Richard."

For a moment I thought she was about to offer herself to me, there and then, but she continued talking.

"But I know what you mean. Until we know more clearly what the future holds, neither of us can afford to make that final step." She looked away, then back toward me, shyly.

"It's not that I don't want to. You know that don't you?"

We kissed and clung to each other in the long grass, knowing we had passed an important and possibly irrevocable step. There was nothing left to say. We both knew that one day we would be lovers. One day, but not yet.

After ten minutes, we recovered our horses and began to ride slowly down the hill, back to the Park, both silent, lost in our respective thoughts. As the house came into view, I could see a horseman riding hard toward the main gate. I shook off my thoughtful mood and called across to Catherine.

"This looks like trouble. We had better get back quickly."

We kicked our horses forward and cantered down the hill.

෨   ෙ

By the time we reached the house, everyone was gathered in the Great Hall, asking the new arrival for his news. It was Mark Cope. Like his horse outside, he looked exhausted, having ridden from London in three days, and he was trying without great success to answer their questions, while eating and drinking at the same time.

"Give the lad a chance," shouted James Ulverscroft as Catherine and I ran into the room. "Let him have his ale and summat to eat, then we can all ask our questions. I expect I have as many as most."

As if in reply, Mark reached inside his jerkin and pulled out a leather pouch, from which he distributed letters to Catherine (who also took one each for Jane and Mary), for James Ulverscroft, for John Aylmer, and, finally, for me. This had the desired effect, for the room fell into an expectant silence as those with letters read them, whilst those without watched them for a response and awaited any announcement of news.

As the senior person present, James Ulverscroft was the first to respond.

"This letter is from his Lordship; I assume the others contain similar information, so I will summarize the content of my letter. His Lordship and her Ladyship are heavily immersed in matters of national importance at Court and require their winter clothing to be despatched to them with speed as they do not expect to return here for some weeks or months, and almost certainly not before the entertainment season commences. Richard and Mark will be returning to London tomorrow with the baggage cart. The rest of us will remain here as before."

He looked at John Aylmer to see if he wanted to add anything from his letter, but he merely nodded and turned away. James then looked at me, but my letter had nothing else I wished to announce to the whole household, and I shook my head in reply.

The group began to disperse, some of the servants looking disappointed, knowing that any exciting news was unlikely to be shared with them.

As soon as it was quieter, Mark Cope caught my eye and beckoned me over.

"Let's go for a short walk. There's something I want to tell you before we leave in the morning."

I excused myself from Catherine, who took her letter and those for her sisters to the family rooms, and joined Mark outside.

"Well Mark, what news have you that requires us to skulk outside like this?" I asked. Mark grinned conspiratorially and drew me away from the windows, just in case anyone in the house should overhear us.

"I thought you should know what's going on in London. I happened to be standing within earshot of a conversation the other night ..."

I interrupted him. "You mean you have been listening at keyholes again!"

"Well, if you put it like that, yes. It's only sensible to be as well informed as possible."

Put that way, I could not really disagree with him, but nevertheless Mark's approach to life stuck in my throat. He was always cheating and lying, but somehow he always had a moral defence whenever you confronted him with his actions.

"Anyway, what did you discover that I should know now, before we set off again for London?"

Mark looked all round us, to ensure that we were not observed or overheard.

"Lord Henry was telling Lady Frances about his various discussions with the Earl of Warwick. Apparently the King is growing increasingly independent and is now attending all Council meetings himself and making his presence felt, so Warwick feels his power may be reduced.

"It seems the King's remaining weak spot is his absolute zeal for religious Reform. Warwick has been working on this to strengthen his position with the King. For the last six months he has been replacing Catholic bishops with Reformers of his own choice; Ponet was moved from Rochester to Winchester to replace Stephen Gardiner in April, Hooper moved to Gloucester in July and Veysey has now been replaced at Exeter by Miles Coverdale.

"Warwick still doesn't trust Somerset, and he and Lord Henry have been plotting his final downfall. Even worse, if anything happened to the King, the next in line for the throne is Princess Mary, and having come this far along the path of Reform, if she came to power, they would all be fighting, not only for continuing power, but for their very lives. Warwick therefore plans to work on the King's weakness by emphasizing the embarrassment caused by his sister's continuing to attend Mass and embrace all the trappings of the Catholic Church, so that the King will be encouraged to sign a new law, passing the crown to a Reformist.

"Four times during August envoys have been sent to see Princess Mary and to ask her to change her ways. Now it has reached the point at which the King has written to his own sister telling her that if she attends Mass (even in private) she and those involved will be guilty of treason. Apparently, Nicholas Ridley, Bishop of London, went to see her privately last week at Hunsdon, to ask her to act more sensibly, but she flatly refused. Now Warwick is confident that, given time, he can get the King to deny her the succession by Act of Parliament.

"If Princess Mary's claim to the throne is denied, so must be Princess Elizabeth's, for their claims are parallel, and the legal ground for denying each of them rests on their illegitimacy. If both of them are out of the way, the next in line is Lady Frances, as daughter of King Henry's sister Mary Tudor."

I listened even closer. I had known that Lady Frances was of royal Tudor blood – she had told me herself – but I had not realized she was this high in the order of precedence. Mark Cope continued, concentrating hard and in full flood.

"Now it seems Warwick has made Lord Henry a proposal. With the death of the Willoughby brothers, the line of the Dukes of Suffolk passes through Lady Frances to her sons (except she hasn't got any). Warwick said he would support a petition to the King that Lord Henry be made Duke of Suffolk, but there's a condition attached. That is, in the event of the King's illness and death, Lady Frances would forgo the crown in favour of her eldest daughter."

I stiffened.

"Lady Jane! Lady Jane to be Queen of England in her own right, and not by marriage to King Edward!"

Suddenly I could understand the whole plot. What a long game they were playing, and what a dirty game it was. Something was still missing however.

"Why did you think it was so important to tell me now, before we set off back to London? We have the whole journey to discuss it."

Mark shrugged his shoulders. "I don't really know. I thought you might want to warn Lady Jane or Lady Catherine, before we left."

I was aghast. "You must be mad. Don't you realize how dangerous this whole situation is? Can you imagine how Lady Jane would respond? She would probably ride to London and confront her parents on the spot. They would of course deny the whole thing and say it was ridiculous, and you and I would be dead within a week. For God's sake Mark, forget this whole story and whatever you do, do not tell anyone else."

Now it was Mark who turned pale. "Sorry Richard. I didn't realize how dangerous it was. I just listened to what they were saying, tried hard to remember it as accurately as I could, and wanted to tell you before I forgot it. I wish I had your skill with reading and writing, I could have written it all down."

I put a hand on his shoulder and led him back toward the house.

"Then we are all blessed that you did not write any of it down and that you remembered it just long enough to tell me. Now, for both our sakes, let it slip out of your mind and forget the whole thing."

We walked slowly back into the house, each as pale and nervous as the other.

❧ CHAPTER 29 ❧

End September 1551 – Dorset House, London

"Richard! his Lordship wants you, quickly."

What now? I thought, as I finished my last mouthful of breakfast and made for the stairs of Dorset House. Since Mark Cope and I had arrived back at the house, after a gruelling seven day journey with a cartload of family possessions, the atmosphere had been awful and the pressure unremitting.

Lord Henry and Lady Frances were both in a frenzy of nervous activity, with meetings and discussions at Dorset House and at Whitehall Palace. Each day began early, and the frenzy did not seem to abate until the couple finally collapsed into bed late at night. Even then, the pressure did not end, for Adrian Stokes, sensing my exhaustion and increasing frustration, had me running around until the small hours, only to be summoned again at first light the next morning with more urgent tasks. Adrian was clearly enjoying his position of power and obviously had no intention of letting me regain his master's or mistress's respect.

It had become obvious to me after the first few days back at Dorset House that Adrian Stokes was jealous and mistrustful of me and would go out of his way to show me in a bad light whenever the opportunity arose.

The atmosphere between the Dorsets was similarly tense. Lady Frances crashed around the house, giving orders to everyone, including her husband, whilst Lord Henry glared at her, but refrained from starting an argument. The source of their respective actions was more clear to me than it apparently was to the majority of the household, for, knowing of the impending petition to the King and it's importance to the family fortunes, I could understand Lady Frances's fear that something might go wrong at the last minute and her frenetic efforts to cover every eventuality to ensure it never did.

His Lordship's passive response to his wife's rudeness was also understandable, for she was key to the whole transaction and without her active participation, he would never obtain his Dukedom.

With Lady Frances's star so clearly in the ascendant, it was perhaps not surprising that Adrian Stokes should use the opportunity to lord it over the rest of us, but the extent to which he went out of his way to belittle me had me at a loss. Why, it was nearly three months since I had bedded Lady Frances (or to put it more accurately, since she had bedded me), and it had been brazenly clear at Bradgate and more recently here at Dorset House that Adrian had regained his previous position and was actively enjoying her favours once again.

161

"Richard. Hurry!"

I ran up the stairs and into Lord Henry's receiving room, overlooking the road outside and the Palace of Whitehall opposite. My master was dressed and breakfasted, the plates pushed to one side to allow him to read the papers before him.

"Good morning, Richard. Thank you for coming so promptly, I wanted to speak to you quietly before my wife arose. I see Adrian Stokes is riding you harder than ever I rode our horses. It's a personal thing, as you have no doubt identified for yourself. Adrian sees you as a threat, and as a potential usurper of his position with my wife and in my household. Regarding the former – yes I am fully aware of what she gets up to with Adrian when I am engaged on Privy Council business – I am content to let matters continue, for it provides me with more than a moment's peace when time to think is precious."

He gave a small, smirking laugh, which I decided would be impolitic to respond to.

"Regarding the latter, you have my assurance that your position in my household remains secure. Both my daughter Jane and John Aylmer have written to me, explaining how you were falsely accused over the business of the book which Jane had lent to you, and I know you to be completely innocent. Contrarily, and by the same circumstances, I now know Adrian to be false and unreliable. It isn't his fault; he has been led badly astray by my wife, but that does not alter the fact that a basic weakness in his character has been exposed, and clearly noted. I am biding my time now Richard, for reasons I cannot disclose, but rest assured, truth and honesty will eventually prevail. Now back about your business before the day warms up."

I thanked him for his support and honesty and left the room. Descending the back stairs, I wondered how Lord Henry, and people like him, could hold an apparently sincere conversation, talk about truth and honesty, and still be hiding plans, which, if they came to fruition, would devastate the lives of those around him. How could he sleep at night when the inner recesses of his mind held such dark secrets? And yet to judge him by his

162

actions, Lord Henry had been more than fair to me, had given me opportunities beyond my wildest expectation, and, even now, was expressing his continuing support.

Just before I reached the bottom of the staircase, at the darkest corner before entering the lower hallway, my way was barred by Adrian Stokes.

"What took you to the upper floors so early in the day, young Master Stocker? Been up to some mischief again no doubt? Stealing family possessions perhaps? Show me your hands. Let me see inside your doublet."

He gripped the leather doublet either side of my neck and began to rip it open. The first button tore away and he pulled again, harder. He had made one tactical error, however, for he had accosted his victim just too soon – while I was still two steps up from the bottom of the staircase. The resultant height difference meant Adrian was now reaching upwards and exposing the whole of his front to me.

It was not that hard a kick as kicks go, but it was well meant and deadly accurate. As Adrian doubled up, holding his private parts, I lifted my knee. The crack, as Adrian's nose broke, surprised even me, as my assailant fell to the floor, blood streaming across the flagstones. In the dark I saw him reach for his dagger, and stamped on his wrist. Quietly, I bent down, took the dagger from the outstretched hand and held the point to the corner of Adrian's left eye. I could see his eyes open wider as the blade glinted before him. With my face no more than inches away from Adrian's I began to speak in a low, confident voice.

"Listen Adrian. I don't know what this is all about, but if you think you can carry on like this, you are wrong. I have done nothing I need be ashamed of, either here or at Bradgate. I have never said a single word against you, and I am not trying to usurp your position with either of our employers. But if you carry on like this, then next time I will break every bone in your body, and that's a promise."

I threw the dagger to the ground, far enough from Adrian's outstretched hand that it could not quickly be retrieved, and walked out into the morning light of the main hallway.

Lady Frances was just entering the main door, removing her riding gloves as she came.

"Ah Richard. Have you seen Adrian this morning?"

I bowed low, hiding the missing button on my doublet with the hand across my chest.

"Not this morning my Lady. Perhaps he is having a slow start?"

I walked though the still-closing front door. Some fresh air was called for. Dorset House was beginning to feel a little crowded.

❧ CHAPTER 30 ❧

4th October 1551 – Dorset House

There were no reprisals and no visible response to my confrontation with Adrian during the week that followed, except that Adrian was conspicuous by his absence. The tension in the household continued to rise until, very early on the morning of 4th October, Lord Henry and Lady Frances, dressed in their finest, left Dorset House and walked the short journey to Whitehall Palace.

They did not return until the late evening, having dined and supped at the palace, the former publicly with the King, in celebration of their investiture, and the latter in private, with the Earl of Warwick. When they did return, as the Duke and Duchess of Suffolk, they were both clearly drunk, although whether with wine and brandy or with the flush of success, was not clear.

Overnight, the atmosphere in the house changed. Gone was the worry, the nervous tension and instead came a new, confident, controlled busyness. There was much to do, for the King had indicated, and Warwick had confirmed, that apartments at Richmond Palace were a more appropriate centre of operations for a Privy Councillor Duke and his Duchess, who was also a member of the royal family of Tudor and cousin to the King himself, than a private house, however conveniently located.

I had not seen Adrian once since our confrontation on the staircase and I was wondering what had happened to him when Mark Cope, with studied nonchalance, paused in the street as we set out on a mission for Lord Henry and looked closely at my doublet.

"Is that a new button Richard? It's a good match, but it looks newer than the others. Have you had an accident perhaps?"

I looked at him closely. What did he know? Mark had an uncanny ability to ferret out information.

"Yes I lost the other one. It must have been torn off somehow."

Mark sniffed. "I heard the person who tore it off is having trouble blowing his nose these days. It used to be quite a big nose as I remember. I wonder what happened to it? Hit by a flying button perhaps?" He looked sideways at me.

"Been listening at keyholes again have you Mark? You will get yourself into trouble, I have told you before."

"And I have told you it's just as likely to keep me out of trouble. Did you know, for instance, that Adrian has been sent to a barber surgeon to have his nose sewn up and set back straight and then told to make his way back quietly to Bradgate Park once his two black eyes have healed?"

"How do you know that?"

Mark tapped the side of his nose. "Her Ladyship has a very loud voice when she is roused. She was not amused about his injuries I can tell you. She sent for Adrian in her bedroom and nearly passed out when she saw him. I heard her screaming. Then he told her he couldn't do it because his balls hurt too much and that was the end. She packed him off there and then. Apparently Lord Henry was all for dismissing him immediately, for putting the great venture at risk with less than a week to go, but Lady Frances argued that he would be more of a risk if they threw him out, so he was put in the charge of a surgeon in Blackfriars and the staff here have been told he's left for Bradgate on urgent business."

"How do you know that?"

"Celestial Edmund told me."

"Who?"

"Celestial Edmund – Edmund Tucker. That's what John and Dick, the wherrymen, call him. They say it's because he looks like an angel. Anyway, I had the job of finding a surgeon and taking Adrian to him when no one was about. He says Adrian is after your blood but he's also mortally scared of you after that beating you gave him."

There was a pause. "Oh, and Celestial thinks you are even more wonderful than before."

He looked sideways at me, and I decided to ignore him. Mark was not above inventing a few 'improvements' to his stories when it suited him.

❧ CHAPTER 31 ❧

14th October 1551 – Richmond Palace, London

"Edmund!"

The shout dragged me from my daydreaming, but there was no reply. I waited to see what would happen

"Richard!"

The rooms of the family apartments at Richmond Palace were not all that extensive and his Lordship's voice echoed through them loudly. I jumped up from the window seat. "Yes my Lord."

I had been looking across the courtyard at the rest of the palace. Once again, my association with the Grey family – since last week now the Duke and Duchess of Suffolk – had lifted me higher up the social ladder, even if it was only as servant and observer.

Now my master had reached the heights, but dangerous heights they appeared to be. There were only four dukes in the land: Thomas Howard, Duke of Norfolk, now in his late seventies, disgraced, imprisoned, and his property attained since the end of King Henry's reign; Edward Seymour, Duke of Somerset, whose position was hanging on a knife-edge; Henry Grey, promoted from Marquess of Dorset to Duke of Suffolk only a week ago; and John Dudley, who had been promoted from Earl of Warwick to Duke of Northumberland only three days ago, on the day before the King's fourteenth birthday.

This last promotion had in one sense been the most dramatic of all. The Howards and Seymours were great royal families, and Lord Henry had achieved his status through Lady Frances who, as a Brandon, was descended from Queen Mary Tudor. The fourth and most recent was of no great family, however, but the son of a lawyer who, in forty-eight hard-working years, had clawed his way up from plain John Dudley to Viscount Lisle, Earl of Warwick, and now Duke of Northumberland. With seven children in tow, he was now trying to create a dynasty of his own.

"Richard. Where is Edmund Tucker?" The words were shouted down the corridor as I approached the doorway.

I ran into the room before replying. The Duke was resplendent in his new attire and looked the picture of confident health. His new status clearly suited him and he seemed to have gained a new authority since his Dukedom had been announced.

Lady Frances, on the other hand, looked pale and diminished, puffy-faced and uncertain. Perhaps she had been crying. This was certainly not the Lady I was used to retreating before. As I looked from one to the other, waiting for the castigation that would surely come (it always did when both of them were in the same room) I sensed there was something else out of order.

Then I realized what it was. The Duchess was not wearing any rings. She always wore a number of rings, some on each hand, but now she was not wearing a single one. Her hands, like her face, looked puffed up. Perhaps she was ill?

"Well?"

"I am sorry my Lord. He went over to the new house at Sheen, very early this morning, and has not yet returned."

Things were certainly looking up in the world. Not only had

the Suffolks been invited to occupy this apartment in the royal wing of Richmond Palace, they had also acquired a new house, The Chapterhouse, at Sheen in Surrey – close by the Thames and conveniently accessible to London. They planned to use it in place of Bradgate Park as their main household, leaving Dorset House as an occasional town base for private meetings in the city.

"In that case, you will have to take charge, Richard. The Duke of Northumberland and his wife are coming to supper this evening. It's too soon to use Sheen, Edmund clearly has things to organize, and so we'll have to hold it here. Rouse the servants – supper for four at five o'clock. The kitchens downstairs will provide."

I bowed and made to depart, in order to make the necessary arrangements.

"Oh and Richard?"

"Yes my Lord?"

"I want you personally to ensure we have absolute privacy. Absolute! Do you hear? This place is a web of intrigue and you can't trust anyone. Once the supper is served I want all servants to withdraw to the servants' quarters – only you should remain here, in case there are any messages. We should not have any interruptions from over there" – he indicated the royal quarters across the courtyard. "The King has gone back to Whitehall this morning, following his discussions with Northumberland last night."

He turned back to me.

"Understood?"

"Completely my Lord." I bowed and withdrew.

This was interesting. How jealous Adrian would have been, to see me asked to remain as the only trusted servant, at a private supper between the two newly appointed Dukes. I went to ferret out the house servants, to ensure all the arrangements were in place.

Northumberland arrived with his wife at four o'clock precisely, the Duke carrying a small bundle of papers, and the four of them withdrew into the dining room. I had clear instructions that I was to wait outside for the whole evening, and that servants were not to enter until I, personally, had knocked and been invited to enter by those inside.

At five o'clock the servants began to arrive from the kitchens and I knocked as instructed. There was a long pause, until, finally, Lord Henry opened the door. I could see papers spread all over the table, which Northumberland was quickly gathering up. I nodded at Suffolk, who opened the door wider and waved the servants in. Trays of broth, bread, meat and cheese were brought, together with ale, wine and a basket of fruit. The sight of the food made me realize I was hungry, but it was clear I could under no circumstances leave my post. As the last servant girl departed I recognized her.

"Anne isn't it?"

She blushed and lowered her eyelids. "Yes sir, that's right."

"Would you like to save my life Anne?"

She leaned back away from me and rolled her eyes. From the look on her face, she was used to advances like this from smooth-tongued courtiers. Her expression indicated that we always wanted the same thing. She blushed again, but her worldly smile denied her blushes.

"It depends what you're after sir."

"Food Anne, for I may be here until very late and I must not leave my post."

Instantly, her mood changed. She sniffed and suddenly looked disappointed.

"Oh that's all is it? Don't worry. Your basket has already been prepared. Molly will bring it in a few moments. We can't do everything at once you know. We only have one pair of hands each." She stamped off down the staircase, her heels clacking down the stone steps as she went.

I rubbed my forehead. Sometimes you could never win. Whatever you said to these girls was wrong. You were damned if you did, and damned if you didn't. I sat on the step to the dining room, leaned back against the door, and waited. The murmur of voices was clearly to be heard from within, but was quickly drowned by the clack of more feet on the stairs.

Molly brought my basket and winked at me. Clearly Anne had said something to her, for she grinned as she put it down, bending slowly toward me and placing it between my feet as I sat on the step, leant back against the heavy door. I looked up to thank her, but she remained bending, the looseness of her plain dress revealing her generous figure.

As if pretending to be unaware of my closeness, she took a slow and deep breath, her breasts rising and falling as she did so. "There should be plenty there for you to get your teeth into," she murmured. "Anne says you will be here until very late. Perhaps you could do with some company later? I shall have to come back to collect the basket and the plates from within." She nodded at the door.

I looked at her smiling face, at her heaving bosom, and again at her eager face. Something was wrong; it was too easy. I was used to getting a favourable reaction from girls, even outright offers, but two invitations in five minutes was unusual, to say the least. I stood up, almost pinned against the door by her presence.

"Yes, that would be nice. But for now I have a duty to perform. Perhaps later then."

She looked at me inquisitively, seemed to make up her mind and nodded, smiling.

"Later then."

Her footsteps retreated down the staircase. For a moment, I thought I heard a second pair of footsteps, the other much lighter, like slippers, and whispered voices, but I was not sure.

$\approx$ $\ll$

Slowly a cold silence fell across the narrow corridor. I lifted the jug of broth from the basket and poured some into the bowl, breaking off a heavy crust of bread to go with it. The soup was not very hot – most of the food in these big palaces was cold if you ate far away from the kitchens – but it tasted good and I sat in the semi-dark, making the most of it. The single rush light at the end of the stone corridor flickered. I hoped it would not go out completely before my vigil was over.

170

Something was troubling me. My mind kept cycling back to an event that had happened earlier that day. What was it? For some reason I kept thinking of my mother, something she had said, years ago.

Rings!

That was it. Years ago, my mother had announced that one of the women in Colyton was with child. When my father had asked how she knew, for nothing had been announced, she said it was because her wedding ring had become too tight and was hurting her finger. "Every woman knows your fingers swell when you are pregnant." I could hear her saying it now. And now Lady Frances had removed her rings and was looking puffy. Was she with child?

Then, with a chill, another thought hit me.

What if the child were mine?

For a second, I panicked, then realized that if it were, the signs would have showed up ages ago. Since then I had been with Lord Henry in London and Lady Frances had been at Bradgate – with Adrian! Of course! What if the father was not Lord Henry but Adrian? That would explain much of the recent events, Adrian's unreasonable behaviour toward me and Lady Frances's active support of everything he did.

I returned to my bread and soup. Time would tell, one way or the other. The rush light flickered lower and the corridor seemed to grow colder by the minute. With a shiver, I pulled my heavy cloak around me.

Still my mind wouldn't rest. My thoughts wandered back to Lord Henry's remarks earlier that day: "This place is a web of intrigue". Then I remembered Anne and Molly – particularly Molly. Was I getting carried away, or was something going on? Were the discussions taking place behind my back so sensitive that someone would send spies to listen in? There was only one way to find out. I found myself eating more quietly, listening.

Slowly my ears grew accustomed to the silence and I began to pick out the odd word from within. Then I heard the scrape of chairs and footsteps coming toward the door. I rose quickly and stepped a respectful distance away from the door. Lady Frances and the Duchess of Northumberland came out, talking hurriedly. They were so immersed in their conversation, they didn't notice my basket of food on the floor, nor acknowledge my presence.

"I am sorry you feel so ill Frances. I know what it's like, I have had seven children of my own," murmured the Duchess. "I was always sick as a dog in the morning and my fingers also swelled up terribly."

They crossed the corridor, rounded the corner, and I heard them turn into Lady Frances's withdrawing room, closing the door with a bang behind them. Silence began to return, but less soundly than before. I realized the ladies had not quite closed the door to the dining room; I could hear Northumberland and Suffolk quite clearly now. Should I step forward and close the door properly? For a moment I hovered, uncertain. It was already too late – if I did so now, their Lordships would conclude I had been listening at the door. The only thing to do was remain where I was, to make sure no one else came within earshot, and to listen as carefully as I could.

I heard Northumberland bang the table in frustration.

"This time Somerset has gone too far. His suggestion at the meeting the other day that we should be more lenient in our dealings with the Princess Mary was ludicrous. She is making a laughing stock of us all – and in particular of her brother the King. She has had her warnings – next time it's treason. I think the King is now angry enough to act. The one thing he does not like is his personal authority being questioned. That, more than anything else, brings out the father in him."

Lord Henry was more subservient. "Do you think we can get him on a charge of treason?

Northumberland's voice was quieter now, but still audible.

"I had a long audience with his Majesty last night. I was able to tell him everything that Sir Thomas Palmer has discovered about Somerset; including how he began a conspiracy on St George's Day, six months ago. I told him that Somerset intended to assassinate you, me and Northampton at a poisoned dinner, then, with Arundel as his second in command, to raise London, seize the Great Seal and rally the apprentices. I told the King his long-term aim was to break up the French alliance and, acting as dictator, marry the King to Lady Jane Seymour."

"What was the King's reaction to that?"

There was a snort of laughter. "I don't know which shocked him more, the thought of organized insurrection or of marrying Jane Seymour. However, he took it all in and wrote it down in that private diary of his. I left him with the clear understanding that Seymour's intention is to overthrow the Reformation and return the country to Catholicism. In short, we can, I believe, now move forward, assured of the King's support against his uncle."

"What is the next step?"

"The Council meeting on the 16th. We will catch him at dinner. I can have everything in place by then. Now, shall we rejoin the ladies? Congratulations on your forthcoming child by the way. No doubt you hope for a boy, to carry on the Suffolk line?"

"Of course," replied Lord Henry as they opened the door. He saw me standing opposite, seemingly close enough to do my duty, but far enough away not to be eavesdropping.

"All clear Richard?" he asked.

"All clear my Lord," I replied, and Suffolk nodded contentedly as he followed Northumberland round the corner.

"Oh Richard!"

The call came from around the corner. *What now?* I thought. *Is there no end to the demands?*

I took a deep breath. "Yes my Lord?"

"You can go now. We scoured the room before we left. We have left nothing behind."

"Thank you my Lord. Goodnight my Lord."

I turned toward the stairs leading to the yard and the servants' quarters beyond, for space in the royal apartments was limited. Half-way down the stairs, I heard footsteps coming up toward me, and ducked into a dark doorway to my left. A man and a girl

173

passed me on the stairs and continued upward. I stood quietly. The man waited on the stairs while the girl continued along the corridor, toward the Suffolks' apartment rooms. I heard her shoes clacking across the flagstones, then, after a pause, returning.

"He's gone, and the door to the room was open. They have all gone." It was Molly – I was sure it was her.

"Too late then," replied the man and I shrank into the shadows as the couple descended the stairs, passing within six feet of me as they went.

I waited a full ten minutes before continuing downward myself. *What,* I wondered, *was that all about?* No doubt I would find out, eventually.

❧ CHAPTER 32 ❧

Late October 1551 – Dorset House

"Ouch!"

For the third time that day, the point of my sharp knife stabbed painfully into my finger. This was harder than it looked. It had started out as a simple idea. A week or so ago I had been told that Mark Cope had (once again) been sent to Bradgate Park, this time carrying instructions for James Ulverscroft to move the main part of the household, including Lady Catherine and Lady Mary, to the new house at Sheen, whilst Lady Jane would attend her mother, whose pregnancy was not proceeding satisfactorily and who was now quite ill, at Richmond Palace. There had been no mention of Adrian Stokes and I hoped this signified that he had either been dismissed, or at least left to rot by himself at Bradgate.

Hearing that Lady Jane would soon be arriving, and realizing that she had probably celebrated her 14th birthday by herself at Bradgate, and without any presents from her preoccupied parents, I had decided to make her a present myself. I had no money to buy her anything in the style to which she was accustomed, but at least I could make her something useful. I bought a slip of dark, polished leather from a stall at Cheapside market, and now I was carefully carving the bookmark with the inscription 'Thus far have my studies brought me' in Latin. The task was taking much longer than I had originally expected, but so far the results did not look too bad and I was determined to finish it by the time I saw her.

I was also excited by the prospect of seeing Catherine again. It seemed an age since we had ridden down the hill to Bradgate and received Mark Cope's news following his previous journey north. I wondered how she was, and whether the recent changes had yet had any effect upon her life.

Much had happened since I had seen her last; Dukedoms to Suffolk and Northumberland, and similar (although less lofty) promotions for their allies, including William Paulet (now Marquess of Winchester), William Herbert (now Earl of Pembroke) and sundry others. Somerset had finally been arrested, as planned, at the dinner on 16th October and his trial was now proceeding, day by day. His second downfall had been a shock to many, for although no longer Lord Protector, he had, since his reinstatement, been a Minister and Privy Councillor and in constant attention upon his nephew, the King.

There was a commotion downstairs and I crossed to the window to see who was arriving. To my delight I saw a tired and dishevelled John Aylmer slide gratefully from his horse and rub his backside before turning into the house. Putting my handiwork away safely, I ran down the stairs and greeted my friend as he entered the door.

"Ha ha. So finally Norfolk comes to Suffolk," I called, referring (rather cleverly I thought) to John's origins and our master's recent elevation.

Aylmer caught the joke with his customary speed and welcomed me heartily, his Norfolk accent still as strong as ever.

"Indeed. And, if my eyes don't deceive me, Devon is still in Dorset by the same count."

I realized he was referring to Dorset House, which Lord

Henry had not yet made any attempt to rename, and laughed. This game could go on for hours.

"Let's hold that match at deuce, for neither of us deserves to lose."

"Agreed," called Aylmer.

"Bring Mr Aylmer some refreshment," I called, as I led my friend, tutor and confidant upstairs. We found a quiet corner from the many now available, for the house had gone strangely silent since most of the family had decamped to Richmond Palace and Sheen.

John Aylmer kicked off his riding boots and threw his cloak over a chair.

"The sisters send you their best regards. Catherine and Mary invite you to visit them at Sheen at your earliest convenience," he tipped his head mockingly, "when State business allows. Lady Jane says she hopes to see you in the next day or so, either at Sheen or at Richmond Palace, once she has seen to her mother's needs. How is Lady Frances?"

I pulled a face. "I am no doctor, but she did not look comfortable to me the last time I saw her. She appeared not to be progressing well. I believe she is frightened of the consequences."

"As well she might be. Then it's true."

I looked at him quizzically.

"Adrian Stokes came to see me shortly after I arrived back at Bradgate. He looked terrible. Someone had given him a mighty beating; he wouldn't say who. His nose was tied and bandaged, his eyes were still black, and he expressed great discomfort in riding. Five days in the saddle must have killed him. He admitted to me that he thought he had put Lady Frances with child and only by her intervention had he survived more serious action by Lord Henry. I must admit I didn't think Lord Henry had it in him, to inflict a beating like that on Adrian, who is, after all, a large and strong man."

I smiled to myself. "Yes it's amazing what angry men will do isn't it?" I said. "How is Lady Catherine?"

"As beautiful as ever, if not more so. She has missed you and looks forward to your meeting again very soon." My heart skipped a beat at the news.

"And Lady Mary?"

"She is growing fast; as inquisitive as ever. Her character was set at an early age – she won't change now. That young lady sees more than she admits, hears more than she acknowledges, and understands much more than others realize. She will, alas, always be a prisoner of her stature, and no beauty, yet she has a reasonable intellect by the standards of all except the truly gifted ..."

"Speaking of which, how is the truly gifted Lady Jane?"

John Aylmer sighed. For the first time since I had known him, I watched him weighing his words and carefully considering his reply.

"She is at a difficult age. She has reached her 14th birthday and somehow seems not to have quite the vocation for her studies she once had. I cannot be specific but I feel my relationship with her is changing. She is more remote – perhaps more her own person."

"That may not be a bad thing, John. Perhaps, indeed, it's a measure of your success as her teacher, for if the fledgling never quits the nest, she has not been fully prepared for life."

Again, John Aylmer sighed. "Those are kind words Richard, and I thank you for them. These next weeks will be telling, for she is invited to Whitehall Palace early in November, to welcome Mary of Guise, who is travelling from France to Scotland. It will be a very distinguished occasion. No doubt the King will make it a special show, to let the Scots know he is in control of his kingdom and that the kingdom, too, is strong, (despite the debasement of the coinage which has made a mockery of all values this ten years). I just hope it does not go to her head."

"Why should it? She has always shown great humility in clothing, surely?"

"Indeed she has, and just before we left Bradgate, a parcel arrived for her from her cousin the Princess Mary containing a dress for the occasion. It was ostentatious beyond comparison and I hate to contemplate the cost. It was made of tinsel cloth of gold and velvet, laid on with parchment lace of gold. She looked at it and stood aback. 'What shall I do with it?' she asked Mrs Ellen. 'Marry, wear it, to be sure,' said Mrs Ellen, who has always loved to see the girls dressed up. But Jane was mortified, and refused, saying, 'Nay, that were a shame to follow my Lady Mary against God's word and leave my lady Elizabeth, which followeth God's word.'"

"That is a good sign isn't it?" I asked.

John still seemed troubled.

"You would think so, but I noticed that she gave instructions for the dress to be packed and carried here with particular care, and I still think she will wear it."

"John, sometimes I think you ride her too hard."

"Perhaps I do Richard, but I can only follow my conscience and what I believe is right for her. Besides, there is another dimension to the issue – a political one."

"What do you mean by that?"

"This country is at a very sensitive stage in its history. At the core of the disagreement is religion. There are strong factions supporting either side. The King, Northumberland and Suffolk side with the Reformists, and Jane's views are if anything stronger held than are theirs. But against them are the traditionalist Catholics, supported by many of the old families and comforted by the public displays of the Princess Mary."

I did not follow the connection. "But surely Lady Jane's position can give you no difficulty in all this?"

"Her position – no. But the family runs with the hare and the hounds. Suffolk joins with Northumberland in making the Princess Mary's attendance at Mass treasonable, yet Lady Frances his wife is a close friend of her cousin, Princess Mary, and visits her houses regularly – and will do again in the near future, I am sure."

"I can't see how you can blame Lady Jane for any of that, John."

John Aylmer shook his head in apparent resignation. "I don't blame her, I am just concerned about her, that's all. I fear she will finish up in the middle of someone else's battle. That's one of the reasons I am going to see Nicholas Ridley, the Archbishop of

London, to ask for his guidance on behalf of us all. When I return from seeing the Archbishop, I shall make my home with the others at the Chapterhouse, at Sheen, and I hope to see you there in the near future."

We talked on for another hour, but the mood of our conversation had become sombre, and we parted heavy-hearted after supper, John Aylmer wanting a good night's sleep before going to see the Archbishop in the morning, whilst I was thinking how I could arrange to see Catherine and Jane and which to see first.

❧ CHAPTER 33 ❧

Beginning of November 1551 – Palace of Westminster

To my great surprise, and deep disappointment, John Aylmer's premonition proved to be correct.

I had accompanied the family, primarily as escort for the sisters, to the Palace of Westminster, for the welcome to Mary of Guise, en passage from France to Scotland. The occasion was on a similar scale to the welcome given to the French ambassadors two months before, and I hoped that again, as then, I might get a view of the King as the reception proceeded.

As with the French ambassadors previously, the reception was proving to be an extended affair, beginning with Queen Mary's arrival at Hampton Court, after a lengthy journey from Portsmouth, then proceeding to Southwark Palace, where she had held a reception for the ladies, which Lady Frances had attended alone, and finally arriving here at the Palace of Westminster, where the King was waiting. The scale of the proceedings did not surprise me, for by now, aided by Lord Henry's explanations, I had seen enough of the process to understand. As the first occasion had been aimed at showing friendship, backed by a less than subtle show of power to the French, this second was designed to pass the same message to the Scots, who were, in their own way, an equally awkward potential enemy, and lurking outside England's back door.

I had arrived early, and was standing in the Great Hall, dressed in the new dark blue velvet that Lord Henry and Edmund Tucker had ordered on my behalf, when the more junior guests began to make their entrances. Quickly the hall began to fill up as, in reverse order of seniority, the great and the good of the land assembled, save the thirty most senior men, who were waiting at the gates of the Palace in formal greeting.

There was a strange and nervous atmosphere in the room. On the one hand, everyone was looking forward to the day; those who had taken part in the welcoming party for the Dowager Queen at Hampton Court a few days earlier realized that she was being given special courtesy, whilst the ladies who had in turn been entertained by her at Southwark Palace had appreciated the style of the Queen and her following of French and Scottish ladies. Against that, however, a shadow hung over the room – that of the absent Somerset. He had been popular with many present, who had always found him charming, if a little self-important, and, although none dared say so out loud, many believed his recent, second, downfall was more a measure of Northumberland's growing power and ambition than it was evidence of any real wrong-doing by Somerset himself.

I saw Lady Frances arrive, still looking pale, but improved over recent days. *Jane's ministrations must have worked well*, I thought. She was expensively over-dressed, as I had known she would be, almost staggering beneath the weight of jewellery she was wearing. Since she and I were both unusually tall in comparison with most of the people in the hall, she caught my eye quickly and I made my way toward her, pushing through the excited and increasingly noisy crowd.

As I approached, I could already see Catherine next to her. I had never seen her looking more radiant, or more extravagantly dressed. She looked the beauty she was, and my heart gave a lurch at the pleasure on her face as she saw me pushing toward them through the crowd. I reached their group and greeted Lady Frances and Lady Catherine in turn, then bent to say hello to Lady Mary, who was looking very self-important in a fine dress that did its best to hide the imperfections in her stature.

"Is the Lady Jane not with you?" I asked, rising again, surprised at her absence after all the discussions in the house about whether she would wear the gown sent to her by Princess Mary or not. (The new house at Sheen was large, but not so large that major family rows could take place without the servants hearing about them within hours.)

"She is right behind you, Richard," laughed Catherine, who had clearly been waiting for this moment. I felt a light tap on my shoulder and turned to see Lady Jane, not only wearing the dress given by the princess, but bejewelled to match. Her hair was lifted high and held in place by a pearl band, supported by a doubled headpiece, with more pearls in two further bands behind. The square neck of her gown was edged in lace of gold and around her neck was a tight choker of pearls and emeralds, supporting a large ruby and emerald brooch at her throat. The effect was outstanding and I stood with my mouth open as she mock-curtsied, her eyes sparkling with amusement.

"I ... you look ... beautiful," I stammered, quickly flicking my eyes toward Catherine, aware that I had responded much more strongly to Jane's costume than her own, but on this occasion, she seemed not to mind, so great was her pleasure that her sister had joined the party spirit.

Remembering little Mary and not forgetting Lady Frances's own sensitivities, I stepped back two paces, opened my arms and announced, "You all look magnificent; what a tribute to the family and its success these recent months."

Just for an instant, I saw a shadow pass across Lady Frances's face and realized that, in all probability, the recent months had not brought unfettered success and happiness to her. I noted that she was, once again, wearing her rings, but whether that was a reflection of the importance of the occasion, or signified a change in her condition, was not clear.

I was just considering this question when I saw Catherine's face light up with anticipation, as she looked beyond my shoulder toward the end of the room. I turned to see what had attracted her attention, and noticed a considerable commotion by the main doors. A new group was arriving, and judging by the amount of rearrangement taking place, the party was both large and important.

"Oh look," called Catherine, "there's Amy Robsart with her new husband – and his brothers, the whole Dudley family are here."

All eyes had, by this time, turned to watch the new arrivals, who, fully conscious that they were the centre of attention, processed down the centre of the room, nodding acknowledgement to left and right as they came. The Duchess of Northumberland scanned the room, and, seeing Lady Frances, the other recently-made Duchess (clearly visible with her imposing height) made toward her. Her husband being in the official welcoming party at the gates to the palace, she was led by the hand by her eldest son, John Dudley – now Earl of Warwick since his father's promotion to Northumberland. Behind them came the other brothers, Henry, Ambrose, Robert, and the still unmarried Guilford.

I had to admit that Robert and his new wife, Amy Robsart, were well suited. Robert was the tallest and handsomest of the brothers, who had been (it was rumoured) allowed to marry for love. Now I understood why Robert had apparently pressed his father so hard, for Amy was, indeed, a beauty: tall, straight-backed, with a long neck and fine features. Together they made a handsome couple, and I immediately decided I liked them.

I decided equally quickly that I did not like Guilford, at sixteen, the youngest, and clearly his mother's favourite. He was good looking enough – fair haired, graceful and elegant – to the point, I thought, of looking effeminate. But it was his self-important manner and spoiled, scowling attitude which made me take an immediate dislike to him. In fact, on second consideration, I decided I did not take to any of them, and would not trust them an inch. They were trouble this lot, I thought. I could smell it.

Lady Jane Dudley, Duchess of Northumberland, was, it seemed, as domineering as Lady Frances, and immediately began the introductions. I dropped back, for servants would not form part of this social etiquette. This was, I realized, the first occasion on which the families of the new dukedoms, Northumberland and Suffolk, had met as a group, and I was quietly delighted when Lady Jane, although making courtesy as good manners required, gave me every indication that she did not like the Dudleys at all.

Catherine, on the other hand, seemed overcome by the occasion, and giggled nervously as Robert and later Guilford, perhaps responding to Jane's evident coldness, focused their charm on her, and told her effusively how beautiful she looked. Perhaps she saw Amy Robsart as representing her own possible position in the future, for the two of them were quickly in deep conversation, comparing notes on gowns and jewellery.

Suddenly there was a fanfare of trumpets, and the King himself entered the room. He walked slowly toward the canopy of state, giving all present time to take in the finery of his clothing, the expense of his jewellery, the elegance of his taste in both, and the evidence of raw power which the combination represented. He turned and stood under the canopy and faced the assembled throng. His gaze alone was sufficient to silence the room in seconds, and the cacophony died to a murmur and then to an expectant hush.

The King, fully aware that all eyes were on him now, and still without speaking, slowly moved his gaze to the great doors at the other end of the hall, and all eyes in the room did likewise. As their attention reached the doors, they opened, and Mary of Guise, the beautiful thirty-five-year-old French widow, walked quietly through the doors and the whole length of the hall, followed in turn by her many accompanying ladies, the rear brought up by the thirty most senior men in England, who had escorted her from the gates of the palace to the hall.

There was no sound, save for the light footsteps of the ladies' slippers, for the men had halted after entering the room, allowing the French and Scottish ladies to dominate the moment. Almost silently they approached the King, who waited, standing on the dais, a smile on his face. As she reached him, the Dowager

Queen and Regent of Scotland knelt on the edge of the dais, to be raised again by the King, who kissed her cheek. One by one she presented her ladies, by name and title, and one by one, the King kissed each of them on the cheek. Surely no one, I thought, could be in any doubt about her welcome after such an introduction.

At mid-day, the King conducted Queen Mary to her apartment to rest. Everywhere was thronged with people, both nobles and serving men – the Courtyard, the Great Hall the staircase mainly with servants, and the King's Presence Chamber, Great Chamber and Queen's Presence Chamber, with nobles. The whole structure of England was effectively on display.

At two o'clock, we were called to dinner. In honour of the ladies, the King was to dine separately with them, and since neither of his sisters, Princesses Mary or Elizabeth, were present, he was to be supported by his two cousins. As a result, Lady Frances was summoned with Margaret Clifford, daughter of Lord Cumberland, and also cousin to the King, to sit behind Queen Mary, whilst the French ambassador would sit behind the King. Jane, Catherine and Mary joined the body of ladies at the three great tables in the Queen's Great Chamber, whilst Lord Henry and the other male nobles ate together in the King's Great Chamber opposite. I and the remaining throng of gentlemen, personal servants and senior courtiers ate at four large tables quickly assembled in the Great Hall.

At four o'clock in the afternoon, the servants were pushed from their places and we waited patiently around the Great Hall as the tables were dismantled. Half an hour later the lords and gentlemen appeared at the head of the stairs, descending slowly and circulating in the Great Hall until the ladies arrived. They were unused to hanging around, waiting for the women – normally it was quite the other way round – and some tempers were beginning to get frayed when the ladies finally appeared at five o'clock, having eaten well, been entertained to music, and followed the King and Dowager Queen as they had walked slowly around the gardens and galleries, deep in conversation.

Lady Frances looked better than she had for weeks – whether it was the good food and wine or the royal recognition of her family status was not clear – and, as always, when she was in a good mood, Lord Henry also relaxed. Catherine and Mary were still as excited as they had been early that morning, talking incessantly with the other young ladies of their age group who had similarly enjoyed a great occasion, made even more enjoyable by its focus on the ladies present.

Lady Jane, by contrast, was a paradox. Dressed more finely than I had ever seen her, she was clearly uncomfortable in gold lace and heavy jewellery. With her retiring manner, small stature and pale, freckled skin, she was overshadowed, rather than embellished, by her clothing, and, as so often when they appeared together in public, looked more like Catherine's younger sister than her elder. With everybody else competing to be the most shining light of the day, the effect was to make Jane retire ever more quietly into herself, seeming (as so often in the past) aloof and remote.

"Did you enjoy the day?" I asked, lightly, trying to jolly her out of her mood.

"It was politics," she replied, "nothing more, but well presented. It was a relief to get away from the men. Those Dudley peacocks are utterly offensive and I would not trust them any further than I could spit."

I could not imagine Lady Jane spitting, even in her present mood of disgust, but instinctively I shared her response to the Dudley men. There was something about the way they stuck together and faced everybody with such confidence. They reminded me of a pack of hunting dogs, scenting for a trail and then hunting together in unison.

"Come family," called Sir Henry. "Let's to Suffolk Place," and with that, we left the palace. As so often in the past, I found myself running ahead to find their horses in the ostler's yard.

The family had acquired Suffolk Place, the traditional London home of the Dukes of Suffolk, with their recent elevation, and had just moved into it from Dorset House which was now left empty, apart from a couple of housekeepers. For the three sisters, the novelty of living there had not yet worn off.

For Lady Frances, it brought mixed emotions, for she and Lord Henry had been married there, eighteen years before, in 1533, when it had been the property of her father, Charles Brandon, then Duke of Suffolk. Since then, the Suffolk line had passed briefly to Henry Brandon, her half-brother by her father's second marriage to Catherine Willoughby, only to be lost when Henry and his brother Charles had so tragically died of the sweating sickness at the beginning of the summer. Now the Dukedom had returned to Lady Frances's side of the family, and with it the house.

I stood with the horses, watching the family walk slowly toward me. Sometimes the world seemed to move in circles, especially the tight world of the Tudors and the great families which swarmed around them. No wonder they jostled for power so continuously; it came and went so quickly.

か　ら

Dawn broke over Suffolk Place, with heavy mists rolling in from the Thames, across the south bank at Southwark, carrying the damp salty stench of the incoming tide, as it brought the last part of yesterday's sewage back upstream.

I had given up trying to sleep. Sometimes, especially on damp days like this, I hated London. If only the Thames was as clear as the River Axe back home in Devon, or the little River Lyn running past Bradgate Park. Now, in early November, it was not as bad as it was of a hot August night, but nevertheless with such a mild autumn as this it was often hard to breathe at all down here by the river.

I heard voices in the hall downstairs and, dressing quickly, ran down to see who it was. Jane, Catherine and Mary were all dressed, wrapped in cloaks against the early morning damp, and chewing leaves of lemon balm to lighten their breath.

"Can't you sleep Richard?" asked Catherine. "We can't either. We need to get some fresh air; this is disgusting. We did not expect the air here to be as clear as Bradgate's, but Sheen and even Dorset House are better than this."

"Are we allowed out so early here in London?" asked Mary. "You remember the warnings Mother gave us about travelling alone in this city, especially on this south bank."

"Do not worry sister, the bawdy houses will have closed their doors hours ago, and in any event, we'll be safe with Richard," replied Jane, smiling confidently at me. She seemed to reconsider for a moment and a small furrow crossed her brow. "Have you got a sword Richard, just in case?"

"No I don't carry one – only my eating knife, but I'll take a stick from the kitchens. We'll be safe enough with that."

We tiptoed quietly out of the house and crossed the muddy street, making our way upstream along the river, and past Winchester Palace. Here the ground rose slightly – it was only a few feet or so but it made all the difference. For a moment, the mist and tidal stink were left behind and we continued upstream in better spirits. Looking across the river, we could see Baynard's Castle and Durham House, both still half enveloped in the swirling mists.

"That's Northumberland's London house," I said, pointing to Durham House. "I expect the Dudley brothers will all be staying there at the moment."

Jane shivered. "It looks cold and horrible. I hope I never have reason to enter that building."

We turned again, upstream, and were dismayed to see the subject of our conversation staggering drunkenly toward us. Robert and John were not with them, but Henry and Ambrose Dudley had abandoned their wives and were leading their younger brother Guilford along the river bank, looking, apparently without success, for a wherrymen to carry them home across the river. Guilford, in particular, was blind drunk, his clothing disarrayed and wine stained, a brandy bottle still in his hand. It was too late to avoid them, and in any event Ambrose recognised the girls as we approached.

"Good morning ladies," slurred Ambrose, hardly upholding

the upright reputation of his non-drinking father. "Have you been out on the town all night?" He looked at me and clearly did not recognize me. "Picked up a nice young boy have you? He looks as if he would keep you warm if you gave him half a chance. Eh Guilford?"

Guilford leaned against a wall and leered at Jane.

"I could look after you Lady Jane. It would be my pleasure. I should know – my cock's still wet from the last one."

Ambrose laughed and winked conspiratorially at me. "He's just been to his first Bankside bawdy house." Guilford grinned inanely and burped loudly. "Made the most of it too, didn't you little brother? Three whores in one night and still ready to go again. A true Dudley!" He turned to Guilford, who by now was clinging to the wall, knuckles white and face pale with concentration. "Your wife will be in for a busy time when you get married, eh brother?"

We would probably have been alright at that point if we had simply joined the laughter and moved on, but Jane, having visibly retreated at Guilford's earlier remarks, now seemed to regain her self-composure. Suddenly, her face white with disgust, she stepped forward toward Guilford and began shouting at him.

"You are disgusting. You are repulsive. You are a disgrace to your family. Look at you, like some filthy animal."

Guilford's drunkenness turned to anger and he swung toward Jane with his brandy bottle. I jumped forward to restrain him, grabbing the collar of his heavy coat, but Guilford, now in a blind rage, smashed the brandy bottle against the wall and tried to push it in my face.

Instinctively, I protected myself with the stick I was carrying, hitting Guilford on the side of the head, so that he fell, heavily, onto the roadway. He did not look as if he was capable of getting up unaided and, though standing over him, I had no intention of hitting him again, but by now the Dudley brothers had moved into action and Henry and Ambrose had their swords drawn.

There was no alternative but to fight. One sturdy stick against two swords should have been very heavy odds against me, but they were both nearly as drunk as their brother. First Ambrose and then Henry fell to a hard blow to the head and quickly the three brothers were lying together in the gutter, sewage-strewn rainwater running down the hill and soaking their clothes.

The first onslaught had been overcome, but now I was concerned about getting my three charges home again in one piece. Guilford was unlikely to be an effective pursuer, but Henry and Ambrose both looked as if, their judgement dulled by drink and their pride enraged by their defeat, they might well recover their swords and pursue us before we reached the safety of Suffolk Place.

There was only one course of action and I did not take it lightly. One after the other, I picked up the brothers' swords and, propping them against the stone wall, snapped them with a diagonal stamp of my boot.

Shepherding the three girls before me, I turned back toward Winchester Palace, and Suffolk Place. They would not pursue us now, for half a sword was no weapon for a drunken man against a sober one with a stout stick, but when the brothers reached home there would be hell to pay with Northumberland. Swords were expensive and in any case, to have your sword broken by another man was an act of dishonour.

We reached Suffolk Place safely without further pursuit, but I was aware I had made mortal enemies in the most powerful family in the land, and knew I had not heard the end of it.

&ewline &

Two hours later, Catherine held my head on a towel in her lap and carefully wiped away the blood.

"You have a nasty cut on your eyebrow. It's short, but deep. He must have caught you with that brandy bottle. You are lucky you didn't lose an eye."

I winced as she cleaned my wound. At the time, I had not realized that Guilford had cut me; it had all happened so quickly.

"What a stupid situation. I should never have allowed it to happen, never have taken you out in this city so early in the morning and without proper protection. I'm sure your father will dismiss me, and if he doesn't, Northumberland's men will find me. In either event, I am in real trouble."

Catherine leaned forward and kissed me on the nose.

"You exaggerate. First our father will not do anything because we won't tell him what happened. There's nothing to show except this cut on your eye and once it has stopped bleeding, your eyebrow will hide that. And if you think the Dudley sons are going to lose face by admitting that they were so drunk you single-handedly overcame three of them with only a stave, and then broke their swords, you don't understand them. No, they'll use their own money to have their swords re-bladed without telling anyone. But you are right about one thing; one day, they will be after you, given half a chance, so be on your guard."

The sharp pain of the cut had eased to a deep throbbing headache now, but I was more than happy to remain in Catherine's lap and made no attempt to move.

"We would have been alright if Jane had not suddenly attacked Guilford like that. I have never seen her so angry. What on earth made her do it?"

Catherine cradled my head in her arms. The wound had stopped bleeding and if I remained like this, on my back, for a little more time, with luck it would not re-start.

"Has Jane ever said anything about the Admiral?"

"The Admiral? Do you mean Thomas Seymour, the Protector's younger brother?"

She tapped the end of my nose in admonishment.

"The *former* Protector's younger brother. Well, has she?"

I could not remember Jane ever saying anything specific or personal about Seymour.

"Well, when she was younger, Jane was sent to live with Queen Catherine. Before the King asked her to marry him, Catherine Parr (as she had been) had been planning to marry Thomas Seymour. When King Henry died, Seymour began to court her again and she agreed to marry him. Jane and Princess

190

Elizabeth were both still living with the Queen when Seymour joined the household. He proved to be a rogue, and used to make lewd suggestions to Princess Elizabeth, visit her bedroom early in the morning and jump into her bed to tickle her. Finally he bedded her – more than once."

"That's outrageous. How do you know?"

"Because Elizabeth told Jane all about it when she was leaving, and told her to be careful. Whilst Elizabeth was in the household, Jane was safe enough, for Elizabeth was thirteen – four years and one month older than Jane – and more fully developed. But then the Queen became pregnant, and she decided enough was enough. So she packed Elizabeth off to live with Sir Anthony Denny, who was married to the sister of Kate Ashley, who had been Lady Mistress of the Nursery and Elizabeth's friend and mentor. That's when Elizabeth gave Jane the warning."

I was now half-seated.

"Did that mean Jane was left by herself – with Seymour?"

"Indeed it did, and with Catherine his wife now pregnant and confined to bed for long periods, she was at his mercy."

I was now fully seated, holding Catherine's hand.

"What happened?"

"The worst. He tried all the things he had done with Elizabeth, visited her bed, tickled and fondled her and finally tried (unsuccessfully I should say) to bed her. The difference was that Elizabeth had enjoyed it – she had encouraged Seymour because she was infatuated with him – some say she was already pregnant when she went to the Denny's. But Jane was only nine. She didn't fall for his charms at all, but was disgusted by him and rebuffed him. It has left her with a morbid fear of being left alone with men she doesn't trust – and that means nearly all of them. Haven't you noticed, if you try to approach her closely, she stiffens in fear?"

I tried to think back. "I don't know, I've never tried to approach her that closely. It's you that I love, not Jane."

As soon as I had said it, I wished I hadn't. I felt like Judas

Iscariot in denying her. For a long while, Catherine looked close into my eyes.

"I don't believe you."

My heart gave a lurch. What could I say now?

"Catherine I do love you."

"Yes I know you do, and I also believe you love Jane – perhaps in a different way, but in its way, equally strongly. I have watched you looking at her when she explains something. Your mouth opens and you stare at her, like an adoring puppy dog."

"Cat, I ..."

"It's alright. I don't mind. I know I don't have her intellect. I know you will never look at me with your mouth open like that, but I also know how you look at me and I don't think you will look at her the same way – at least I hope you won't."

It was a difficult and sensitive moment and both of us were aware of it. I took her hands and looked at her with all the honesty I could muster.

"Cat you have my word, I would never ..."

She laughed, the tension relieved. "It's alright, you wouldn't get anywhere if you did."

"If she hates men so much, how does she feel about being betrothed to the Earl of Hertford?"

Catherine smiled, paused, deep in thought, and then gave a little laugh.

"Edward Seymour is different. He has had an excellent education and loves books. He and Jane get on really well. They discuss books, religion, philosophy, everything, and he's never ever tried to put a hand on her. He is charming – really nice. Mother likes him too; she calls him 'son' – I think she still grieves for the son she bore and who died, aged two months, long before Jane was born. Since then she has borne one more daughter, who was stillborn, followed by the three of us. I think she still wishes she had had a son."

For a moment she looked wistfully toward the window, lost in her own thoughts. Without looking at me and half-talking to herself, she murmured, "I must admit, I wouldn't mind being betrothed to Hertford myself."

Catherine turned back to me, a strange, almost combative look in her eyes. "You obviously haven't met him."

I suppressed the surge of jealousy which I felt instantly welling up inside me. For what seemed like a long time, we sat, holding hands, looking at each other, but with no words coming. A realisation began forming and fading, going round and round in my brain. Finally, picking my words carefully, I spoke.

"Have you always had to share things with your elder sister – precious things? Things that should be your own?"

She smiled. For a moment she looked a million miles away. Then, as if making up her mind, she shook her head. She could not face me but spoke away from me, as if addressing someone across the room.

"It's not like that. She is the eldest, and the eldest gets everything. But she doesn't take anything from me, she doesn't compete, she doesn't try to overshadow me. She doesn't need to, she really is different; not just intelligent, but outstanding, of another world. She understands things that are beyond my comprehension, not just foreign languages, but matters of religion and philosophy."

Now Catherine turned her head slowly toward me. There were tears in her eyes.

"She really is very unusual."

A large tear welled up and ran down her left cheek.

"And very unhappy."

I felt such a strong bond for both of them that my chest felt tight. For a moment I felt as if I couldn't breathe.

"You love her, don't you?"

She nodded, gulped, wiped away a tear and lifted her head. She sniffed, loudly, wiped her nose with the back of her hand, and turned to me, smiling, her eyes still wet.

"Yes." There was a long pause, then Catherine gave a little forced laugh. "Yes – like a sister."

At that moment, I felt envious of them both. I realized now, if I had not known it before, that I loved them both, in different ways. I also knew I was excluded from their inner lives, and, in particular, from that unique bond that held them together, and I knew that, whatever happened, I would always remain outside it. At the same time, I felt intensely happy for both of them, for the relationship that held them so strongly together, that supported each other and that kept both of them strong. I just hoped that nothing would ever take that away from them.

❧ CHAPTER 34 ❧

18th November 1551– Clerkenwell, London

We had arrived at Martinmas, eleven days after All Saints had heralded the arrival of winter, and after a long, humid autumn it had suddenly turned bitterly cold. Overnight, the streets of London, awash with mud for the last two months, had changed to ice, and our horses had slipped nervously as we made the short journey across London to the former priory of St John of Jerusalem, in Clerkenwell, now a London home for Princess Mary.

We had been welcomed in, and as I had led the horses to their new stabling, I had seen the princess embracing Lady Frances like a long-lost sister. Lady Frances and the princess were about the same age, had grown up together, and largely shared the same values. Only in religion did they differ. Lady Frances accommodated the Reformist influences in her household – it kept everyone quiet and didn't get in the way of hunting, so what did it matter? The princess, on the other hand, remained a fervent Catholic, and, despite threats of treason from her brother the King, continued, it was said, to say Mass in the traditional fashion, three, sometimes four times a day.

I had been aware of a tension before the household had left Sheen. Both John Aylmer and Dr Haddon (with Bradgate almost deserted, now household Chaplain at Sheen) had pleaded other engagements, making it pretty plain that they did not want to spend even one night under the same roof as the Catholic princess.

I had recalled an earlier conversation with John Aylmer when he had made reference to 'running with the hare and the hounds'. It was difficult. Apart from being cousins, the princess was a very old friend of Lady Frances, and loyalty to one's friends was important. At the same time, the family owed all its newfound power to Northumberland and the King. And King Edward was not only fiercely Reformist, he did not take kindly to having his personal authority questioned – even (perhaps especially) by his sister.

The house was cold and damp. Her servants had explained that the princess had spent most of the summer at two of her houses in Essex (Woodham Walter, near Maldon, and her favourite, Newhall Boreham), and this house, the former priory at Clerkenwell, had been left virtually unattended for months. Now, it appeared, for the week since their guests had arrived here, the servants had been keeping the fires going day and night, in a desperate attempt to warm the place up.

I was bored. Apart from eating, sleeping and shivering, there was not much else to do. I was expected to be on hand in case I was required, and as a result, I could not explore the City of London which was only a couple of miles to the south and within easy walking distance, even in this weather.

But I had not been required; the family had spent most days partying and playing games with their host, and I had been reduced to filling the time looking after the horses. I was returning from the stables when Catherine found me.

"Hello. You look bored."

"Hello. I am bored. This is the coldest, dampest, most boring prison I have ever been in."

"Have you ever been in one?"

"What?"

"A prison. Have you ever been in a real prison?"

"Well … no."

"Then I suggest you hold your judgement until you have. Our father took us to the Tower and we saw some real prisons. They were horrible – terrifying. And the really frightening thing is that people can get put in there for years without really having done anything wrong."

I laughed. "Thank you very much. Now I feel much better."

Catherine grinned and took my arm. "I'm bored too, and so is Jane. We are missing our studies with Mr Aylmer."

She laughed and, holding my hand high, as if in a galliard, spun round under my arm in mock dance. "I never thought I would say I am missing my studies. For years I have plodded through them, watching Jane run on ahead, and wished I could stop. Now I have no one to give me lessons, and I am missing them."

She danced around under my arm again, turned and curtsied.

"Thank you kind sir. I name this dance the Stables Galliard, always to be danced in muddy boots, and with hands smelling of horse sweat."

"I am sorry." Embarrassed, I pulled my hand away and attempted to wipe it on my breeches. "I have been doing the horses. I didn't know you would come out."

Catherine slid daintily under my arm and brought her face as close to mine as the difference in our heights would allow. "I like you smelling of horses. Will you kiss me?"

Now confused and embarrassed, I stood back, uncertain of the game, for clearly that was what it was.

"Will you kiss me if I give you a present?"

I was taken aback. First came the criticism, then the invitation, then an offer of presents. Would I ever understand women? "But my hands ..."

"I don't want to kiss your hands, I want to kiss your mouth. Hold your hands behind you and bend forward."

I did as she instructed and she reached up and kissed me, gently at first, then with increasing passion. "Close your eyes," she instructed, and I obeyed. I heard a rustle of her cloak and for a moment thought she was removing it, but she took my left hand in her right and turned it palm up.

"Open your hand, but keep your eyes closed." Again I obeyed, and a small but heavy parcel was placed in my open palm. "Now you can open your eyes."

Intrigued, I looked down at the parcel. She nodded and I

began to open it. It was a dagger, with a fine sharp blade and a leather scabbard with the letters RS engraved on the side.

"It's beautiful, but I can't accept it. Someone – you know which someone – would say I stole it."

"No they wouldn't, because it's from all of us, including Father ... and Mother." The way she added the last name made it pretty clear the Duchess was the one person who had not participated.

"Do you like it?

"Like it? It's beautiful. It must have cost a fortune. How did you get it?"

"We knew there would be giving of presents today, so Jane, Mary and I asked Edmund to buy it for us. Jane teased him. She said 'Edmund, be an *angel* and buy a dagger for us to give Richard as a present.' She was giggling like mad as she said it."

I looked at her out of the corner of my eye. "You mean she thinks Edmund is ..."

Catherine spun round delightedly. "Of course she does. We all do. You don't think you are the only person the wherrymen confide in do you? Anyway, Celestial Edmund was worried so I asked our father if it was alright and father not only said 'yes', but agreed to pay for it."

I was suspicious. "He doesn't know anything about the Dudleys at Bankside does he?"

"No he does not. Some things are better left unsaid."

"Then why ...?"

She looked at me carefully for some time, as if trying to make up her mind. Finally she said, "To thank you for your loyalty this autumn, when some very sensitive things were happening," there was a pause, "and to make a point to our mother." She nodded in affirmation as she said it.

I looked at her. Did she mean what I thought she meant? I couldn't ask her. It was too delicate; once started, the conversation could not be ended. I need not have worried, Catherine clearly understood my dilemma and decided to release me from my embarrassment.

"Yes. To make a point about you … and about Adrian. In father's eyes it's about taking sides, and he has decided that you are on his side, whilst Adrian is on his own side and, if you will forgive the indelicacy, at our mother's side more than he should be."

She looked at me, searchingly. "You did realize she was with child I assume?"

I nodded. "The rings," I said.

Catherine smiled knowingly. "Ah, the rings. I didn't think a man would notice that. And of course you realize it was Adrian's?"

I nodded again. "It had to be didn't it? Lord Henry simply was not there at the time when she must have conceived."

Catherine took a deep breath. "That's the conclusion Jane and I came to as well. But it was a bit of a surprise when little Mary told us she had drawn the same conclusion."

I raised an eyebrow in surprise. "She is frighteningly forward that one."

Catherine laughed aloud. "You don't know the half of it. Do you know what she said?"

I shook my head.

"She said she could not decide which of us it would be first, mother, with Adrian, or" – she looked at me from beneath lowered eyebrows – "or me … with you."

I let out a long breath. "God's teeth. So both of your sisters now think we are lovers."

Catherine took my hand. "I think so too, in my mind and in my heart. It's just … well, you know."

I put my arm round her. "I know," I said, but each time I said it, I was less sure that I did know.

She broke the moment by dancing away again. "Ask me about our presents." For ten minutes she described the presents given and received, including a fine black stallion presented by the Duchess to her husband. When she mentioned this, I could not hide a sharp intake of breath.

"Was that a message also?" I asked.

"I fear so," she replied. "At least she didn't name it Adrian."

"Why does she torment your father like this?"

"She wasn't tormenting him. It's her way of apologizing, but she is incapable of retreat, so she always pushes back. Talking of which, I would like your opinion whether our beloved Jane is retreating or rebelling."

Neither sounded like Jane to me. "I don't understand."

"Well you remember how surprised (and if I may say so, delighted) you were when you saw Jane at the welcome for Mary of Guise, dressed up like a peacock, and wearing the gown her godmother Princess Mary gave her? Well, today the princess gave her a beautiful necklace of rubies and pearls. I thought she would shun it, but she seemed overjoyed and wore it immediately. Everyone was delighted, and she looked wonderful."

"That sounds more like retreat than rebellion to me," I replied, disappointed that Jane seemed finally to have forfeited her principles.

Catherine wagged her finger in admonition. "It all depends who she is responding to. Just wait until John Aylmer and Dr Haddon hear about it. There will be more than one sermon on the subject of appropriate dress, I can tell you. Do you think Jane is finding Mr Aylmer a little old-fashioned these days? She seems to be letting go some of her hard-held principles?"

I thought for a moment before replying. I was ashamed of my first thought. Jane was made of sterner stuff than to let her principles slip that easily. We had to be misreading the signals.

"No I don't think so. I think she is taking her lead from the King. For all his fervent Reformism, he, of all people, dresses like a peacock, and I know Lady Jane likes and respects her cousin, and takes his example seriously. To me the more worrying aspect is whether Princess Mary is using her presents to try to convert the family back to Catholicism, or at least to associate you with her point of view. You did say she gave your mother a set of crystal rosary beads with gold tassels? In view of the King's edict and letters to her over recent months, that's a pretty pointed present to give anyone."

Catherine nodded. "I had not considered that. If that is her objective, she will, of course, fail entirely, for our mother and father will take their lead from the King and Northumberland, and it would take more than a few expensive trinkets to change Jane's view of her religion."

I felt reassured, for my own leanings toward the Reformist church had solidified in the last three months and I would have been very concerned to see Lady Jane moving in the opposite direction.

As if to reinforce the point, I asked, "Surely Lady Jane has not celebrated the Mass since she arrived here at Clerkenwell?"

Catherine nodded slowly. "Perhaps you are right. She certainly has not gone near the princess' chapel, but prays alone in her room morning and evening." She took hold of my arm and we walked across the stable, back toward the house. We reached the door and it was time for each of us to return to our separate worlds. She grimaced and gave me a short peck on the end of my nose.

"Somehow, Richard, I think it's going to be a long and trying winter."

❧ Chapter 35 ❦

Christmas 1551 – Tilty, Essex

It certainly had the makings of a long, cold winter.

Snow was already falling heavily in the second week of December, as we rode north through Barnet and turned east to the ancient Saxon cross at Waltham. Here we crossed the River Lea – no longer in flood, but gripped by the ice – and rode past the old Abbey of Waltham, into Essex, first east, through the Norman hunting forest of Theydon Bois, and then north, following the Lea valley to Bishop's Stortford. After the soft going in the Lea valley, the ford over the river Stort that gave the village its name brought the old Roman road of Takely Street to our aid and this gave us a short and relatively comfortable run east again, to the lovely Essex town of Great Dunmow.

It was market day and the town was buzzing with activity. The opportunity was taken to buy last minute Christmas presents and we all had a warming glass of brandy before riding the last few miles north to Tilty.

We received a warm welcome at Tilty – a real family homecoming, with Lord Henry's two younger brothers, Lord Thomas and Lord John Grey, already there and talking to the Willoughbys. The family maintained an open house atmosphere, with local friends and the more senior servants joining in the food and the entertainment. As the Grey party entered the Great Hall, Lady Frances rushed across the room to greet Catherine Willoughby and they embraced, both bursting into tears.

"Who is that?" I whispered to Catherine, who stood alongside me.

"That's Catherine Willoughby," she whispered back. "Since her sons died in the summer, everyone calls her My Lady of Suffolk. She doesn't look too bad does she? We thought she might put a dampener on the party, for she was terribly upset when the boys died last summer, but she seems to have recovered now. You should make a point of getting to know her. She's lovely, with a really refreshing view on life. Although she's technically my mother's stepmother, she's two years younger than her and, as you will see if you talk to her, much more easy-going."

We watched as My Lady of Suffolk crossed the room and welcomed Lady Jane and young Mary.

Catherine continued. "Henry Brandon, our grandfather, was her guardian, and soon after our grandmother, Princess Mary Tudor died, he married her."

I was looking at the striking young woman across the room and found the explanation difficult to believe.

Catherine caught my look and giggled. "He was forty-eight when he married her – but she was only fourteen."

I looked at her quizzically, an expression of disgust on my face. Catherine shrugged philosophically. "It's politics; power, money and land – she brought all three, and grandfather, as always, was a bit short."

I looked again across the room at the handsome figure. She had small, delicate features, a small nose and a tiny but mischievous mouth. Her eyes, although smallish, were bright, and flicked round the room, missing nothing. I was entranced. As I looked at her, she seemed to catch my gaze, stared briefly at me, and smiled fleetingly.

"She's a very attractive woman isn't she?" I commented, without thinking.

Catherine dug her elbow into my ribs. "You're not allowed to take a fancy to her Richard. You are spoken for."

I looked down at her, unsure what that really implied. She shrugged, embarrassed.

"Well, sort of. You know what I mean"

Once again, I realized I was not really sure what she did mean.

☙ ❧

"Will you take me riding please Richard?" My Lady of Suffolk looked up at me, her lack of stature no constraint on her physical presence.

It was two weeks since I had first met her eyes across the room. Despite an almost continuous party atmosphere from that day to this (or perhaps because of it, for our Lady of Suffolk, as bridge between the Grey and Willoughby families, was virtually acting as hostess) we had had little opportunity for real conversation.

I looked down at her delicate features. On closer examination, I realized that her eyes were not small, but that she was short-sighted, and tended to squint at distant objects and people. Now, standing before me, her eyes were wide and clear.

Still I hesitated.

"You are quite safe. I shall not burst into tears over the death of my sons. I shall miss them for every remaining day of my life, but life is precious and must continue. I pray for them in private, and trust in God that my prayers help them in the afterlife, but in public I give my attention to the living, for their lives I may be able to influence, not by prayer, but by conversation."

202

It was an unexpected line of discussion and I did not know how to respond.

She smiled at me, teasingly. "Nor will I pursue your virtue behind the hedges of the Essex countryside. My appetites are less raging than my niece's. Besides, she tells me you are honourably chaste."

"Often chased but rarely captured," I replied, immediately regretting the attempt to sound clever as soon as I had uttered it. Why did my mouth always run off unbidden when I was in the presence of attractive women?

To my relief, she laughed, and pinched my elbow. "You have developed the Grey facility with words Richard. Has our Lady Jane been tutoring you?"

"On occasion, yes my Lady. I am also lucky to have my education developed by Mr Aylmer."

"I hear your education is also developed with my namesake, Lady Catherine?"

I sensed a trap coming and decided to avoid it. "I believe that Lady Catherine treats me like a friend, rather than a servant. The whole family have been generous and honourable toward me since I entered their employ nine months ago. In turn I try to repay them by hard work and loyalty."

She seemed satisfied. "Then we are both on safe ground. Now, will you take me riding, for two weeks of continuous partying have left me precious short of air."

         ∾   ∿

"Bloody hell it's freezing."

We lay in the flat-bottomed punt, waiting for dawn to break. Like Our Lady of Suffolk, John Aylmer had become stifled by too much food, too much wine and too much indoor activity, but whilst Lady Suffolk had opted for riding as her solution, John Aylmer had returned to his Norfolk roots and brought me out here into the Essex marshes to shoot geese and ducks.

The gun was huge – almost like a small cannon – and fixed down the centre of the punt, so that the only way to aim it was to aim the boat itself. At the first grey light, the mudflats of the estuary began to appear, first murkily, then with greater clarity. This was the moment we had waited three hours for, and as the contented gabble of feeding wildfowl ceased and was replaced by visible movement in a growing part of the flock, John pushed on his punt pole and, very gently, brought the muzzle of the gun into line with the centre of the flock. It seemed we could not miss, for there were thousands of birds right in front of us, and we crouched down, our only cover a few tufts of marram grass.

"Now!"

At the cry, the flock erupted into a cloud of wings, shaking off water and mud as they lifted.

I lit the fuse and the gun roared.

For a moment, I thought it had exploded, for the noise was deafening, but an instant later I was aware of John standing in the boat shouting gleefully.

"Good shooting. We will feast tomorrow!"

Standing now, for the only birds within sight were dead or wounded, we poled the punt forward into the estuary and collected the slain, aided by John Aylmer's three spaniel dogs, which, slithering through mud and swimming through water, gathered the ducks and geese and brought them back to the punt. We dispatched the injured birds and counted them into sacks. Seven geese and sixty one assorted ducks from one carefully planned explosion. The power of these new guns was frightening, but their size and lack of flexibility made me wonder if their military potential was not being a little exaggerated.

We punted the boat back to the raised shoreline, where farmland met wild marsh, and with considerable difficulty, carried the gun ashore and hefted it into the waiting cart. The geese and ducks followed, but John and I preferred to ride our horses back to the house, rather than sit in the cart, for our bones were chilled to the marrow and the ride would warm us up.

"How did you get on with my Lady of Suffolk?" enquired John as we ambled back, looking forward to a well-earned breakfast.

"I could listen to her for hours," I replied, "she has such modern ideas. We discussed marriages – whether they should be arranged or ordered by love – and I expected her to have the same attitude as Lord Henry or Lady Frances, but she didn't at all. On the contrary, she said. 'I cannot tell what more unkindness one of us might show the other, or wherein we might work more wickedly, than to bring our children into so miserable a state, as not to choose by their own liking such as we must profess so straight a bond and so great a love to, for ever.'"

"Indeed," replied Aylmer, "well she should know, having been married at fourteen as fourth or fifth wife to a man aged forty-eight. What brought you onto that subject?"

I tried to remember. "I think she brought the subject up. She was talking about her sons and what might have happened if they had not died."

John Aylmer smiled. "Aye perhaps. My guess is she was put up to it. She and Lady Frances are very close and always have been, having married into different branches of the same family within a couple of years of each other. I would not be surprised if Lady Frances asked her to try to find out what you and Catherine have been up to."

"What do you mean ... been up to? Lady Catherine and I have not done anything we need be ashamed of."

"I'll take your word for that Richard, but please don't tell me you are indifferent to each other. Any fool can see the attraction between you. In fact Lady Catherine hides it less well than you do."

I pulled my horse to a stand and turned toward my friend.

"John, I believe I can confide in you as in no man. I truly love Catherine, as I believe she loves me. But strongly as my heart desires her, my brain tells me there is no hope; that she is a daughter of a powerful landed family and, despite any liberal attitudes Our Lady of Suffolk may hold, the present Duke and Duchess of Suffolk will trade her to the highest bidder when the time comes. Convince me I am wrong and I shall be the happiest man in Christendom."

John Aylmer shook his head.

205

"Much as I would like to tell you it is otherwise, I am afraid you are right Richard. Your only chance would be if Lady Frances gave birth to a healthy" – he raised his eyebrows – "and legitimate, son. That would move Jane, Catherine and Mary down the pecking order and then, perhaps – but only perhaps, mind, they would allow Catherine to marry who she wished."

I listened, nodding. The chance of Lady Frances producing a son after all these years was, surely, unlikely. And if recent events were what they appeared to be, the chance of a legitimate son was even smaller.

John Aylmer continued, looking across at me in the damp morning light as we rode.

"But even then, my young friend, I have to tell you that when the time came to choose, I think it's likely that Catherine's love for you would be tempered by your lack of land, of money, or of real prospects of betterment. It's hard, but true. Realistically, what could you offer her?"

I rode on in silence. John was right of course. I had never wanted power, or wealth, and had despised those who openly pursued them. My mother, and in a different way, Dr Marwood, had both pushed me to better myself, but in the direction of knowledge and education, rather than the pursuit of power or wealth. But when faced with the harsh reality that the lack of these things might get in the way of love, or happiness, then perhaps I had to reconsider.

A year ago I would have dismissed the thought in an instant. Back home, any girl in the valley who did not want me for myself but for what meagre wealth I possessed would have been rejected as a gold-digger, and the value of our relationship questioned to destruction. But what about Catherine? She did not care about my wealth, but in all reality, even with the blessing of her family, how could I offer her the prospect of continuing to enjoy any of the day-to-day comforts which, unimagined luxuries to me until a few months ago, were to her the normalities of life? It was one thing not to move forward, but another entirely to be asked to step backward.

I remembered something John Aylmer had said to me months before, that travelling through life is like walking down a long hallway, with many doors to right and to left. To the lucky, and those with opportunity, most of the doors are already open – or at least can be pushed open with a little effort – but to the less fortunate, most of the doors are closed and will remain so. Education, Aylmer had said, was a key which unlocked many doors, but now I realized that money and power were more powerful keys, and likely to open more doors than anything else. No wonder some people pursued them with such persistence.

I was not in a party spirit when we returned to the house. But who knew? A well-earned breakfast and I might feel better. Somehow, I always bounced back, but this time the thoughts lay heavily with me for days.

❧ CHAPTER 36 ❧

End of January 1552 – Walden, Essex

The Christmas party season seemed to go on forever, and well into the New Year. Princess Mary came for dinner on Christmas Day and again on New Year's Eve, each time riding over from her home at Newhall.

The Willoughbys had gone to great lengths to make everyone's stay enjoyable, from the princess to Dr Haddon, although his reaction to what he called "these mummeries" was predictably negative. To James Haddon, Christ's birthday was an occasion for Christian rejoicing in the appropriate and religious manner, not for the nobility to reduce themselves to (or even below) the standard of the uninstructed country people, by indulging in endless and often drunken partying.

Not that his salt-tongued expression spoiled the party for everyone else. With the great freeze continuing, there was less and less incentive to go outside, except to throw the occasional snowball in the garden, and most of the party settled for late nights and equally late starts the next day, with partying continuing in its alternative forms downstairs by day and upstairs by night.

There was no end of entertainment, from tumblers, jugglers and a singing boys choir. Perhaps most enjoyable of all was the Earl of Oxford's Company of travelling professional actors, which put on plays every evening after supper. The plays, in particular, upset Dr Haddon's sensibilities, for they were more Mummers than Miracle Plays, and the jokes grew more ribald as each evening progressed and the drink flowed freely.

Nevertheless, by the end of January, despite the best endeavours of the players and musicians, the party had begun to go stale, and Lady Frances decided that we would all visit the Duke's sister, Lady Audley, at Walden. At least it was not a long journey.

Spirits revived with a new environment, only to be dashed.

We had been there less than a day and the great chests had hardly been carried to the respective bedrooms when the messenger arrived from London. He and his horses were frozen and he had to be thawed out with brandy and hot soup before he could impart his message to Lord Henry with any semblance of order. The two of them disappeared into a side room and the door was firmly closed. The effect was immediate – everyone in the house wanted to know what news the messenger carried, and we all scurried around, apparently busy, but always within earshot, in a mood of nervous expectancy.

After half-an-hour, the messenger emerged and, to my great surprise, I was summoned into the room in his place. Lord Henry sat beside the fire, looking lost in thought.

"Richard, come closer. While we have been partying here in Essex, great events have been taking place in our absence. The deed is done – Somerset has finally been executed – on the 22nd of January, and by all accounts it did not go as planned. There was confusion with the late arrival of troops, the crowd mistook them for a reprieve party and all hell broke loose. Needless to say, it was Somerset, of all people, who held his nerve and calmed the crowd, and he finally went to his maker as a man of stature;

the last thing we wanted. If we are not careful he will be remembered as a martyr."

I was not overly surprised at the news – I had known from previous comments by Lord Henry that Somerset's execution was being held back until Christmas was over – but I was surprised that Lord Henry had chosen to inform me before his own family.

My master continued.

"The King seems to have accepted the demise of his uncle with equanimity – Northumberland must have convinced him well of Somerset's guilt. However, the mood of the people is ugly and we will have to enter the New Year with care. There is much to be done and we will not serve our King, our country or" – he smirked – "ourselves by continuing to play in the country when there is work to be done in the city."

"You did well last summer and autumn Richard and I have already thanked you for it. Now I need your hard work and loyalty to continue, for with Somerset out of the way the path is clear for major reform, and that will require a special effort by all of us. The new Book of Common Prayer is due to be published soon and it is vital that it is well received by the people. Can I have your assurance that I can rely on your continuing loyalty and discretion throughout this New Year and for the future?"

I gave the assurance – what else could I have possibly said? I could not understand why Lord Henry should even have asked me. There was something strange about the whole conversation. Finally, it was clear I was about to be dismissed.

"Richard I am glad we have had this conversation. Tomorrow we must return to Suffolk Place. For now, I need to speak to my wife. Would you be so good as to ask her to join me? And while I am speaking to her, perhaps you would be good enough to inform my daughters of the situation before the messenger does?"

I left the room and found Lady Frances, asking her to join her husband "at her convenience". She was clearly angry at receiving the message from me but I could see no alternative – I had been asked to pass on the message and I had done so.

As instructed, I looked for the sisters and found them playing music in a small room at the end of the house. I entered and explained that their father had asked me to inform them of the situation whilst he spoke to Lady Frances. Catherine and Mary received the news of Somerset's demise with equanimity. Death by execution was a fairly normal hazard to a Tudor family and the first reaction normally seemed to be 'Thank the Lord it was not us'.

Lady Jane, however, paled, and sat down in the window seat, looking as if she was going to faint. I was concerned at her reaction and not sure what to do, but Catherine put an arm round her shoulder and held her until she recovered. I stood, awkwardly, waiting to continue, until Jane signalled for me to do so.

"Don't wait for me Richard – I am alright. It came as a shock, that's all. Pray continue."

I began speaking again, but immediately Jane stood and, with Catherine assisting her, made for the door.

"Excuse me Richard. I feel a little sick. I think I will go and lie down for a while. Please excuse me."

I waited for ten minutes, chatting awkwardly to Mary, until Catherine returned. She went as if to say something, looked at me, then at Mary, and appeared to change her mind. "She will be alright. Jane always takes these things badly. She has such a fertile imagination."

I felt awkward at the whole situation and wanted to apologise.

"I am sorry, ladies. I feel I have been put in a difficult situation. For some reason, when the messenger arrived, your father decided to speak to me first, even before speaking to your mother." Catherine and Mary glanced briefly at one another, without comment.

"He is speaking to her now, and asked me to inform you of the situation while he did so. It seems there is much afoot in London and we need to return tomorrow at the latest. We shall be leaving for Suffolk Place at first light."

Mary jumped up. "I am going to help Jane. She will need a

hand with all her books. She has only just finished unpacking them again."

As soon as she had left the room, Catherine signalled me to sit with her in the window seat. For a while, we held hands, she apparently lost in thought and I, also silent, not knowing what to say next. Finally Catherine spoke.

"He still hasn't forgiven her."

I looked at her quizzically. "Who?"

"Our mother. Father hasn't forgiven her for renewing her affair with Adrian and (perhaps worse) for being stupid enough to get pregnant. That's why he spoke to you first. He has always had Mother as a confidante and advisor. In fact, most of the time, she tells him in no uncertain terms what to do. But now he is sulking, so to make the point, he has banished Adrian to Bradgate, and will not have his name mentioned in this house. Did he have anything specific to say to you?"

"No. Not really. It was strange. He told me the situation, said we would all be very busy on important work, and asked for confirmation of my continuing loyalty – as if I would say no?"

Catherine nodded. "I thought so. It all revolves around his relationship with Mother. He is so dependent on her strength, even if he sometimes resents her dominance. He is using you as a substitute for her and for Adrian." She paused, and then looked at me from the corner of her eyes. "And for the surviving son he never had. You do realize that don't you?"

I was astounded. "What do you mean?"

She gripped my hand.

"Our father is a lonely man. He craves male company, and in particular has always wanted a son who he can take riding, hunting and so on. Instead he has a domineering wife, and three independent daughters."

There was a pause, and I realized she was mulling something over, as if deciding whether or not to mention it. Finally, she appeared to make the decision and looked away from me, embarrassed.

"Why do you think he has always sponsored young men?

211

First there was John Aylmer, then Adrian, and now you have donned the mantle. Yes I have heard the rumours that it's because he is a secret pederast, but that's ridiculous. To my knowledge" – she looked at me a little uncertainly - "he has never made approaches of that sort to any of you?"

I shook my head – perhaps too emphatically, but Catherine appeared reassured and continued.

"Exactly. He simply wants a son – a male friend he can trust and share the burdens of life with. He looks at Northumberland and sees him with his Dudley boys, all of them, even Guilford the mother's boy, respectful and totally loyal and he wishes he had the same. It's sad really, but very understandable – you have quite an opportunity – and quite a responsibility."

For some time, I considered what she had just said.

"What about your mother – doesn't she wish for a son also?"

Catherine moved round in front of me and held both my hands in hers, looking deep into my eyes.

"Of course she does. It must be worse having had a son – her first born – and having lost him so young in life. Sometimes she talks about it – especially after Lord Hertford has visited us. She calls Edward her son. Perhaps that's why she had Jane betrothed to him when she did – it was Mother not Father who wanted it. Now, with this news, who knows? Seymours will be worth nothing from now on."

I put my arm round her shoulder and hugged her. It was so unfair. The lives of Catherine and her sisters were so dominated by politics. Why couldn't they just be allowed to live their lives in peace and tranquillity? I knew the answer as soon as I had asked myself the question, and for a moment I recalled a cold morning's ride with John Aylmer across the Essex marshes only a week before.

But it still seemed unfair.

Ω Ω

The news spread rapidly throughout the house, and, as it did so, everyone went quiet, lost in their own thoughts.

The power battle between Northumberland and Somerset had been public knowledge for months. Some thought Somerset was guilty of the charges against him, but more were convinced that the evidence against him had probably been trumped up or bought. Most had put the issue aside before Christmas, however, comfortable in the knowledge that the King would not execute the man who had, for so long, been his favourite uncle.

Now the news had come that Somerset had, indeed, faced the axe in front of an angry crowd, who had publicly blamed Northumberland afterwards for what they shouted was an act of great wickedness. The consequences were anyone's guess, but for the Grey family one thing was clear – they had partied too long out here in the country – they needed to be back in the thick of things for their own protection.

Early next morning, in heavy frost, we set off across the Essex countryside, hoping the cold and the ice would not prevent us from reaching Suffolk Place by nightfall.

❧ CHAPTER 37 ❧

February 1552 – Suffolk Place

The news about Somerset had finally killed off the Christmas spirit and we returned to Suffolk Place thoroughly depressed. Perhaps everyone had been compressed for too long into too small a space, for as soon as we reached what we now called home, the members of the party went their different ways.

Lord Henry, as always, immersed himself in his work, maintaining the closeness of his relationship with Northumberland and attending to Ministerial matters. The King had had a new burst of energy, in part, it was said, inspired by the expected publication of the new Book of Common Prayers, which came out during the month.

Toward the end of February, Nicholas Ridley preached on the plight of the poor, in front of the King, who was so moved

213

he immediately commenced a series of new works, including two charitable foundations in empty religious houses in London: St Thomas's Hospital in Southwark, not far from Suffolk Place, and Christ's Hospital in the old convent of the Greyfriars in Newgate. Needless to say, the detailed work to turn royal concept into operational achievement fell to the Council, and Lord Henry became embroiled in the detail.

James Haddon returned to Sheen to write letters to Henry Bullinger and his other Reformist contacts on the continent. The festive season had convinced him the whole country was going to the dogs, a view shared by John Knox, who had arrived from Scotland to be appointed Chaplain at court.

John Aylmer's reaction was to try to re-establish the comfortable, and satisfying, process of educating Lady Jane and her younger sisters, but for the first time he was finding it difficult. Trying to be helpful, he had spoken quietly to Catherine along the lines of his conversation with me on our return from the wildfowling trip in Essex. The result had not been what he expected, for Catherine, having solved the problem by simply refusing to address it for months, now became distraught and took to her room, too upset to talk to Aylmer, who she thought had betrayed her, or to me, out of sheer embarrassment.

Jane was no help to her either, for she too had locked herself in her room and refused to speak to anyone, except little Mary, who emerged as the main channel of communication within the family that month.

"What on earth is wrong with her?" I asked Mary, when Lady Frances had had to excuse Jane from three successive court occasions on the grounds that she was "exhausted from too much partying".

"She's very upset," explained Mary, whose powers of diplomacy seemed to have developed extensively over the winter. "She tries so hard to please. Everyone is demanding things of her: God, the King, our parents – especially Mother of course, for Father keeps out of the way when there's a shouting match – and Mr Aylmer. She has fallen out with him very badly."

"What happened?" I asked, alarmed, for the close relationship between my two good friends was a comfort to me, and the thought of it breaking down was a real worry.

Mary sat me down and began to explain, wagging her finger, and using the simple language, spoken slowly, which she used when explaining something important to Floppy, who in the last six months had grown from a lovable bundle of fur into a characterful spaniel, always on the lookout for mischief.

"It's all Princess Mary's fault. It started when that gown arrived, before the reception for Queen Mary of Guise – you remember?" I nodded. "Well Jane thought it was too rich and not at all to her liking. Mr Aylmer agreed with her and she told Mother she would not wear it. Then Mother got some of the court ladies to explain that the purpose of the occasion was to impress the French and the Scots, and it was important that we all dressed up, as the King intended to do. They said the King would be upset if anyone let the side down, so Jane agreed to wear it and you saw the result – she looked beautiful."

I agreed. "She really did – I remember it very well. You all looked wonderful."

Mary continued wagging her finger. I was clearly not allowed to interrupt any more than Floppy was when she was in full flow.

"Well, after that occasion, Mr Aylmer told Jane he didn't like her in that dress and that Princess Elizabeth had looked much more fitting in a plain dress when she attended the reception given by Mary of Guise for the ladies at Southwark. Jane lost her temper and said she was following the King's command, which had not applied at Southwark, as Mary herself was hosting that occasion.

"Then came the Christmas presents. Mary again. This time she gave Jane a ruby and pearl necklace, which was really lovely – not too gaudy and it suited Jane's colouring perfectly. So she wore it over Christmas as Mother and Father wanted the other side of the family, and My Lady of Suffolk in particular, to see how well we were doing, and that we could carry off the Suffolk name as well as she and her husband had. It was a bit delicate, for mother and Aunt Catherine have always been really good

215

friends and none of us wanted to upset her by appearing to take over her title – and of course, this house also, from her family.

"This time Mr Aylmer had grumpy old Dr Haddon with him and the two of them really had strong words with Jane. She decided they are dried up old prunes who have lost the ability to enjoy themselves, but at the same time she is ravaged with conscience about dressing in an ungodly manner. Poor Jane, all she wants to do is the right thing, but, as always, whatever she does, it's wrong. She is used to arguing with mother – she has no respect for her opinions anyway – but now that she has fallen out with Mr Aylmer, she is distraught."

I was about to say that I understood, but Mary had still not finished. As I leaned forward toward her and tried to speak, she pushed the palm of her hand toward me, as if telling me to 'sit'.

"But there's worse. It was when we were in Walden, and we heard that Somerset had been executed. You remember Jane suddenly went cold and said she felt sick? That was because she realized that her betrothal to dear Edward Seymour, Lord Hertford, who she really likes (so do Catherine and I and so does Mother, by the way), well that will certainly be ended. Now Somerset is disgraced, attained and executed, Hertford is worth nothing and association with him is considered dangerous, so the family will look round for someone else. Jane is terrified it will be Northumberland's son, for father is closer and closer to him as the weeks advance."

I understood it all now. It was as if the moon had come out from behind a cloud and flooded the place with light. Why hadn't I realized it before – it was obvious.

"Guilford Dudley! Of course – the only unmarried one. And after that morning we met them, and her earlier experiences with the Admiral, I can understand. Poor Jane, what can we do?"

Mary shook her head. "I don't know. Just to understand is a start I suppose. I will tell her you understand and ask her to talk to you. She trusts you and says she doesn't think you're repulsive like other men."

It was a strange compliment, but somehow a satisfying one.

216

Mary was as good as her word, and Jane opened her door and began talking to me again. She agreed with Catherine that their father looked upon me as the son he had never had and that he was likely to draw me ever closer into his world. She decided my education was in danger of lagging behind my growing responsibilities, a situation she planned to redress.

"I shall teach you Italian," she announced at the beginning of our third meeting. "You may be my mentor and share my troubles, and in return I shall take responsibility for your further education. I believe you have a flair for languages – your Latin really is excellent these days – and Italian is such a useful language in diplomatic circles. You will be able to understand the Venetian ambassador."

For the next six weeks, we met for an hour every day (except Sundays), and by the end of that period I had a smattering of Italian phrases and the beginnings of an accent that owed more to Venice than to Devon, while Jane had recovered her equanimity and her sense of humour. Suffolk and his wife were pleased with the improvement in Jane and gave much more of the credit to me than to the visiting apothecary, most of whose potions Jane had, in any event, poured out of the window.

In early March, the cold weather, which had gripped the country for so many weeks, finally thawed, and with it the relationship between Suffolk and his wife. Lord Henry was immersed in the King's various projects – his latest was a planned reorganization of the Council into committees – and when Lady Frances suggested she and the girls should go to Sheen to enjoy the spring air and, with the King's permission, hunt in Richmond Park, he agreed, and even suggested she might invite Catherine Willoughby to join them there, if only to thank her for her hospitality over the Christmas period.

In view of the urgency and delicacy of his business affairs, Suffolk declined Lady Frances's invitation to accompany them to Sheen, and said he would remain at Suffolk Place, working. So great was the workload, and so sensitive – being at the personal prerogative of the King himself – that he asked me to remain with him at Suffolk Place, and to accompany him to the various meetings as his Secretary.

In many respects, I would have preferred to remain with the ladies, for my studies with Lady Jane were proving enjoyable and, it appeared, beneficial to both of us, whilst Catherine's mood was so fickle that I wanted to keep in close touch with her. On the other hand, Suffolk's work was directly at the King's request, and as Secretary, I would be attending some of the meetings and taking notes – a significant promotion from Second Master of Horse – and the thought of perhaps seeing the King at work was very exciting indeed.

It was therefore with mixed feelings that I waved the ladies off, one sunny spring morning, on their short journey to Sheen.

ॐ Chapter 38 ॐ

March 1552 – Whitehall and St James's Palace

Suffolk's work with the King progressed well enough, although the young sovereign was bubbling with more ideas than could be implemented at one time, and eternally frustrated that he could not achieve all of them immediately.

One afternoon, I was walking rapidly along a corridor in Whitehall Palace, excited because I was carrying a bundle of important papers. I was approaching the room where Suffolk was in committee with the King and others, when I was met by loud ranting and swearing of oaths. This time I knew immediately that it was the King who was swearing and my pace slowed to a walk and finally to a complete halt, just outside the door.

It was just as well I did, for a very noble Lord emerged red-faced from the room, muttering to himself, followed by cries of "Incompetent bloody jug-head" from inside. I was just on the point of deciding that the documents could be delivered later, when the King, whose moods could apparently change as fast as his father's had, shouted a further obscenity, and the whole room burst into manly laughter.

Gathering up renewed courage, I entered the room, just as the King was holding forth for the benefit of all present. There must have been something about my demeanour, carrying a large pile of rolled up drawings and other papers, which found its reflection in what the King was saying, for, on seeing me, the King burst into uncontrollable and infectious laughter, so that the whole room finished up laughing until they had tears in their eyes. Uncertain what the joke was, I joined in, and laughed too.

The room grew quieter and all eyes were on me, as I stood half-way between door and table, the pile of drawings heaped in my arms.

"Forgive me young sir," called the King, still chuckling, "you have arrived at the end of a jest. What have you there?"

"Drawings your Majesty," I replied, for that is what I understood most of the papers were.

"Drawings!" howled the King, slapping his thigh and howling with laughter again, until he nearly choked.

Once again, the room erupted in merry laughter, leaving me, bemused, standing with a silly grin on my face, awaiting instructions. Finally the King recovered his self-control and beckoned me to approach.

"Put them here on the table," said the King, looking at me closely. "I know you, don't I? Never forget a face and I know yours. You remind me of my Yeomen of the Guard, six feet tall and long blonde hair, you could be one of them, but I know you are not, for I know each of them by name. What is your name sir?"

"Richard Stocker your Majesty."

Now I was the real centre of attention and feeling distinctly uncomfortable.

The King clicked his fingers, as if capturing a memory from the past.

"Richard Stocker? Horses! I was with the Maréchal – my horse fell and threw me on a hunt, and you came to my aid.

Devon accent isn't it? You are one of Suffolk's men – is that right?"

I was impressed that my King should remember one ordinary subject from only a single short meeting. "Yes your Majesty, that is right in every respect – at Windsor it was, on 19th July last. I am indeed originally from Colyton in Devon, but now with the Duke of Suffolk."

King Edward slapped his leg and looked round the room, eyes twinkling.

"Bull's-eye! Did I hit the target gentlemen?"

Everyone in the room applauded, as they were clearly meant to, and I, my task completed, bowed and retreated to the door, looking at Suffolk for instructions. Lord Henry smiled, nodded, and signalled that I could leave.

Anyone who bumped into Richard Stocker as he returned from that encounter might reasonably have wondered how I could walk those stone corridors with my feet six inches from the ground, and why I had such an inane grin on my face.

❧ ❧

It was the 15th of March, and the sun was shining as Lord Henry and I, accompanied by two lesser servants, rode through the crowds north from Suffolk Place, across London Bridge, and turned left through the City of London, toward our planned destination at the Palace of Whitehall.

The recent fine weather had lifted everyone's spirits and there was a general mood of bonhomie in the air as we headed northwest. We were early for our appointment – London Bridge was usually so crowded it could take half an hour to ride its length, especially if a merchant's cart lost a wheel half-way across, as had happened the other evening, but today the bridge had been strangely empty and we had crossed in minutes.

As we entered Cheapside, we were engulfed by an army of horsemen and women – (unusually, many of them were women – I estimated there must have been 200 women alone) – following a large troop of yeomen making their way up the hill toward the wooden tower of St Paul's Cathedral. The yeomen, being on foot, were making hard work of the slope and we were able to push our horses past them before the road turned downhill again after the cathedral, and narrowed at Ludgate.

"Kick on," shouted Lord Henry, for if we did not get through the gate before this crowd, we would likely be held up for over an hour and lose all the benefit we had gained on the bridge.

"What is this army?" I shouted, alarmed to see so many armed men marching through the City with such a huge following.

"It's the princess," shouted Suffolk in return.

This alarmed me even more. The bad feeling between the King and his sister, Princess Mary had, if anything, worsened over the last six months and I was not only surprised to see her in London at all, but alarmed to see her apparently leading an armed guard.

"Won't there be trouble, with the Princess Mary leading an army into London?" I called to Lord Henry, but Suffolk only laughed.

"Wrong princess Richard. Up ahead is the Princess Elizabeth – quite a different kettle of fish, a Reformist, and a favourite with the King. You will see a very different reception for her than was meted out for her half-sister. I did not expect her until late this afternoon or tomorrow – she has come from Hatfield and is bound for Durham House this night, from whence she will progress to the Palace of St James on the 17th. We will accompany her from there to Whitehall on the 19th – you will see."

We rode on, making steady progress past the throng, and then slowly overtaking the yeomen, who, thoughtful of the congested London streets, had reduced their marching file from four to two abreast.

By the time we breasted the hill with the cathedral of St Paul's on our right, we had worked our way to the front third of the army and Suffolk began to greet nobles he recognized, whilst carefully avoiding getting into real conversation, which would force us to maintain our present positions.

Suddenly a thought hit me and I leaned over to Lord Henry's side to speak as quietly as possible, whilst still being heard in the middle of 300 mounted people, riding on cobbled city roads.

"How are we to move ahead of them? Won't it be considered bad manners to overtake the princess?"

Suffolk laughed and edged his horse on past another mounted party of gentlemen, all dressed in their finery.

"You are right. We shall have to approach delicately and await a suitable opportunity. At least if we get through Ludgate toward the front of the group we can take our opportunity there, for the princess will certainly halt to thank the Lord Mayor for her safe passage through the City. In any event, she will be stopping at Durham House at the end of the Strand, so we can continue alone to Whitehall. Stay close to me and keep those two behind as tight in as you can. I know your horse is steady in a crowd, but theirs might not be as reliable."

It was skilful riding, and I was glad to have the ever-reliable Jack under me as we tickled our way forward, never seeming to be pushy, yet at the same time steadily improving our position, socially as well as geographically, as we did so.

By the time we reached the bottom of Ludgate Hill and the great City gate, we were in the front fifty of the group and finally close enough to see the princess herself, riding at the front. She cleared the gate and waited for the first group – nobles and City Aldermen – to do likewise. Suffolk and I managed to stay with the party and were outside the city walls when the princess turned and stopped.

"Good Mayor and Aldermen of the great City of London," she called in a strong, almost masculine, voice. "Once again, I thank you for safe passage though this, your city, and, as always, for your continuing support. I look forward to seeing you at Westminster in four days hence. In the meantime, may God bring success to your ventures and may your City continue to prosper."

The Lord Mayor bowed, whilst the Aldermen removed their velvet caps and waved them in support.

The princess turned west, toward the bridge over the Fleet

River and the Strand beyond, and began to walk her horse slowly forward, taking time to allow the following throng to take shape again as the backlog streamed through the City gate. Suffolk took his opportunity and rode forward, raising his hat.

"Good morrow your Royal Highness. It is a pleasure to see you here and in such good voice. I trust your journey from Hatfield was safely completed without discomfort."

The princess turned in the saddle and greeted him.

"My Lord Suffolk. Well met indeed. Our journey has been uneventful and comfortable to the degree to which one is accustomed. Whither do you ride?"

"We are to meet the King within the hour at Whitehall, Ma'am."

"Then I shall not detain you. Give my brother my best regards and tell him I look forward to our meeting four days hence. Shall I see you then Suffolk?"

"Indeed so your Grace, I shall accompany you from St James's on the morning of the 19th. Until then, Ma'am, God speed." He raised his hat.

The princess inclined her head and turned back to her party, which had used the delay to re-form.

"Come on, quickly," called Suffolk to me. "Let's move forward and get clear of this mêlée or we shall be late for the King's business and that will never do, princess or no princess."

Four days later we arrived at the Palace of St James in good time for the planned procession. Suffolk had moved with his usual attention to detail and Edmund Tucker had been brought back from Sheen to attend to our clothing. I was now resplendent in black once more: black velvet doublet and black hose with long black riding boots and a black riding cloak. Edmund had said that the formality of the clothes made me look older than my sixteen years (I would be seventeen in June) and I rode with a confidence that also belied my age. I was pleased that Celestial Edmund had opted for the formal, unadorned, look. I was looking forward to Jane, Catherine and Mary seeing me in my new clothes, and the last thing I wanted was for Jane to think I had let the side down by over-dressing.

In view of the importance of the occasion, Lord Henry had also presented me with my own sword, which I wore opposite the dagger I had received at Christmas, with style and pride. All in all, the Richard Stocker, Secretary and Personal Assistant to the Duke of Suffolk, who rode to meet Princess Elizabeth on the morning of 19th March 1552, was a very different young man from the junior servant who had first met the Grey family at Shute House in Devon just under a year ago. In truth, I was proud of what I had achieved, but still a little nervous.

The occasion proved to be as impressive, exciting, and memorable as I had hoped. We arrived at the low, red brick building early in the morning. It had been built by Henry VIII for use as a London residence for Edward as Prince of Wales, and had been used by Thomas Cromwell prior to his fall from grace in 1540.

The morning was cold and sharp, but with the promise of a wonderfully crisp but sunny early spring day. It was an important occasion, and planned meticulously well in advance. Northumberland and Suffolk, now the two premier peers in the land, took the lead in the train and awaited the princess at the gates of the palace. She did not keep them waiting, but (no doubt having received the appropriate assurances that all was in place) swept out of the palace gates at the allotted time, riding a huge white hunter covered in gold embroidered cloth.

We rode the short distance toward Whitehall Palace, passing the tiltyard, and entered King Street, one of the largest streets in London, which bisected the palace of Whitehall and which had, specially for the occasion, been strewn with soft sand to reduce the noise. Just as well, I thought, for there must have been at least 400 mounted people in the princess's train and without the sand, all discussion within the palace would have been impossible for the half-hour it took for us all to ride through.

We processed the length of King Street, under the arched gateways which housed the two private galleries of the palace and joined the two halves together, and turned into the palace yard.

Here was a special occasion indeed, for the King, breaking all normal protocols, met his sister at the gate itself, calling her "my sister Temperance" before kissing her on both cheeks and leading her by the hand into the Great Hall of the palace, where even more of the great and the good were waiting to greet her.

ও ৯

Riding home at the end of the day, tired but contented with both the splendour and the warmth of the occasion – an unusual combination it seemed to me – I found myself privately comparing the two princesses.

I had only met Princess Mary at private family occasions – first at her own home of St John's Palace in Clerkenwell and later at Tilty with the Willoughbys – so in that sense the comparison was unfair, but I could see enormous differences between the two half-sisters and I knew clearly which one I preferred.

Mary had been straightforward and friendly. She had spoken to me on a number of occasions and even once served me wine at Clerkenwell, but at thirty-six years old, she was to me no more than a drab, middle-aged lady, who seemed to like children because they did not demand more from her than she was capable of giving. On the occasions I had been in her company, I had seen no sense of humour, little show of intellect, and, despite her royal upbringing and evident poise, little evidence of any qualities of leadership. Somehow, even putting aside her Catholicism, which I instinctively feared and disliked on behalf of the Grey family, I could not see her as heir to the throne if, God forbid, anything happened to the King.

Elizabeth, on the other hand, had real stature, even though she was not yet nineteen years old. I realized with a jolt that the great princess I had seen dominate the proceedings for the whole day was less than two years older than I was, yet she seemed, of all the people I had met in the last year, except the King, Lady Jane, and My Lady of Suffolk (who had made a particular impression on me), to be in a class of her own. When I took into account the merits of her Reformist philosophy, which both Jane and John Aylmer had spoken about on many occasions, I had to conclude that here was someone the country could fall in line behind in the unhappy event of the demise of the King.

It was strange, I told myself, as we finally reached Suffolk Place that night: a year ago I would have been wondering how the spring weather would influence the year's harvest, and now I was worrying about the succession to the throne. How times changed!

&✦ CHAPTER 39 ✦&

10th April 1552 – Palace of Westminster

Had it been a presentiment? Less than three weeks ago, I had left this palace and ridden home, comparing the two princesses as heirs to the throne in the event that anything should happen to the King.

Now, with the first spring flowers emerging, and at a time when we should all have been rejoicing the arrival of another cycle of nature's growth, we had received (in great secrecy) the news that the King had been taken ill a few days before with a deadly combination of smallpox and measles, and was sorely ill.

Suffolk had been in deep conference with Northumberland for most of the day and everyone here in the Palace of Westminster was whispering.

It was a worrying interlude, and, more than any time I could remember, I felt the need to pray – for all their futures.

The only good news was that Lady Frances and the girls were expected to return to Suffolk Place within the next two days. I could not wait to see them.

CHAPTER 40

April 1552 – Suffolk Place

"Richard!"

For a moment I thought she was angry, but it was pure exasperation.

"Who is Fergal Fitzpatrick? Come on Richard, tell me what has been happening?"

Catherine gripped my hand and stared at me excitedly. The ladies had only returned late the previous evening and as soon as breakfast was finished, Catherine had pounced on me, wanting to know everything that had happened since they had left for Sheen nearly a month before. So much seemed to have happened, I didn't know where to start.

"Fergal is my new friend. He is Irish; cousin to Barnaby Fitzpatrick, the King's best friend, and he works in the royal household as Master of the Bedchamber. I met him one day when I had to deliver some private papers to the King himself, and we have since become good friends. He has the most irreverent sense of humour. It is impossible to be with him for ten minutes without laughter. Even the King says he is irrepressible."

"Is he good looking? Has he got wild red hair? I've heard the Irish always have red hair – and green eyes."

I tried very hard to look serious. "He is very well read, speaks Irish as well as English and Latin, and" – I leaned over to her confidingly – "he has green hair – and red eyes."

Catherine's eyes opened wide for a moment, then she screamed and punched me on the chest.

"You pig. You horrible pig. That's really unfair. You are laughing at me."

"Not at all," I said, mimicking the Irish accent as best I could. "Not at all. I'm laughing with you, not at you." I put my arm round her shoulder and kissed her gently. It was so good to be close to her again. The month had seemed to last an age.

For an hour we sat quietly in the window seat, happily

remaining undisturbed, for everyone seemed to have rushed off to attend to their own urgent business.

I told her my news, about my new role and the opportunities I had had to meet the highest in the land, including being spoken to by the King and becoming the centre of one of his jokes. Catherine said they had had a pretty miserable time at Sheen, for, although the air was better than it was here in central London, much of the time it had been windy, wet, cold and unpleasant, with little to do but study and play music.

"In that case, I assume Jane was happy?" I asked, remembering her hatred of hunting and outdoor pursuits, but Catherine pulled a face.

"Not entirely. She has still to make her peace with Mr Aylmer. He has put out the hand of friendship often enough, but you know how stubborn she can be, and he will not bend his principles or swallow his pride. If you ask me, they are as bad as each other."

I put my arm round her shoulder, more brother than lover, and promised to talk to Jane as soon as the opportunity arose. But if she was still sulking, that might be some time in the future.

    ∾ ∿

On the 14th of April, as expected by those in the know, Archbishop Cranmer read his proposals for Reform of Canon Law to both Houses of Parliament, and the Act of Uniformity was duly passed. It was supported by a doctrinal statement and found its practical focus in the new Book of Common Prayer which, it was hoped, would be better accepted than the first, published in 1549, had been.

Suffolk took the proceedings in his stride, for although the event had seemed of great significance in the planning, when it actually happened, there was little initial reaction. He was, in any event, far more concerned about the King's recovery, for if, as had been believed, he did have smallpox and measles at the same time, his chances of survival were slim indeed.

"Richard – can you talk to your friend Fergal Fitzpatrick and confirm the King's recovery. We are getting so many different messages, and he won't see any of us, even Northumberland, at the moment."

This was the request I had been dreading. Fergal's cousin Barnaby had been the King's best friend since he had acted as the King's unofficial whipping boy when they were children and shared a classroom. He had got his position purely on the strength of his relationship with the "Royal Imp" (as his father had apparently called him) and it was well known he was totally loyal to the King and would not let any private information at all leak from the royal bedchamber. I knew that even to ask him was to put our own relationship at risk, and, if the conversation were reported back to his Majesty, could, in the most unfavourable circumstances, be construed as treason, and cost me my head. But a master is a master and Lord Henry had been more than good to me, so at least I had to show willing.

"I shall try to see him in the morning, my Lord, when we go to the palace," I agreed.

ℜ ℞

As luck would have it, I was not required to choose between my loyalty to Lord Henry or to my friend, for Fergal was in high spirits when he saw me the next morning.

"I bring yer good tidings of great joy," he said, as I approached. "The King's surgeons have frightened themselves unnecessarily. He has the measles and only the measles."

Fergal took me to one side and looked up and down the corridor before speaking further.

"Yesterday morning he said his balls hurt something terrible!" he confided, laughing.

I looked nonplussed. "Why are you laughing? Isn't that serious?"

"The King says it's good news. He says if your balls hurt it must be measles."

Laughing myself, not because anything said was really funny, but in response to Fergal's infectious giggles, I cast my mind back to conversations with Dr Marwood, when I was quite young.

229

"I thought that was mumps. What if it's smallpox then?"

"He says if it's smallpox you can't feel your balls at all!" He started to laugh harder and grabbed my arm, pulling me closer. "Even with your hands. Ha ha!"

By now we were both rolling around, laughing, with tears in our eyes – in part with relief that the news was good.

Fergal was in full swing now and making the most of it.

"He must be getting better because he was teasing me about it first thing this morning, as soon as he woke up. He said it couldn't have been the women because I wouldn't let him have any, so it must be the measles. He was relieved I can tell you – it was the King himself who first thought he had smallpox as well as measles. God he looked rough for a couple of days – red all over and sweating like a bull! But yesterday the fever broke and by tomorrow he will probably reach the itching stage. I tell you Richard, that man is so much fun in private; we have such a laugh when the watchers aren't around."

"Who are the watchers?" I asked, confused.

"The old men. Northumberland and that lot in the Privy Council. That's what the King calls them – 'the watchers' – because they are always watching and plotting. He is pushing Northumberland to give him his majority, so he can rid himself of them, at least some of the time, but he has not been successful yet. But I tell you, he will, for King Edward is persistent as well as intelligent. He will get his own way in the end, you mark my words."

There was a pause, while we both tried to get our breath back.

"Can I tell anyone?" I asked, carefully.

Fergal was still grinning. "You can tell your master about the measles, but don't tell him about ..." he started to snigger again " ... about the King's balls! That's called privileged information."

The two of us sat and sniggered in the long stone corridor until the approaching footsteps of a pair of the King's Yeomen of the Guard brought us quickly back to our senses.

Fergal watched them walk past, sternly, their polished halbards a frightening reminder of their potential role as the Kings personal bodyguard. Fergal was a familiar face and they ignored the two grinning youths as they passed. When they were out of earshot, Fergal took a deep breath, leaned over and said confidingly, "Oh God I'm glad you are involved in the King's business now Richard. We have such a bloody good laugh, the two of us. And will do in the future I hope."

I grinned and shook my friend's hand. "You're right, we will Fergal. We will."

❧   ❦

The news got better, for so did the King. By the end of April he was feeling strong enough to move to Greenwich, following his customary seasonal circulation, and was able to review his men at arms at Blackheath, without looking too frail in public.

By mid-May, Fergal said he was feeling fully strong again, but the illness had frightened him. The fear was not of illness itself, which might have caused him to take it easy for a while, but quite the opposite – the King was afraid of losing time, and now had a renewed sense of urgency. It was as if he believed he had a limited time in which to accomplish all the things he wanted to do, and as a result, worked everyone harder than ever as the latter half of the month progressed.

Lord Henry and I were caught up in the mainstream of the workload and neither of us saw much of the family at all until the end of the month, when, in any event, they were due to leave for Newhall, to visit the Princess Mary once again. Finally, the party left Suffolk Place on the last Monday of the month, with no farewells from Lord Henry or from me, for once again we were absent, attending to the King's needs, this time at Greenwich.

❧   ❦

So it continued until the beginning of June – the King driving everyone forward with his various programmes of Reform and the members of the Council and their retainers trying to turn the King's dreams into manageable – "appropriate" – solutions, even if on occasion that meant emasculating them completely.

Early that month a letter arrived from Lady Frances at Newhall. Lord Henry took it and disappeared. An hour later he called me to him.

"The King's business seems to be abating and he is soon to commence his progression around the south of England. However, I have decided to join the family at Newhall and to travel with them to Bradgate Park for the summer."

I must have raised my eyebrows at the mention of Bradgate, for Lord Henry caught the look and responded.

"I know you and Adrian will fight if you spend too long together at Bradgate Park. Frances insists I keep him on there, despite his demonstrable unreliability last summer. I, of course, insist I keep you, for you have by now fully outgrown Adrian in reliability and usefulness – in any event he does not have your education or experience at Court. The result is stalemate.

"Nevertheless, we need to be represented with the King when on his extended progress this summer. Northumberland will be joining the party later – he has to visit the fortifications in Scotland first – and I can't continue with the Court all year round, or the family will suffer. The progress will be informal and almost entirely taken up with sports – particularly hunting and hawking. You excel at both of those and have made the King's acquaintance on the sports field, and at Court, so you are a natural choice. Northumberland has agreed that you can go and represent the family, and I will try to join you later."

I did not know what to say.

"Thank you my Lord. It's a great honour and I thank you for your trust in me. Will there be great expense?"

Suffolk smiled expansively.

"That's one of the nice things about it. It won't cost you a groat, for the King will pay for everything, apart from your own equipment and clothing, and I shall provide for those. You will need a spare horse also. Jack is a treasure, but you will not be able to stay up in the hunt with just the one. Ask Edmund to go with you to the horse-market." I must have glared at him, for he added immediately, "Not to choose, Richard, only to pay. And get a good one, for the summer will be long and anyway – you deserve it."

I was about to thank him, but Lord Henry was in one of his busy moods and clearly did not want to be interrupted further.

"Don't delay with your arrangements. The Progress commences on the 27th of June, and you will need to join the party at least a day before. No doubt your friend Fergal Fitzpatrick will be able to tell you the latest plans" – he smiled – "straight from the horse's mouth, as it were."

ﺷ ﺷ

Two days later, Lord Henry left for Newhall, wishing me an enjoyable and productive summer and promising to catch up with me some time during the back end of the Progress, perhaps in early September.

ﺷ CHAPTER 41 ﺷ

June 1552 – Suffolk Place

With Lord Henry's departure, and with the rest of the family already at Newhall, I assumed that life would be quiet at Suffolk Place, and so it proved to be, apart from Celestial Edmund, who seemed to feel the need to fuss over every detail of my clothing, hunting equipment and general arrangements for the Progress.

Then, on the day after Lord Henry's departure, Edmund appeared, looking very sheepish and embarrassed.

"Richard I have a confession to make. Last week, when Lord Henry received his letter from Lady Frances, there was one for you also, which he asked me to give you. In all the rush what with one thing and another, I completely forgot. Here it is, I hope it wasn't urgent."

I took the letter. I could recognize Catherine's writing immediately, but somehow I did not want to open it with Edmund standing over me like that. As soon as I had the opportunity, I found a private corner and opened the letter. Inside, the writing looked hurried, and not up to her usual precise standard.

Dearest Richard,

I am having to write this in a great hurry as I have just heard that mother is sending a messenger to our father within the hour, and I wanted you to know about something important which happened, and which they will probably avoid telling you, out of embarrassment.

As you know, the Princess Mary still clings vehemently to her Catholicism, which does not overly concern our parents but which Mary and I disapprove of and Jane absolutely hates. Despite it being illegal, with regular browbeating from Northumberland, and direct instructions from her brother the King (both of which she openly admits to in the privacy of this house) the princess continues to say Mass daily. Of course, the Host remains on the altar when she is here alone or sharing the house with people she trusts – like us, and it is clearly visible if you go into the chapel.

Well, the day before yesterday, Jane was passing through the chapel with Lady Anne Wharton, when she saw her curtsy. So Jane, ever ready to start a row about religion – especially in this house – pretended to be stupid and said to her, "Why do you do so? Is it because our Lady Mary is in the chapel?"

Of course, Lady Anne walked straight into it and said, "No madam, I make my curtsy to Him that made us all."

So Jane looks at the altar, sees the bread and says, "Why, how can He be there that made us all, and the baker made Him?"

Of course, Lady Anne squealed and ran to tell the princess what had happened and there was a terrible row between her and Mother. Princess Mary told Mother her daughter was being blasphemous and she would not have her in the house any longer. Mother, who normally lets all religious things slide over her shoulder, started to defend Jane and reminded the princess that the King himself has instructed us – and her

234

in particular – what is correct in these matters, and that Jane was in the right, if a little tactless.

The end result was that our visit here has been cut short and we leave for Bradgate Park tomorrow. Mother is writing to Father to ask him to come here before meeting us in Bradgate, in order to smooth the princess's feathers, for she remains next in line to the King, and not the sort of person you want to make a life-long enemy of. In any case, mother is upset at their falling out, for she and Princess Mary have been close friends since they were very young.

No doubt father will use his diplomatic skills to smooth it all out when he gets here, but Jane is in real trouble and will be in their bad books for weeks for creating this whole mess. Guess what the atmosphere will be like when we get to Bradgate?

If you get a chance, please write a short private letter to Jane – pretend you don't know about all this – but just show her the hand of friendship, for at the moment, she is feeling pretty lonely.

As am I!

I miss you, Richard, and wish you were coming to join us in Bradgate and not charging round the south of England with the King, but no doubt you can recognize a better offer when you see one and summer with the King at his expense does not sound like a bad proposition, I suppose, especially if you ride as well as you do.

Please write often and tell me everything. I must go now, as mother has summoned the messenger.

I love you, more than you appreciate.

Cat

Twice I re-read the letter, then folded it into the inside pocket of my jerkin. So Lord Henry had, after all, not told me the full truth. Even that relationship, good as it seemed to be, needed some watching. The harsh lesson was, when the pressure was on, you couldn't trust anybody.

❧ Chapter 42 ❦

Summer 1552 – Petworth House

"We need you to keep an eye on the King's Progress."

When the words had been spoken, I had not appreciated the pun, but now, with the arrival of Suffolk's letter, I realized what my role really was. The letter made everything clear. When Lord Henry had said 'Keep an eye on the King's progress', just as he was leaving for Newhall, I had assumed he meant that Suffolk and Northumberland wanted to keep in touch with the royal party and to know where they had reached in their journey round the south of England.

Now I realized that when Suffolk used a phrase like "Don't forget your responsibilities", he was not (as the rest of the letter before me implied) telling me to give the King my fullest support, but to spy on him on behalf of Suffolk and Northumberland – the king's 'watchers'. In particular, it was clear to me (if carefully coded in the letter) that the main concern of the two powerful Dukes was the King's health, not for his sake, but for their own.

"The King! The King!" shouted the halberdier Yeomen of the Guard. I jumped up and stuffed the letter into the inner pocket of my jerkin, as the King rushed enthusiastically into the room. We had arrived here at Guildford from Oatlands the previous day and the King was in high spirits.

Just as we had been about to leave Hampton Court on our journey, with many of the Council, including Northumberland and Somerset already departed elsewhere, de Scheyvfe, the Emperor's envoy, had demanded a meeting to discuss English support against the activities of the French in the Low Countries. King Edward had allowed a meeting and had read the Emperor's letters of protest – privately, to himself, not to the remaining council members present as was customary – before announcing that the envoy would receive his reply in a day or two. De Scheyvfe had retired, satisfied.

The departure of the royal party on the summer Progress had

then been hastened, the King laughing in private at de Scheyvfe's attempt to arrange a further meeting. Finally we had departed, with one of de Scheyvfe's gentlemen trailing along with our baggage, trying unsuccessfully to send his master meaningful reports on our activities – activities to which he was carefully not invited. "The Emperor can wait with the others," the King had said to Fergal Fitzpatrick. "I am on my holidays and we will not be troubled by the affairs of state here or abroad." Now the game continued, always on the move, remaining ever-active, and the King never found time in this busy schedule to attend to the Emperor's representative or any of the other supplicants who, for the remainder of the year, hung endlessly to the King's coat-tails.

The King's sense of freedom had the result of rearranging the social order for the duration of our travelling holiday, and as if to emphasize the break from the imprisoning formality of the court hierarchy, his closest companions became those who rode fastest, shot their arrows most accurately, or handled a falcon with the greatest style, and with little or no consideration given to their usual social status.

"We are the Lords of Misrule!" shouted the King as he rushed into the room. "Come, who will ride with me to the top of yonder hill? His eyes flicked merrily round the room, looking for those companions of the previous day who had best lasted out to the end.

"Ah! Now we have a true companion! Lionfart! Will you entertain us again at supper tonight Richard?"

I grinned sheepishly, but secretly more pleased to be recognized by the King than I was embarrassed by the memory of the previous night's revelries. The combination of a day's active hunting and too much hurriedly eaten food at the noontime dinner had confused my insides and, in the King's presence, and to the enormous amusement of all gathered around them, I had broken wind noisily, and more than once.

"Who did that?" the King had shouted on the second occasion, a huge smile on his face.

Fergal, always ready for a joke, and the shrewdest judge of the

King's mood, had pointed to me and shouted, "He did – Richard!"

The King, laughing, had taken off his hat and put it on my head saying, "I appoint you Richard Lionfart. May your fame remain behind you."

The joke had been well received, especially by Fergal, who had set it up for the King's opportunity, and I wondered if I would ever live the name down. Now was the time to retire gracefully from my moment of fame.

"If it please your Majesty, I hope to contain myself with a little more decorum today."

King Edward turned his head to one side and smiled. "Decorum. That's a nice word. Yes decorum it shall be, but let us not bring with it too much formality, for we are, gentlemen … ON HOLIDAY!" The last two words were joined by the whole room, who, over the past few days, had picked up the endlessly repeated phrase and now used it as a rallying cry.

"Let's to horse!" cried the King and with that we streamed into the July sunshine, hoping that the hunting at Petworth, where we were now bound, would provide as much exercise and fun as had that at Oatlands in the previous week.

❧ ❦

We arrived at Petworth – one of the most magnificent houses in England it was said, and certainly even more grand than Bradgate Park – on July 20th. Since our original departure on June 27th, the weather had been continuously hot and dry. The party had been on the road for four weeks and in that time we had hardly paused for breath. Now we had dismounted on a hilltop. The King, looking over the dry fields, turned to me.

"This land looks dry, Richard. Will the people have taken a good hay crop before this dry weather overcame them?"

I shook my head. "It has been a difficult year, your Majesty. Wet autumn, cold winter and wet spring, now followed by the hottest summer I can remember. They may have saved some hay but no doubt that will be sore needed for the winter."

King Edward nodded thoughtfully. "How many are we in this party?" he asked.

There was some turning of heads before somebody had the courage to reply. "We are four hundred your Majesty."

The King addressed his Chief Steward. "We are eating the country dry. That will not do. I will not have my people starved because of me. We will reduce numbers to a hundred. I want all my hunting friends retained. The Council followers can return to London or to their homes – they will have their own harvests to attend to, no doubt."

He turned to the assembled throng. "Any man who wishes to attend to his family's needs has my blessing to do so. I shall not feel deserted and will think no less of you for considering your families." He turned back to me, standing beside him. "Will you be returning to Bradgate, Richard?"

"No, your Majesty," I replied. "The Duke has a full complement of servants there and Adrian Stokes now manages the Park on his behalf. I am not required."

King Edward smiled and nodded. "Good. Then I shall at least have one companion who will still be in the saddle by my side when the day ends. You ride and shoot well Richard – like the true countryman you are, and you do not fill your head with politics. Would that we had more like you."

🙐 🙑

My Lord Suffolk,

We are arrived at Petworth, a magnificent House and are to stay here for five days before departing for Cowdray, where we shall be entertained by Sir Anthony Browne. I am looking forward to seeing its Buck Hall, where, it is said, they have eleven life-sized stags, brown, bay and trey, carved in oak.

The weather here remains very hot and the land is parched dry. His Majesty has ordered a reduction in our numbers for fear we starve the land as we progress through it, and this afternoon, after much argument, we were reduced from four hundred to one hundred and fifty. Those remaining are, in the main, hunters and shooters, not diplomats, for this royal party is indeed on holiday and affairs of state have been left behind.

The King is in mighty spirits, riding well every day and looking a picture of health and strength.

I believe we are intending to progress into Hampshire by the end of the month, and expect to reach Portsmouth by the end of the first week in August, thereafter to Southampton.

I trust all is well with you and the family at Bradgate and wish you a fruitful harvest.

Your loyal servant

Richard Stocker

I sealed the letter and went to look for Fergal, who had told me that the King was taking the opportunity to write some letters including a long-overdue one to Fergal's cousin Barnaby, and that the messengers would be departing before supper commenced.

* CHAPTER 43 *

12th August 1552 — Portsmouth

"I wish he would pause to catch his breath now and again."

Fergal Fitzpatrick shook his head and nudged me with his elbow. The King was certainly looking tired again.

Cowdray had, indeed, been magnificent in every respect, but Sir Anthony Browne's hospitality had, if anything, been too much for a number of us, including the King. Day after day we had risen early, hunted extensively and dined and supped excessively, staying up half the night in the process. Our host was rich, his lands were rich, and his food was rich. Although the King had thanked Sir Anthony effusively on our departure, Fergal had confided to me that he was among the many who were pleased to end that stage of the progress and to take to the road in hopes of plainer fare at our next destination.

The King's stomach had been badly upset by the endless richness of the food and it had not fully recovered when we had arrived at Portsmouth four days earlier. However, instead of resting quietly, as many of us would have been happy to do for a few days, the King had commenced a detailed tour of the fortifications and dockyards, each of which was woefully in need of modernization. In the last three days he had been tireless, arranging for new bulwarks, and two strong castles to be built, one either side of the harbour entrance, as well as ditches and rampiers to better protect the town itself.

Now Fergal and I leaned against the outer harbour wall while the King, followed by the harbour master and his engineers, paced from end to end, sketching alternative designs and reviewing the effectiveness of alternative solutions, the King in the middle of the discussions, animated in his freedom to talk direct to the people who built things, rather than having all his ideas reviewed, filtered, and often smothered by members of the Council.

As we watched, the wind blowing refreshing salt spray into our faces, a group of newcomers marched along the sea wall and joined the King's party. There was a shout of welcome and the King could be seen throwing his arms round the tallest of the newcomers.

"It's John Cheke," called Fergal, "the King's old tutor and, after Barnaby, his closest friend."

I looked at the scholastic figure as he knelt on the sea wall with the King, drawings held down by large stones in front of them, and both of them talking animatedly. "The King says, 'He doesn't teach me – we discover together,'" said Fergal. "The man's great company, religious but not serious, informative but not patronising, and totally without the mannerisms of a courtier. He has more influence over the King than any man, including ..." he nodded, knowingly, "you know."

I nodded in return. The atmosphere of recent weeks had indeed been so much lighter without Northumberland's presence. Now, with Cheke's arrival, it might lift again, so long as the King didn't overdo it. Perhaps Cheke would calm him down.

The next morning we were off again, this time to stay with the Earl of Southampton at Titchfield, and to visit the famous city. As a result of the long hot summer, the roads were unusually good and the faster riders (as always, including the King) raced ahead of the dust raised by the carts. We had nearly reached our destination when the King, pausing for some cattle to be cleared from the road ahead, noticed that he had lost a large pendant pearl from his gold collar. As I rode up to him he was turning his horse this way and that, staring at the ground in obvious concern.

"Can I be of service, your Majesty?" I asked.

"I have lost my pearl. It is a good one and it was a present. Perhaps you could help me look for it," replied the King, clearly now worried.

"When did you see it last?" I asked, and the King replied that he was sure he was still wearing it at dinner, some ten miles back.

"Then I will take three bright-eyed men and we will re-trace our steps to that place," I replied, and selecting three of the younger and sharper-eyed youths in the party, I began to ride back slowly.

Our way was hampered by the stream of riders and carts following the King, each of which was treading down the road which we were searching, but after five miles, breasting a hill, and at a place where I remembered galloping with the King, Jack Varley, one of the youths, cried out and jumped from his horse. We were in luck; it was the pearl, still with its gold clasp, the gold wire which had held it to the collar twisted and broken.

"Well done, Jack," I called, slapping him on the back. "Keep that safe now and you shall present it to the King yourself, when we reach Southampton."

We did not rush the remaining journey but took our place in the dust of the throng and made sure the pearl was not lost again. It was clear, when finally we arrived in Southampton, that the citizens had made a real effort in preparation for the visit, for the walls were newly repaired and ramparted and a smell of new paint hung in the summer air.

The King was being entertained in the castle by the Earl of Southampton, in the midst of a great display of welcome by the people of the city, and I hesitated before pushing myself and Jack forward. I need not have worried, for the King recognized my golden hair over the heads of the crowd and called to me.

"I can see by your expression that you have been successful Richard. Come forward."

I pushed through the crowd, indicating to Jack Varley to follow me.

"Did you find it?" asked the King, a small frown on his forehead the only remaining sign of his concern.

I shook my head. "Alas no your Majesty, I did not."

The King shrugged his shoulders in resignation. "In any event I thank you for the attempt," he replied.

I smiled. "But Jack Varley here did better, your Majesty, and has the article safe and sound."

I pushed Jack forward, who fumbled with the prize, then held it aloft for the King and everyone else to see. The pearl was the size of a Robin's egg and, together with its gold clasp, represented a lifetime's wages to many of those standing on the edge of the crowd. A gasp went up as it glistened in the evening sun.

The King took it gracefully and passed it to Fergal Fitzpatrick for safe-keeping. "Thank you Jack," he announced in a clear voice. "You have the eyes of a falcon and the honesty of a wolfhound." As Jack stammered his embarrassed reply, King Edward turned to his Steward, who was standing nearby, and in a loud voice, clearly aimed at the citizens of Southampton, rather than his Steward, said. "This man is to be given gold to the value of a falcon and of a wolfhound, in recognition of his service."

It was a huge sum – enough to buy a small farm in his native Kent, and Jack was overcome. He sat down on a nearby bench and gratefully took the flagon of ale proffered to him by one of the stallholders. The King waved me over and leaned toward me confidentially.

"That was well done Richard. A lesser man would have taken

credit for the recovery of that jewel himself. You shall be rewarded on another occasion, for today is Jack Varley's day."

I bowed and smiled in deep satisfaction. This was a King indeed, and he knew how to motivate his people.

❧ CHAPTER 44 ❧

Summer 1552 – Bradgate Park

Dear Richard,

I have addressed this letter to Southampton as our father's information is that you and the royal party will soon reach there. The same messenger will carry letters from Father to Council members in your party, so I am confident this will eventually find its way to you safely.

I hope you are enjoying the high life with the King's party. Father says he heard that many of the party were sent home the other week but had an assurance that you were still continuing with the Progress. Your riding and archery (not to mention your size and good looks) should make you stand out in front of those soft courtiers. I do hope you get to speak with the King again, it could be to your advantage, unless you blot your copy book, which I am sure you will not do.

Please do write if you get an opportunity, for I miss you terribly and long to know what you are doing.

This is proving to be a strange summer here in Bradgate, not at all like the summers of our childhood. There is a heavy atmosphere hanging over the place, although I am not sure why. Mother and Father have been strangely remote this last few weeks. Whether it is still to do with the affair with Adrian, or something else, I cannot tell, for they will not discuss anything with us but tell us everything is alright.

I do know that Jane is in their black books after the row with Princess Mary at Newhall. Father visited there before joining us here in Bradgate and it must have gone badly, for he was still in a black mood when he arrived here. Normally the hunting at Bradgate soothes him, but this year it doesn't seem to be having its normal effect. Father just seems to lose his temper all the time – last week he threatened to horsewhip Zachary Parker for something quite trivial, and Zachary said if he did he would die by his own (that is Zachary's) hand. Naturally that dampened the party at supper that night.

Adrian said he should get rid of Zachary immediately but father reminded him that his own sin had been much greater than Zachary's and that he should treat others with the clemency which had been showed to him. That put him in his place and he has been less arrogant since, although how long that will last is anyone's guess. I don't think he has been running the Park very well since he was sent back from London.

Mother, I am sure, still dotes on him, but plays the meek wife these days – quite a change from her old domineering ways. She has changed since Father's elevation and so has he. In fact their roles are almost reversed since his Dukedom, and he now rules the family with a quiet confidence – or at least he did before this latest row boiled up.

Jane has retreated to her tower (as little Mary calls it) and her books. I don't know why she comes here at all, for she rarely ventures into the Park, but she says she likes the air, so I suppose it's up to her. She has John Aylmer for company and that's all she needs. They seem to spend their days writing letters to Switzerland and reading the replies from Bullinger and the others. The same letter seems to get read and re-read as if it was a wonderful new truth or a piece of the Bible. I am sure the Genevan school has taken a real hold over Jane. Of course, the New Book of Common Prayer and this year's Act of Uniformity have tended to show her in the right – or at least to hold the same views as the King – but Jane does not think the Act or the prayer book went far enough.

I think Jane is becoming a bit of a zealot – it's a Greek word which she has taken a liking to, and keeps using. Mary and I feel as if we are losing touch with her. The only person who seems to be able to understand her is dear Edward Seymour. He visited us last week and spent most of his time with Jane, which is reasonable enough I suppose, as they are betrothed to be married. I must say, I think she is very lucky – he is not only handsome but really charming and very kind; just the person for Jane. Even father brightened up while he was here.

I pray for your safe return at the end of the summer. Please look after yourself and don't take any unnecessary risks. We all want you back in one piece. Are you able to see much of Fergal Fitzpatrick? He seemed such a good friend.

I must stop writing now as the messenger is below and must depart soon.

Your ever loving

Cat

I closed the letter and looked out of the heavily leaded window, lost in thought. Life seemed to be changing rapidly for the three sisters. Sadly, but perhaps inevitably, as they grew, they were also growing apart. Even in the year-and-a-half I had known the family, I had seen the changes.

Catherine had probably changed the least. She was still excitable and impetuous, with wild mood swings on occasion, which I sometimes found hard to keep up with, but her basic fun-loving nature had not changed and I hoped life would never cause it to do so. She was rapidly growing into a beautiful woman and would soon, no doubt, make someone a good wife. How I wished it could be me. I had not given up hope. Lesser men than I had been raised high by the fountain of court life (some, it was true, to be splashed onto the stones later) and I had, I realized, already come a long way from the farm boy Catherine had first taken a fancy to. But I was setting my eyes very high with Catherine, and the chances of being able to offer her the access to power and fortune she had grown up with and took for granted were remote indeed.

Mary had not changed much physically. Her diminutive size was now clearly not going to change and her hunched back showed no sign of straightening, despite her own characterful efforts at standing, walking and riding upright. Her eyebrows had thickened even more and the eyes were as dark as ever, but still bright and observant. The main change I noticed was that she had developed a controlled guile, with an awareness of the world's difficulties more commonly found in a middle-aged courtier than a young girl. No longer would she chatter away to me like a young magpie, in the process letting out a number of little secrets and indiscretions. In fact, the reverse – in recent months, I had learned to be wary of her, as her ability to seek out information was well in excess of her willingness to impart it. The world has dealt her a poor hand of cards, I thought, but at least she is not in pain, is well fed and has the protection of a generous, if not truly loving, family.

Jane was the odd one out. I picked up the letter from her which had arrived together with Catherine's. The handwriting, like everything she did, was almost too perfect. Yet her striving for perfection was my inspiration, the one thing more than any other that made me want to reach higher, to improve myself and to make the most of my life.

But there was one enormous difference between us. Whilst my search for improvement gave me a growing – a gnawing – sense of urgency, Jane seemed to lift herself intellectually with the benign peace of a nun. It was almost as if, while I strived to improve myself in this life – and in this world – Jane had already entered that other world, in which everything was subservient to God and the Truth, and man's scrabbling efforts were like a dirty floor – to be stepped over as daintily as possible.

It was that, I realized, which made her so unworldly, for she always believed the best of people, even when they had let her down on numerous occasions. It was also that attitude to the world which isolated her from others, which made so many think of her as cold and aloof, when I now knew her to be both caring and warm.

As I opened the letter, I realized that I did so with an even greater sense of anticipation than I had Catherine's before it. I could have guessed what Cat would say, but with Jane, there was always the expectation of a new idea, a different perception or a greater understanding.

Dear Richard,

I hope this letter finds you well in mind as well as in body. It pleases me that you may be in the active company of our dear cousin King Edward and may have an opportunity not only to share his enthusiasm for the chase but also his commitment to the reformation of our church, a subject which remains in the forefront of his attention, as it does mine.

It has pleased me considerably to see the fruits of his efforts, expressed through the good Bishop Cranmer, take form in the publication of the New Prayer Book. Although I fear the reforms contained therein do not go far enough, I am content to see progress in the right direction and in particular to see the position regarding the Eucharist finally expressed with truth and clarity.

How can people misunderstand so patent a truth? For surely it is evident that the Body of the Redeemer was ascended into heaven and placed on the right hand of God the father; therefore it cannot be situated upon earth in the sacrament of the altar.

On that subject you would do well to listen to our cousin the King, who summed up our shared distaste for the Catholic desecration of the most sacred of all rites into an act of cannibalism when he wrote:

> Not with our teeth His flesh to tear,
> Nor take blood for our drink;
> Too great absurdity it were
> So grossly for to think.

If only my parents could understand the immensity of this difference more clearly, they would not feel it necessary or appropriate to rebuke me for my recent comments when staying with Princess Mary. She is, I realize, a royal princess and a great lady, but in this matter of religion, she is misled and misguided, and the issue is of such significance that compromise is retreat, and retreat is unthinkable.

This thing is causing a rift in our family, for our mother would remain friends with the princess whilst our father – a more robust adherent to the Reformist cause – recognizes that she is not only wrong and stubborn, but politically dangerous. Our father is now, after only the King and Northumberland, considered internationally to be third most powerful supporter of the English Reformist movement, and my frequent correspondence with Zürich reminds me with regularity of the great responsibility our family faces in assisting the King's people to find the real truth.

I, for my part, strive to find that truth for myself, and have recently undertaken the study of Hebrew, that I may read and understand the scriptures in their original form. Bucer, Bullinger and Ulmis have been a great support in this and Bullinger in particular has written many times to me, telling how I may undertake this study. With Dr Haddon and Mr Aylmer at my side, I am confident that I shall prevail.

It concerns me that your own study and education, which were progressing so well, may now be dissipated by the pleasures of the flesh. You are in good company, but nevertheless, I am concerned for your welfare. No doubt the King's Progression will require you all to travel many miles day by day and with that and the daily hunting, you will be preoccupied by matters physical at the possible expense of matters of the mind.

Please do not allow too great an imbalance to arise, for you will surely find the effort to buckle down upon your return a heavy burden. Observe the King and his daily devotions and make sure you allocate part of every day to prayer, contemplation and study. I promise you that upon your return you will experience a greater richness than would another who merely galloped across the country every day.

I pray for your health and happiness and look forward

to your safe return. In the meantime, remember, labour always to learn to die, for that way is the promise of eternal salvation.

Your loving friend

Jane Grey

Silently I folded the letter and put it down on the table before me.

How strange she now seemed. It was as if she had retreated entirely into her world of books, study and religion. Since I had known her, Jane had always been intellectual, studious and a trifle unworldly, but she now seemed to be retreating away from me – perhaps from us all. Piety was a virtue – especially in a young woman – but she seemed to be losing the balance between ... striving and living.

In the year-and-a-half since I had first known her, Lady Jane had grown more and more important to me. At first I had thought her priggish, remote and self-important. But over the months I had realized that this assessment was wrong. She had no regard for herself at all – did not care for possessions, fine clothes, money or power. The one thing she did care about was ideas. Although she was normally very calm and quiet – some said cheerless, even melancholic – she could be a she-cat in defence of ideas, and in particular what she believed to be the truth, and she pursued the expression of those ideas with a fervent, almost messianic, zeal.

Perhaps it was that eternal confidence in the rightness or her opinions (for that, I realized, is all they were) which so irritated some people, who found her oppressive, self-occupied and over-bearing. Yet I knew her well enough now to recognize that she herself, would be appalled by such judgements. She simply wanted to find the truth, and having (as she believed) found it, to share it with others.

In the end, what it came down to was simple – almost naïve – honesty. It suddenly dawned on me that for all her learning and languages, she was actually a poor missionary, for her commitment to her own ideas was so strong that her attempts to bring them to others (who in most cases did not have her outstanding intellect) took the form of bludgeoning, rather than coercion. Yet strangely, the more I could see her faults, the more I loved her for her imperfections.

Love? Was it love that I felt for Jane? It was hard to know.

It was certainly not love in the same way I loved Catherine – not physically. I loved Catherine for her beauty, her earthy femininity and her easy companionship. When we were together there was a vibration which joined our bodies, so that both were aware of it and we felt as if we were sharing a common space which others always remained beyond. In Cat's presence I found it difficult not to touch her, and I was always aware of waiting to feel her touch in return.

But if Catherine fed my body, Jane fed my mind, and in her case, the mechanism of feeding was the eyes.

When I was with her, I could not take my eyes off her and when she looked at me it felt as if something had passed between us, so that something which had resided in her mind seconds ago now found its place in mine. When we studied together, she would look at me, as if willing the thoughts across the air between us, and I could feel my mind filling, almost as physically as I could feel the air I breathed entering my lungs. Sadly, I did not feel as if I was able to reciprocate. Perhaps I did not have the skill to transmit thoughts? Or perhaps I simply had nothing to teach her, and nothing to offer her.

Despite these differences, I realized that my love for them also had two characteristics in common. The first was my willingness to emphasize their strengths, to forgive their weaknesses, and to take continuing pleasure in the warmth of their presence.

The second thing was harder to identify. When I was away from them, and thought about them, I was always overcome by overpowering feelings of simultaneous pleasure and pain – warm pleasure at the prospect of being in their company again, offset by a gnawing emptiness in the pit of my stomach at the thought – the fear – of losing them.

I moved toward the window, for it was evening and the light was beginning to fade. Sitting in the window seat, I reopened Catherine's letter. There was no time to pen a reply tonight, but I could read them both again, at least once, before retiring for bed.

❧ CHAPTER 45 ❧

August 1552 – Southampton

The following morning the King was up early and visited the shipyards. He was appalled by the number of men hanging around, apparently not fully employed. "These men are needed elsewhere," he announced, and by the next day many of the local carpenters had been sent off to work temporarily on the King's new men-of-war in the Port of London.

King Edward's enthusiasm seemed to know no bounds, but day by day his activities took their toll, and he began to look more and more tired. We moved on to Beaulieu, where the King suddenly admitted he was exhausted and needed to rest. But just as before, he bounced back the next day, and by mid-morning was leading the hunt again.

However, the courtiers in the party were becoming increasingly concerned and each day one or another of them would sidle up to Fergal or (to a lesser extent) me, to ask whether the King had showed signs of weakness during the hunt. Both of us could honestly say 'no', for the King's sense of freedom was at its maximum when out hunting and his energies revived. But the courtiers could see for themselves how tired the King was when he returned home from the hunt and the excitement wore off, and they began to lay plans to curtail the Progress.

The first approach was to tell the King that there was a risk of contagion with the sweating sickness. This the King refuted, saying the country in general was clear of infection and that the only towns where contamination had even been rumoured were Bristol (which was miles away) and, some said, Poole. However, as the King explained, he had recently been within three miles of Poole or even nearer, "and yet no man feared it".

The courtiers waited a day and then tried again. This time they returned to the issue which the King himself had raised at the beginning of the journey – that the expense of the Progress was crippling both those taking part and those acting as hosts. Reluctantly, the King agreed, and arrangements were made to return home by way of Wilton and Salisbury.

🙠   🙡

At Wilton house, the Earl of Pembroke's hospitality was the most lavish yet. We hunted for hours every day – over the rolling Wiltshire countryside, which gave everyone a good gallop and tremendous views, but which invariably seemed to involve a long hack back when finally we decided to call it a day at some remote point way across the county.

On one occasion we lost the King completely and the party was split to search the surrounding lanes to see if he had been sighted. I was riding down Felstone Lane, near the village of Bowerchalk, when I came across a little girl – she could not have been more than five or six years old – standing in the lane as if she had seen a vision of an angel.

"Have you seen a well-dressed gentleman riding past here?" I asked, as the girl stared down the lane. She did not speak, but merely pointed with her right forefinger in the direction she was facing, and continued to stare, the thumb of her left hand firmly in her mouth.

"What is your name?" I asked. For a moment she took the thumb out of her mouth. "Dew," she said, then put her thumb back again and would not speak any more.

I followed the lane to the bottom of the valley and found the King, leading a sound but tired horse towards a nearly-empty dewpond by the side of a white cob cottage, for a well-earned drink.

"Richard! Well found," called the King. "I was wondering why everyone except me had got himself lost. Now there are two of us." He grinned boyishly. "Do you by any chance know the way home?"

I dismounted, watered my own horse, and together we walked slowly back up the lane to the top of the hill and the way home. There was no sign of the little girl.

❧ CHAPTER 46 ❦

September 1552 – Windsor

At Salisbury, the King's Progress was joined by Northumberland, who, as usual, immediately took control. With his support, the courtiers finally had their way, the King lost interest, and the Progress quickly became a retreat, planning to make its way back home through Winchester to Windsor.

Pembroke's entertainment was lavish to the last. Those at the King's table had eaten off plates of beaten gold, the Councillors off silver gilt, and all members of his household, down to the very least, was reputed to have eaten off solid silver. Now, as a final leaving present, he gave the King a travelling bed, decorated with pearls and precious stones, and made to fold up and be carried by a mule.

The King thanked him for it, and promised that next summer, when again he made his Progress, he would use it. As he made the promise, I looked hard at Fergal's expression. What I saw there was disbelief. What I could not read, and dared not ask, was whether Fergal did not believe the King would use the bed on next year's Progress, or whether he doubted that there would be a Progress at all.

❧   ❦

Passing through Salisbury, Winchester, Newbury and Reading, our party finally reached Windsor on September 15th.

Fergal said the King had written to Barnaby to say how much he had enjoyed the whole summer and that he was in

254

good health, but Fergal knew the truth, and confided in me that he was concerned for the King's health. He also admitted that King Edward had asked his cousin Barnaby to seek leave of absence from King Henry II of France, with whom he had been serving since December 1551 (and in the process, acting as the King's private informant).

"I think he's missing Barnaby," admitted Fergal, in a quieter voice than usual, "and in my book, that means he feels the need of some close, friendly support. I think he's sicker than he admits."

For a long moment, he looked at the floor. Then he spoke again, this time in an even quieter voice.

"You know Richard, in his heart of hearts, I think he knows he is very ill indeed. But don't say anything. He wants to see you. Come on."

We climbed the stone steps together, into the royal apartments. At each door the Yeomen Guard recognized Fergal and held their halberds at the salute. We moved closer to the inner sanctum, through the Presence Chamber and finally to the King's bedroom itself.

The King was sitting near the window, coughing heavily. When he saw us approaching, he waved us forward, still coughing. We were motioned to sit and did so while the King held his chest and got his breath back.

"Another cold I fear. My breath has quite gone."

Slowly the colour came back to his cheeks and he seemed to get his strength back.

"Richard, I am so pleased to see you. I made you a promise at Southampton and now it's time to keep it. You proved not only your resourcefulness but your honesty and loyalty when you retrieved my lost pearl pendant. Most of all, I appreciated your willingness to give the credit to another when most men would have taken it for themselves."

I could not think of anything to say, so I didn't say anything, but smiled and nodded.

"Here – take it!"

The King handed me a rolled parchment. I looked at him, confused, and opened the legal document.

"It's a bill of transfer. Without it you would be arrested as a horse-thief. I am giving you my horse – the white one – the Spanish stallion, together with the saddle and harness."

I was overcome. The horse was a pure-bred Arab stallion, raised in Spain and specially imported as a present from the Emperor in Brussels to King Edward. I had ridden alongside it on many occasions that summer and had openly admired it. The horse was worth a fortune. The king's saddle and harness were likewise worth a lifetime's wages.

"His name, as you will remember, is Ventura. Enjoy him, as I know you will. I can think of no man who would sit him better, ride him with greater style, or look after him with more care. You deserve him Richard, and in any case, it's in the horse's interests – he will get more exercise with you now than he will with me."

I was about to express my thanks when the King started to cough once again. He wiped his lips with the back of his hand and I thought I saw a smear of blood. The King saw my look and waved it away.

"It's nothing. Ignore it. I have bitten my tongue that's all. Now go and enjoy the horse before Northumberland finds out and becomes jealous."

Rising to my feet, I thanked him as best I could, and began to leave the room. As I reached the door, the King called out.

"Richard!"

I turned. The King was leaning against the back of a heavy oak chair, coughing again. Slowly he recovered his breath and lifted his eyes towards the door, where I stood, patiently waiting. For the first time that day, I saw King Edward smile. It was a forced smile – he was clearly in pain – but genuine for all that.

"Thank you for your company this summer. You have been a good companion. Have a safe journey back to London."

It was a strangely personal thing to be said by a King. As I walked slowly down the cold stone steps, in something of a daze,

I realized that this was another of those moments I would remember to my dying day.

❧   ❧

The following morning, armed with the bill of sale, I retrieved Ventura from the royal stables, together with the saddle and harness, and rode slowly down the steep hill towards the Thames and the road to London. Behind me, two servants rode Jack and Vixen, the mare I had bought at the beginning of the summer, one also leading two mules carrying my small document chest and other possessions. My large chest, with most of my clothing, would be sent down-river by boat later in the day.

I watched as others from the Progress picked their way away down the hill ahead of me, most turning towards London, but others turning up-river, towards Oxford and the West. Having shared the hottest, and for many, the most enjoyable, summer we could remember, it was a very muted party which finally broke up and went our various ways from Windsor Castle in the third week of September 1552.

❧ CHAPTER 47 ❧

20th September 1552 – Suffolk Place

It was strange, I thought. The more you look forward to something, the more it seems to be a disappointment when it happens. I had so looked forward to arriving home, for home was what I now considered Suffolk Place, but now that I had arrived here, none of my dreams could be fulfilled.

Being honest with myself, I now realized that I had largely been looking forward to showing off. How I had looked forward to seeing all of their faces – especially Lady Frances' – when I showed them my still-unbelievable present from the King. I had dreamed of their reactions.

In my dream the whole family would be standing near the

gates when I clattered into the cobbled courtyard on Ventura, with Jack and Vixen being led behind me. How they would gasp at the new horses, for none of them had seen Vixen either, and then they would see the new saddle, and marvel at its design, its quality, and its origins.

Catherine would be delighted and proud of me, Jane would, I hoped, be impressed and see me in a better light. Finally, Lord Henry would see my prizes as evidence of my growing closeness to the King and therefore be more attentive to my opinion when he asked — as I knew he would — after the King's health.

Now I sat, nearly alone in the kitchen — before the only fire alight in the building — and drank a pot of mulled ale as I wondered when the family would finally return.

"They went to Sheen three days ago." Celestial Edmund seemed to share my disappointment that I could not have arrived back in style.

"I expect them back before supper this evening, for his Lordship has to ride to Whitehall in the morning for a meeting with Northumberland and he has not taken his Court attire with him to Sheen. They just wanted a day or so hunting before everyone prepared once again for the pressures of work at Court."

I nodded, absent-mindedly.

"They say the King is unwell, Richard. Is that so? How was he during his Progress?"

I looked up at him. Edmund was alright — a good friend when few of that kind were to be had in and around the Court — but he was given to trading confidences. After the King's treatment of me, I was not of a mind to spread tittle-tattle about his Majesty's health to Celestial Edmund or anyone else.

"He was in excellent spirits throughout the Progress, led the hunting and stayed up and feasted alongside the best of them."

Edmund smiled and stood up. "I am pleased to hear it. He is a good King and supports the true faith with the stamp of his authority. If anything happened to him, the alternative doesn't bear thinking about."

He gave me a direct and provoking look, but I refrained from

258

responding. Speculation about the King's health was treasonous, and contemplating the choice of his successor doubly so. The awkward silence which ensued was finally broken by the sound of running feet above us.

Edmund turned quickly. "Quick Richard. They are returning. I must shake the house into activity."

❒ ❓

"If you carry on like this, I shall have to extend the house or find somewhere larger. I swear the stables are full of your horses."

Lord Henry swept into the room, beaming, and slapped me on the shoulder. "How are you Richard? How was the Progress? By the look of that saddle you made a good impression on someone – someone of the very highest. Come, bring that jug of wine over to the table here and tell me about it. How is the King?"

For nearly an hour, I gave a step-by-step account of the Progress, being as factual and truthful as I could, and trying not to embellish the tale as so many at Court were prone to do. Suffolk sat and listened, feet spread out and crossed before him, wine glass at his elbow. Occasionally he would interject with a question of detail, but in the main, he was careful not to interrupt my flow, or to steer me off my own view of the events of the last three months.

I talked easily and honestly, only starting to pick my words carefully when I reached the arrival of Northumberland at Salisbury. Lord Henry picked up my hesitancy straight away and pressed me on the point.

"What was the King's reaction when Northumberland joined you?"

This was a difficult one.

"I am sure he was pleased to see the Duke, but his arrival did seem to signal the end of the holidays – it was as if Northumberland had rung the school bell and we were all required to return to our studies."

I looked at my master to see his reaction. It was hard to tell

259

one Duke how the King responded to the arrival of another. I appeared to have got the tone right, for Lord Henry smiled and said, to no one in particular, "He can be a bit heavy-handed on occasions. Northumberland works too hard, but he has the interests of the King and the nation at heart. However, I feel a growing sense of urgency from him – as if time were running out."

Suffolk looked up sharply at me.

"How is the King's health? Think carefully before you answer, for it is important."

I looked at him and paused, thinking. The Duke's eyes – always attentive – were now half-closed, a sure sign he was concentrating really hard. I had noticed him do that in meetings at Court – it meant he was concentrating on receiving as much information as possible, whilst giving nothing away himself.

I tried to concentrate equally hard.

"It is hard to describe. Early in the Progress, he woke well, and was rested. During the day, he led from the front, riding fast and with an abandon which frightened his keepers. At dinner he ate and drank well and was funny, joining in the laughter as well as any man. Fergal said on more than one occasion that his father, King Henry, used to refer to him as 'the Royal Imp', and during this summer, he appeared to have returned to that role."

I paused and looked at Suffolk, who was watching me attentively, sitting unmoving, his eyes still half closed. "Go on."

"But by the end of August his stamina seemed to be wearing down. Whereas at the start of the Progress he would party until after midnight, this month he was different. By supper time he was tired and beginning to cough. Once the cough started, he tired even more quickly, and frequently had to excuse himself and retire early."

Suffolk leaned forward and pushed his wine goblet away, lest it interfere with the directness of our conversation. "When he coughs, is there blood?"

I nodded slowly. "The last time I saw him, at Windsor on the 16th of September, there was, yes. He said he had bitten his tongue."

Somerset sat silently for some time, staring across the empty room, thinking. Then his eyes – still half-closed – turned toward me again.

"He knows he is seriously ill, doesn't he?"

For an instant, I could see the King, wiping his mouth with the back of his hand. The image had remained with me since that last meeting. I could not bear to answer, but simply nodded.

Suffolk sat back in his chair, breathing slowly but deeply. After some minutes he stood up and walked toward the window. Almost under his breath he murmured, "The alternative doesn't bear thinking about."

I sat still and avoided catching Suffolk's eye. His mood had been prickly for days; most of us had tried to avoid him, or at least had been careful to pick our moments when we did have to speak to him. Now, perhaps, the reason for his moods was beginning to emerge.

The alternative doesn't bear thinking about. It was the same phrase Celestial Edmund had used. So this was the issue troubling Suffolk's mind and making him so short-tempered. He thought the King was dying, and, as leading Reformists, he and his family would be finished if the staunchly Catholic Mary came to the throne. No wonder everyone was preoccupied.

෮ ෴

"By the Saints, you look well!"

I put down the brush which I had been using to groom Ventura's coat, and turned round. "He does doesn't he?"

"Not the horse, silly. You." Catherine ran across the stable and into my arms, kissing me hard on the mouth until I was short of breath. She released me and held me at arm's length, looking at me intently. "You do look well. Given half a chance I would let you carry me up into that hay-loft and ravish me as I am."

Somehow, I knew she didn't mean it. I raised my eyes toward the hay loft. "We might give Mark Cope a fright. By the rustling noises, he's up there with young Molly the housemaid already."

Catherine gave a giggle and led me through the yard into the small garden at the rear of the house, where we would not be overheard.

"Well? How was the Progress? How was the King? How was the hunting? Did you meet any beautiful women in all these mighty houses you visited? Come on Richard – tell!"

We sat on a little seat in the deep shade of the huge plane tree at the end of the garden and talked, on and on. By the end of an hour, I had relived my whole journey, and arrived at the gift of the horse and saddle from the King. Catherine gushed her admiration, taking every opportunity to hold my hand or touch my arm, and I made sure the opportunities were many and long. It felt so good to be together again after a whole summer.

Finally I was able to turn the conversation towards her. "But what of you Cat? Did you have a torrent of handsome and charming men visiting Bradgate Park this summer?"

She shook her head, coyly. "No not a torrent, not even a stream; there was a little trickle, but he was visiting sister Jane."

I raised an inquisitive eyebrow. I did not associate Lady Jane with handsome visiting men.

She saw my surprise and laughed. "Edward Seymour – Lord Hertford! He came for a week, and we all fussed over him. He was especially kind to little Mary and took her riding every day, but I cannot think of him as a brother, even though he may still be married to my sister one day."

I frowned. "I was surprised when you suggested as much in your letter. I had understood from Jane that she thought the betrothal would be denied, once Somerset was beheaded?"

"So did I," nodded Catherine, "but it seems it is safe. He stayed a week and we all parted on the best of terms. Jane is so lucky. I only hope they find someone as kind and nice for me."

As soon as she said it, I felt her loosen in my arms. She turned to face me.

"I am sorry Richard. That was clumsy of me. But you know the situation; I love you and always will, but one day I shall be promised to someone else. That's how it works. That's what we both have to learn to live with."

She snuggled back under my arm and gave me her best friendly squeeze. "Until then, we can make the most of what life offers."

I sat, woodenly, my arm around her, but unable to respond to her movements. She sensed my change of mood and loosened her grip on me, turning to face me, suddenly angry.

"Oh come on Richard. We both know the reality. Nothing has changed – either way. Please don't be sulky like that, I have been looking forward to seeing you for ages, and now it's all gone wrong."

I wanted to smile. I wanted to hold her and to know that it would one day be alright, but I felt as if I had just fallen off a ladder, and was lying on the floor, bruised in body and spirit.

"But I hoped …"

"I know … You hoped if you studied, rose higher, gained position and wealth, we might escape, and marry and live happily together with our children."

I nodded, my eyes now close to tears – of sadness, of disappointment and of frustration. I could not say anything. There was nothing to say. I should have been the strong one, but just for the moment, I didn't have it in me.

We stood, and began to walk slowly back towards the house, not touching, the inches between us a chasm a mile wide. Halfway back she stopped and turned to me.

"Please Richard, believe me. Nothing would please me more than to run away to Devon with you and to live in a little house like Shute House, with just a few servants and our own farmland. I have dreamed of it, night after night. But that's probably what it is – a dream. We must keep dreaming, both of us, for this world is so uncertain, it's the dreams that sustain us, but we must also not let go of reality, and reality is that I, who am arguably fifth in line for the throne, may never be able to determine my own destiny" – she gripped my hand and looked deep into my eyes, her own expression totally sincere – "however much I want to, and I do my love, believe me."

At the door, she paused and kissed me gently, knowing I

would now return to my reality – to the stables and my horses, and my secretarial responsibilities with her father, as she did to hers inside the house.

Just as we were parting, the door opened and Lady Frances emerged, her husband close behind. With one sweeping look she took in our wretched expressions, our slumped shoulders.

"Come to terms with reality at long last eh Richard? It took you long enough." She swept off into the garden.

Lord Henry paused and looked at his daughter, then at me, compassion on his face.

"It's a difficult world for all of us, but remember, there are many people over there" – he looked across the river Thames at the City of London opposite – "who are much worse off than either of you two are. We must play the hand of cards God deals us. All we can do is play them honestly and to the best of our ability."

He turned to follow his wife. Catherine, with one long, sad look back at me, stepped into the house. I was about to retreat to the stables when Lord Henry called to me from the lawn.

"Early start tomorrow, Richard. We meet Northumberland at Whitehall at nine. Let's leave at seven – Court attire, the holidays are over for all of us."

☙ ❧

I had finished the horses, had my supper and retired to my room to read, but however hard I tried, the same paragraph came and went and nothing went in. My brain was dead. I could not think. One phrase kept echoing, just out of reach, at the back of my mind. Suddenly I had it.

"A little house. Like Shute House, with just a few servants and our own farmland."

That's what she had said, and in one phrase she had summed up everything. For Shute House and its estate were beyond the ultimate dream for me, whilst she used it to represent the minimum – the theoretical minimum – which she would be satisfied with. The dream had finally cracked and proved itself a nightmare. She was, and always would be, beyond my reach.

There was a gentle tap at my door. In a daze I opened it and held it wide.

Lady Jane entered the room with her customary quietness. As soon as she looked at me, I knew she had been talking to Catherine. Embarrassed, I beckoned her to my bed, the only piece of furniture in the room apart from the chest which held all my belongings apart from those in the stables and tack rooms. Awkwardly, she perched on the corner of the bed whilst I looked at her. I could not bring myself to sit on the bed beside her — it would not be seemly — and instead I dragged the used clothing from my chest and sat uncomfortably on the end of it.

"I am so sorry Richard. It seems you had every reason to expect a proud homecoming and a happy reunion with our family. Instead your dreams have been dashed. Please do not blame Catherine, for she is distraught with grief and does not know what to do now. She only spoke the truth and you must never blame anyone for doing that. The truth is sacrosanct, although the telling of it may sometimes be tinged with generosity or malice."

I sat with my head bowed, unable to speak, just nodding to indicate that I had heard what she said and accepted it.

"You know my view of life Richard. For most, it is simply a struggle for existence — you have seen that on the Devon farmland and in the back streets of London. For some who have been raised higher, those burdens are removed, but only to be replaced by others — the burden of responsibility being the paramount one. Just as the farmer's destiny is tied to his land, and the need to preserve it for future generations, so the destiny of great families is tied to the family name and its preservation and continuation."

She signalled me to sit beside her. Obediently, for I had no will left, I did so, and sat, leaning my head against her shoulder for comfort. She put her arm around me, and let me lean heavily against her, my breath turning to the sobs of a confused child as I let go. Absent-mindedly, and with a maternal instinct perhaps neither of us realized she had, she stroked my head as I calmed down.

"Your father has his destiny and is, so you have told me before, content with it, even though it acts as a prison around him. Similarly, Catherine, Mary and I have our destinies – larger, better furnished, and with more generous provisions perhaps, but our prisons nevertheless. The reason you are confused Richard, is that you have escaped your former destiny but not yet identified or come to terms with your new one."

For some time she held me as I slowly relaxed, stroking my head, as a mother would an upset child.

"I have never held a man like this before, felt his warmth next to me, felt his heart beating. I have only sisters and have never even held a brother closely. For reasons I cannot bring myself to explain, I am normally unable to stand close to men, never mind let them touch me, but you are different Richard. You have honesty, strength, and vulnerability, and I feel safe next to you. When we study together, and I look into your eyes, it is as if the window of your prison is opposite the window to mine, so that we are able to see each other, and by looking at each other, to communicate, and to enjoy the freedom of the space in between."

I lifted my head and looked at her. I had never been this close to her before, and I felt her pull away from me, instinctively afraid again now that my vulnerability had been put to rest. I edged back to the other end of the bed, giving her space, and saw her visibly relax.

"What you say about the windows – that's exactly how it feels for me – exactly the same. When you teach me Latin or Italian, but most of all rhetoric, I can sense something almost physical, joining our minds together, through our eyes. Do you think it is some physical but invisible force?"

She smiled, now relaxed again. "I don't know. All I do know is that if you sense it, and I sense it, then it must be real. What it is, I care not, but I would wish it to continue."

We sat opposite each other, at either end of the small bed, eyes locked together.

"Do you expect to be happy?" I asked her.

"Eventually. Of that I have no doubt, for I trust in God, do not fear death, and am confident of eternal salvation. Before that happy moment of release, during this life, I am less sure, but I think it will be so. I am betrothed to Edward Seymour, Lord Hertford, with whom I also have that same sense we have just described. He shares my love of God, of books and of learning, and apart from yourself he is the only man I can be still beside. I hope and trust we shall be married and will be able to distance ourselves from Court life and live quietly, in a small cathedral city, with a chapel and a library."

I smiled at her. For a moment I wanted to move forward and give her a hug, to express my pleasure at her company, but I was afraid it would be misinterpreted and did not want to spoil the moment.

"Do you think I will find happiness also?" I asked.

She looked hard at me, but her expression was clouded. The "feeling" had gone, but still she tried.

"I believe you will, but where I do not know. Your life has changed so greatly in the last year and a half. I am reminded of an image you once conjured for my sisters and for me – that you are far out to sea, beyond sight of land – but in my image, you are lost, and must find your own way of navigating to your destination – wherever that may be."

It was an incomplete answer, but an honest one. I smiled at her in thanks. "When sailors are out of sight of land, they sustain themselves by thinking of their loved ones, knowing they are not forgotten. When I am far out at sea, may I believe you have not forgotten me?"

She stood and leaned over to me, taking my strong hands in her tiny ones. "Yes you may, so long as I may be comforted by the same thought."

A wave of warmth swept over me. I tried to stand, but in the little room, with my much greater height and size, I would have threatened her. Instead I dropped to my knee, as a knight doing obeisance, and took her hand again.

"My Lady Jane, you have my sincere and everlasting promise of that."

CHAPTER 48

November 1552 – Palace of Westminster

"Holy Mary, Mother of God, what a month this has been."

I winced. *I wish the Irish did not swear in this blasphemous way quite so vigorously*, I thought.

I considered Fergal Fitzpatrick one of my closest friends and one of the funniest men at Court, but he did make free with the language on occasions. The King admonished him on the subject at least once a week and once a week he apologized, but it made little difference. Now we sat in a secluded corner of the Servants Hall below the Palace of Westminster, speaking quietly, for, if overheard, our subject matter could have landed us both in prison.

"Between them they nearly killed the man. You know how ill he was when you last saw him in September?"

I remembered well enough. I had not seen the King at all since that memorable day, and now the news was, if anything, worse. "Who nearly killed him?" I asked.

"Well, we got him to rest at Windsor, though God knows he hates the place with a vengeance, and we had him moved and settled at Hampton Court before his birthday on the 12th of October. He seemed better then, for he likes Hampton Court as much as he dislikes Windsor, but then we had the silly arguments with that pompous fool the Spanish Ambassador."

"What was that about?" I had not heard this story.

"Oh the Ambassador called when we were at Hampton Court, and the King performed his role as he always does so well – you know, make them think he's their best friend, laugh at their stupid jokes – all that stuff. Well the Ambassador says he has a new son, and would the King be a godfather? 'Yes,' says the King, friendly-like. So the Ambassador, getting a bit pushier, says will you attend the christening? 'No,' says the King, seeing he was being manoeuvred into attending a Catholic ceremony, 'it's against my coronation vows, but I will send the child a present.'

At this, yer man loses all sense, absents himself from the Court and stays away for weeks, in a sulk. Well, you can imagine, the King was not too pleased and had a relapse."

"Is he alright now?" I asked, concerned.

Fergal gave me a long, frustrated stare. "Will you let me tell the story?"

"Well," Fergal settled to his task, "the next thing is Northumberland starts to worry because the King is coughing badly again, so he arranges for the King to be brought downriver to Westminster. It turns out what he really wants is for the King to meet some Italian doctor called Giralomo Cardano, who had just cured the Bishop of St Andrews of asthma, when it had been wrongly diagnosed by everyone else as consumption."

I began to relax. Some of Fergal's stories rambled on inconsequentially for hours, but this was making sense, for I knew the private view of the King's inner circle was that his cough was caused by consumption of the lungs.

"Well, we go through this long rigmarole about exchanging scientific ideas – although it was a farce because both of them knew why the doctor was there. Anyway, they met about four times altogether and got on really well, except the doctor let slip he thought the King was a bit deaf. Deaf? Of all things! I'll tell you what that was, for the King told me himself he could not understand Cardano's Latin, because, he said, he spoke it with such a strong Italian accent. Italian accent? Ha Ha."

For once, my patience was beginning to run thin. "Did he find a cure?"

Fergal spread his hands palms upward and pulled a false smile: "Is the Pope a Catholic? What do you think? The poor man had no chance, for if he had cast an honest horoscope they would have thrown him into the Tower and he could not recommend medicine as he had to maintain the pretence he was just a visiting scientist. They all think the King does not know what's wrong with him. Ridiculous – the man's not stupid and he knows the history of the male Tudors when they start coughing blood. He knows alright. All Cardano could do was privately warn Cheke about what he already knew, that the King had a bit of consumption of the lung and needed as much rest as he could get."

Sometimes this Court ritual made me very angry. "So did the King get the rest he needed?"

Fergal shook his head in resignation.

"No, that's what I was getting to, if only you would stop interrupting. The King tried to rest, but then, half-way through October, when the New Book of Common Prayer was at the printers and almost ready for publication, John Knox preaches in front of the King at Westminster and argues strongly against the Table Gesture."

"What's that?"

"Exactly. What he meant was you shouldn't kneel to receive the sacrament as that implies idolatry or adoration, which, as a Catholicism, is banned."

I shrugged. "I can see the point. What support did Knox have?"

"Northumberland, for one, and your master, Suffolk (no doubt aided and supported by the good Lady Jane), and Archbishop Hooper. They all took a strong stand, thinking we would please the King, who seems increasingly swayed by Calvinist arguments – and also, no doubt, because Archbishop Cranmer and most of the other Bishops argued the other way. You know how Northumberland hates Cranmer."

"What was the King's view?"

Fergal gripped my arm, to emphasize his point. "Well that's what threw the cat amongst the pigeons, for the King did not want to delay the Prayer Book any longer – you know he wrote a good part of this edition himself – in his own handwriting. So he was willing to let the matter slide, in the interests of publication, but Knox made such a fuss that it could not be passed over, so they held a great debate at Windsor."

"Did that mean the King had to return to Windsor?"

"Exactly, now you are catching on Richard. He had to go to Windsor and sit through this debate – which turned into a shouting match. I'll tell you how tired the King was, he didn't even make any notes himself – and you know he always makes notes – but instead he asked Cranmer to summarize the arguments on both sides."

"What was the outcome?"

"As you would expect, the King got his way in the end, and the New Prayer Book was published on the first of this month, albeit with a thing called a Black Rubric, amending it in respect of the Table Gesture, and saying that the communicant knelt to receive the sacrament in reverence, not in idolatrous adoration."

I leaned forward over the table, conspiratorially. "It all seems a bit of a fine distinction to me."

Fergal nodded. "It's a fine point to worry a King over, having him rushing here and there and getting himself all wound up over the delayed publication of his Prayer Book. It has all taken a lot out of him. It was the last thing he, or anyone, needed."

"How is his Majesty now?"

Fergal pulled me closer to him, for reporting on the King's condition was a dangerous occupation. He looked round the empty hall to be sure no one had recently entered.

"Between you and me, I think he's worse. He has his good days and his bad days. But month on month I think he's declining. I only pray for a short winter and an easy spring, so he can get some sun on his back."

I nodded. "Amen to that. Will the King remain at Westminster now and have a chance of some rest?"

"Hardly. We move to Greenwich in a couple of weeks, in preparation for Christmas. At least the King likes Greenwich and he can watch the ships going up and down the river. That always pleases him. But it does tend to be damp, with the winter mists coming off the river, and that often makes his cough worse."

"Well I hope he does get the rest he deserves. And you too, Fergal. All this has taken it out of you too by the look of things."

Fergal shrugged his shoulders. "Ah. I will be alright. It's the King you should think about over Christmas. What are you doing for Christmas Richard?"

"I'm not sure, although I have a suspicion that the whole family will attend on the King at Greenwich. Suffolk has not told us yet, but something he said the other day suggests he is thinking in that direction."

"Well I hope so," Fergal grinned. "If you do get to Greenwich we should get a chance to sneak off and have some fun of our own somewhere along the way."

His eyes lifted, more serious now. "Assuming, that is, the King is not so unwell he needs me all the time. If that is the case, we will have to let fun wait."

I understood. It was the threat which hung over everything nowadays.

❧ CHAPTER 49 ❧

Mid-December 1552 – Palace of Westminster

A grey dawn was just breaking across a drab December morning, as Lord Henry Grey sat at the desk of his private study at Suffolk Place, looking out over the Thames at the walls and spires of the City of London. As Christmas approached, he might have had reason to feel satisfied with the year's work, for just over a year ago he had been elevated from Marquess of Dorset, to Duke of Suffolk, and now, at only thirty-five years old, he was a Privy Councillor and, after Northumberland, second most powerful lord in the land.

To his left, and taller than him by some four inches, sat I, his protégé, Richard Stocker. I too might have been pleased with the year, for the last twelve months had seen me rise from erstwhile Second Master of Horse at Bradgate Park to scribe, personal secretary and increasingly, private confidante to the Duke, and I now moved in the company of Kings and princesses.

It was not really cold – the shallow water at the edge of the Thames showed no sign of freezing, as apparently it often did by this time of year, but the sky over London had turned a threatening steely-grey and it was clear we were in for a wintry patch of weather in the run up to Christmas.

Two trading vessels, both recently unloaded at Poles Wharf,

opposite and upstream from where we now sat, were being warped out into the current, no doubt trying to catch the out-going tide before the squall hit the river.

Upstream again from this activity, I could see the bleak but imposing river frontage of Baynard's Castle, standing powerfully just below the Temple and Blackfriars. The owner and occupier, William Herbert, was another of Northumberland's inner circle of supporters and had gained his elevation to Earl of Pembroke in October of last year, at the same time Suffolk, and Northumber-land himself, had been elevated.

If you want to succeed, I thought, *the pattern is clear: you scratch my back, I will scratch yours, and we will both scratch the King's — the ultimate source of power.*

I looked at Suffolk's face. It was lined, tired and troubled.

"I shall be glad to see the back of 1552," he sighed. "It has been a long, uphill struggle, which has taken its toll on all of us. The King is tired, I am tired, and Northumberland admitted to me last night that, having seen the organization of this year's Christmas festivities put into place, he is so exhausted that he hasn't got the energy to attend them himself. Which means," he turned to me with a look of resignation on his face, "that we shall have to attend in the place of honour and keep the King's mind off his ailments."

I looked into his worn-out eyes. Yes, that was it, I thought. Keep the King going at all costs, for if he dies now, the legal next in line is Catholic Mary, and with her in place, the whole power-house will collapse. Northumberland, Suffolk, Pembroke and the rest will be thrown out of power, with their very lives at risk, and Durham House, Baynard's Castle and this great house of Suffolk Place, will all find their way into the hands of Catholic sympathizers. When looked at like that, it was clear how fragile the whole edifice was.

"Are you thinking what I'm thinking?" asked Lord Henry.

I nodded, with a heavy heart. "Yes, I think so."

Suffolk sighed. "It's all so vulnerable — the future good of the nation — all dependent on one man's life and failing that, on his successor."

"But the King will live?" My tone of voice gave away my misgivings, for what was meant as an emphatic and supportive statement had come out as a question.

"God willing he will," grunted Suffolk, "and to give him the incentive, Northumberland has promised he will attain his majority early – in October next, on his sixteenth birthday. It will be confirmed when Parliament re-sits in the spring, and will be announced immediately." He shook his head, as if the prospect of the approaching year weighed heavily upon him.

"This coming year is going to be a test of us all." Suffolk looked more like fifty-five than his thirty-five years as he spoke. "I am concerned about Northumberland. He has been a tower of strength these last few years, but the battle with Somerset took it out of him and this matter of the King's illness and the succession must be preying on his mind, as it preys on mine."

"How old is he now – Northumberland?"

Suffolk thought for a minute. "He must be about fifty, or fifty-one. Why do you ask?"

I shrugged. "No real reason. It's just that you said he was getting tired and I wondered how old he was." I looked across the river at Baynard's Castle. "How old is Pembroke then?"

"Five years younger – forty-six. What is all this about Richard?"

I gave him my most disingenuous smile. It usually worked. One of Suffolk's weaknesses was that he was so totally caught up in his own elevation and social progress, he tended to underestimate others. "You seem to have got to the top quickest my Lord."

Suffolk began to turn toward me, seemingly about to preen himself, but paused and looked across the river. "Yes, well ..." there was a pause, as he looked across at his associates' houses. "It does help if you marry into the royal family of course, as Pembroke did with the Parrs and as I did with her Ladyship. But Northumberland! He did it all by himself. Fought for everything, clawed his way up from the bottom – a real self-made man."

I had not realized the extent to which my master was over-awed by the older man.

"But you are right," went on Lord Henry. "Northumberland

is a lot older than I am and exhausted to boot. Should anything happen to him, and the King were to survive, then I am much closer to your – and the King's – generation, and might ... who knows?"

I caught the look. It was at moments like this that my master was prone to think out loud and to share confidences.

"But if the reverse were to happen and Northumberland survive the King, then what?" I asked, hoping I had picked my moment correctly and not overstepped the mark.

"Then," said Lord Henry, "we all face a very difficult prospect and one we shall have to think long and hard about. The key to the whole process is being aware of the reality of the King's health at all times. It is for that reason I need you to continue to cultivate your relationship with your friend Fergal Fitzpatrick, for within that relationship may lie the future salvation for all of us. I suggest you try to see him later today, after we have attended the Council meeting."

༄ ༄

"What's up with you then Fergal? You look very down in the dumps." It was probably the first time I had ever seen my friend without a smile on his face.

Fergal sat with his head in his hands, looking very down-hearted indeed.

"It's my cousin Barnaby. For the last four or five months he has been negotiating his departure from the French Court, as King Edward was missing him and wanted him back here. Finally he managed to get away, only to be summoned to Ireland where his father, my uncle, is dying, so he has to put his affairs in order. He is obviously upset because of his father but also feels he is letting the King down. I am upset because of my uncle dying and because the King is feeling lonely and, if the truth is told, a little bit frightened, and there's precious little I can do about it."

I sat down beside him and for a few moments the two of us remained lost in our own thoughts. Finally I nudged Fergal's elbow with mine.

"By the way, it's confirmed that the whole of our family will be attending the Christmas festivities with the King at Greenwich. Apparently, Northumberland has arranged it all and now feels too weary to attend himself, so Suffolk will be the senior Lord present."

Fergal tried to smile. "I am glad you will be there Richard, but I fear you will find me poor company this year, unless the King's health improves dramatically. Northumberland! I so hate that man. He claims to have done all the work, but that's rubbish. George Ferrers has planned most of the festivities. I know because one of his writers John Heywood – a Catholic, but good at what he does – was imprisoned, and the King had to get him out again. He has been working on the designs with Sir Thomas Cawarden, who is to be Master of the Revels this year. They are trying to make a really big show of it, to 'take the King's mind off his troubles' – but that will never work, for the King is more ill than they realize, and in any event, is fully aware what they are up to."

I looked across at him gently. "How bad is he?"

Fergal lifted his head wearily. It was clear he had been missing a great deal of sleep, for his eyes were all puffed up.

"I'll tell you how down he is Richard. On 30th November he wrote his last entry into his private diary. I have asked him many times since if he wants to write more but he says he hasn't the energy. That's bad, I can tell you, for it means he is beginning to lose the fight for life inside. I am worried Richard. Very worried."

✦ CHAPTER 50 ✦

Christmas and New Year 1552 – Greenwich

Everyone said that this year's pageant was on an unusual scale, and one which had rarely been seen since the death of King Henry himself.

We stood, perhaps 400 strong, on the banks of the Thames, as the ship, draped in blue and white, glided silently though the winter mists towards the pier at Greenwich, where the King's Master of Horse attended. As the ship slid silently against the pier – Fergal told me they had hung inflated pigs' bladders against the pier to ensure the theatrical effect of the noiseless arrival – George Ferrers, Lord of Misrule, disembarked. He was dressed in midnight blue, to represent (it was said) outer space itself, and was preceded by two lines of drummers, dressed in Turkish costumes of white and gold.

The "arrivals from outer space" were met by Sir George Howard, the Stage Manager for the revels, with a horse, pages of honour, and men-at-arms. They presented themselves to the King, Ferrers announcing, "The serpent with seven heads is the chief beast of mine arms and the holm-bush is the device of my crest. My motto is *semper ferians* – always feasting and keeping holydays. Upon this Christmas day I send a solemn ambassade to the King's Majesty by a herald, a trumpet, an orator speaking in a foreign tongue and my translator."

There followed a number of complementary verses, the crowd, wrapped in their furs and well-fortified with mulled wine and brandy, cheering each verse in turn. Finally, as the brandy wore off and the damp cold began to creep into our bones, we were led in procession into the Palace of Greenwich for the revels to continue.

"I was about to say that Northumberland does not know what he is missing, but of course he does, for he has planned this Christmas entertainment with Ferrers there and authorized the funds to boot." The Duke of Suffolk was as splendidly dressed as everyone else as we followed the King's party into the palace.

"The Duke has chosen not to attend?" I asked slyly, for I knew the answer full-well.

"I fear he is starting to feel his years," replied Suffolk. "You remember our conversation at Suffolk Place? He is, as you so kindly reminded me at the time, considerably older than I am, and this last year, especially, has taken its toll. He has worked wonders and secured a strong basis for King Edward's reign. Now Parliament has agreed – not yet formally of course, but we have an understanding – that the King will attain his majority next October, on his 16th birthday, so Northumberland may be able to rest a little. He told Cecil that he was not well enough for the revels – 'like the faithful servant in the Italian proverb, I shall become a perpetual ass,' he said."

I nodded my understanding. All this I knew already, but as I had hoped, it led the Duke to continue.

"Northumberland also told Cecil that he longed to retire from the world, that every night he 'retired to bed with careful heart and weary body, and yet abroad no man scarcely hath any good opinion of me.' It's true he is not popular, but strong leaders never are – the people want progress but without the discomfort of change."

We trudged along the gravel path, our feet crunching in the frosty evening. The path was well lit by cresset lamps and ahead of us the gates to the palace glowed with light from hundreds of torches.

"What shall we do if Northumberland does retire or is taken ill before the King attains his majority?" I asked.

Suffolk half-turned to ensure no one was within earshot. "Careful Richard, these are difficult questions," he replied under his breath.

I waited. I knew Suffolk by now. Like the King he was overawed by Northumberland, but in his absence and in the company of those he trusted, he could not endure a silence. Sure enough, after a few paces, he continued.

"If anything does happen to Northumberland before the King attains full authority, the Privy Council will continue to bear the burden of policy guidance."

I raised an eyebrow. "And in Northumberland's absence, who would bear the mantle of leading the council in its deliberations?"

Suffolk took a deep breath of apparent resignation. "Well, then, I suppose, as senior present, that burden would fall to me." His face had the expression of a martyr.

I could not contain myself. Something made my face soften – just a little – betraying the slightest small grin and merriment of the eyes. Suffolk caught it, looked round again for privacy and, satisfied, laughed.

"Yes, I suppose I should have to accept that burden, but God willing, not in the manner of a mule or pack-horse." He smiled conspiratorially at me, and I grinned back, nodding.

"Quite!"

ॐ ॐ

"Who is that stupid old man? Don't you think he's getting a bit old for this sort of thing?"

We had lived through two weeks of festivities and now, on Twelfth Night, the climax was a "Triumph of Cupid", showing the gods in a torchlight procession, accompanied by dancers dressed as monkeys in grey rabbit skins, and carrying the musicians. We, in turn, were surrounded by cats, Greek worthies, satyrs, monsters, soldiers and 'wild Irish savages' carrying clubs. It was a strangely mixed collection, but colourful nonetheless.

Lady Frances Grey signalled to her daughter to be quiet. "Shush Catherine, that's the famous Will Somers, Court Jester to His Majesty King Henry VIII. We have brought him out of retirement for this season's festivities."

Catherine glared. "He's not very funny is he? He's ugly too – he looks like a monkey."

I sidled up beside her and nudged her elbow. "I think that's the point," I whispered, "but don't underestimate him. He was the only man who could shake the old King from one of his moods without risking his life in the process. He is also the man who befriended the young prince Edward at Court and, it is said, developed his impish and irreverent sense of humour." For a moment we watched the pageant, then I leaned across to Catherine once more. "But I agree, it's a bit sad to see an old man brought back like this, trying to jolly the King back to full health. It does not seem to be working does it?"

"The bloody ould fool's past it."

We were joined by Fergal Fitzpatrick, who had been allowed to leave the King's side for a while. He nudged my elbow as a

279

sign of friendship and reached up to whisper in my ear. I lowered my head to catch the words.

"He's past it. Not funny anymore. Too old to be a Court Jester, and besides, this form of over-organized revelry is out of date and a waste of money."

I leaned down and cupped my friend's ear for my reply, for this was a risky conversation.

"How do you know that, you little Irish whippersnapper? You aren't old enough to remember Will Somers at King Henry's court."

Fergal signalled me to lean down, for there was at least a foot difference in our heights and, risk-taker as he was, he also recognized the dangers of the conversation.

"I'm quoting the King. He remembers. He also knows the country is desperately short of money – in part thanks to his father's own profligacy, although he would never admit that publicly. The King is increasingly sick of Northumberland trying to buy his favours with his own money – the nation's money. 'Why,' says the King, 'spend eleven months of the year trying to control the exchequer and then one month throwing it all away? It doesn't make sense and it's ungodly.'"

I rolled my eyes around the room, anxious to make sure our conversation was not being overheard. It was alright for Fergal, he was only short and could mutter away like this for hours without being noticed, but I was (as usual) one of the tallest men in the room, and when I stood for minutes on end with my neck bent downward to hear someone's whispers, it was pretty obvious something was going on. As usual, however, Fergal was undeterred, and continued his commentary without pause.

"The King says Northumberland has created all this frivolity in an attempt to keep his mind off his illness. He says if he believes that will work, he is not only stupid but patronizing. The King increasingly resents Northumberland's hovering by his shoulder, watching every move and manipulating every decision. He wants to be a great King – like his father – and to make his own mark. As you have seen in the past, Richard, he's full of ideas for change and has a great sense of urgency – even greater now that he knows he is ill. On good days he rallies and believes he will soon get better – as he did from the measles last year and never felt better afterwards – but on bad days, he gets very depressed. I am sure he knows he has the consumption and we all know how few men recover from that, especially when the weather is cold and damp as it is now."

I put a hand on his shoulder, partly to reassure him and partly to silence him. This was not a conversation we should have at all, and certainly not in a room full of people, even if they were distracted by the festivities. I looked round furtively to see if anyone had noticed. Most, including Catherine, were laughing at the entertainment, but I noticed Lady Frances was glancing in my direction and from me to the other side of the room. I looked across the room, following her gaze. It led me to the King who, I realized with a shiver of fear, was looking right at me, and very intently.

"The King is watching us," I whispered out of the side of my mouth, toward Fergal, gripping my friend's shoulder hard in warning as I did so. Carefully and slowly, Fergal swung his eyes toward his master. The King made an imperceptible nod of instruction with his forehead and Fergal responded by nodding back.

"I have to go. The King wants me," Fergal replied and quietly began to make his way through the crowd toward the corridor and his way back to the King's side.

I chatted to Lady Frances and Catherine for a few moments, as the next entertainment was being prepared, all the time keeping my eyes on the King. Eventually Fergal appeared at the door behind King Edward and regained his side. I saw the King lean over and ask Fergal a question, looking across the room toward the Suffolk family party as he did so. I gave a shiver of apprehension as the King's eyes met mine, but then they moved on to Lady Frances and her daughters. The King seemed to be looking at Lady Jane and as he did so, leaned over to speak to Fergal again. I saw Fergal cup his hand to the King's ear and whisper a reply. Whatever he said had clearly captured the King's sense of humour, for he let out a great guffaw of laughter which seemed to please and entertain the room considerably, even through only Fergal and the King himself knew the source of the laughter. *Please God, he's having one of his good days,* I thought.

"It seems your friend has the King's ear – almost literally!"

Lady Frances had, as usual, missed none of the interplay. It was clear from her relieved expression that, like me, she had perceived the risk, and judged it had receded when the King's laughter had echoed across the room.

"Yes my Lady, he is in a privileged position in that respect, but he has the sense, I believe, not to abuse that privilege."

Lady Frances looked me straight in the eye, as only a woman of her mighty stature could, and smiled a cold smile. "I am sure he does not Richard, but a useful friend nevertheless in these uncertain times."

"Fergal and I do not discuss the King," I replied, in careful tones.

Lady Frances gave me a withering look. "Of course you do not, Richard, for that would indeed be improper. But it seems your friend and his monarch are not beyond discussing us." Her eyes swept the room, taking in every nuance and expression as she did so.

"Take care, Richard, you are swimming in deep water."

I bowed my understanding. It was an admonishment. I must remember to tell Fergal not to speak out in Lady Frances's presence again. And what, I wondered, had Fergal said to the King about Lady Jane?

❧ CHAPTER 51 ❦

11th February 1553 – Suffolk Place

"And how is the King's health? I assume you asked your good friend Fergal Fitzpatrick and that, like a good friend, he told you?"

I sat opposite Lord Henry Grey, Duke of Suffolk, in his study overlooking the Thames at Suffolk Place, as my master continued the inevitable questions.

"I understand he is unwell my Lord and much troubled by his sisters."

Suffolk nodded, as if his own information had been confirmed. "How does Fergal describe his condition?"

"He caught a heavy cold on Tuesday of last week, and by Thursday it had gone to his chest and he was too unwell to attend the Candlemas celebrations."

"Yes, yes, which is why they were cancelled – exactly," replied Suffolk, suddenly appearing somewhat irritated. "I know all that, but how has the King progressed this last three days? I cannot rely on Northumberland's public reports, as well you know."

"It appears he has worsened my Lord. The doctors fear for his life, for his coughing fits have become so violent and extended. Fergal says he only has to succumb to one other ailment before he has shaken this one off and he may die. Worse still, the King himself thinks he is dying already."

Suffolk looked at me hard, saw truth, and sat back, thinking. He looked across the Thames, as if seeking inspiration. When he spoke, his words were heavy, as if all the cares in the world had suddenly landed on his shoulders.

"Northumberland is exhausted and unwell and the King may be dying. These are burdensome times Richard, times to tread carefully, to seize opportunity and to avoid error."

I nodded, trying to show I understood the full portent of what Suffolk was saying.

"But how to identify which course of action is opportunity and which will lead to disaster. There's the rub." As if to emphasize his point, Suffolk wrung his hands together and hunched his heavy fur coat around his shoulders, for the fire in the room, although large, was fighting a losing battle with the cold coming in off the river.

I shivered in response, and in turn wrapped my own cloak around myself, although whether as a comfort against the cold, or against the uncertainties of life, I could not really decide. I looked at Suffolk. Was he in a talkative frame of mind today, I wondered. It was sometimes hard to tell, and the mood could go badly wrong if I misjudged the occasion. On balance, I decided, it was worth a try, as I had just the right introduction.

"Why should his Majesty be troubled by his sisters my Lord?" I spoke in as light a voice as possible, to avert suspicion.

Suffolk did not respond, but continued looking across the Thames. I knew better than to pursue the matter – his lordship would reply in his good time or nor at all. Suffolk drank from the pot of wine in front of him and continued to look across the river. It was a good sign.

"The King thinks he's dying. You said so yourself. What does a king think about when he is dying?"

"Salvation, my Lord?"

"Pah." Suffolk spat the response. "The succession. That's what dying kings think about, the succession. And what does he face when he thinks about it? Mary his sister, first in line and ready to tear down everything he has believed in, everything he has worked for, since he, himself, succeeded to the throne. Is he going to throw everything away? Of course not."

He threw another log on the fire and shrugged back into his coat.

"And could he consider Elizabeth as a safer pair of hands? Not if you were King Edward. She's too clever by half that one – neither Reformist nor true Catholic, and as likely as anything to marry a foreigner, and then where would we be – eh?"

"What alternatives does he – do we – have?" I suddenly had a horrible feeling I was not going to like the end of this conversation.

"He must be encouraged to look further, to reconsider the true precedence. Let me put an idea to you Richard. I know you and Lady Jane like to discourse together with rhetoric and to play consequences, so think about this one. What would be the consequence of a clear ruling by the King that both of his sisters are bastards? Think about it. Mary is illegitimate because her mother Catherine of Aragon had been previously married to King Henry's elder brother Arthur, making her marriage to

Henry illegal. And Elizabeth is illegitimate because King Henry's marriage to Anne Boleyn, her mother, was null and void. Where do we go next?"

I was sure I knew the answer, but was less sure it was the answer I was being asked to find. I remembered John Aylmer's advice: "If unsure, answer a question with a question."

"Who is next in line of succession?"

Suffolk nodded enthusiastically. "Yes exactly."

This was not going as easily as I had hoped. "But who is …?"

Without further delay, and with a conspiratorial smile on his face, Lord Henry signalled with his thumb over his shoulder at the next room.

"Lady Frances?"

Suffolk spread his hands wide, palms upward. "The Duchess, my wife, exactly, and by direct line of descent from Mary Tudor. No uncertainties, no arguments, no doubts."

I took a deep breath. "Then that would make you …?"

Suffolk removed his velvet hat, then replaced it. However, instead of replacing it with a dragging action with one hand, he lifted it high with two hands and placed it, slowly, and oh-so-delicately on his head, as if it were a crown.

"You got there in the end, Richard. It makes me – powerful!"

"That would indeed be an achievement my Lord."

There was a long, congratulatory pause, for it was hard to follow the conclusion that one of those present in the room might shortly be King of England.

Suffolk smiled at me, a smile of solid satisfaction. He had clearly enjoyed sharing the dream and teasing it out of me as he had, but I remained troubled by a loose end.

"My Lord, can you help me with one thing please?"

Suffolk opened his hands expansively. "Of course."

"Why did the King refuse to see both princesses when they came to visit him at Candlemas, but agree to see Princess Mary and only Princess Mary the following Monday?

Suffolk's eyes were gleaming with intrigue. It was clear he not only knew the answer, but was going to enjoy telling it to me.

"Perhaps as a result of his illness, King Edward had been missing his sisters and had expressed his disappointment that neither of them was present at Greenwich over the Christmas festivities. So before he returned to Westminster in the last week of January (and unknown to Northumberland, who, as we know, wasn't there) he invited both of them to attend a children's masque at St James's Palace at Candlemas – on the 2nd of February. When Northumberland heard that they were making their preparations, he was faced with a problem, for the King might say anything to either of them if they all got together, and they to him. So he instructed the Princess Elizabeth not to attend, and used the King's illness as the excuse."

"But why did he allow Princess Mary to come to London, only to prevent the visit when she got there, and then, on the Monday, allow it to take place after all?" I had heard all this from Fergal Fitzpatrick, but whether as a result of Fergal's excitable description, or the true complexity of the situation, had not followed it at all clearly.

"You have to look at it from Northumberland's point of view. Princess Mary believes (as do many others, by the way) that she is the true heir to the throne of England. If we are to replace her with someone else, the last thing we want to do is to send her signals to that effect. She may not have the Princess Elizabeth's brains, but she is not stupid, and would smell a rat immediately. So Northumberland agreed to let her come.

"However, by the time she arrived at her house in Clerkenwell, the King had already taken ill again and was in a very sad condition – indeed he was genuinely too ill to attend the children's Candlemas masque. Northumberland did not want Princess Mary to see him in that condition, as she would immediately begin thinking about the succession, so he told her the King was too ill to see her.

"However, she remained in court, asking awkward questions, and as soon as the King got a bit better, it seemed safer to let her see him. In case she realized how ill the King was, and to put her off the scent, Northumberland started being really nice to her.

Yesterday she rode out from St John's Clerkenwell, to Whitehall, where she was greeted with all honour, Northumberland gave her back her old coat of arms that she had worn in the 1520s as her father's heiress, and the exchequer paid over £500 for repairs to dykes on her Essex estates. She saw the King again and this time he was reported to be much improved, and was able to greet her in the Presence Chamber. That was why I was asking you about the King's real condition – behind the scenes, so to speak his public face was clear for all to see, but we cannot rely on that – from now on we need the private picture."

Suddenly I felt uncomfortable. I felt as if a noose was tightening around my neck. All this was too fluent – too clearly understood, too well-rehearsed. With a sick feeling in the pit of my stomach I realized that Suffolk had been in the middle of this plot with Northumberland for many months – perhaps years – and saw himself as the main beneficiary. Only now did I realize my own sordid role in the plot.

"Has the plan worked?" I asked, as enthusiastically as I could.

Suffolk pulled a long face. "I am not sure. Northumberland may have overdone it a bit, for I heard this morning that Princess Mary was suspicious of his generosity and may have associated it with her brother's illness, which apparently shocked her when she finally saw him. Did Fergal Fitzpatrick have anything to say about that?"

I shook my head. "No, he did not mention the Princess Mary at all. All he said was that the King had received a letter from Princess Elizabeth, from Hatfield, saying that she was very upset at being sent back when she was half-way to see him, and hoping that he would soon be recovered enough to receive her. He said the King was sorry to have disappointed his sister Elizabeth, with whom he has a special rapport, both in learning and in religion – neither of which he has with his sister Mary."

Suffolk stood, arched his aching back and prepared to leave.

"Thank you Richard. As always you have been most helpful. Now don't forget, this discussion did not take place and the thoughts expressed have never been uttered – not even thought – by me or by you. We live in hard times, and although the path of life's mountain may occasionally lead us quickly upward, the slippery slopes can throw us down and asunder even more quickly. I bid you good day."

↦ ↤

I climbed slowly up the back stairs towards my own room at the top of the house. What a world we inhabited! They were all scheming – the lot of them. Perhaps it was unavoidable. If you had nothing, nobody was going to spend any time trying to take it from you, but it seemed the more you had, the more you wanted, and at the same time, the more you had to work to protect what you had already won.

I thought of Lord Henry's analogy of the mountain path. It seemed, once you had started on this path, there was no standing still to enjoy the view, it was onward ever upward, or slip back down again. Sometimes, on days like this, I wished I were back in the Coly valley, watching the kingfisher catch minnows.

I reached my room and sat on the bed. My sword and dagger were hanging behind the door. I looked at the heavy chest which almost filled the remainder of the room at the end of my bed. My fine clothes were in there, reminders of what I had achieved, where I had been, who I had met and the ideas they had shared with me. Exciting ideas, which exercised my mind as effectively as my horses exercised my body. My horses, which were my friends and now ate quietly in the stables below, and my saddles, which were in the tack room beside them. These were my possessions now, and I did not want to lose them.

It was nearly two years since I had first met the Grey family. In that time I had grown from six feet to six feet three inches tall, had increased in weight to twelve stone and six pounds (I knew because Celestial Edmund had wagered he weighed at least two stone less than me and taken us both to the vegetable market to prove his point and win his wager). I had also (despite losing a tidy sum to Edmund), increased in wealth over the last two years beyond my wildest dreams.

But the biggest changes had taken place inside, in my head,

288

and in my heart. I knew I now had a level of courage beyond all my childhood expectations. Not just boyhood bravery – the courage to snatch a burning stick from a fire or to stare down a snorting bull – I had had those in Devon. But now I had moral courage – the strength to fight for what I believed was right, to defend the weak against oppression, and, I hoped, the humility to listen to the views of others and to admit that I was (sometimes) wrong and they were right.

I had learned from them all. From John Aylmer, Lord Henry, Lady Frances and Lady Jane – especially the latter, whose moral strength outmatched anything I had seen in anyone else. But as Lady Jane (and Catherine) would quickly remind me, I had also learned some lesser skills and less worthy instincts, political guile, cynicism, and perhaps – now for the first time in my life – greed, and the hunger for power.

Perhaps the price was beginning to get too high? How I wished I could talk to Dr Marwood. He would be able to put it all in perspective.

❧ CHAPTER 52 ❧

2nd March 1553 – River Thames near Whitehall

I shivered in my heavy cloak. It was late and it was cold here on the river, as the wherry carried me the short distance downstream and across the river from Whitehall Steps to the small pier at Suffolk Place, on the south side of the river, and just upstream of London Bridge. I had been at Whitehall for the last two days, attending the beginning of the new parliament, and now felt cold, hungry and drained of energy.

During February, I had kept in touch with Fergal almost on a daily basis, and for the last three weeks, each report had confirmed that the King remained confined to his bed. Then, toward the end of the month, Fergal had told me that the King was determined to participate in the opening of the new parliament, which had been announced by Northumberland on the 21st of February and was due to take place on the 1st of March. As a concession, in view of his illness, it would be held at Whitehall and not at Westminster, as was customary.

I had reported back to Suffolk, who was to attend the parliament as a member of the Council, and was told to attend myself, with the specific responsibility of watching the King's every move and, if possible, obtaining a more recent and accurate description of his illness from Fergal Fitzpatrick, my private source in the royal bedchamber.

The meeting had started well, and parliament had ratified the Council's decision, announced by Northumberland before Christmas, that the King would attain his majority on his forthcoming sixteenth birthday. Then, for two days I had watched the King presiding over the parliament, looking very weak, white and thin, and still troubled by the recurring cough, but managing, nevertheless to play his part to the full. He had arrived wearing a ten-yard-long train of crimson velvet and had patiently signed the documents for seventeen new statutes, for despite his illness, his appetite for reform had remained undiminished.

Everyone was waiting to see how the King's temper fared, for it was well known that at a Council meeting during February, which the King had attended from his bed, there had been a disagreement with the King's point of view, and he had gone into a rage, shouting, "You pluck out my feathers as if I were but a tame falcon – the day will come when I shall pluck out yours." The meeting had, apparently, broken up in sombre mood shortly afterwards.

But now the strain of presiding over the large meeting was beginning to tell on Northumberland. When Cranmer had risen to read out his measures for the reform of canon law, Northumberland had shouted out, "You bishops, look to it at your peril that you touch not the doings of your peers. Take heed that the like happen not again – or you and your preachers shall suffer for it together." Cranmer had protested and it had turned into a shouting match, until the King had silenced them both.

The whole episode had surprised me, for in my limited experience, the King was always a master of self-control and Northumberland likewise. I had asked Fergal what he thought, and, as usual, Fergal had had the answer.

"The King's illness is making him really bad tempered, and he has taken to disagreeing with the Duke on numerous occasions. The trouble is, the Duke has become used to dominating him – although quietly and subtly – and now feels threatened when the King shouts him down. His response is to shout back, and, as you can imagine, that does not work with our King Edward, who, when pushed, has a very well developed sense of his position, and exploits it quite as well as his father did.

"I'll tell you something else Richard. The King has changed his view about Northumberland. At one time – particularly around the time when his uncle, Somerset, was executed, the King believed the Duke was his most loyal servant. But now he realizes that Northumberland has his own objectives, and increasingly he resents them."

I shrugged myself down in my cloak and shivered again. I hated the position I had been put in, using my relationship with Fergal almost to spy on the King, and then reporting most of it – I had found myself increasingly selective in what I passed on – to my master. But in one respect Suffolk's instincts had been proved right. It was clear to everyone that the King was ill, and obvious to anyone who knew anything about court life that that meant the issue of the succession – and all the changes in patronage which would accompany it – was of paramount importance to all of them.

But Lord Henry had sniffed out something else. He had realized that Northumberland was controlling the news about the King's health to his own advantage. That had no doubt been true for some time, but the most recent change in my master's perception seemed to be the realisation that, although he was Northumberland's staunchest – and most powerful – ally, he was no more privy to the truth than anyone else.

It was, I believed, that realisation which had prompted Suffolk to push me so hard to develop my relationship with

Fergal Fitzpatrick, for as a member of the royal bedchamber, Fergal saw the King when his defences were down, saw him cough blood and sputum into his handkerchief, and smelled the suppurating stink of what emerged from his insides. Only he and his colleagues in the most private positions saw the swelling of the King's legs and lower abdomen, for the royal clothing allowed much of this to be hidden from the visitor or the casual observer in public meetings.

One thing, in particular, that Fergal had told me, I held back from Lord Henry. That was Fergal's belief that the diagnosis of the King's illness, made initially by Cardano last autumn, was wrong. Cardano had cured the Bishop of St Andrews of asthma, when everyone, including the Bishop himself, thought he had phthisis, or consumption of the lungs. Fergal knew that was what he believed troubled the King, for he had read his private notes when Cardano had left them on a table. But Fergal disagreed. This, he said, was worse.

"What can be worse than the consumption," I had asked Fergal, "for surely few men, if any, survive that illness?"

Fergal had been very certain in his reply.

"I sit there, quietly, as one doctor after another pontificates. I remain with them, as their assistant if required, when we retreat from the King's presence. That is when they speak their minds, for to do so in the King's presence would be treasonable. Listening to the doctors, I tell you that consumption takes a man slowly, and if he eats well, avoids arguments and upset and gets out into the fresh air, he may not outlive it, but he can extend his period of tolerable living for many years. That's what the King believes – that's why he will retire to Greenwich as soon as this parliament has completed its responsibilities, and try to enjoy the springtime. But I do not believe he has the consumption; there is an evil, a poison, something more pernicious than the consumption, inside him, and Richard" (he had gripped my arm tightly as he had uttered the words) "I believe he will not survive until his majority is reached."

The words had hit me like a stave to the head. The enormity

of the situation had left me stunned and I had staggered to the wherry steps in a dream of fear and confusion. Somehow I had found a wherry going downstream immediately and now I sat, head in hands, cloak pulled tight around me, wondering where my life was leading and what I should do next.

The incoming tide was running strongly and we were making slow progress downstream, but I was in no hurry to reach Suffolk Place. I needed time to think, to decide what to do next.

"Don't hurry boatman. I am early for my appointment. Just let her ride the current for ten minutes will you?"

The aged boatman touched his cap. "Very well sir. Ride the current it is sir."

I shook my head, trying to clear my brain. The implications were too enormous to take in. If the King died, unmarried and without children, and if, as Lord Henry had suggested, the Princesses Mary and Elizabeth were both pronounced bastards, then the crown would go to Lady Frances, and as her husband, Suffolk would surely be King. Where did that leave me? Surely as the trusted close employee of the King – a powerful and well rewarded position. Perhaps under those circumstances I might after all …?

Catherine! Where would she be in all this? With a lurch I realized that, if I understood the protocols, Lady Frances's elevation to Queen would make Jane, Catherine and Mary princesses.

Catherine a royal princess and further out of reach than ever! If she was already a commodity in the power market, to be traded with the highest bidder, think how much greater her market value would be if she were a princess and potentially (unless Lady Frances produced a boy heir) second, after Jane, in line for the throne. Queen Catherine! It all seemed crazy, yet suddenly it was not beyond the bounds of possibility.

What was I supposed to do? With every month of my life, whatever I did and however high I progressed, she seemed to move further out of my reach, rather than closer to me.

Suddenly I made a decision, punching one hand into the palm of the other. The boatman, who had been resting on his oars, holding the wherry steady in the slack current at the river's edge, jumped at the sudden movement. "Anything wrong sir?"

"No, boatman. Nothing. I have made a decision that's all. Take me in to Suffolk Place if you please."

The boatman pulled the wherry into the current and slid her the remaining few yards to the waiting pier. I paid him generously and jumped up. I stood alone on the pier, as the wherry pulled across to the public steps, for, as always, there was a queue of people willing to pay his price to cross the river quickly, rather than spend up to half an hour fighting their way through the throng and the market stalls on London Bridge. I had made my decision. From now on I was going to be my own man, pursue my own interests and make what I could of this topsy-turvy world.

For a start, I was not going to tell Suffolk what Fergal had said. After all, it was only an opinion, and I had not been asked for those. Privately, however, I was sure Fergal's judgement was sound. If the King's life could not be saved, and if his death was to take place before the autumn, I might as well consider how that information best served my own interests, before passing it on to others.

❧ CHAPTER 53 ❧

Third week of April 1553 – Suffolk House

"NO!"

It was the terrible, sickening, frightening scream of a person in abject terror. The whole household stiffened and waited. What in God's holy name was that?

"You selfish hussy. Know your duty – you will do as you are bid!" Suffolk's voice bellowed through the house.

"I will not, Father. On this I cannot obey you. You can call me all names, but I WILL – NOT – MARRY – GUILFORD – DUDLEY!" Each word was screamed aloud and echoed around the house, where all the staff were frozen, listening.

Jane's voice now dropped in pitch and became more supplicant. "In any event, I cannot, for I am already betrothed to Lord Hertford."

"That arrangement has been withdrawn Jane. It is no longer appropriate. This agreement is much better – for all concerned." Lord Henry's voice was controlled and clearly trying to be conciliatory.

"I am sorry, Father, but the answer is no. Not him. Not Guilford Dudley. I could not bring myself to …"

"Know your position, daughter. You will do as you are bid or take a whipping!" It was Lady Frances now, screaming at the top of her voice.

"I will not, and that's final. As God is my maker, I refuse." Jane's normally quiet voice was now ringing through the stone corridors of the building.

"What can we do? I fear for her very life, for she will never give in, and neither will they." Catherine ran into my arms and clung to me, terrified.

"There is nothing we can do. This is between parents and daughter, and any interference on our part will only make it worse." I held her close to me and together we quaked at the sound of the argument in the nearby room.

"Get on your knees girl and pray for God's forgiveness. You will obey or I will make you obey."

"I will not!" There was a sharp slap, followed by a dull thud.

"Get up girl, or I will hit you again. Henry – take your belt to her, for if you have no taste for discipline, by God I'll do it myself."

Jane's voice was quieter, between sobs, but still defiant. "You can cajole, you can argue, you can shrill and you can hit me, but I WILL – NOT – MARRY – GUILFORD – DUDLEY."

Catherine stiffened again, as the sound of whipping came from the room.

"Enough, woman," called Lord Henry. "You will kill her if you continue, and then where will our alliance be?"

There was a dull thumping noise, as of someone being kicked.

"Get up girl, or by God I will thrash you again."

Silence.

"Frances, I do believe you have killed her."

"Nonsense. Meg! Meg! Bring a bucket of cold water – as cold as possible."

Whimpering with fear, Meg the maid ran down the stairs and returned with a pail of cold water and a towel. She entered the room and there was a splash, as the water was thrown over the beaten girl.

There was a gasp of breath as Jane felt the freezing water hit her.

"Do you obey, or shall I send for another bucket of water?"

"I cannot obey mother. Not Guilford Dudley. Not him. Please mother, anyone but him."

"We have made the best arrangement we can girl. For you, for the family and for the future. You have been accepted by the most powerful family in the land and you should be grateful. I will brook no argument and we will not discuss this further. You were called into this room to be told of our decision, not to participate in a debate on the subject."

"But mother, please …"

"There are no ifs and no buts. You will obey me and you will not leave this room until I have your acceptance. I do not need your agreement, for we have already agreed this matter with Northumberland. Now decide. Accept, or we shall start again."

"I cannot …"

There was a further sound of whipping, then the maid ran out, crying, carrying the bucket. Absolute silence reigned through the house as Meg ran to the yard and refilled the bucket at the pump. The silence from the room continued as she returned, running up the stone staircase, trying not to spill more water than was necessary in her haste. She entered the room and the door was slammed shut; the household held its breath waiting for the splash of cold water.

Minutes later it came, and was followed by quiet sobbing and the murmur of conversation. Finally the door opened and Meg appeared, carrying the empty bucket and the towel, now sodden with water. Through the open door, Lady Frances's domineering voice could be heard above the sobbing.

"Good. Then it's agreed. That's more sensible. Now go to your room and put on dry clothes before you catch your death of cold."

Jane emerged from the door, soaked, her face puffed with tears and a large bruise on her cheek. She was holding one arm with the other, as if in pain, and limped off up the stairs without looking at Catherine or me, as, horrified, we watched her from the open doorway of our hiding place.

"This is wrong Richard. It's all wrong." Catherine had tears in her eyes and she was shaking with repressed anger as she watched her elder sister limp away upstairs. She seemed so diminished. Jane, who was always so correct. Somehow it was more difficult to accept such rough treatment being applied to her than, say, a disobedient servant.

I put my arm round Cat's shoulder. "I agree, my love, it is all wrong, but I fear the deed is done and neither you or I have any power to undo it."

Catherine twisted in my arms and looked up into my eyes. "When do you think my turn will come?"

I thought about my boat journey back from Whitehall six weeks before, and for a moment contemplated sharing Fergal's thoughts about the King's health with her. Should I, for example, tell her how close I thought her mother might be to the throne of England? No, it was too dangerous, she was impetuous and was quite likely to share the information with Mary, or even ask her father questions about it at dinner. That would ruin everything; Lord Henry would want to know where she got the information and would then want to know why I had not shared it with him as soon as I had received it. No, silence was the best policy.

"I have no idea, Cat. But I hope when and if that time does come, you are less unhappy about the choice than poor Jane. Guilford of all people – after that disgusting episode at Bankside. It doesn't bear thinking about."

She looked at me sharply. "Indeed it does not. You should not even contemplate such thoughts Richard. I hope you do not lie awake at night thinking about me with another man?"

I kissed her on the end of the nose, and tried to conjure up a grin, but I was too unhappy inside for it to work. "No, I don't." I looked deep into her eyes. "Not with another man I don't, no."

❧ CHAPTER 54 ❧

End of April 1553 – Suffolk House

In the event, it was only three days later that Catherine sought me out in the stables, where I was cleaning the saddle the King had given me, and broke the news.

"I have been told."

"Told what?"

"You knew it would happen. That I am to marry – William, Lord Herbert – Pembroke's son. Jane and I are to have a combined wedding, in a month's time. And Mary is contracted to our cousin – Lord Arthur Grey. Father and Northumberland are making a joint announcement this afternoon."

I felt my heart sink. I took her hand and kissed it, formally. "I wish you well, madam. I hope you will be very happy."

She took her hand away and looked at me wistfully. "Come on Richard. We both knew it would happen one day. Don't sulk. Not now."

I tried to smile but only achieved a twisted scowl. "I know. I'm sorry. I do wish you well – all the good wishes in the world. But it hurts, just the same."

She kissed her fingertips, then brushed them against my lips. "I understand. Now we will never know, will we?"

"Know what?"

"What it would be like to lie together, to be lovers together."

Without thinking I gripped her arms and pulled her close. "We still could. We could here, now."

She pulled away from me. "I thought about that Richard. As soon as I was told that was the first thought I had, that we should love each other, just once, before we go our separate ways. But it would not work."

"Why not?"

"Without a future in front of us it would simply be lust. Just taking, me from you and you from me, rather than giving, as it should be. I would rather remember the dream, and the moments when we nearly …"

"At Shute Hill?"

"Yes, and that afternoon on the hill above Bradgate. I was so close to giving myself to you that afternoon."

I looked at her, already retreating from me, and nodded, my eyes wet.

"I'm glad we didn't – that day" she whispered.

"So am I," I replied, but as with so many things I had had to say to her in the last year, my heart was not really in it.

❧ Chapter 55 ❦

21st May 1553 – Durham House, London

"Why did Northumberland not arrange this wedding at Syon House? It's a better setting than Durham House and we could have progressed across the deer park from Sheen. It would have been beautiful on a day like this."

I sat in the stern seat of the following barge and looked over Celestial Edmund's shoulder at the family barge in front of us, steadily being rowed the short distance upstream and across the Thames from Suffolk Place. I had to admit, they looked beautiful, Jane and especially Catherine, without boat cloaks, braving the gentle breeze in their wedding finery. Suffolk and Lady Frances were, as I had expected, dressed up to the nines and wearing such a weight of jewellery that I feared for their lives if the barge were to overturn.

Lady Jane looked pale and grimly determined. Since that terrible argument, she seemed to have accepted her fate and, supported as always by her religion, had knuckled under to do her duty for the family's sake. She had also dressed to please others, not herself, and looked surprisingly comfortable in a closely tailored gown of gold and silver brocade, sewn with diamonds and pearls. I knew it had been provided by Sir Andrew Dudley, who had been empowered by Northumberland to scour the royal wardrobe, in search of the very best that he could find. Her hair was left loose to the shoulders, to signify virginity (though none would question it in her case) and plaited with pearls, which shone gently in the warm morning light.

Catherine, on the other hand, looked utterly radiant. She had taken to William Herbert in the short time since their betrothal and seemed settled on the idea of marriage into the Pembroke household. I could see her absent-mindedly trailing her left hand in the Thames as their barge neared the pier of the great house. Since our last conversation at Suffolk Place, when she had told me of her betrothal to Lord Herbert, she had avoided my eye and had hardly spoken to me. I was resigned now to the reality that she was to be married to someone else, and would never be mine, but it did seem a pity we could not go on being close friends. I had to admit, however, that had the roles been reversed, had I been marrying Catherine and she had tried to continue a close friendship with another man, I would have been more than troubled by jealousy.

I looked back at Edmund Tucker, sitting facing me in the second barge and unable to see the wedding party behind his back.

"Northumberland chose this house because he wanted the King to attend and with his present illness it was deemed too far from Greenwich to Isleworth."

"And in the event, will he attend here?" asked Edmund.

"I believe not. His recovery has been slower than expected and he remains at Greenwich." I spoke in as measured a tone as I could, but Edmund knew me too well.

"His recovery?" Edmund lived up to his name and produced

a questioning expression of such angelic proportions, that few who did not know him well would have seen the cynicism behind it.

"Yes, his recovery," I hissed, indicating quickly to Edmund that this was not a line of discussion to be pursued in public. I half-stood, and leaned forward putting my mouth close to Edmund's ear. "He remains very ill, I understand. But don't ask me further."

Edmund nodded, red faced at the sharp rebuke. His relationship with me had changed a great deal in the year we had known each other and it was now I who was the dominant party. I looked at his expression as we faced each other. Although I had realized as soon as I met him that Edmund was different from me in his relationship with the ladies, I had always found him kind, knowledgeable about the ways of London society, and solicitously helpful to the young new arrival – especially when it came to the purchase of clothes. As I had grown, both in physical stature and in position in the family, Edmund's approach to me had changed. He had become more – more what? Perhaps more *feminine* was the best description: he now responded to me with the same kind of submission he had formerly reserved for our employer, Lord Henry.

Since the announcement of Jane and Catherine's betrothals, he had seemed even more attentive. Privately, I wondered if he hoped to replace Catherine in my affections, and questioned (not for the first time) whether at some time in the past, he had had a similarly close relationship with Lord Henry himself. I looked across at Edmund, who smiled and reddened, as if he had read my expression. To my embarrassment I felt myself flush in return. Edmund reacted immediately, and sat back in the wide seat of the barge, smiling contentedly, as we pulled alongside the pier of Durham House.

The house was huge, built around a large central courtyard and garden, and covering all of the land between the Strand roadway and the banks of the river. I had visited it before, accompanying Suffolk on business, and remembered in particular the hall with its lofty ceiling, and pillars of what had looked to me like Beer stone, but which I had been told by the Steward, was a superior stone, from the Isle of Purbeck. Well, I had thought, Beer was close to the Dorset border, so they were probably pretty much the same thing. It was certainly not worth arguing about.

As we approached the house over the freshly cut lawns, it was clear that no expense had been spared in decorating the house and grounds for this great occasion. We were welcomed on the lawn by the Northumberlands, the Huntingdons, the Warwicks, Pembroke, Winchester and other members of the Council and the Dudley family. I kept a wary eye on the latter, for I had no wish to fall foul of the Dudley sons again, and on their own ground, after the thrashing I had given them eighteen months previously. Luckily my humble position as a minor guest meant I was not introduced to anyone and was able to remain quietly in the background as the great families played out their pageant together.

Jane and Guilford Dudley were married that afternoon in a wedding service in the chapel of the house. This was followed by great celebrations, including jousting and masques, both held on the lawns beside the Thames. Afterwards, as the May sunlight began to cool, we returned inside to the Great Hall for a sumptuous feast. We had been at table for some two hours when Celestial Edmund, who had spent much of the day with my counterparts in the Northumberland household, slid next to me and, cupping his hands against my ear, whispered, "Whatever you do, don't eat the Oyster Pie" before slipping quietly away again.

I shrugged my shoulders and at first thought little about it – perhaps one of the cooks had admitted that he had let slip the salt too freely in its preparation. However, Edmund's warning had sounded surprisingly urgent, and I was careful to avoid the dish when it arrived. It was a strange dish to serve, I thought, for it was well known that the younger members of the Suffolk family, having been brought up far from the sea in Leicestershire, could not abide the taste of oysters.

Guilford, on the other hand, seemed to relish the dish and I guessed it had been put on the menu especially at his request, for he remained his mother's favourite and was openly spoiled by her, even though he was now eighteen years old.

The feasting continued and the oyster pie was forgotten, as I watched intently the family on the high table. Jane was bearing up well and responding to everyone – including the members of her new family – with her customary good manners. Catherine seemed openly flirtatious with her husband-to-be, and I felt the burning pangs of jealousy more than once that night.

❧ ❧

I blamed that jealousy the following morning, when I awoke with a heavy hangover. I had drowned my sorrows too well and my head hurt like hell. Edmund found me walking the lawns beside the Thames, drinking boiled water infused with honey and mint leaves.

"How do you feel?"

"Terrible. I started on the brandy and finished most of a bottle I think. I have a headache to drop an ox."

"Oh is that all? Thank God. I thought you had not heeded my warning."

I peered at him, red-eyed. "Why, what has happened?"

Edmund grinned triumphantly. "Food poisoning. I have it on good authority that little shit Guilford Dudley has been as sick as a dog all night, and so have a number of his so-called friends."

"Are the girls alright?"

"Yes of course, you know they won't eat anything with oysters in it."

My head began to clear rapidly.

"You knew about this didn't you? It was no accident was it? What happened."

Edmund looked around us before replying.

"Well, they are putting out the story that a cook plucked one leaf for another, by mistake. But what cook worth his salt does not know the difference between bay leaves and laurel?"

"Laurel? That's a deadly poison isn't it? Who would put that intentionally in someone's food?"

"One of the kitchen maids, so I am told. It's said that Guilford Dudley took advantage of her, and made her pregnant, but would not help her and she lost the child. She vowed to get even with him. She put the laurel leaves in with the bunch of bay being prepared for the oyster pie that Guilford had specially requested. She knew the greedy little bugger would eat it to excess, as he had been heard telling one of his brothers he was building up his virility for his bride to be."

I felt a sense of revulsion at the thought of Guilford Dudley and Lady Jane. It was so unfair. But at least someone had fixed him.

"Will he die? Guilford I mean."

"Sadly not. It seems the cook was sparing with the spices as the oysters were fresh and well-flavoured."

I looked him straight in the eye. "You are very well informed Edmund. You knew about this didn't you?"

Edmund looked away. "Not fully, I was just asked what, if anything, our family was unlikely to eat. Oysters were mentioned and I said the girls would certainly not eat them, and Lord Henry and his wife probably not either."

He gripped my arm tightly. "You won't say anything will you?"

I ruffled his hair. "Of course not. Your secret is safe with me."

A look of total relief swept over Edmund's angelic face. He reached up to me – "Thank you. Oh thank you!" – and before I could respond, kissed me full on the lips, then, as if realizing what he had done, made his way quickly back to the house.

Doubly confused now, I continued my slow walk along the bank of the Thames. The view was less attractive from this north side, I thought. I would rather sit in Suffolk Place, on the south bank, looking across at the City of London, than here in fashionable London, looking across at Bankside and the Lambeth marshes.

જ⁊   ৶

"Catherine, you look beautiful. I wish you a memorable wedding day and a happy and contented marriage thereafter."

She stood before me, Lady Frances on one arm and Lady Jane – I could not think of her as Lady Jane Dudley – on the other. Truly she did look beautiful. Whilst Jane could wear expensive gowns and jewellery and look elegant in them when duty called, Catherine positively glowed with happiness, health, beauty and apparent contentment.

"Thank you Richard. I know this is not an easy day for you and that you will have found those fine words most difficult to say with conviction. I appreciate them all the more for that. Yes I believe I shall be happy and I am confident that you, too, will, in due course, find your ideal partner and make her very happy, as surely she will you. Please promise me that when that happy day comes, you will invite me to your wedding."

I smiled and kissed her, for the last time and more formally than either of us was accustomed to, then withdrew. It was her day and I would not get in the way. Perhaps I would join Edmund and discuss everyone's clothing. I did not think I had ever attended a better dressed gathering, even in the King's presence.

It was Whit Sunday, and the third day of the celebrations which had commenced with Jane's wedding, progressed through the marriage of Katherine Dudley and Lord Hastings, Huntingdon's eldest son, and was now to be rounded off by Catherine's marriage to Lord Herbert.

The process was repeated once again, but by now the assembled stomachs were over-full, the masques beginning to be repetitious, the jousts a little tired and the lawns very much the worse for wear.

At the end of the day, the weary celebrants all went our separate ways.

Northumberland left within the hour to return to Greenwich where, I had been told secretly, the King's condition had worsened over the weekend.

Catherine was to go to Baynard's Castle, just along the river, where she and William Herbert could be chaperoned by his parents. They had been forbidden to consummate the marriage, on the argument that she was still only thirteen and he but fifteen, although everyone present was secretly aware this was a political move, in case the political situation around them changed dramatically and it was deemed necessary to annul the marriage in the near future.

On similar grounds, Jane was to accompany her parents to Sheen, where they had decided to rest after the preparations (in particular the negotiations) for the wedding. She seemed relieved that the evil day of being forced into the same bed as Guilford was to be delayed, and asked me to go first to Suffolk Place and to bring her boxes of books to her at Sheen, where she could retreat into her studies again. She also asked me to bring with me the various letters from the pastors of Zurich, that she might continue her correspondence with Bullinger and the others.

Little Mary, who had enjoyed the celebrations immensely, but who was missing her pets, asked her father if she could accompany me and travel to Sheen by way of Suffolk Place and he and Lady Frances readily agreed, their focus remaining on Jane.

By the time I had organized the wherries to take Mary, myself, and the many returning possessions to Suffolk Place (for Suffolk and the rest of the family were taking the barges upstream on their way to Sheen) I felt drained. Edmund Tucker had been dispatched forthwith to Sheen, to prepare the house and to send messengers back to Suffolk Place for all those items he felt the family would need to be transferred for their stay in the country.

"Don't you wish we were going back to Bradgate Park?" asked Mary as we skimmed across the Thames toward Suffolk Place.

"I loved Bradgate. Everything was easier to understand when we were there. Since we all moved to Court, life has become too complicated and ..." she looked at me uncertainly "too political. It's frightening. They still ignore me most of the time – I suppose they always will – but I still watch what's going on and think about it. Even you seem to have abandoned me, Richard. You were my friend once."

I smiled, ruefully. It was true. When I had first joined the family I had felt lost in its size, its wealth, its newness and its complexity. Mary had been a friend, an informant, and a lifeline. Now the harsh truth was that I didn't need her. I was the one who knew the family secrets – or most of them – and my ability to understand political events – within and outside the family – had outgrown my dependence on her. Nevertheless, I felt badly that I had allowed what had once been a valued friendship to become diluted by other needs, and other priorities. It really was a tough world, I thought, and participating in it made you tough in turn.

"I still am, Mary," I replied. "But you have seen what has happened in the last year. Our world has turned upside down. Sometimes I feel that we have all tumbled downward in a waterfall and are now being churned about in the troubled waters beneath."

The eight-year-old watched me carefully from beneath her heavy eyebrows. It was sunny and the light reflecting from the river made her frown more than ever, and those black eyes even harder. She spoke in careful, measured tones.

"I think we are still falling in the waterfall and have yet to reach the bottom. Furthermore, I don't believe there is a deep pool churning away at the bottom of the waterfall but sharp rocks, on which some (or perhaps all) of us are going to be damaged – and quite soon. I fear for the future, but feel powerless to do anything about it."

Although it was a warm spring day, I shivered. Her words had chilled me, for in my heart of hearts I knew she was right. The Suffolks had not finished plotting yet. They were still after the crown, and almost certainly pursuing their objective in partnership with Northumberland. But suppose Northumberland had his own purposes – undeclared to Suffolk? I knew that Suffolk's greatest weakness was his vanity, which often led him to believe he had more command over situations than was the case – especially when he was dealing with Northumberland, as devious a man as any at Court.

The wherry reached the pier at Suffolk Place and I stood to help Lady Mary out.

"We must talk some more my Lady. You are very perceptive."

She did not smile, but climbed to the top of the pier steps and looked back down at me in the wherry. Once again she stood above me.

"Don't make the same mistake as my father, Richard. Don't get so preoccupied with your own thoughts that you forget others are present, and may have purposes and objectives of their own, which may not coincide with yours. The Raven sees all. Yes Richard, I know what you all call me, the Raven. Well, remember where the ravens live most close to power – at the Tower of London. Perhaps this raven will finish up there too? Perhaps we all will? Who knows?"

Mary turned her back on me and walked confidently into the grounds of Suffolk Place, where the servants were beckoning to her. I shivered again. It was as if a ghost had just walked over my grave. I felt very uneasy, but why I was not too sure.

⚘ CHAPTER 56 ⚘

6th June 1553 – The Chapterhouse, Sheen, Surrey

"How is she?"

Lady Mary had just returned from visiting Lady Jane at Durham House.

"She is terribly ill. In pain and frightened beyond belief. She is also embarrassed, so much so that she will not let Mother bring her back here or to Suffolk Place as she cannot face the family, you, or Edmund, or the servants. Mother has taken her to Chelsea – to Catherine Parr's old home, as she says she will feel safe there."

"But what happened?"

"What do you think? It was as bad as she had feared it would be. You know she has been sick since the wedding. She has pain when she … I can't."

"I was brought up in the country and I have sisters Mary, I am not completely ignorant."

"She has an illness – here inside. It makes her want to – you know – to pee all the time, but when she does, it hurts. And the more she thought about having to – to let her husband do it, the more she worried, and the worse it got. She wasn't at all well when she left here last Monday, but Northumberland had instructed that they were to consummate the marriage and mother said she should just get on with it."

"And did she? With Guilford I mean."

"She wouldn't talk to me about it, but I heard her tell mother he was like an animal. She pleaded with him not to hurt her but she said he took her like a Bankside whore. Five times in one night and painfully. No woman should be abused thus, by her husband or by any man."

I was shaken, but not, in truth, surprised. I had watched Guilford Dudley, seen his selfishness and cruelty, and seen him emulate his father's total lack of respect for others. Edmund's story rang even more true now.

"It's a pity the kitchen maid didn't kill him. It's what he deserves."

Lady Mary looked up at me sharply. "What did you say?"

I shook my head. "It's nothing – a rumour, that's all. Over and done with some time ago." I regretted mentioning the incident and wanted to return to the issue we had been discussing.

"Were none of you able to prepare her – beforehand I mean? To allay her fears or give her – you know – advice?"

"We tried. Mother had a long talk to her, and I mean a proper mother's talk, not the usual shouting match. I told her privately (not in mother's presence) that I had heard from Catherine, who was in the reverse situation. They told her and William not to consummate the marriage, but William managed to find a way to her room by the balcony and she says they did it every night. She said it was better than she had ever believed and to tell Jane she would enjoy it after the first one or two times, which might be a bit uncomfortable."

I never ceased to be amazed by this strange hunchbacked child. "You told Jane that?"

"Well somebody had to pass on the message and I'm sure you

wouldn't have wanted to do so, even if Catherine had been willing to tell you. By the way she asked me especially not to tell
you, as she didn't want to hurt your feelings, but, well, I sort of
had to say it didn't I? So please forget I told you."

I snorted. First she tells me the person I respect most in the
whole world has been mistreated by the man she is imprisoned
with, and there's nothing we can do about it. Then, in the same
breath, she tells me the love of my life is enthusiastically making
love every night with another man, and promptly tells me to forget she told me.

I looked out of the window. Outside, the park at Sheen was
green and lush. The deer ambled gently through the parkland
and at the bottom of the valley I could see circles in the lake as
the fish rose to feed on summer flies. It was the 6th of June, my
eighteenth birthday, although, like the last, it had proceeded
unrecognized. Under other circumstances it might have been
such a happy day.

❧ CHAPTER 57 ❧

1st July 1553 – Greenwich Palace

The letter had been addressed to Suffolk Place, but one of the
servants had ridden over to Sheen with it the same day.

Dear Richard,

There is something I need to tell you and you alone. If you
have any opportunity, please, please come to Greenwich
Palace as soon as possible.

Your friend
Fergal Fitzpatrick

I had made my excuses to Edmund, for Suffolk was already
with the King at Greenwich, and Lady Frances was with Jane at
Chelsea.

310

Edmund had realized my difficulty, for what would I say to Lord Henry when we met at Greenwich, as surely we would? Thoughtfully, he had given me some documents, books, and other possessions which Lord Henry had asked to be sent to the palace with urgency. "There you are – that is your excuse. Godspeed."

I delivered the papers to Suffolk as soon as I reached the palace of Greenwich. Lord Henry did not question my bringing them – I was after all his secretary – and made short enquiries about Jane's condition and how long Lady Frances expected to have to stay at Chelsea. Then to my relief, Suffolk was called away by Northumberland, and I was able to make my way quietly to see Fergal Fitzpatrick.

My friend, when I reached him, was distressed beyond belief.

"Richard. You must believe me. This is God's truth and very important, though who you can tell I do not know. They are poisoning the King." He blurted the words out as if we, too, were being poisoned.

"Who is, Fergal? Who is poisoning the King?"

"Northumberland's people. He has spies everywhere, I no longer know who is on whose side, so trust no one – except you, Richard. He has dismissed all the true physicians and brought in a woman – she's a quack Richard, a charlatan of the first order, who promised she could save the King. But he is beyond saving. John Banister, one of the junior physicians, told me while you were at the wedding that the King was, in his opinion, steadily pining away."

For a moment, Fergal was too upset to continue. It was clear that the day-by-day experience of seeing his King and friend dying so horribly and in such pain had taken him to the end of his tether. I shook my head in disbelief.

"The sputum which he brings up is livid black – I see it every day Richard – it smells beyond measure, as if he is rotting away from the inside. His feet are swollen all over and he is growing more swollen in his stomach every day. This is no case of consumption, it's something even worse – more pernicious

311

even than that. It's truly pitiful to watch. They should work to make him comfortable, to let him sleep until blessed relief finally comes, but they are not – the woman is giving him arsenic, I am sure of it. It's keeping him alive, but causing him intense pain. It's wrong Richard, but who can I tell? I fear for my life every day."

We sat together, quietly, as Fergal went over and over the same fears and concerns, worried that he had omitted some important detail. Finally I took his hand and lifted him to his feet.

"Do no more Fergal. Wait. Just wait. For surely the King will die soon and your loyalty to him will be unquestioned. What will you do when the King dies?"

"I shall wait a decent interval, so it does not look as if I am running away, then probably return to Ireland until the future is clearer. My cousin Barnaby, who has now become Baron of Upper Ossary on my father's death, is back here, in case he can give comfort to the King, and so is Thomas Butler, our other cousin, the Earl of Osmond, who was also a schoolboy with the King. We will stick together until a successor is in place, then, I expect, travel back together."

"By a successor, I assume you mean Princess Mary, for she is, I believe, first in line?"

Fergal nudged my elbow, as he had done so often back in happier times.

"C'mon now Richard. You must know full well what your master and Northumberland have been plotting with the King. I wouldn't be surprised if you had written most of it out in your own fair hand."

I shook my head. "Truly Fergal, I have not. What have they been agreeing?"

Fergal looked around to ensure we were not overheard. "The King's Device it's called. A document now written in the King's own hand, which seems to get amended every few days. Its main purpose is to ensure that neither Mary nor Elizabeth succeed to the throne, but that it goes to the House of Suffolk through Lady Frances's line."

I nodded, comforted that the plan remained unchanged. "Yes

I was aware of that proposal, although I did not realize the King had consented to it."

"Consented perhaps, but this King is more independent with every last uncomfortable breath. The document is not signed yet, and even if it were, it could be modified or replaced tomorrow. Only the King's death will end the discussions and finally determine what the succession will be, and even then, there may be argument and doubt."

"May I see him?" I suddenly had a strong desire to see for one last time the King I had grown so much to admire.

"I'll see," said Fergal, "but only if the quack's not there, for she believes we are all spies, acting against her. Wait here."

I waited for ten minutes, until Fergal returned. "C'mon now. Quickly. We only have a few minutes." He led the way through a dark corridor into an even darker room. The room stank like an open sewer. I gagged and put my hand over my mouth, but Fergal gently took it away. "Please don't do that. He doesn't realize how bad it is for the rest of us. Let him believe it's otherwise."

We approached the bed where a small white-faced old man lay dying. At first I could not believe this was my King, and younger than I was – the body in the bed looked eighty years old. He coughed, and the bloodshot eyes slowly opened.

"Not more of the medicine. Please, not more, not yet."

Despite the smell, I leaned closer. "It's not your nurse your Majesty, it's Richard Stocker, Suffolk's man."

The eyes opened a little more and focused on me.

"Lionfart! Richard the Lionfart! How good of you to come. I fear we shall never hunt together again, for I shall be dead within a week and sooner, and out of pain at last, God willing, if this quack stops pickling me alive."

"I am sure we will hunt together again your Majesty." I had tears in my eyes as the lie emerged.

"Yes we will Richard. But not in this world. In the next. Yes, in the next."

His head fell back, clearly exhausted, and Fergal signalled it was time to leave. As I withdrew from the bed, the eyes opened again.

313

"Richard."

I stepped forward, the breath hitting me. "Yes, your Majesty?"

"Make me a promise, Richard."

"Anything your Majesty. What is it?"

"Don't say 'Suffolk's man'. Don't even think it. Be your own man. Always be your own man."

I nodded, tears in my eyes, I could not speak. Fergal approached the King from the other side of the bed. "He has agreed your Majesty. He has agreed. He will be his own man. He has made a solemn promise to do so, and I am its witness."

There was an imperceptible nod of the head. "Good."

❧　❦

I left Fergal to his responsibilities and made for the river. Walking back down the gravel path from the Palace of Greenwich to the pier, where I hoped to find a wherry to take me back to Suffolk Place and my horse, I felt overcome with grief and foreboding. To me, the King had always been the representation of life's pinnacle. In the last year, I had not only seen my king, but had met him, spoken to him and, in a small way, shared experiences and moments of humour and pleasure with him. Now the King, become man, become friend, was going to die, and very soon, leaving a vacuum of fear, uncertainty and doubt.

As I walked down toward the river, I thought I could hear angels, and stopped, listening. The King's choir was practising, and the sound, floating from the chapel windows on the evening air, enveloped me like smoke. The voice of a single alto echoed round the chapel roof and escaped across the grass. I recognized the music as Thomas Tallis's *Spem in Alium*. The number of voices grew, and the sound swelled. I had a strange sense of distant time – of my ancestors in Devon talking to me.

Instinctively, I left the gravel path and continued walking on the grass, to prevent the rhythmic crunch of my feet from interrupting the clear sound of the voices. Quietly, my mood changed. I stopped and stood on the grass, the first swirls of a cool evening mist beginning to waft in from the river.

Now the whole choir lifted. The music was confident, triumphant, an expression of an absolute faith:

Domine Deus, Creator coeli et terrae
respice humilitatem nostram.

Immediately I could see Jane's face and I found myself translating:

Lord God, Maker of heaven and earth,
be mindful of our lowliness.

It seemed appropriate. For a moment I felt I shared the faith which sustained Lady Jane and (I knew from Fergal) the King. In that moment, I was comforted by a thought. If the King departed this place carried aloft by that degree of support, then surely the pain of the world departed would be as nothing to the pleasure of the expectation of the world to come.

But as the choir stopped singing, and the enveloping smoke of the music cleared, my former mood began to return, and once again, I felt vulnerable, and alone. "Be your own man," the King had said to me, and I had made a solemn promise to do so. All my childhood, I had wanted to grow up. Now, nearly one month past my eighteenth birthday, I knew I really was in a man's world, and the reality of it dismayed and frightened me.

❧ Chapter 58 ❧

9th July 1553 — Suffolk Place

"Come to my study please Richard. I have grave news and we have much work to do."

I prepared myself. This was going to be difficult, for I knew the grave news and thought I could guess the work that had to be done. However, it was essential that I did or said nothing which might compromise my friend Fergal Fitzpatrick, whose brief letter sat deep inside the pocket of my jerkin.

Dear Richard,

The King finally died last evening, in the arms of good
Henry Sidney, in great pain to the last, but upheld as always
by his faith. I was out of the room when he finally expired
and cannot tell you his last words, but his valet Christopher
Salmon (whom you have met often with me), and
Dr Wroth, a worthy physician, were also with him and told
me he went well. It was a blessed relief, but a disconcerting
occasion, accompanied as it was by a raging storm, the sky
all afternoon remaining black as night and showering blood
red hailstones as big as pigeon's eggs upon all who ventured
out. The Lord is watching over these dark deeds. Of that I
am certain.

It appears I must thank you. I do not know what you
were able to do, or whether, indeed you were able to
influence events, but the quack disappeared as suddenly as
she had come on the 2nd of July, and the King's
discomfort, although grave, was, at least, not made worse by
that woman's poisons any longer. I pray that the wicked
woman was made to drink the remainder of her own
potions before departure, for she deserves no less.

There was much scurrying about the King in his final
days, almost all of it concerning the King's Device or
Book, which (as I am sure you know well) has been drafted
and modified time and again, largely by the King's own
hand. Being close to the family, you will know that Lady
Frances visited the King recently, and in my presence and
that of Northumberland and her husband Suffolk, formally
renounced the succession to the throne in favour of her
daughter Jane. So finally your friend will become your
Queen, much as my King finally became my friend.

We are all imprisoned here in body, spirit, and speech,
for Northumberland seems undecided how to act and has
refused to announce the King's death. We are all sworn to
secrecy, but as you will be informed anyway, as part of the
family group, I wanted you to know the situation direct
from me. The servant who carries this can be trusted with
your life, but you might be better not to reply; simply tell

him you have read the letter, and then, if you will, destroy it for both our sakes.

I have no idea what will happen now. We are all sitting around, unhappy and, in the main, nervous for the future, but not allowed to do anything. Part of the purpose of this letter is to warn you not to be shocked at the appearance of the King, should you see his body. All I will say is that the embalmers have been extraordinarily diligent and the body which may be showed to the people is greatly different from that poor soul you spoke to only a week ago, may he rest in peace.

Perhaps we will meet again in the next few weeks. If not, I hope, in your exalted new position, you will remember your old friend kindly and pray for me in these troubled times, as I pray for you.

In sorrow for the past and in hope for the future

Fergal Fitzpatrick

I followed Suffolk into the study, uncomfortably conscious now of the rustling paper in my pocket, and wishing I had destroyed it already. As always, when he wanted to discuss something important, Suffolk did not face me, but stared absent-mindedly out of the window and across the Thames to the City walls.

"Our King is dead, Richard. He went to meet his maker confident that he had put in place arrangements for the future which ensure the succession is safe from popery and from the risk of foreign domination of our fine country."

I nodded sagely, trying to indicate that this was all a lot to take in, but I hoped I understood.

"The Council met early this morning and decided to inform the chosen successor of her accession. Lady Mary Sidney (Northumberland's daughter) has, this minute, left for Chelsea, to inform our daughter Lady Jane Dudley that she is to be Queen of England and to go to Syon House in Isleworth. There she will be received by her husband, the Northumberland family, ourselves, and leading members of the Privy Council, and will receive the news formally. Tomorrow, the whole party will take barge to the Tower, where the official ceremony will take place. I want you to find the boat-master and have our barges readied forthwith. You may then proceed direct to Isleworth by wherry and do what you can to assist there."

I tried to look overcome with surprise, but at the same time, to appear strong enough to withstand the shock and a reliable servant in the events to come.

For fifteen minutes Suffolk and I discussed the details – numbers, who was travelling, which clothes would need transporting to Isleworth for the following day's progress by barge and what needed to be sent to the Tower. Quite a few of the family possessions were still at Sheen, and messengers were sent there to inform Edmund Tucker (who had remained there) what arrangements he should make for forwarding them to Syon House, to Suffolk Place, or to the Tower, as appropriate.

❧   ❧

Syon House, the former convent at Isleworth, on the Middlesex bank of the Thames, and opposite Richmond, was the largest of Northumberland's properties, having been sequestered following the execution and attainder of Somerset. It was well known that Somerset had spent a fortune on the place and that, more recently, Northumberland had done likewise, stamping his own mark on the property. The result was certainly impressive and a more than suitable venue for a major affair of state.

I disembarked at the water gate and offered my services to Northumberland's stewards, but they declined my offer, saying that they were fully able to organize an event on this scale, and I was left to wander the grounds awaiting the arrival of the royal parties.

The Dudley family soon began to arrive and make themselves at home. The last thing I wanted was to cross swords with the brothers in the grounds of their father's estate, and I made myself scarce as they and their retainers arrived and swaggered confidently from the watergate building to the great house.

Sitting on the river wall, I recognized the Suffolk barges approaching, and moved back down to the watergate to help. Lord Henry and Lady Frances disembarked carefully, closely observed by the waiting officers of the Dudley household. It was immediately made clear that the Suffolk family was on show today, and that I was not part of it. Lord Henry gave me a curt nod of recognition and Mary and Catherine waved nervously to me, but Lady Frances ignored me completely.

All that was left to do was to await the arrival of Lady Jane. I returned to my riverside wanderings. Eventually a barge appeared, closely followed by a more military-looking craft, clearly filled with armed yeomen. I looked back toward the house, to see how the welcoming party was to be organized, but no one was to be seen. Clearly this occasion was to be held inside.

As the barge approached the pier, it slowed, allowing the yeomen's craft to overtake and disembark what quickly turned into an armed welcoming guard. There was something about their practised efficiency which warned me to keep my distance, and I walked slowly back along the tree-lined path towards the house as Lady Sidney stepped ashore and handed Lady Jane onto her family soil with the dominant manner of a gaoler, rather than the welcoming supplication of a host.

The guard remained at the watergate, as if to signify that no one left here except with Northumberland's permission, and the two ladies, now sisters-in-law, walked purposefully towards the house. Jane's face was paler than usual and drawn – she seemed even thinner than normal, perhaps as a result of her illness, but she held her head high and, eyes firmly forward, walked toward whatever the day held for her.

It was clear that the final guests of honour had now arrived, for the officers of the Dudley household made their way to the house by another door, and disappeared. I followed the ladies at a respectful distance and after an appropriate pause, followed them into the silent house. I could hear the quiet murmur of voices ahead of me and walked slowly forward toward the Great Hall. It was empty, apart from the two ladies, who stood at the far end speaking in near-whispers, apparently inhibited by the huge tapestries all around them. I retreated into the corridor and waited.

A few moments passed before Northumberland himself entered the room, followed by a growing group of worthies. I waited for the families to appear, but they did not. It appeared this part of the ceremony was to be limited to the Councillors themselves. Northumberland stood to one side, talking seriously to Northampton and Arundel, whilst Huntingdon and Pembroke engaged Jane in a long conversation. Pembroke bowed low and, taking Jane's hand, kissed it. He seemed to be honouring her as one would a queen. *This is the moment,* I thought, but Jane responded with embarrassment and went bright red, pulling her hand away in obvious discomfort.

A few moments later, Northumberland came across to Jane and, taking her hand, led her to the Chamber of State, followed by Lady Sidney and the assembled Councillors. As the Great Hall emptied of Councillors, other servants like myself, but mainly Dudley men, sidled into the hall from both entrances, and began, gently, to follow the departing Councillors. Thus emboldened, I decided to do the same.

Looking round the door into the Chamber of State, it was immediately clear that this was the place where Jane would effectively become Queen. At the far end of the room was an empty throne, covered by a canopy of estate. Arranged in strict order of precedence on either side of the throne were the two families, Guilford Dudley, and a number of nobles who were not members of the Privy Council. They were now joined by the Councillors, and as Jane passed them, all the company bowed or curtsied.

Northumberland led Jane to the throne and turned her before it to face the now considerable throng. "As President of the Council," Northumberland announced, "I do now declare the death of my most blessed and gracious Majesty King Edward VI." As he continued, reminding those assembled how good the King had been and how he would be missed, I saw Jane shudder. Surely by now she realized what this whole proceeding was about – the trail to this day was clearly to be seen. But it seemed not – Lady Jane was looking around her now, a wild and frightened look on her face, as if the full consequence and, it appeared from her expression, horror, of the proceedings was only now dawning upon her.

"His Majesty hath named your Grace as the heir to the crown of England," continued Northumberland. Lady Jane jolted backward, apparently shocked to hear the words spoken, and incapable of reply.

"Your sisters will succeed you in the case of your default of issue." I looked immediately at Catherine and realized by her expression that she had been equally slow to recognize the implication of the proceedings for her, and for her sister Mary.

Northumberland turned to Jane and, addressing her, but in a tone and volume clearly meant for the room, continued.

"This declaration hath been approved by all the lords of the Council, most of the peers, and all the judges of the land. There is nothing wanting but your Grace's graceful acceptance of the high estate which God Almighty, the sovereign and disposer of all crowns and sceptres – never sufficiently to be thanked by you for so great a mercy – hath advanced to you. Therefore you should cheerfully take upon you the name, title and estate of Queen of England, receiving at our hand the first fruits of our humble duty – now tendered to you upon our knees – which shortly will be paid to you by the rest of the Kingdom."

The room knelt in reverence, as Northumberland continued, reassuring Jane that each one would shed their blood for her, "exposing their own lives to death". I watched from the doorway as Jane, clearly overcome by the terror of the occasion, looked round the room, as if for assistance and, receiving none whatsoever, glazed over and passed out on the floor.

She lay there for a few seconds only, then, appearing to recover herself partially, sat up and tried to get to her feet. Still no one moved. I wanted to run into the room and pick her up, take her from this imprisonment and return her to the quiet of her studies and the comfort of her books. But I knew it would be impossible. I was an interloper at a ritual which would be played out, whatever the consequences to the country or the participants. The abject loneliness of her situation seemed to hit Jane again, and she fell back to the floor, lying there, sobbing uncontrollably.

The throng stood, coldly, patiently – some, perhaps, believing that Jane was sobbing for her recently departed King, but the rest remote, as the spectators at a bear-fight, letting a fifteen-year-old girl meet her destiny alone and making no attempt to help her along the way. For a few moments there was an embarrassed silence, as the lone girl lay in the middle of them, sobbing. Eventually there was a sigh of relief, as, slowly, she got to her feet, wiped away the tears with the back of her hand and gulped a number of deep breaths.

I watched as she took one, two, three large breaths. I saw her expression change and suddenly knew what was going to happen. They would not overawe this Lady. Jane would not retreat passively in the face of what she believed to be an untruth. I saw her eyes get larger, her back straighten and I looked at Northumberland as if to say, "I have seen that look before. I hope you know what's coming."

Jane glanced at Northumberland, then around the room. Most of those present avoided her gaze as she took them all in, one after another, before returning to Northumberland.

"The crown is not mine by right, and pleaseth me not. The Lady Mary is the rightful heir."

There was a stunned silence throughout the room.

"Your Grace doth wrong to yourself and to your house!" shouted Northumberland, but still she flatly refused to cooperate. Suffolk stepped forward and spoke cajolingly to her, but with no effect. Her mother shouted at her, but she simply glared back coldly, and silenced her without even speaking.

Guilford Dudley now sought to influence his new wife the only way he knew – by sharp rebuke and direct instruction, but she turned her back on him as an irrelevance. It was an impasse.

"I will pray for guidance."

Jane fell to her knees and began to pray, seemingly able to become oblivious of all around her. The crowd stood silently around the kneeling girl, waiting with growing impatience, yet unsure what else to do, for only she could break the impasse. Eventually she rose, and turned to Northumberland.

"After humbly praying to my God and beseeching Him to give me guidance, I am guided that I should accept. If what hath been given to me is lawfully mine, may Thy Divine Majesty grant me such spirit and grace that I may govern to Thy glory and service, and to the advantage of the realm." Carefully, she rose and seated herself on the throne.

There was an audible sigh of relief all round the room, not least of all from Northumberland, who was clearly unused to people refusing him direct. He stepped forward to kiss her hand, followed, with increasingly scrabbling enthusiasm, by the whole sorry crowd.

I tiptoed away in disgust. I was ashamed of the so-called nobles who had engineered this whole situation for their own power and betterment, uncaring for the consequences for a fifteen-year-old girl. I was ashamed of the Councillors, declaredly leaders of men and highly regarded representatives of the country, but proven to be a bunch of craven, self-serving cowards. But most of all, I was ashamed of myself, for surely I had known, in my heart of hearts, what all these signs and signals, moves and steps had meant over the last four months, and I had never made a move to save her, to warn her, or even to prepare her for what was to come. I was as bad as them all.

I made myself a promise: if the opportunity ever arose again to help Lady – no, Queen Jane, and if she asked for my help, I would assist her, regardless of the price to me or the discomfort involved.

• CHAPTER 59 •

10th July 1553 – Grounds of Syon House, Isleworth

The next morning was hot and sunny, which was just as well, for I had spent the night curled up in one of the barges in the water-gate. I had not been invited to join the dinner arranged for the official guests and had not felt able to invite myself to join the Dudley servants for fear of being recognized and reported back to the brothers. As a result, I realized when I woke cold and damp that morning, I had not eaten for twenty-four hours.

I was rescued by one of the barge masters, who took pity on me and showed me the back entrance to the house, where a small hall had been made available for "merchants, visiting servants and the like". Breakfasted, dried off by the warmth of the crowded room, and with my cloak thoughtfully dried by a buxom maid from the kitchen who appeared to have taken a fancy to me, I felt considerable better as I joined the throng preparing to depart for the river journey to London.

"Ha Richard!" called Lord Henry disingenuously. "We missed you last night, where were you?"

"I ate with the servants my Lord," I lied, "and breakfasted with them this morning also."

"Excellent. I am glad Northumberland's people looked after you properly. Knew they would of course. Now, for today's plan. The families will take barge at mid-morning and stop for dinner at Durham House. We will then continue downstream and expect to arrive at the Tower at three o'clock." He thrust a piece of paper into my hand. "Will you travel on ahead to Suffolk Place and collect these things from there, then bring them down to the Tower? The guards have been told to expect you, but just in case, carry this note with you."

The paper had a long list of items and at the bottom was written, "To be delivered to the royal apartments at the Tower by the bearer", together with the Suffolk seal.

"Oh and Richard? Try to have it all there before three o'clock will you? We may need to change some clothing after two boat trips. Although the weather looks good now, you never know – think what it was like last week."

I nodded, remembering the storm the day the King had died. I looked at Suffolk for further instructions, but he was already deeply involved in a conversation with Huntingdon. I was forgotten already.

It had gone well, and I had done it all, as instructed. The Suffolk seal had, to my surprise, opened the door of the Tower – even of the royal apartments – and I had been able to deliver my list and to return to the riverside before the barges arrived.

The crowds outside had been surprisingly small, and surly. I had heard many a muttering that "Mary is the true Queen" and that "this Dudley Grey woman is not a proper Tudor", but in the main they seemed to think there was nothing they could do about it and that life would go on being short and hard, whatever happened. Nevertheless, I decided to use my wayleave to remain inside the Tower, to find a good viewpoint, and quietly await the arrival of Jane, the new Queen.

Having just come downstream from Syon, with the boats arriving and departing at its watergate, I had initially positioned myself close to the watergate at the Tower. But seeing the crowds were all massing elsewhere, I had asked one of the yeomen why I was standing alone to await the new Queen's arrival. "Surely, good sir," he had replied, "our new Queen will not be entering the Tower by this gate, for this is Traitor's Gate. At this stage of the tide, I think you will find the party will pull in tight against the wharf." I thanked him and found myself a reasonable vantage point further along.

It was well after three o'clock when finally they arrived. The crash of guns giving the royal salute along Tower Wharf signalled their impending arrival, and some arrival it was. Upwards of a dozen barges shot London Bridge in close formation – it was still half-tide and therefore not too dangerous – and swung skilfully into order of reverse precedence against the wharf. This enabled the men to form a welcoming guard and to receive their Queen, who alighted last.

She looked so small, although I noticed they had tried to make her look taller for the crowds by binding chopines – three inch wooden clogs – to her shoes. She managed very well, and alighted delicately and without a wobble or any return of the nervous fear she had shown the previous day. Her brocaded kirtle and long sleeved bodice were in white and green – the Tudor colours – and were embroidered with gold. Her hair was set high, within a French hood, again to increase her height, and set with emeralds, diamonds rubies and pearls. Alongside her, resplendent in white, gold and silver, Guilford Dudley was clearly enjoying his role as consort and paying her all the attention this theatrical act required.

Jane walked confidently, head held high and back straight, through the Tower precincts to the royal apartments, where the keys were presented by the Marquess of Winchester, who waited in attendance with the Lieutenant of the Tower, Sir John Bridges, and a detachment of the Yeomen of the Guard. The keys were received (some would say snatched) on her behalf by Northumberland, and the party proceeded to the White Tower.

I followed, with the small crowd of onlookers who had access to the Tower fortress, as Jane approached the White Tower, to be met by her father, and sister Catherine, with her new husband, Lord Herbert, and a great number of peers. The party climbed the stairs to the small and easily defended doors of the White Tower – the keep of the Tower of London and, in itself, as domineering a fortress as I had ever seen – and I paused outside. Just at the last minute, Lord Henry turned at the top of the steps, as if searching the crowd below. He saw me and beckoned me to follow. "Come, Richard, this is a working day and we may well have tasks to perform ere the day is out."

Inside, Jane led the way confidently to the Presence Chamber and seated herself on the throne. Gone was the hesitancy of yesterday. She had clearly decided that if God wanted her to perform the role of Queen, then she should do so to the best of her ability and with the dignity the highest office in the land clearly demanded. No sooner was she seated, than Northumberland and Suffolk fell to their knees and bade her officially welcome.

The royal families then proceeded to divine service in the White Chapel – the chapel of St John, high up within the White Tower, whilst I and the lesser mortals waited in the Presence Chamber.

An hour later Jane reappeared and seated herself beneath the canopy of estate. Guilford, seated next to her called solicitously, "Who will you have to attend you my Lady?" Queen Jane looked around her and at Guilford. This was one of her first decisions, and, as I knew from my many conversations with Fergal Fitzpatick, an important one, for it determined who had close access to the Queen thereafter, and clearly this was a decision which she did not intend to have made for her by her husband, by her parents, or by Northumberland.

She looked round the room and announced, "I shall have my nurse, Mrs Ellen, and my Gentlewomen, Mrs Tilney and Mrs Jacob."

Guilford put his hands on his hips and snorted. "Shall you have only women in your circle, Lady? No men in your life – except your husband of course." He managed to make the last part of the comment sound lascivious, to the clear embarrassment of all present, particularly Queen Jane, who understood fully the inflection in his voice. She looked around the room, and, finally, at me.

"I had not finished. I shall, indeed, have a man to be my trusted servant. I shall choose" – she looked slowly round the room, pausing for effect. "I shall choose Richard Stocker." She turned to Suffolk and inclined her head regally. It was the first conversation between them since their respective positions in the order of precedence had been reversed. "That is, allowing my father the Duke of Suffolk can spare him?"

I took a deep breath. Would I, indeed, be chosen and accepted as a personal servant to the Queen when her husband surely remembered the beating I had given him? Perhaps he had been so drunk on that occasion that he could not remember?

All eyes, including mine, were on Suffolk now. He inclined his head back to his daughter. "My Queen invites and her father, her servant, obeys." He bowed low to his new Queen.

"Come ladies, Richard, join me here at my side," called the Queen and, showing our embarrassment as well as our delight at being chosen, the four of us took our places beside her.

The Marquess of Winchester entered the room with three servants, carrying between them on silver trays what seemed like most of the crown jewels. Hesitantly he lifted the crown and held it above Queen Jane's head, but she refused to let him put it on her, reminding him that she had not asked for it.

Winchester, not in the slightest put out, replied silkily, "Indeed Majesty, it was only my intention to try whether it becomes you or no, for it is a man's crown, and likely to be both large and heavy. But your Grace may take it without fear."

The Queen allowed him to lower it slowly onto her head but the very process clearly distressed her. Winchester deftly removed it before there was further upset and gently remarked that it could certainly be modified to make it fit better, and that at the same time, a suitable crown could be made to fit Guilford. The Queen did not reply, but I saw the steely glint in her eye as the throwaway remark was made. *We shall have fireworks before that matter is resolved*, I thought.

Dinner that night took the form of a great banquet and for the first time in my life I found myself seated at the high table, although, it was true, at the very end of it.

The meal was in full swing, and everyone seemed relaxed after the tensions of the last two days, when a man, announcing himself as Thomas Hungate, entered the room, looking concerned, saying he had an urgent letter to the Council from Princess Mary and asking Northumberland whether he should read it out. Northumberland took the letter and read it quickly before returning it. "Yes, read it," he rasped, clearly upset.

Nervously, Hungate began to read.

"My Lords, we greet you well, and have received sure advertisement that our dearest brother the King is departed to God, which news, how they be woeful unto our heart. He wholly knoweth to whose will and pleasure we must and do humbly submit us and our will.

"But in this lamentable case, that is to wit now after his death, concerning the Crown and governance of this realm of England, what has been provided by Act of Parliament and the last will of our dear father, the realm and all the world knoweth, and we verily trust that there is no good true subject that can or will pretend to be ignorant thereof. And for our part, as God shall aid and strengthen us, we have ourselves caused, and shall cause, our right and title in this behalf to be published and proclaimed accordingly.

"And albeit this matter being so weighty, the manner seemeth strange that, our brother dying on Thursday at night last past, we hitherto had no knowledge from you thereof. Yet we considered your wisdoms and prudence to be such that, having eftsoon amongst you debated, pondered and well-weighed this present case, we shall and may conceive great hope and trust and much assurance in your loyalty and service, and that you will, like noble men, work the best.

"Nevertheless, we are not ignorant of your consultations and provisions forcible, there with you assembled and prepared, by whom, and to what end, God and you know, and Nature can but fear some evil. But be it that some consideration politic hath hastily moved you thereto, yet doubt you not my Lords, we take all these your doings in gracious part, being also right ready to remit and fully pardon the same freely, to eschew bloodshed and vengeance. Trusting also assuredly you will take and accept this grace and virtue in such good part as appeareth, and that we shall not be enforced to use the service of other our true subjects and friends, which in this, our just and rightful cause, God in whom our whole affiance is, shall send us.

"Wherefore, my lords, we require and charge you, for that allegiance which you owe to God and us, that, for your honour and the surety of your persons, you employ yourselves and forthwith, upon receipt hereof, cause our right and title to the Crown and government of this realm to be proclaimed in our City of London and such other places as your wisdoms shall deem good, not failing hereof, as our trust is in you. And this letter signed with our hand shall be your sufficient warrant.

"Given under our signet at our manor of Kenninghall, the 9th of July 1553

"Mary"

Hungate put down the letter. There was a stunned silence, and then, to my amazement, the Duchess of Northumberland began to snuffle, quickly joined by Lady Frances. Both ladies continued whining, "We are lost, all is undone," until Northumberland's glare silenced them. The Queen herself did not speak, but remained silent and deathly pale.

Northumberland tried to recover the situation by assuring the Queen that Mary was a woman alone, powerless and with no following, but his actions gave lie to his words, for his anger was so great at hearing that the princess had evaded capture by his troops, that he had Hungate thrown immediately into the dungeons.

The evening was ruined and the party broke up, Queen Jane retiring to her private chambers, calling, "Come ladies, Richard, follow me," and followed by a nervous-looking Guilford.

Arrangements for sleeping were made and the Queen and her husband retired to their bedchamber. Within half an hour, however, shouting could be heard from inside and Guilford stormed out, in shirt and loose breeches, crying his eyes out and calling for his mother.

Within minutes he had returned, the Duchess of Northumberland at his side. She stormed straight into the Queen's bedchamber, demanding that her son would be made King and immediately. "I will not be a Duke, I will be a King," wailed Guilford's voice from within the room. Immediately the Duchess could be heard to reply in high dudgeon, "Guilford, you are to abstain from the bed of so undutiful a wife. Now follow me. We are leaving and returning to Syon House this very night."

I sat quietly in the corner and rolled my eyes. That was not the way to get agreement from this Queen, I was quite sure. As if to prove my point, the Duchess reappeared, but walking backwards, Jane pursuing her in a cold anger, the forefinger of her right hand in the centre of the Duchess's bodice, and her advancing nose only inches from the Duchess's retreating one.

"Madam that is the first time, and the last time, you invade a Queen's bedroom. Do that again and you will be removed to a less comfortable place by my armed guards and thereafter you will remain there at my pleasure. Thanks to your husband's scheming, I have been made Queen of England, and by arrangement between our families, wife to your youngest son. But be clear madam, I have no need of my husband in bed, but by day his place is by my side, and BY – MY – SIDE – HE – WILL – BE!"

The Queen had won the day. Guilford was found a separate bedchamber, and sent into it like a naughty schoolboy, whilst his mother retreated from the royal apartments, flushed and surprised that so small a person could wield so forceful an argument – and against her of all people.

❧ CHAPTER 60 ❧

11th July – Tower of London

"Thank you ladies. You may leave me for a while now. I shall read my book."

Mrs Tilney and Mrs Jacob bobbed their heads and withdrew, smiling indulgently at their Queen as they did so. We looked like proud parents whose child had won a prize for recitation at school. I began to follow them.

"Richard. Tarry awhile if you will."

I paused and turned back into the room. "Your Majesty?"

She giggled. "It still seems strange to hear you address me so. Come sit with me Richard, I would like to talk to you."

I crossed the room and sat in the window seat beside her. The royal apartments at the Tower were more than comfortable, but there was something about the atmosphere which made me want to shiver. All the time I had the feeling that the real purpose of the fortress was not to keep the State's enemies out, but to keep them in.

Queen Jane looked at me with that soft but penetrating gaze she used when she was listening to you or concentrating on something important. Back in Bradgate – it seemed so long ago now – when she had first joined John Aylmer in helping me with my education, I had found that look disconcerting, and had felt she was interrogating me, looking for weakness or ready to find fault. But over the months I realized that this was not the case; she took no pleasure in correcting my errors – only in seeing me improve month by month, and as my confidence in our relationship had grown, I had got used to it, and now enjoyed the feeling of unity – of closeness, which that look inspired.

"I don't think you realize, Richard, how important it is for me to have you here with me. For most of my life I have felt there were few I could trust, and life's experience has sadly proved me right. But you are one person I feel confident I can confide in, trusting, as I do, both your integrity and your competence to understand the issues we discuss and to avoid communicating them to others by expression or manner, let alone by actually speaking of them. The ladies are wonderful – from an emotional point of view, Nurse Ellen is in many senses my true mother, and Mrs Tilney and Mrs Jacob I would trust with my life. But they do not have your experience of the affairs of men – of power, of politics, of greed and of corruption, which you have witnessed and understood whilst in my father's employ. I have to admit to you Richard, that the events of recent days have left me tired and disconcerted – not to say frightened. I realize now that this whole affair is a plot, designed by Northumberland purely for his own betterment and protection, and I, along with so many others, am a mere pawn in his Machiavellian schemes."

I hated to see her so discomforted and was more than a little embarrassed to hear her speak so openly. "But your Majesty, you are the rightful heir, according to the King's wishes."

She took my arm and, despite the smallness and delicacy of her hands, gripped it tightly.

"Please, Richard, promise me this. Will you, of all people, treat me as a person and not as a status? Do not butter me up as the others do. Do not give me 'Your Majesty' when no Majesty is present. Do not tell me lies – even kind ones – and tell me they are truths. Not you Richard. Please, not you."

I swallowed hard at being so rebuked, and nodded to show I had been found out and accepted it was so.

"May I call you 'your Grace', for grace is surely present?"

Queen Jane smiled at me. Her grip slackened, but still she held my wrist, gently now.

"Nicely said Richard, and yes you may. But please be aware of this. I do not believe I am the rightful Queen of England. I loved and respected our cousin King Edward and believe them when they tell me he signed a 'device' declaring the princesses bastards, and that my mother – and through her, I – was the next in line to the throne. I know he did it in God's name, to prevent Princess Mary from undoing all the Reformist good he managed to do during his sadly short reign. It was for that reason – perception of God's will – that I accepted the crown when they forced it unwillingly upon me. But I have thought hard and long since then, and although I fear for what Princess Mary might do to the religion of this country, I have reverted to my original view, that it is she who is the rightful heir to this throne and not I."

"Jane – your Grace, it grieves me to do so, but in my heart of hearts I agree with you. However, you have now been appointed, the deed is done, and you have accepted it. Surely the right thing to do now is to try to contain Northumberland's ambitions, and, if I may say so, those of your own parents, to reign as fairly and honourably as possible, and to continue the work your dear cousin our King began."

She looked at me for a while, then out of the window, across the courtyard and towards the White Tower.

"I understand what you are saying, Richard, but deep down I do not believe the deed is done. Mary has made her position clear, and the people have yet to speak. Did you hear the cheers of the crowd when I entered the Tower?"

I shook my head. "No Lady, there were none."

She, in turn, shook her head, very slowly and almost imperceptibly. "Precisely. There weren't any, were there? The people are for Mary and she may yet win them. How feel the common people for Northumberland, Richard?"

"He is unpopular but greatly feared, your Grace. Few will speak out against him, for he has informers everywhere, and his power is absolute – he appears to have taken effective control of the Council. The Treasury, the Army, and even the Church fears him. But neither the people, nor, if my observations are right, do most of the nobility or the Council love or respect him. If he shows any weakness, I sense the removal of their fear will also be the destruction of their loyalty, and he will fall fast and far, as if from that flagpole on the White Tower."

"Is he that unpopular? Have the people seen through him so clearly?" She looked up at the royal pennant, fluttering above the White Tower, nodded and let go of my wrist. "You are right, Richard, I am sure of it. Now everything depends on the people." She turned to me, a smile on her face for the first time that day.

"It's just like old times – when we were at Bradgate – you, me, Catherine and Mary. It's just the same."

I looked at her, confused. "How so your Grace?"

"Once again, our lives are in the hands of others. All we can do is live them from day to day, pray, and see what God has planned for us. In the past our futures – even yours Richard, were all in the hands of my parents. But now my future, and yours, and even my parents' and Northumberland's, all hang in the balance, and all are in the hands of the people. We must sit and wait. In the meantime I must play Queen."

❧   ❧

The days that followed fell into a pattern. The Tower itself seemed to be holding its breath, waiting to see what news arrived from outside.

Queen Jane and her personal servants spent much of their mornings in the royal apartments, occasionally walking within the Tower precincts, or along the walls, but not venturing out into the City beyond. Meanwhile Guilford presided over the daily meetings of the Council, which took place in the White Tower, with Northumberland as Lord President of the Council driving the real decisions from behind his chair.

Dinner was a large and formal affair, and taken at noon, Queen Jane sitting at the centre of the high table, beneath the canopy of estate, flanked by the Duchesses of Northumberland and Suffolk. I used the opportunity to watch the nobles and Council members, trying to determine what was in their minds, and their intentions for the future. As far as I could judge, most of them were doing likewise, for nobody wanted to step out of line, or make himself too visible, when the future was so uncertain.

In the afternoon, the Queen returned to the royal apartments and was brought news of the events taking place outside and of the decisions which had been taken that morning in her name, and which, having been duly inscribed whilst we ate, were now ready for her signature.

On the afternoon of the 11th we learned that Princess Mary had evaded the pursuing Robert Dudley and was still at large. Northumberland went into one of his rages, yelling at everyone to act. I could not follow his rantings. Very aware, as were many present, that Northumberland was by far the most effective military leader amongst them, I thought he seemed notably unwilling to leave London and lead the troops himself. Instead, that evening, he arranged a general muster of troops at Tothill Fields near Westminster, offering unusually generous pay to those who would volunteer.

The following evening, the relative peace of the Tower was disturbed by the arrival at the Tower gates of three cartloads of guns and other ordnance, to which were added thirty of the great guns from the Tower itself. Northumberland reported to the Queen that 2,000 additional troops had been mustered in London and that five warships had been instructed to patrol the coast near Yarmouth, to prevent the princesses' party from escaping to the Low Countries. He did not, however, inform the Queen that Robert Dudley had been beaten soundly at King's Lynn and had had to retreat to Bury St Edmunds, or that the City of Norwich had officially recognized Mary as Queen. I picked up both of these snippets of news by listening to the conversations of the Councillors as they sat at supper that evening, many containing their nerves by downing more glasses of strong wine and brandy than may have been prudent.

At an ad-hoc Council meeting later that evening, Northumberland pressured Suffolk into leading the supporting army, and even suggested that he should, on Northumberland's authority, replace his son Robert when the two armies joined up. The Queen, however, had finally seen through Northumberland's guile and insisted that Northumberland himself was the greatest man of war in her realm and he should go. There was a furious argument, but eventually the Council backed the Queen's judgement and Northumberland had to accept the responsibility with as much good grace as he could feign.

Looking around the room, I could now see the final stage of the plot begin to unfold. It was clear, and becoming ever more so day by day, that more and more of the Council believed Mary was going to win and that their personal priority over the coming days was to ensure they emerged on the winning side, with an acceptable story to tell.

It was also clear that, almost to a man, they hated and distrusted Northumberland, and had little respect for Suffolk, whose power base was seen to be diminishing quickly, and who, when the pressure was on, and with Northumberland distracted, made no real contribution himself to the solution of the problem, the furtherance of their aims, or their personal protection. As I heard one of them admit to another late at night in his cups, "We accepted him when he was useless but well-connected, but now he is useless and of no value to us, we are ready to let him sink with that tyrant Northumberland, while we get busy to save ourselves."

❧ ❧

Early the following morning, Thursday the 13th July, the Queen decided to take the air on the Tower walls. It had been agreed the night before that Northumberland would leave the Tower and prepare to lead the army from Durham House toward Newmarket, and after all the recent uncertainties, Jane wanted to see his departure for herself.

336

Queen Jane was restless and nervous. Before leaving her the previous night, Northumberland had told her that arrangements were being made for her and Guilford to be crowned at Westminster Abbey in two weeks time. Not only was this completely contrary to her wishes – she had specifically refused to allow Guilford to be made King – but for Jane, who believed absolutely in the sanctity of the Church, the coronation at the Abbey would be the final, irrevocable, step in her acceptance of the crown which she now firmly believed was not hers by right.

She and I had discussed this late the night before, after Northumberland had left, for the Queen had said she could not sleep until she had it clear in her mind. My concern was for her safety should Princess Mary win the crown, for I had seen sufficient of the Court battles to know how ruthless the process was.

Queen Jane was not in the slightest worried about her present position. In fact she hoped that Mary would supplant her in the role she had never asked for, and that she could then return to her studies in peace and quiet. Secretly, she admitted to me, she hoped that if Northumberland's plot to place her on the throne, and to put Guilford in the position of consort, were overtaken by events, with Mary successful, and Northumberland's power destroyed, her arranged marriage might also be put aside. She had, she felt, been duped into both by a ruthless man without conscience and she prayed that God (and Princess Mary) would recognize the falsity of both positions in which she had been placed.

"The princess knows full well that I did not seek this crown, did not wish to accept it, and stated in public that I believed it was rightfully hers," she had said. "She also knows I did not want to marry Guilford Dudley and will, I am sure, understand the duplicity of the arrangement made between our families for their own betterment and, God willing, will relieve me of that burden also."

I had not been so confidant, but hoped she was right.

We followed Northumberland's departure with ease, for he was dressed in his armour and accompanied by a large detachment of men at arms in his own livery. He disappeared along Thames Street in the direction of Blackfriars, to muster with his troops in the Strand, directly in front of Durham House. For half an hour, we waited in the cold early morning, hoping to see Northumberland reappear in front of his troops before taking the Chelmsford road, but apart from a lot of military-sounding noise, nothing appeared, and Queen Jane finally suggested that we should breakfast instead of standing there catching cold.

We were in the process of returning to the royal apartments when we were surprised to see a large group of privy Councillors walking quickly and, we thought, rather furtively, towards the White Tower. Even more surprisingly, they appeared to be accompanied by the Imperial ambassadors, who looked equally furtive as they entered the huge building. However, we thought nothing more of it and settled for our breakfast.

Later that morning there was a mighty commotion, with horses being galloped across the courtyard below, and a great deal of challenging from the guards and shouting in response. Queen Jane decided to ignore the interruption, but I, leaning out of the window, was surprised to see Northumberland, accompanied by his sons, returning and entering the White Tower, clearly in an angry mood.

It was not until dinner at twelve o'clock that the source of the argument emerged. Apparently, Northumberland, still unhappy at his commission, had returned and told the Council that in his absence he feared they would more easily be "wrought upon to deliver up the Queen". He had then harangued the Council with warnings of his retribution in the event of their infidelity, to which, unsurprisingly, they had responded with their undying support. I had wondered how many of them had made the sign of the cross with their fingers behind their backs as they did so, for it was well known that an oath so sworn was invalid in God's eyes. Finally, Northumberland had asked for, and received, promises of reinforcements to be sent following close behind his army and, in view of his impending departure, had instructed that Suffolk should head the Council while he was away.

After dinner Northumberland received his commission from Queen Jane and left, bidding a warm farewell to Arundel and saying, "In a few days I will bring in the Lady Mary, captive or dead, like a rebel, as she is."

စ~ ~ဇ

On the Friday morning, messengers arrived, saying they had witnessed the departure of the army through Shoreditch, riding on the Cambridge Road. They reported that Northumberland had been in the lead, accompanied by his sons, except Robert and Guilford, and wearing a scarlet mantle over his armour. It was said the army had been seen off by a large crowd, but a surly one, with no one calling "God's speed" as was customary when friends departed.

Within an hour, the level of activity in the Tower had increased dramatically, with horses and carriages summoned and servants running hither and thither; Suffolk could be seen in the courtyard, trying to stop Councillors from leaving. Word reached us in the Queen's chambers that there was news of a mutiny amongst the sailors of the five ships anchored off Yarmouth and that all of their crews had finally defected to Mary's side.

An hour later, the Captain of the Guard came to the royal quarters and asked to see the Queen. She admitted him, but remained accompanied by me, for she feared something was afoot. In the event, he had come to do her no harm, but to report that the Treasurer of the Mint had escaped, laden with all the gold in the Queen's privy purse.

For the first time, Queen Jane now looked frightened and as soon as the Captain had departed, clung to my hand. Without thinking, I put my arm around her, in a protective gesture and pulled her to me. In all the many months I had known her, this was the first time I had held Jane closely, and I was surprised how small and delicate she was. We were still clinging together when the door burst open and Suffolk ran in, shouting.

"I cannot control them Jane – your Grace. The members of the Council have fled, and it is said that broadsheets supporting Mary are appearing all over the streets of London."

He was frightened and diminished. Gone was the puff and bravado, gone the swaggering confidence. The man seemed to have lost two inches in height overnight and his eyes had the hunted look of a man who sees enemies everywhere, and no support on any side.

"What can we do?" he shouted almost hysterically.

Jane pushed my protective arm aside and emerged, energized.

"Govern. That's what we can do, Father, we can govern. Actively govern. Give the people the leadership they want and deserve. I will not sit here and whimper."

I stood back as she turned, sweeping her responsibilities before her, seeming for the first time in her life to relish a fight.

"We need to swing the balance of opinion back to us, and to do so quickly. We need followers – men of influence. Who are the most powerful men left who have not already defected?"

Frightened eyes flashed quickly around the room; they were not used to this Jane.

"Norfolk is the most senior Duke, but imprisoned here in the Tower," I said, uncertainly.

"Bring me paper and my seal. I shall write to him this very morning, offering to release and pardon him if he will make public his support for me."

Mrs Tilney ran to find writing materials and the great seal.

"Bring me Bishop Ridley. I am determined his sermon will go ahead this Sunday. We must maintain our reforms of the Church at all costs."

Mrs Jacob called for a messenger, to find the Bishop and bring him here at the Queen's pleasure, this afternoon.

Queen Jane continued in this fashion for a number of hours, her fear galvanized into energetic activity, although how effective most of it was, I was unsure. Certainly the letter to Norfolk was delivered within the hour, but he, a known staunch Catholic, chose to ignore it, and no reply was received.

One effect of the Queen's outburst was to shame her father back into activity, and by the end of the day he had prepared proclamations in her name, ready for issuing in the morning before the first church services, stressing the merits of her title and calling for the preservation of the crown "out of the dominion of strangers and papists".

We took to our beds early and in poor spirits that night. All night there were sounds of shouting and cheering from the city and we awoke early the next morning thick-headed from lack of sleep and heavy-hearted at what the day would bring.

We spent most of Saturday waiting, and it was nearly midnight when Northumberland's messenger finally arrived, calling urgently for the reinforcements which the Council had promised would follow him. The Council duly gathered after midnight, but their hearts were not in it and their reply to the Duke was described by one of them as a 'slender answer'. By now it was every man for himself, and if any capacity existed for helping others, Northumberland's name was unlikely to be on the list of priorities.

இ ௸

By Sunday 16th July, the news, if anything, was worse. Overnight a placard had been nailed to a church door in Queenhithe, stating that Mary had been proclaimed Queen everywhere except in London, whilst word reached London and the Tower to the effect that Mary's army had now grown to 30,000 men and there was widespread support for her.

In the morning William Paulet, Marquess of Winchester, was nowhere to be found and it was believed he had gone to his house in London. Distrusting his loyalty (even more than some of the others) Suffolk sent for him to return to the Tower immediately and to attend upon the Queen, which he eventually did just before midnight.

After dinner, Suffolk had begun to search for Pembroke, in order to discuss some urgent business, but once again, could not find him anywhere. Eventually a guard admitted he thought he had seen the Earl leave the Tower an hour earlier and had not seen him return. The Queen, now seriously concerned and not a little angry, sent armed guards to bring him back, and, in order to avoid

341

any more defectors, Suffolk ordered the Tower locked. Hearing of this, and not trusting her father any more than any of the others, the Queen ordered the keys to be brought to her personally.

She summoned the Captain of the Guard and asked him, "Captain, what have you there?"

The captain, slightly bemused, held up the ring of keys and said, "The keys your Grace."

"Whose keys are they?" asked the Queen pointedly.

The Captain, who was not stupid, understood immediately and held them forward. "Your keys, your Grace – the Queen's keys."

The Queen took them with a nod and ordered that the Tower would be unlocked again in the morning and the guard would collect the keys from her rooms at fifteen minutes before seven o'clock and not before.

Monday and Tuesday remained strangely quiet. Most of the Council had by now succeeded in creeping away by one means or another, the final excuse being the need to wait on the French ambassador in order to procure his support and help. Only Suffolk, Cranmer and Cheke remained and the atmosphere in the Tower changed from that of a fortress to that of a prison.

On the morning of Wednesday 19th July, it was clear that something had to happen. The atmosphere in the royal apartments had become stifling. The Queen and our group of her immediate followers were in the royal apartments, but regularly visited by Suffolk and Guilford, both of whose earlier preoccupation with the affairs of the Council had now ended, as there was no one left to preside over. They spent most of their time arguing with each other, fretting over what the Council were discussing in their absence, at their meetings which were known to be taking place at Baynard's Castle, under the leadership of Pembroke. They finally came to the conclusion that everyone outside the Tower had now defected to Princess Mary, and unless Northumberland pulled off a military miracle, all was lost. But since they had no allies outside the Tower, and nowhere to go in their absence, there was nothing to do but wait. With every inactive hour that passed, they became more despondent, and with no one else to vent their frustration against, they spent most of their time arguing with each other. I decided to keep well out of their way and to concentrate my attention on giving Jane what support I could.

Next door to us, in the state apartments, the two Duchesses similarly circled each other. The Duchess of Northumberland had always considered herself to be superior to Lady Suffolk, whilst Lady Frances, with her royal blood, apparently considered Lady Northumberland an upstart and rude to boot. As each day passed, it became clearer and clearer that these two proud women realized they had backed the losing side. It was an insufficient basis for a relationship between them and the atmosphere in the apartments was vibrant with a combination of resentment, hatred and fear.

There was a small diversion in the mid-morning, when Mrs Underhill, whose husband was a Tower warder related to the Throckmortons, gave birth to a son. Edward Underhill asked the Queen if she would stand as sponsor to the child in his christening, which was to take place later that day. Jane agreed and the Underhills asked for, and received, her permission to name the boy Guilford.

Sitting in the outer room and listening to the conversation, I smirked. If only they knew how much dear Jane hated that name and how thin a spider's web now held her to the throne of state. I hoped that little baby Guilford would not rise so high, or have as far to fall when the time came. Somehow, it did not seem that we would have much longer to wait now.

ବୈ CHAPTER 61 ଈଔ

19th July 1553 — Royal Apartments, Tower of London

"What do you mean I cannot leave these rooms? I am to attend a christening in the chapel yonder."

Queen Jane was indignant. "Richard, please tell this guard who I am and that I am to be given leave to pass this instance. The Underhills will be waiting."

I opened the door to the apartments and spoke to the guard, who stood nervous but adamant that he had his orders, and that Queen Jane was not to leave.

"Does that apply to all of us?" I asked, in as friendly a fashion as I could.

The guard looked uncertain. "I was only told that the Queen was not to leave here, sir. I have no orders for the rest of you."

I thanked him and returned to the Queen. "It appears the guards have orders only for you, your Grace."

Queen Jane nodded, bewildered. "Lady Throckmorton, I wonder if you would be so kind as to act as my proxy at the christening of the Underhill child? It appears I am unable to attend."

Lady Throckmorton, made Lady in Waiting when Jane was made Queen, in recognition of her family's loyalty to Northumberland, dipped a curtsey and left. Queen Jane watched her go, a look of sadness on her face. "She has been a good friend ever since I lived with Catherine Parr," she murmured to herself. "I hope this affair does her no harm."

For a while the room went quiet, but Queen Jane was not by nature one to be downcast.

"If we cannot attend on Mrs Underhill, we might as well attend on our supper," she suggested a little later, trying to maintain a degree of levity.

Having said grace, we began to eat in silence. Although the windows were all open, to let in as much fresh air as was available on a humid July evening, everything was strangely quiet. The Tower, normally humming with activity, seemed empty. Inside the apartment the atmosphere was tense and no one spoke. For ten minutes we picked at our food, trying to maintain the pretence of normality, but in truth nothing had been normal since Lady Jane had been brought to the Tower and proclaimed Queen.

"What is that?"

Queen Jane cocked her head and we all listened. The sound of cheering could be heard coming through the window from the city, outside the Tower walls. It grew louder and we went to the window to listen.

"It sounds as if a great crowd is rejoicing your Grace," said Nurse Ellen, nervously. "Pray God we are saved and that Princess Mary is defeated and captured."

Queen Jane looked at her sadly, then flicked her eyes across at me, seeking confirmation. "I fear the opposite is more likely Ellen. I believe the nightmare may be coming to an end and swiftly at that," she said.

As if to confirm her words, the door burst open and Suffolk appeared, eyes wild with fear.

"You are no longer Queen," he blurted out to Jane and began, himself, to tear down the canopy of estate. "You must put off your royal robes and be content with a private life!" he shouted, his voice sounding strangely excited in his nervousness.

Jane put down her knife and, calmly pushing her platter away from her, rose from the supper table. "That I will gladly," she replied, "for you know I did not seek either the position or its attendant fripperies. I much more willingly put them off than I put them on. A private life, in quiet and contemplation, is all I have ever asked for, and if I may return to that now, I thank God for it."

She walked across the room and stood before her father, who twitched and shook in nervous excitement. In contrast, Lady Jane was calm, almost relaxed.

"Out of obedience to you and my mother, I have grievously sinned. Now I willingly relinquish the crown. May I now go home?"

Suffolk stared at his daughter, seemingly traumatized with fear. He opened his mouth, but no words emerged. His wild eyes swept round the room, as if for one final time, then he left as abruptly as he had entered, with no farewells or goodbyes.

No sooner had he left the royal apartments than a troop of guards arrived. "My Lady," the Captain of the Guard addressed his words to Lady Jane, "we are instructed to escort you from this place to the Deputy Lieutenant's House, for your own comfort and safety."

Calmly, Jane cast her eyes round the room as if to remember a place visited, to which she would not return, and she followed the captain. Lady Tilney and Nurse Ellen followed, but Lady Jacob was absent from the room. She would, no doubt, find her way later, I thought, as I brought up the rear of the party, the ladies crying, in contrast to Lady Jane, who, in her customary fashion, held her head up and walked confident and dry eyed, down the steps behind the relieved captain.

"Where are my husband and my mother?" asked Lady Jane as we crossed the cobbles towards our new place of imprisonment. The captain slowed to walk beside her, confident now that he would not have a group of screaming women trying to quit his command and escape from the Tower. "I believe they remain in the White Tower my Lady," he replied.

"Are we prisoners?" asked Jane.

"Only you are under my protection my Lady, I have no orders regarding them," he replied, in carefully measured tones.

๛   ๛

The following morning, our quiet contemplation was disturbed by the Marquess of Winchester, who demanded the return of all the jewels "and other stuff" which he said Lady Jane had falsely purloined from the Crown, under pretence of being the Queen.

"Please seek what you will my Lord," replied Jane, shrugging her shoulders. "As you see we have brought with us only the most basic of clothing and possessions to this small house. All the royal frippery you require remains in its rightful place in the royal apartments."

Winchester insisted on going through the wardrobes in our rooms in the Deputy Lieutenant's house and picking over the ownership of one item after another, but if his charade was intended to belittle Lady Jane, it failed entirely, for she merely repeated her instruction to "take what you will".

Watching her, I thought I understood. They had forced these things upon her and she had accepted them unwillingly. Now they wanted to make a play of taking them back, but in so doing they could not reach her. She had withdrawn again into her own world, and if I understood her at all, she would never again be dragged from it by her parents, her husband, her gaolers or her future Queen. In God had she put her trust and in God it would remain. She was invincible, untouchable and for most of them, unreachable.

I hoped, however, for my own sake as well as hers, that she still might open the door to me, for somehow I felt she might need me before, as she dreamed, she was "allowed home." In this matter, I felt, as in so many recently, we were not dealing with honourable men.

☙ CHAPTER 62 ❧

28th July 1553 – Gentleman Gaoler's House, Tower of London

"Mistress Partridge, you have made us feel most at home here and I thank you for your kindness."

The Gentleman gaoler's wife bobbed her head – nobody was clear nowadays how to treat Lady Jane, but Mistress Partridge's natural good manners and kind spirit had prevailed and the atmosphere in the house since we had been moved there across the Tower Green a few days previously was more like that of a family home than a gaol.

Since our arrival, we had established a comfortable routine. Jane was seated in the place of honour, at the end of the table, with me at her left elbow and Nurse Ellen and Lady Throckmorton to her right. Mrs Jacob sat next to me, with Mrs Partridge next to her, and Mr Partridge sat next to his wife, at the other end of the table, opposite Jane. To the casual observer, we might just as well have been a happy country family enjoying Sunday dinner together.

The house, unlike the majority of the massive old stone fortresses in the Tower of London precinct, was a newly built two-storey Tudor house, half timbered, with fine open windows, and the upper floor overhanging the lower by some three feet.

347

It was on the north side of the Tower, to the left after entering the main gate and past the Beauchamp Tower, hard under the wall itself, overlooking a large courtyard just below Tower Green. It was one of a small row, catching what sun found its way inside the Tower walls. Into this 'family' environment, the news was filtering day by day. Some of it lifted our spirits, only for them to be dashed by other news hours or days later.

Soon after our arrival, we had been shocked to hear confirmation that London had declared for Princess Mary and we had officially become prisoners. Meanwhile Jane's parents had quietly slipped away from the Tower and were said to be in Sheen, although nobody seemed very sure.

Outside the Tower, it was said that Pembroke, too, had declared himself for Queen Mary, showering the crowd outside Baynard's Castle with gold coins. Immediately afterwards he had declared his son's marriage to Lady Catherine 'annulled before consummated' and she had been thrown out onto the streets, to find her own way to Sheen alone.

I hoped in all the upset and confusion she had kept her wits about her enough to walk the couple of miles from Baynard's Castle to London Bridge and across to Suffolk Place. No doubt the servants there would have helped her and, if Edmund had been resident, he would certainly have organized horses and protection for the journey to Sheen. I assumed she had successfully completed the journey, and was desperate to visit her there and see if she was alright, but my responsibility was to Lady Jane now and here in the Tower I must stay.

The changes were affecting everybody. Two days previously, we had heard that the Duchess of Northumberland had been released, and had left the Tower to pay a courtesy visit to Princess Mary, who was understood to have slowed her travels toward London and was still at Newhall. Jane had reminded me that she herself had somewhat blotted her copybook during her last visit to Newhall, but was confident that Princess Mary would not hold her remarks in the chapel against her so long after the event. She had, after all, showered expensive presents on Jane on many occasions, although, as I reminded her, not since the argument in the chapel and Lord Henry's subsequent visit to apologize. Now all we could do was wait and see.

Guilford Dudley had not been as fortunate as Jane and had been moved to the Beauchamp Tower immediately to our right. Here, he had been joined the previous day by his elder brother Robert, who had been brought from the prisoners camp in Cambridge.

Now came more worrying news: the Duke of Suffolk had been arrested at Sheen, where he was with Mary and Catherine, awaiting the return of Lady Frances, who had gone to Newhall, petitioning for an audience with the Queen, no doubt to remind her of their longstanding friendship. It was said that Suffolk was to be brought back to the Tower this very afternoon.

I found it very hard to see any clear pattern in all this to-ing and fro-ing. It appeared that no one, including the new Queen to be, had any idea who they could trust, and everyone was making up the rules as they went along. Under these circumstances, it was almost impossible to guess what the eventual future might hold. One thing my instincts and recent months' experiences told me was that everyone outside the Tower would be ducking and diving like feeding water birds, and their priority would in every case be to save themselves. It was unlikely, I thought, that any of them out there would be thinking of Jane or the rest of us incarcerated here in the Tower.

Jane must have been having the same thoughts. While the others were walking in the Tower grounds (after discussion with our guards, it had emerged that only she was house-bound) she took me on one side and began to talk earnestly.

"I believe we are here for a long time Richard. There is such confusion that I cannot see any clear resolution in the short term. No one will have the courage to make decisions on the Queen's behalf and she will be so overcome by the enormity of what she faces that she will proceed slowly and with infinite caution. That being the case, I cannot hold you here indefinitely. You are free to go if you want to, for what can I offer you now?"

The idea was unthinkable. I felt so sorry for her, I crossed the room and instinctively took her in my arms, pulling her close to me. She did not resist, but clung there, like a young bird put inside my shirt to keep warm. Only once had I been this close to her before. As before, she was so slender, so small, that I wondered where, in this tiny frame, that steely toughness was hidden. Yet holding her now, so slight she could become lost in the folds of my shirt, feeling her tremble beside me, I understood how brittle was that strength, and how easily the shell of toughness could be broken.

I found myself stroking the top of her head, putting my face down into her hair to nuzzle the smell of her. For the first time I thought of her as a woman, but the thought as it came made me check and begin to pull back. I must not think of her like this; Catherine was my love and Jane had made it clear on so many occasions that she rejected the advances of men and was disgusted by them. The last thing I wanted to do was to incur her disgust, and I began to release her before she rejected me.

But she didn't reject me. On the contrary, she clung to me tightly, so that I could feel her heart beating. "Don't let me go Richard. Hold me for just a moment. I feel so safe here. Oh how I wish my father had held me like this when I was a child. I longed for him to do so, but he never did. All my life I have wanted my father to love me, to be proud of me and to hold me like this. Instead I felt I was a disappointment, rejected for not being the son he so desperately wanted after losing the firstborn. Then, to make matters worse, I couldn't even play the role of a son. I hated hunting, fishing, horses, fighting, jousting and all men's games. I loved books and music and quiet and my religion."

She pulled away from me, tears running down her face, then looked up at me, as I bent to sooth her. "I wasn't much of a son was I?" she sniffled.

I bent further, until my face was level with hers. Gently I kissed her on the nose. "No, how could you be? But you were a perfect daughter. It's just that he couldn't see it."

She pulled herself back into my arms and drew them around

her. "Oh Richard. Please stay with me, at least for the next week or two. I need my 'gentle giant' to protect me. I don't find all this at all easy and I must admit, I am frightened."

I hugged her as gently as I could, afraid of squeezing the breath out of her. "Don't be afraid Jane. I will be here. I will remain here until all this is resolved. That's a promise."

Slowly she unfolded from my arms and stood back, facing me.

"Thank you Richard. I am so grateful. You don't know how much it means to have you beside me as a constant and honest companion. But please remember, I shall not hold you to a promise you may live to regret. Any time you want to leave, you must do so and I shall understand. But until you do, I shall be grateful for every day of your support and companionship."

The door below banged. The others were returning. She pulled me forward and kissed me on the lips.

"We must go down."

❧ CHAPTER 63 ☙

5th August 1553 – Tower of London

It was early in the morning and, as usual, I was awake. The note was close at hand; quietly, I opened it and read it again.

How many twists and turns was this story to take?

Dear Richard,

In view of the many honest conversations we have had in the past and your friendly understanding and acceptance of my little difference, I felt I must write to you to tell you what has been happening here at Sheen.

Lord Henry and Lady Frances arrived here on 21st July with Lady Mary, a day after Lady Catherine, who was distraught at being rejected by her husband, whom she had grown very fond of during their short marriage.

Lady Frances left again almost immediately in order to

351

seek an audience with the Queen at Newhall. Just before she returned, Lord Henry was arrested and, I understand, taken to the Tower. I don't know whether you were able to see him? I imagine under present conditions, everyone is carefully kept apart to avoid conspiracies, or attempts to escape. It seems that her Ladyship was successful with the new Queen, for Suffolk was released again after three days and returned here, much relieved.

Imagine his shock when he arrived back here to find Lady Frances in bed with Adrian Stokes. Their intimacy has grown more – what shall I say? – more urgent these last days, and Lord Henry's arrival could not have been worse timed. How the world has changed! In the past (and this has happened many times before) his Lordship would have created a great row and shouted at her. Not this time. To my embarrassment, he simply cried and left the room.

I think he is missing your support and companionship Richard. You know he finds the affairs of state more difficult than he admits in public, and since Northumberland was arrested and taken to the Tower with his sons last week, our master appears to feel alone and lost. Needless to say, he is isolated from the rest of the Council, who protect themselves by emphasizing his association with Northumberland. Judge, therefore, the effect of returning home from such a situation, and finding yourself rejected by your wife and your servant also.

I think of you often, and our sweet Lady Jane, when occasional news of the Tower reaches us here in Sheen, and hope you are able to survive in a degree of comfort. Please remember me to Lady Jane. She is a fine lady and people should not speak of her as they do in the market or the alehouse. I do not believe she ever sought the crown, or even wished it.

Each night I go to bed with a heavy heart, thinking about the future, but all we can do is soldier on and do our best. Should you be released from the Tower and need help, do not fail to contact me, either here or at Suffolk Place or Dorset House. Your horses, saddles and other bits and pieces (but not your sword and dagger which I assume you

took to the Tower with you) are safe at Suffolk Place and I
shall look after them for you until I hear from you or my
master gives me other instructions. However, at the
moment he seems too preoccupied with his own affairs to
worry about the cost of looking after a few of your
possessions, and anyway he can afford it.

I hope you occasionally think of me in your quieter
moments.

Edmund Tucker

I had no idea how Celestial Edmund had got this letter to me,
but I was grateful. Now I appreciated a little more how my support might be helping Jane, for the knowledge that Edmund was
there and willing to help me, was a real comfort to me in these
difficult times.

Try as I might, I could not bring myself to feel sorry for Lord
Henry. Not after what he had done to his daughter. The man was
inadequate as a person, and I had lost any respect I had had for
him. It had been a shock when Suffolk was arrested and brought
to the Tower, and a blessed relief when he was released again
three days later. A surprise, too, with Northumberland still next
door in the Beauchamp Tower with his sons, and expecting to
be tried and executed any day now. I felt sick to realize how
close I had been to so many of these men, who were now fighting for their lives. If Queen Mary gave as much thought to them
as they, in pursuit of power and influence, had given to others,
she would execute them tomorrow.

But the signs were the other way. Dishonourable men seemed
to have a way of surviving.

Queen Mary's arrival at the Tower two days before had been
quite a ceremony. The atmosphere in the Tower had been fairly
relaxed, only the most important political prisoners being kept
in their cells. Sadly, Jane was considered one of them. I was not
considered by the guards to be under house arrest and had been
allowed to walk across to the main gates and to witness the
Queen's arrival.

It had been an affair of some pomp and ceremony. She had entered the Tower to a salute of guns, with an oration from a hundred children before she entered the gates. No one was left in any doubt about her position as rightful Queen, and she rode in a dress of purple velvet and satin, covered with gold and jewels, and a thick gold chain of office around her neck. Even her horse was covered in embroidered cloth of gold.

Before her had ridden the Earl of Arundel, pleased to demonstrate his support for the new Queen by carrying the sword of state, with a thousand men and women in velvet coats. Behind her had ridden Sir Anthony Browne as train-bearer, followed by all the names necessary to confirm her position: Princess Elizabeth, Anne of Cleves (a surviving wife of Henry VIII), the Duchess of Norfolk and the Marchioness of Exeter.

But the event we all remembered had been the affair of the prisoners, for Mary had been met on the lawn in front of the main gate by four prisoners of her father or brother: Stephen Gardiner, Bishop of Winchester; Thomas Howard, the eighty-year-old Duke of Norfolk; the Duchess of Somerset; and Edward Courtenay, the last of the Plantagenets, who had spent more than half of his twenty-seven years in this royal prison.

Each, in turn, had knelt to ask her forgiveness. "These are my prisoners," she had announced to the guards. "Set them free." The Queen had then dismounted and embraced each of them, before giving them their freedom. Gardiner was made a Councillor on the spot and Norfolk was told the attainder against him by Henry VIII would be reversed. Knowing that he had at one time been the most powerful Duke in England, I wondered just how many other lives and livelihoods would be turned upside down by that one easily announced decision.

As I had walked back to Partridge's house, I had tried to decide what I could report to Jane. Finally, I chose to emphasize the new Queen's apparent compassion for prisoners whose main crime was to be facing in the wrong direction when the political wind had changed.

Now I lay in bed wondering how much my words had influenced Jane, for today she planned to write a long letter to the Queen, begging her forgiveness and her pardon. I had better rouse myself, I thought, for this could, literally, be the letter of a lifetime and she might need my moral support. One thing was certain, however, she would not need my assistance in writing the letter itself.

❧ CHAPTER 64 ❧

23rd August 1553 – Tower Hill

At nine o'clock on the morning of the 23rd August, the mood in the house was sombre, as Northumberland was taken from the Beauchamp Tower and led across Tower Green, directly in front of us, to the chapel of St Peter Ad Vincula for a final Mass, prior to his execution.

They said his trial had been a show event, and had taken place at Westminster Hall five days earlier. When the news had come, it was as expected: Northumberland had been found guilty and given the usual two days before his execution. Apparently, however, he had tried to recant and obtained a delay of execution for a further three days to make his peace with God, and this had finally been granted.

As a result, the previous morning he had attended a full Mass in St Peter Ad Vincula, together with the Marquess of Northampton, William Parr, his son Andrew Dudley, Henry Gates and Thomas Palmer, his prime co-conspirators.

Mrs Partridge had attended the service, as she explained to Lady Jane, "in the role of observer only", and had reported that Northumberland had made a full and seemingly genuine conversion back to the Catholic faith of his childhood. Not surprisingly, the service, also, had been a show affair, for it gave an unexpected opportunity for a political statement on behalf of Queen Mary, with the elevation of the Host, pax giving, blessing, crossing, and "all the other rights and accidents of the old church", as Mrs Partridge had described them.

"The Duke made a full conversion," she said. "He even made a speech to the congregation, saying 'My masters, I let you all to understand that I do most faithfully believe this is the very right and true way, out of the which true religion you and I have been seduced these sixteen years past, by the false and erroneous preachings of the new preachers. And I do believe the holy sacrament here most assuredly to be our Saviour and Redeemer Jesus Christ; and this I pray you all to testify and pray for me.'"

Jane had given Mrs Partridge a withering look. "I trust you were not taken in by these rantings?" she had hissed.

Mrs Partridge had gone pale and bobbed a nervous curtsey, replying, "Of course not my Lady, I just repeated what the accused said."

Jane had watched the rest of the party return from the service, as Mrs Partridge finished her description, and was disgusted. "I pray God that I, nor no friend of mine, die so," she said, and turned away from the window.

❧ ❧

Now, the following morning, the time had finally come and Northumberland was to meet his end as befitted an unpopular commoner, on Tower Hill, just outside the Tower walls, and in front of a crowd reputed to be 10,000 strong, with every man and woman amongst them fully convinced of his guilt.

Perhaps to make a point, the Queen had eased the restrictions on Jane's movements and now she was allowed to walk in the Tower grounds and along many parts of the Tower walls. At first she said she would remain indoors while the execution took place, but after watching Northumberland walk to the chapel, she had announced that she would walk on the walls, "just to see the crowd".

We climbed the steep steps just at the side of the Gaoler's House, and reached the wall part way between the Beauchamp Tower (where Northumberland and his sons had been held, including Guilford) and the Deveraux Tower. The permanent scaffold on Tower Hill was a good arrow shot away from us, but the crowd was truly enormous and reached right back to the moat below the walls of the Tower itself. We stood close to the Beauchamp Tower, but to one side, so that, by turning, we could look down on Tower Hill beyond the walls or to Tower Green within them.

Jane drew a hood over her head, so that she would not be recognized, as below us, Northumberland, Gates and Palmer with their escorting party came out from the Chapel and walked, seemingly in circles, on Tower Green. Northumberland could be seen talking to Lord Hertford and his brother. He seemed to be asking for their forgiveness – perhaps for his part in their father Somerset's death – and they appeared to give him their blessing.

"What are they doing?" asked Jane. It seemed, for a moment, that they were waiting for a reprieve, and that the crowd outside would be denied their spectacle. But it was not the case.

"They are waiting for the due time, my Lady," explained Partridge, "The execution is arranged for ten o'clock, and no doubt the Duke prefers to remain here until the last minute, rather than spend more time than is necessary in front of that crowd. I am sure I can hear them, even from down there."

Jane shivered at the thought. "Do you want to go down my Lady?" asked Mrs Tilney, who also seemed uncomfortable with the whole thing.

Jane shook her head. "We cannot now," she pointed out, for their only way back to the Gaoler's House was by the steps we had ascended and that would take us onto Tower Green and right past the condemned men.

Northumberland walked toward Sir John Gates and they spoke together, gravely, for two minutes. Then they bowed to each other, notably refraining from shaking hands, and Northumberland followed the guards through the gate of the Tower, slowly climbing the slope of Tower Hill ahead of them.

The crowd was in angry mood, clearly blaming Northumberland for Somerset's death and surging forward against the halberdiers to get at him. He climbed the scaffold and stood, making his last speech to the murmuring crowd. From where we stood, we could not hear what he was saying for the baying of the crowd. Finally, Northumberland removed his surcoat of pale grey damask and handed it to the executioner, who limped forward in his white apron. The Duke could be seen to pay the traditional fee to the executioner, and to receive the blindfold. He took the one step forward and knelt before the block, feeling for it with his hands.

There was a gasp from the crowd as the bandage slipped and Northumberland, confused, had to stand and have it re-tied. Then his courage, which up to that point had been exemplary, seemed to fail him. He cried out a confused mixture of Hail Mary and the Lord's Prayer, half kneeling before the block, then, decisively, put his head down and clapped his hands. The axeman struck him with one terrible blow and his head fell, spurting blood, into the straw-filled basket below the block.

I looked at Jane as the moment came. I had expected her to turn away, but like me, she was drawn by the terrible fascination and horror of the occasion, and was watching, her hands to her face. As the axe fell, I could feel her stiffen and her sharp intake of breath made a small whimper of sound. I stepped across to her and raised a protective arm, and she turned into it, burying her head in my chest and letting out a long moan.

"It's barbaric," she whispered hoarsely into my chest. I held her there, letting my body shield her from the cheering of the crowd below.

"He did great harm to many people my Lady, not least to yourself, and tried, and very nearly succeeded, in stealing the crown and the country, first from the King and then from his successor."

She raised her head, eyes red with shock. "I know. He deserved it. I hated that man like no other in the country. It's not me I am appalled for, it's the others, Gates and Palmer, having to stand on the scaffold and watch him, knowing their turn will follow."

I looked across at the ladies, all of whom seemed equally affected by the sight below, and equally unwilling to watch two more executions. "Come ladies, let's inside. This is no place for us here."

Slowly, I led Jane down the steps and beside Tower Green, where the dead man and his soon-to-be-dead companions had been walking only minutes before. Already it felt as if Northumberland's ghost was watching us. I shivered and led the ladies into the house. *God willing*, I thought to myself, *the Queen will be more merciful and forgiving to the innocent Jane than she has been to the true source of all our problems.*

❧ CHAPTER 65 ❧

29th August 1553 – Tower of London

Less than a week later we knew. On the morning of the 29th of August the Queen's response was made clear and it was with lighter hearts that we welcomed a gentleman visitor that day.

Rowland Lea, an official of the Royal Mint, who lived in the Tower, was a close friend of Master Partridge and had been invited by him to dinner. He was good company: educated, thoughtful, and knowledgeable of what was going on in the world, whilst sensitive to our situation as prisoners of the Queen. Tactfully, he asked Jane of our position, which he understood had now been clarified.

"Indeed so, sir, and kindly. I remain here as the guest of Master Partridge and his good wife, who make us more than comfortable. The Queen has promised me life and liberty, but has explained that it will be necessary in the interests of the people, and for the guidance of others, to keep me (and my husband) here in the Tower until a formal trial can be held. My husband remains in the Beauchamp Tower and at present I am unable to speak with him, although I do have considerable freedom to walk in the grounds and gardens. I am allowed to keep my four trusted servants and both they and I have an allowance from the Queen, with which to ensure that Mistress Partridge is properly rewarded for her daily kindness."

The Partridges beamed their support for the arrangement. In truth, Mistress Partridge, having no children, was pleased to have Lady Jane as a surrogate daughter, and fussed after her as much as the competing attentions of Mrs Tilney, Nurse Ellen and Mrs Jacob would allow.

"Do you want for anything my Lady?" asked Rowland kindly.

"Not that I can think of, thank you sir," replied Jane. "I have my books and can buy all the writing materials I require. Richard is allowed to leave the Tower during the daytime and can acquire all that I, or we, need." She turned to me.

"I believe Edmund Tucker is sometimes able to help you Richard?"

I inclined my head in agreement. "Indeed, my Lady. When he is at Suffolk Place he is most helpful, but he is spending much of his time at Sheen these days."

Lady Jane lifted her glass of wine. "Sheen. How I look forward to returning there – and, hopefully, to Bradgate before this summer is out. The air in the Tower here has given me a new enthusiasm for the countryside."

We all drank a toast to the countryside and its merits, then Rowland returned to his concerns.

"How do you spend your time here my Lady?"

Lady Jane looked at me, as if searching for a reply. "In reading, in studying, in debating and in teaching. Richard here is learning Italian and I am writing a denunciation of a fallen priest."

Rowland Lea raised an inquisitive eyebrow.

"Dr Harding. Formerly our Chaplain at Bradgate and my tutor. He has fallen by the wayside and reverted to the Catholic faith. A cowardly runaway, a deformed imp of the devil indeed."

Rowland raised an eyebrow. "There are many now doing so, Lady, for their own protection."

Jane looked at him, eyes narrowing. "What need of protection? I pray you, have we Mass in London now?"

Rowland nodded. "Aye Lady, in some places."

Jane sniffed gently. "It may be so," she said, "for it is not so strange as the sudden conversion of the late Duke – for who would have thought he would have so done?"

"Perchance he thereby hoped to have had his pardon?" suggested Rowland, carefully. He regretted it as soon as the words were uttered.

"Pardon?" replied Jane. "Woe worth him! He hath brought me and my stock in most miserable calamity and misery by his exceeding ambition. But for the answering that he hoped for his life by his turning, though other men be of that opinion, I utterly am not – for what man is there living, I pray you, although he had been innocent, that would hope of life in that case, being in the field against the Queen in person as General, and after his being so hated and evil spoken by the Commons? And at his coming into prison, so mistreated as the like was never heard in any man's time? Who was judge that he should hope for pardon, whose life was odious to all men? But what will ye more? Life as his life was wicked and full of dissimulation, so was his end thereafter."

Rowland Lea leaned forward as if to reply, but Jane was in full flood and continued.

"Should I, who am young, and in my few years, forsake my faith for the love of life? Nay, God forbid! Much more he should not, whose fatal course, although he had lived his just number of years, could not have long continued."

Rowland leaned forward, as if to reply. Seeing Jane's mood, I tried to dissuade him, for at times her conviction was such, there was no arguing with her, but Rowland ploughed on, regardless.

"I believe only, Lady, that he wished for his life and sought to save it."

"But life was sweet, it appeared, so he might have lived you will say, but he did not care how," Jane seethed. "Indeed the reason is good for he that would have lived in chains to have had his life, belike would leave no other means attempted."

Realizing that the room had fallen into a passive quiet in the face of this onslaught, Jane eased back in her chair and turned to me.

361

"But God be merciful to us. For He sayeth, 'Who so denyeth Me before men, I will not know him in my Father's Kingdom.'"

The ladies nodded in agreement, crossing themselves. Rowland looked across the table at me, hoping for some indication of what lay behind these strong words, but I (who had heard a lot more, and a lot worse, on this subject) gave him a long dead look as if to indicate that this was not a path to be pursued lightly. This time, he read the signal correctly and rapidly changed the subject.

"We shall have further excitement ere the week is out, my Lady. Queen Mary having taken up residence here two days ago, I am informed we can expect her coronation on the 1st of October. The Tower will soon be full again, with competing voices."

I looked across the table at Jane. I hoped the Queen's coronation would signal the end of this interregnum and that life proper could be resumed, including Lady Jane's release from the Tower. If that did happen, where would she go? With her husband, or was that enforced relationship to be seen as the sham it was, its validity having died with Northumberland? If not, where? And in any event, what would happen to me once we escaped this place?

Somehow I felt some more dramatic changes were coming soon. I just hoped the recent favourable trend would continue – for all of us.

❧ CHAPTER 66 ❧

1st October 1553 – Tower of London

The excitements had indeed begun. The following day, Queen Mary went in formal procession from the Tower through the streets of London. Lady Jane and her small party were "advised" to remain inside as the procession was being gathered together in the Tower grounds ("for fear of danger to your goodselves") but I managed to get onto the walls to see the party leave and turn into the city streets.

At the head of the party were all the newly elevated:

Courtenay, Gardiner, Winchester, Norfolk and Oxford, the latter bearing the sword of office. They were accompanied by the newly appointed Knights of the Bath, and the Lord Mayor and Aldermen of London.

Queen Mary rode in a chariot, wearing blue velvet and ermine, with a tinsel and pearl headdress which looked as if it would roll off her head long before she got to Whitehall. Behind her I could see Princess Elizabeth and Anne of Cleves in a second chariot followed by over forty gentlewomen, walking in procession.

Judging by the cheering I could hear as the procession made its way through the city, Mary's popularity had, if anything, increased and it was clear that the coronation procession the following day was going to be a huge celebration. I was disappointed I could not attend and made my way back to Lady Jane to see what her reaction was.

"Richard you cannot know with what comfort I hear the rightful Queen of England process through her great city of London toward her coronation. You know that Northumberland threatened that occasion for me and my husband, and although I may have relished the prospect, you of all people, know how strongly I did not want that final step to happen, for that would have sealed an agreement between myself and the will of God that I be Queen, and I never wanted that, not ever."

"I am sorry you cannot attend the coronation in your true right, my Lady, representing the Suffolk family," I replied, "particularly as your sister Catherine is to attend."

Jane smiled at my naivety. "Come Richard, you should know by now the reality of politics. It would be an impossible show of weakness for the Queen to allow me to show my face on that, her day. Enough that she enjoy it, as I am sure she will, and that the dust be allowed to settle. Our time will come, but first she has to establish her own position."

She looked at me wistfully across the room.

"What a strange, unexpected and frightening year this has been. Tomorrow is the 1st of October and in a week it will be my 16th birthday. Sometimes, when I was younger, I used to dream that I might be Queen of England, hanging onto the arm of my cousin King Edward. It was my parents' dream for many years and I believe they may have been close to achieving it on occasions. On more than one occasion I was aware of the King looking at me with an appraising eye, like a Leicestershire horse dealer. But it seems in the end he did not find me suitable."

I crossed the room and held her hands in mine.

"I cannot believe that my Lady. The King had not yet chosen and had he survived I think he might still have chosen you, had your own marriage not intervened. And if not, I believe it would have been the need for foreign alliances and affairs of state which made the decision for him, and not any question of your suitability."

She shrugged her shoulders. "Now we shall never know. I have had my closeness to power and authority. From now on I shall be satisfied with quiet, and my learning."

She let go of my hand and skipped across the room, looking happy for the first day in many weeks. For a brief moment I imagined myself looking after her in a small country house, as she concentrated on her studies and I ensured her life remained safe, untroubled and calm. Then I brought myself up with a jolt. *What are you thinking of? Only a few weeks ago she was Queen of England and now you are day-dreaming about keeping her safe in a little country house.* I remembered Catherine's remark, that Shute House was the very smallest house she would ever consider living in; Shute House that still represented an aspiration far in excess of my wildest prospects.

I looked at her and smiled. "I hope so my Lady. I think it might suit you, given time to adjust."

❧   ❦

The following evening we received our description of the Queen's coronation from Rowland Lea, who returned to the Tower somewhat exhausted after a long but enjoyable day, and made a special effort to visit us before the dusk curfew.

"Westminster Abbey was entirely floored in blue cloth, my Lady, and the Queen wore a purple robe, as befits a Queen (although I must admit privately, the colours did clash horribly). Princess Elizabeth wore a scarlet and ermine mantle over a white gown, embroidered with silver, and carried the Queen's train. Close behind her were Anne of Cleves and your sister Catherine. She looked very beautiful in red velvet."

Jane put her head on one side, thoughtfully, and smiled. "Catherine loves red; the brighter the better." I nodded my agreement, remembering occasions from the past.

"We began in Westminster Abbey at ten in the morning and finished at five in the evening, before retiring for a banquet in Westminster Hall," went on Rowland. "I can tell you, the Queen was staggering beneath her huge coronet, but she managed it, to the end."

"Pride makes the strongest of muscles," murmured Lady Jane smiling.

"While we ate, Derby, Norfolk and Arundel rode round the Hall on their chargers, organizing everything, and after the second course, the Queen's champion Sir Edward Dymoke, challenged anyone to dispute her title, on pain of personal battle. Needless to say, there were no takers to his challenge."

"What was the reaction of the people outside?" asked Jane.

"The Queen is very popular with the people my Lady. They believe she is the rightful Queen and" – he reddened – "should have succeeded immediately after the King died."

I was angered at this gross insult but Jane had seen it coming and held out a restraining hand. "We are amongst friends here Richard, and you remember our rule – the truth, even if it hurts."

Rowland Lea sat back in his chair, relieved. It was evident that the last thing he wanted was an argument at this late stage of the evening.

"I am sorry to be so blunt, my Lady. It has been a long day."

Jane rose to thank him. "Not at all Rowland. It is we who should thank you for thinking of us, and for coming here to give us the news at the end of your long day. It is much appreciated."

It was quite dark and well beyond the curfew when Rowland left to walk the few hundred yards to his small apartment on the other side of the Tower. I knew the guards well enough. They would probably think he had been dallying with a woman at this late hour. I watched him disappear into the dusk and turned back into the house. The Partridges had thoughtfully gone to bed soon after Rowland arrived, leaving Jane to ask her own questions, and the house was still, as was the Tower precinct around us.

"It is done then," said Jane. "Mary is crowned Queen and we are left alone until our trial, and eventual release. How long I wonder? How long?"

She walked wearily to the staircase. "I am so pleased Catherine was able to wear red. That will have pleased her."

I followed her up the stairs, thinking and remembering.

❧ CHAPTER 67 ❧

October 1553 – Tower of London

Lady Jane's sixteenth birthday came and went, as had my eighteenth – unnoticed.

On the 5th October the Queen opened her first parliament and we waited to hear something, but little happened to affect our position. Instead, an Act of Restitution was passed, which declared that King Henry's marriage to Catherine of Aragon had been legal, and therefore Princess Mary was their legitimate daughter.

Two weeks later, Huntingdon, who had very publicly converted to Catholicism, was set free, whilst Suffolk, who had been freed earlier, was promised his pardon. For some of those who remained in the Tower, life also improved. Amy Robsart was allowed to visit Robert Dudley and later to stay with him, and the privilege was extended to Ambrose's wife also. We and the Dudley brothers, including Guilford, were allowed to walk on the leads (the roof of the Beauchamp Tower) and in the Lieutenant's garden. Master Partridge was kind enough to allow Jane to walk in the garden at the same time as Guilford, but it was not a privilege she took advantage of very often.

In Parliament, further legislation reversed the attainder on the Courtenay family, amongst others, and Edward Courtenay became Earl of Devon. This interested me, for unsurprisingly, many of the Courtenay lands lay in Devon – not only round Tiverton, but also in my own Coly valley. Colcombe Castle, the Courtenay stronghold in the valley, had for years maintained a competitive and somewhat uncomfortable partnership alongside the Shute estate, which it bordered, and I took a personal interest in anything which affected it.

"That will change a lot of people's lives back at home," I commented, but Jane and the ladies seemed uninterested and I did not press the point. I did, however, comment on the appearance of the former Marquess of Exeter's son, whom I had seen at the time of his release from the Tower by Queen Mary. As the last of the Plantagenets, Courtenay was a perceived threat to the Tudor dynasty. As a result, the new Earl had spent the last fifteen years of his life in the Tower, but having had the services of a tutor, he had been able to develop his learning, languages, music and artistic skills. It was an object lesson, I thought, that with self-control, and a little flexibility by one's gaolers, it was possible to maintain health and sanity over a long period of incarceration in this gloomy place. It was an example for us all.

Then, toward the end of the month, came the news we had been awaiting and dreading. Lady Jane, Guilford Dudley and his brothers Ambrose and Henry were to be tried for treason on 14th November, together with Thomas Cranmer.

From then on, try as we might in the little house, we could not prevent the tension from building as the day came closer.

❧ Chapter 68 ❧

14th November 1553 – Tower of London

They fussed over her dress that morning. It was hard to know which of them was the more upset – Nurse Ellen, who kept dropping things and apologizing, Mrs Jacob, who kept finding minute creases in the dress and arguing that if she would only remove it, they could "be pressed out in no time", or Mrs Tilney who was trying to dress her and make sure she ate a good breakfast at the same time. The one person who remained calm was Lady Jane herself, who understood the source of the ladies' concern, and remained totally composed as they dithered and chattered nervously around her.

I had known she would emerge this morning prepared and focused. I had seen it coming. For three days now she had withdrawn into herself, reading, endlessly reading, her Bible and prayer book, lips moving in silent prayer, totally unaware of the rest of us tip-toeing around her. Now she was like an experienced soldier prepared for battle, at peace with herself and ready to face what the day threw at her.

"Fear not ladies. Today is a formality. A dreadful formality it is true, for you will hear me tried and found guilty of treason against the Queen, and in all probability sentenced to be burned, as is the law for such crimes. But trust in the merciful word of our cousin the Queen, for she knows I played no part in the planning of that event, nor did I want it, nor wish to accept it when it was thrust upon me. I have her solemn promise that in due course I shall be pardoned and spared."

I felt my heart turn over as she said it. I had seen enough of the Court at work under Northumberland and the young King to know how fickle these decisions could be. The Queen might be sincere today, but I knew there would be people of every persuasion whispering in her ear recommendations, mainly for their own betterment, and to hell with the consequences for others, especially those who were not present to argue for themselves.

368

Jane picked up her prayer book, straightened her back and took a deep breath.

"Come ladies, let's walk through the city and show that we are not ashamed. God is on our side, as is our merciful cousin the Queen. Let's proceed."

She kissed Nurse Ellen, who ran into the next room, crying. Turning to me and speaking quietly, so that the ladies could not hear, she whispered, "Pray for me Richard, that this thing does not get out of control. I beg you also to pray for my husband who will stand beside me today, sharing in closer intimacy than we have ever done as man and wife, the events before us. I know you hate him, and I cannot bring myself to admit love for him, but compassion yes, for he is what his mother has made him and he has been manipulated into his imprisonment above us here" (she indicated toward the Beauchamp Tower) "just as much as I have."

I bowed, avoiding her eyes, for I did, in all truth, find it difficult to share her compassion for the nasty, greedy, wheedling spoiled brat she had been forced to marry. In my heart I knew lay the hope that when both of them had been found guilty, and it was a foregone conclusion that they would, only Jane would be pardoned by the Queen.

I watched her walk out into the weak winter sunlight, striking in her black velvet gown and black satin hood trimmed with jet. It was a perfect choice – martyr's wear, proud yet repentant, and I was sure it would win the hearts of the people as she took barge to London Bridge steps and then walked the half mile to the Guildhall, through what I expected would be crowded streets.

As she walked toward the gates of the Tower, the heavy doors to the Beauchamp Tower opened and Guilford, Ambrose and Henry Dudley emerged blinking into the sunlight to join her, whilst Archbishop Cranmer was brought from the other side of the Tower precinct. As they turned through the gate, I climbed the steps to the Tower curtain wall, and watched them disappear towards the barges and the day ahead. I looked to my right, at the scaffold on Tower Hill, remembering Northumberland and the limping axeman only a few weeks before.

369

Hearing the cry of a red kite, I looked up at the sky. It was a crisp, clear November day. I hoped Jane would not shiver in the barge. Once walking up the slope through the city, the exercise would keep her warm and perhaps calm her mind. I turned slowly, taking in the huge Tower of London castle whose complex had become my voluntary prison and would remain so as long as she was here. It was so much more difficult to see her go than it was to accompany her, but the Captain of the Guard had been very specific – two lady attendants only. I would just have to wait and pray.

～ ❦ ～

They were back by early afternoon, protocol destroyed, as the ladies, unable to contain themselves any longer, burst into the house, collapsing with tears, leaving Lady Jane calmly to thank her escort and enter the house alone.

"Guilty," sobbed Mrs Jacob. "All found guilty, including her Ladyship."

"God save us all!" cried Nurse Ellen, staggering faintly towards the wall and reaching for support. I felt my heart beat faster and my chest constrict, so that, for a moment, I was unable to breathe. I looked at Jane, the only one in the room remaining calm.

"It was as expected. The court was honest, the process fair and the judgement and sentence correct according to the law. We knew it would be thus. We now await the mercy of our Queen. It will come, of that I have no doubt. Once again, we must wait."

I took her hand and helped her to a comfortable chair. Now the immediate occasion was over, now the expected performance had been given, now the required control had been exercised without weakness, now, suddenly, her strength would fail her and she would need my support.

As if to confirm my thought, she did not take the chair, but put her arms round me and buried her head in my chest.

"Hold me Richard, please hold me as I recover my strength."

I held her with both arms, my right hand curved over the back of her head to stroke her hair, as she wished her father had done. I smelled her hair, washed and perfumed by Nurse Ellen. I felt her breathing slowing down as the fear and tension ran out of her. We were prisoners here, that I knew, but sometimes I wished it could go on like this forever.

❧ Chapter 69 ❧

November 1553 – Tower of London

As the days went by following the trial, and news from outside continued to trickle in to our little house, we became increasingly aware that the acceptance of Queen Mary as the true daughter of King Henry and the heir to King Edward's throne under King Henry's will, was beginning to wane. Her initial popularity had reflected a general understanding, carefully supported by statements from the royal court, that she would be tolerant of religious diversity and not force men into the Catholic church against their will. But as time went by, with high profile Lords publicly converting back to the Catholic faith, the political reality became clearer.

That, in itself, did not seem to create an insurmountable problem, but ever since the Queen had announced her betrothal to King Philip of Spain on the 8th November mutterings had been growing.

It was said that even as late as the 16th November, Bishop Gardiner had been arguing with the Queen against marrying a foreigner, who would, in all probability, then reign over the country. A petition of both houses of Parliament had been presented, asking her to think again, and to marry an Englishman. Edward Courtenay's name had even been bandied about, but it was the principle which was really important, rather than the individual.

By November 26th it was clear that the Queen had made her mind up. As a thirty-seven-year-old virgin who had spent most of her life living quietly, the issue of her marrying had been a difficult one to broach, not only for the courtiers and ambassadors, but for the Queen herself. Her initial reaction to a twenty-six-year-old Spaniard had apparently been coy – "A man of twenty six is likely to be disposed to be amorous, and such is not my desire, not at my time of life and never having harboured thoughts of love."

However, it was said the Queen was increasingly swayed by the desire to produce an heir, in order to prevent her (increasingly hated) half-sister Elizabeth from inheriting the Crown and dragging the country back into the Reformist direction. Now, having made her mind up, and decided on Philip of Spain, she could not be budged. On the 26th November, therefore, Bishop Gardiner reversed his earlier position, and preached the benefits of Queen Mary marrying the Catholic Philip of Spain by emphasizing "the dowry of 30,000 ducats with all the Low Countries of Flanders".

The argument failed; the money made no impression on the mood of the people, and a counter-swell of opinion began to spread further.

        ❧   ❧

At about this time, I was approached by a messenger wearing the emblem of the new Earl of Devon. I was instantly suspicious, but mention of my old mentor Dr Thomas Marwood as a common acquaintance was sufficient to maintain my interest a little longer.

Jane shared my suspicion, and warned me that the news of dissatisfaction with the Queen – leading in some places, it was said, to near-open revolt – worried her and, she felt, put her in imminent danger.

"How do you revolt against a Queen's wishes except by treason?" she asked. "And if you mount a treasonable revolution, you must have an alternative ruler in mind. Some, it is said, are now naming Elizabeth, but I would not want any of them to harbour dreams of resurrecting my name in that direction. I have had my proximity to the Crown and do not wish to repeat it."

It was with these risks in mind that I walked out of the Tower gates and took a wherry upriver to my meeting with the Earl.

❧   ❧

"Master Stocker — well met indeed. May I call you Richard, for we Devon men must stick together?"

I bowed and shook his hand.

"I believe we have a mutual friend in Thomas Marwood?"

"Indeed my Lord, Dr Marwood is a neighbour of my father, at Blamphayne, in the Coly valley, above Colyton."

The Earl signalled his recognition. "I have a place there — Colcombe Castle. Sadly I have not visited it since I was eleven or twelve years old. The good Doctor has been of great service to my family recently and they have commended him to me. You will appreciate that, having been languishing in the Tower for the last fifteen years, I have somewhat lost contact with my home community in Devon — a limitation I am keen to redress as a matter of urgency."

The young Earl was even more handsome face to face than he had appeared to be on the day I had observed his release from the Tower. He was tall — nearly as tall as me, but much slimmer. He had light brown hair and hazel eyes, his chestnut beard carefully trimmed. Next to my breadth and solidity, Edward Courtenay's slight figure was elegant and graceful, his hands long and noticeably slim, and his head was always held high, in the manner of a born aristocrat.

"Does the good Lady Jane know you are meeting me here?" he asked conversationally.

"Indeed she does my Lord, I would not do anything without her knowledge and agreement."

"She does not mind our meeting?"

It was a tricky question. "Of course not my Lord. However, my Lady has experienced a very difficult few months and would not take any action to reduce her position with the Queen, either by intent or misunderstanding. I would hope nothing we may need to discuss would be detrimental in that respect?"

Courtenay smiled. "Having just been released from the Tower myself, I do understand the niceties of the point you make. Believe me, I am not about to involve you in a Reformist action against our Queen. You know, of course, that like all of my family, I was baptized a Catholic, and remain a committed one?"

"I was not so aware my Lord. I believe a man's religion is his own thing and not to be enquired into."

Courtenay tipped his head to one side, questioning. "A liberal and creditable view Richard, but hardly a fashionable one, I think. Many men around us would deem it the first question to ask and would presume to answer almost all of their further questions from the answer to the first."

He led me to a window seat and offered me wine, which I refused.

"I will come straight to the point. My life in the Bell Tower did allow me to develop many skills: languages, music, painting, and so on. However, there is one rather essential skill which you cannot develop in a small prison cell. Do you know what that is?"

I could think of a few deprivations which might have limited the Earl's pattern of life whilst in a small cell of the Tower, but none of those which sprang to mind would be described as a 'skill'. I shook my head.

"Horse riding, Richard. I can do many things with a degree of style, but I cannot ride a horse properly."

I sat back, amazed. Having ridden from the age of two, I could not contemplate anyone being unable to ride a horse.

"Of course I could ride well enough when I was a small boy, but for fifteen years of my life I did not see a horse; just heard them below me, arriving and departing the Tower courtyard. So I need some lessons, but discreetly, for the news that a twenty-seven-year-old Earl is taking riding lessons could be used to ridicule me, and ridicule is not something I enjoy."

I laughed. "I understand fully, my Lord. Where and when would you wish to ride? I am, as you know, limited in my movements around the Tower on Lady Jane's account."

The Earl stood. It was clear the interview was coming to an

end. "Shall we try to make it twice a week, here at my house, early in the morning – say Wednesdays and Saturdays? Would you ask your mistress if she could spare you then?"

I agreed to ask Lady Jane for her support for such an arrangement. I was just about to leave when the Earl sprang a surprise on me.

"I may be visiting my estates in Devon in the spring – perhaps in March. I am sure Lady Jane will have been released from the Tower and pardoned long before that. The Queen seems minded to ensure it. If so, and you are released from your obligations, you might wish to travel down with me? Dr Marwood says he has not seen you since you left for Bradgate Park three years ago."

It was a nice thought. Not just the idea of travelling home to Devon with the Earl of Devon, but doing so in the knowledge that Jane was released from prison and safe. Yes, on reflection, that *was* a comforting thought.

∾ CHAPTER 70 ∾

18th December 1553 – Tower of London

"Thank God for fresh air. It is so wonderful to be outside again, and so fortunate that we should have regained our minor liberty on such a day as this."

Lady Jane opened her arms and breathed deeply. There had been a heavy frost the night before, but now it was being burned off rapidly by a warm sun, which was making its way up into a cloudless winter sky. It was, indeed, a glorious day and all the more pleasing for being our first opportunity in three long weeks to walk the walls of the Tower.

This will put colour back in her cheeks, I thought, delighted to see her smiling for the first time in twenty days. It had been hard on us all, to be told, shortly after the trial and the promise of release, that Lady Jane's privileges had been withdrawn, and that once again she was in house arrest in the Gentleman Gaoler's house. She had fallen into a slough of despair, writing fatalistic verses:

> To mortals common fate thy mind resign
> My lot today tomorrow may be thine.

My visits to the Earl had not been constrained, and Jane had not asked me to end them. I had managed to leave the Tower twice a week to develop his Lordship's riding abilities, and had to admit I looked forward to escaping from the place.

For me, it was of triple value, for not only did I have an opportunity to escape the Tower, but in teaching the Earl, I myself had an opportunity to ride and to exercise the muscles which, over the last few months, had begun to get soft. No wonder the Earl had found it so difficult, after fifteen years. Perhaps the greatest benefit, however, was the access to information which my visits provided, for the Earl was very well informed and highly aware of the political scene, and more than willing to talk about it in privacy with his riding instructor.

It appeared that Queen Mary was becoming increasingly unpopular since her announcement that she planned to marry Philip of Spain. Priests had been stoned, and a dead dog with a shaven crown had been thrown through the Queen's bedroom window, turning her into a gibbering wreck for over an hour. Courtenay, whose tongue seemed to be loosened by the action of riding a horse, had told me that the Queen was increasingly reliant on the advice of Simon Reynard, the Habsburg envoy from the Emperor Charles V, whose primary responsibility was clearly to ensure that her planned marriage to the emperor's son, Philip of Spain, went ahead, thus drawing England into the Habsburg empire.

It was this source, more than any other, which had caused the discomfort to Lady Jane, for Reynard had planted in the Queen's mind all sorts of ideas about plots and counter-revolutions. Initially, Reynard had seen Lady Jane as the likely focus of these uprisings, and it was for that reason, Courtenay believed, that her pardon had been delayed and she had been returned to house arrest. The effect on Jane had been swift and unhappy. She had immediately taken ill, believing that her promised pardon was now at risk, and that she might, after all, be burned at the stake, as her sentence had promised.

Now, three weeks later, it appeared that Reynard had moved his attention to the Princess Elizabeth. As a result, she was now subject to intense pressure from the Queen, whose long-established dislike of her half-sister had turned to a seething hatred. With Elizabeth as the primary source of their suspicions, attention had fallen away from Lady Jane, and this had finally led to instructions being given to Sir John Bridges, the Lieutenant of the Tower, to renew her privileges at his discretion the previous evening.

The result had been immediate: Jane had slept well for the first time in three weeks, and her first desire on seeing a bright crisp sunny day this morning had been to walk on the walls and in the garden once again.

One shadow hung over my happiness as I watched her walk smilingly along the wall and descend, almost dancing down the steps, into the rose garden below. At first, the Earl had limited our conversation to horse riding and general trivialities, but as the lessons continued and we got to know each other better, Courtenay began to make references to activities taking place in Devon. For example, he had asked me if I was acquainted with Sir Peter Carew, and had repeated his earlier remark about visiting the West Country, probably in March. I had told the truth – that I knew Carew by reputation only, but was certainly interested in the possibility of a visit home in the spring, if Lady Jane's affairs had been satisfactorily brought to a conclusion and her release achieved. But something from these conversations was beginning to leave me feeling uneasy.

"Jane! – My Lady!"

She turned, smiling. One solitary red rose had decided to leave its opening until mid-December, and had been encouraged by the warmth of that morning's sun to do so. Jane bent over and smelled it.

"Richard. What is it? There is a little frown on your forehead. Why so, on this lovely morning?"

Following her example, I bent to smell the rose, gathering my thoughts as I did so.

"Seeing your pleasure at being returned your privileges, I am concerned not to become responsible for their removal once again."

She looked at me carefully, the light mood replaced by a suspicious gaze. "Richard, I do not believe you would intentionally do anything, or omit to do anything, which would harm me in any way."

I stood close to her and took her hand. "No, nor would I, Jane. My fear is that I might have risked your position by unintentional actions."

Gently she removed her hand from mine and began to walk. I fell into step beside her. "What unintentional actions are you referring to Richard?" she asked, conversationally, but underneath her tone I could hear her fear returning.

"I believe it is possible that suspicious persons might misunderstand my regular visits to the Earl of Devon and use them to create evidence of a link between you and him. When I first met him, he told me he was a strict Catholic and I deemed there to be no risk of such a misunderstanding, but of late he has begun to refer to 'common interests' and 'meetings' in a way that has raised my suspicions. He has spoken of Sir Peter Carew and of Thomas Wyatt, from Kent, a neighbour of the Boleyn family at Hever Castle, and associated with them since my father's time. It's nothing specific, but in these difficult times, I am becoming concerned."

Jane walked on, her tiny feet crunching in the cold gravel, then stopped and turned.

"I believe you are right to be suspicious, Richard. Last night, when Sir John Bridges came to give me the good news that we could resume our walks, he told me there were rumours of a Reformist plot and he mentioned Wyatt. He warned me to keep my distance from him, as he is under suspicion, and associated with Antoine de Noalles, the French ambassador. The latter has reportedly been visiting the Princess Elizabeth at Ashridge. It is also known that Courtenay has had what he thought were secret meetings with de Noalles."

We walked on, through the rose garden. The single flowering rose proved to be one colourful exception, but the frosty stems of those rose bushes which were still in shadow made attractive patterns, and here and there, early buds gave a pre-Christmas promise of the spring to come. Jane was now tense again, her mood of the early morning dampened.

"I think your suspicions are probably right, Richard. By all accounts, the Duke has sought to enter the power game more quickly than his limited experience makes wise, and is heading for a fall. He is not the only one who seems to be out of his depth in the intrigues of Court. Sir John told me my own father's name has been mentioned in relation to Courtenay's, though why he should be so stupid as to get involved in anything I do not know, only weeks after being pardoned by the Queen and his fine reduced to £20,000. You would think he would have learned his lesson and kept quiet."

I looked at her standing in the sun, against the white stone wall of the Tower. She had never, to my knowledge, done anything to hurt anyone, yet once again there were men, including her own father, risking her life as they struggled greedily to better themselves. It was disgusting. She looked up at me, squinting against the unaccustomed bright sunlight.

"On balance, Richard, I *should* prefer it if you would sever the connection with Courtenay, in all of our interests, at least until we know what the situation really is. As for my father, surely he cannot put my life at risk a second time?"

છે ન

That afternoon, I penned a short note to the Duke of Devon, telling him how well he was now riding, pleading a need to spend more time with my mistress, "following her recent illness" and recommending some final riding exercises, "to perfect your Lordship's mastery".

It was a bit weak and I hoped I would not get on the wrong side of the "handsomest man in England", as he was regularly referred to, whose name had been linked in marriage with the Queen, Princess Elizabeth and Jane Dormer over the last three months. Running with the hare and the hounds in the game of court politics was all very well, and, when successful, certainly had its rewards, but Jane's life was still not secure and I could not risk that. Hopefully, we would be allowed to enjoy a quiet Christmas and, in the spring, Jane would be pardoned.

❧ CHAPTER 71 ❧

17th January 1554 – Tower of London

"Thank God we acted when we did."

Jane looked pale as she watched Rowland Lea walking back to his apartment on the other side of the precinct. I had been out when he had called, and had arrived back just as he was leaving.

"It was just as we feared. Sir Peter Carew has been inciting the people of Exeter to rise up against the 'Spanish Invasion' as he calls it. An arrest party has been dispatched to bring him to London."

I took a deep breath. This was not good. "Any mention of Sir Thomas Wyatt?"

"Rowland said he has been inciting similar revolt in Kent. It's happening Richard. The Queen's signature of the marriage agreement has broken the dam of discontent. The Lord only knows what will happen now."

"What news of the Princess Elizabeth, for in her active involvement lies your salvation."

"I know it, Richard. Rowland knew little specific. Only that she is gathered at Ashridge, with de Noalles visiting her there, and her followers armed, they say, for her protection. Is there anything we can do?"

"I believe not, my Lady. Indeed our best tactic is to do nothing, for quiet inactivity signals against involvement and we are surely being carefully observed."

She nodded. "You are right. We should remain quiet and private, calm and uninvolved."

It wasn't easy. Inactivity did not come easily to Jane or to me, but if I were the government, I would be watching us like hawks, and the less activity there was from us as any plot developed, the more clear it would be that we were not part of it. Surely the Princess Elizabeth was the key to the future, but everyone said she was difficult to read, too clever to give out signals or to be caught talking to the wrong people.

"What of Courtenay?"

She shook her head. "Nothing. He remains in London. But Sir James Crofts has left the city for his lands in Wales and there is great suspicion of him. The government fear a simultaneous uprising in Kent and the West Country."

"And your father?"

"Again, nothing incriminating I understand, but Reynard, who has the Queen's ear more than anyone now, has his suspicions, according to Rowland Lea. How I wish this were all over."

There was nothing we could do. We must simply wait until the future unfolded.

❧   ❧

If we could not see the future unfolding day by day, we could certainly hear it. When news reached London late on 26th January that Wyatt had taken Rochester, and that the crews of the royal ships in the Medway had gone over to his side, there was near panic. The noise was easily heard in the Tower and Jane and our party spent many cold hours wrapped in our warmest clothes on the Tower walls, trying to get a glimpse of what all the noise was about.

With Jane's agreement, I left the Tower and walked the half mile to London Bridge to see what was happening. The Duke of Norfolk, now aged but considered a safe Catholic pair of hands, was leading the city militia and Queen's Guard across the

381

bridge to reinforce the army trying to defend the city from the rebel advance. They did not look a very confident lot to me and I was not in the slightest bit surprised to hear two days later that the majority of them had defected to the rebel side, shouting, "We are all Englishmen".

On 30th January the noise once again reached fever pitch. The guard at the Tower told us the rebels were camped at Blackheath and Greenwich, and much of the day was spent looking for the arrival of the mutinied fleet in the Pool of London, in front of the Tower.

Visitors to the Tower told us of Queen Mary's impassioned speech at the Guildhall, which resulted in a change of heart for many and the decision to close London Bridge against the advancing army. Across the bridge, and along all the city streets leading from it, shopkeepers and stallholder were closing down and boarding up their premises. I wondered if Suffolk Place would suffer any ill effects, for it was only a short distance from the southern end of London Bridge, where the gates were closed. There was no doubt that some members of a frustrated army would find themselves outside its gates.

Back in the Tower, the guns were trained on the opposite bank of the river, where the rebel army was clearly to be seen, but the Queen forbade them to fire, for risk of killing the ordinary people of Southwark, most of whom were making a good show of welcoming the rebels with ale, bread and the produce of the Borough Market, which sat a few hundred yards from the bridge end. Welcomed they may have been, but in their frustration, the rebels sacked both the Priory of St Mary Overy and the Bishop of Winchester's palace, the latter virtually next door to Suffolk Place.

For three days we watched and listened and then it went quiet. Wherrymen reported that the army had gone upstream, and now planned to cross the Thames by the next bridge, at Kingston.

In all, it took the army four days to march upstream, cross at Kingston, and march back and on the morning of 7th February they staggered, rather than marched, into Knightsbridge. Taking little heed of the royal palaces and Whitehall buildings, they continued toward the City of London and came face to face with Pembroke's defending forces early in the afternoon, at Charing Cross.

London held its breath, and we in the Tower, having little alternative, did likewise.

ᕗ CHAPTER 72 ᕤ

7th February 1554 – Tower of London

"It's all over."

Sir John Bridges stood in the doorway, wearing his official half-armour. He sounded breathless and was red faced.

"I cannot stay, my Lady. Wyatt has just been arrested at Temple Bar, and is being brought here to the Tower. I must receive him."

Calmly, Jane rose and faced him. "Is the revolt put down then?"

"Aye lady, Wyatt's army has given up. They were stopped at the Ludgate by the Lord Admiral, William Howard, and pursued back to Temple Bar by Pembroke. There they surrendered, with minor bloodshed."

Jane crossed herself. "God be praised there was not great loss of life. Too many men have died already in these arguments."

Bridges shuffled awkwardly. "Your father is also here my Lady – just arrived. He was arrested with your uncle, John Grey, near Bradgate Park and brought here in chains. I understand your other uncle – Thomas, has escaped and is being pursued into Wales."

Jane put her hand to her mouth. "My father and uncle arrested. Were they actively involved?"

"It seems so Lady, they were spreading revolt through Leicestershire, timed to coincide with Wyatt in Kent and Carew in the West Country. It was all part of a single plot against the

Queen's marriage, even Catholics and Reformists coming together. We have it all explained; Courtenay has told the Lord Chancellor everything. He says Sir Peter Carew tried to get him to lead the western revolt, but as a good Catholic he stood by his Queen."

He turned to me.

"And if you believe that, you will believe anything. If you ask me he was as fully involved as anyone, but just lost his nerve. He always was a weak one. I should know, I've seen more of him than most people this last ten years."

Sir John bowed to Jane. "I apologize for my haste my Lady, but I must be at the gate."

Jane put a hand on his arm. "I understand, Sir John. You must go. I know you are busy, and I am grateful that you took time to tell me the situation. Thank you."

Bridges departed, leaving Jane, the ladies and me, standing in a circle with a nervous-looking Mistress Partridge, not sure what to do or say next.

It was Jane who broke the ice. "Richard. Can you go to the gate and see if my father is held there. Find out if he is wounded and how he fares, will you?"

Nodding, I left the house, walking quickly down the short slope of Tower Green toward the main gates. When I reached them, there was no sign of the new prisoners, but a large welcoming party of yeomen guards, awaiting the arrival of Wyatt and his rebel leaders. Standing in a doorway, watching the approach road outside the gates, was Sir John Bridges, who saw me coming and walked towards me.

"Have you come to see the rebels put away?" he asked, jovially, for imprisonment was his daily work and he tried to handle it in as light a manner as he could.

"My Lady Jane asked me if I could speak to her father, who is, as we understand, newly arrived."

Bridges jerked his head toward the Beauchamp Tower. "I've put him in the Beauchamp Tower. The same room as Northumberland used to occupy. He always followed the Duke and continued to do so even after Northumberland was dead. It seemed appropriate somehow. No doubt he will follow his leader up yonder hill when the time comes." Again he jerked his head, this time in the direction of the scaffold on Tower Hill.

"May I speak to him briefly, Sir John? He is your prisoner's father and was my own master before I served her."

Sir John, who liked Jane and showed her every kindness his instructions allowed, called to a nearby gaoler guard, who was carrying a ring of keys.

"Thomas. Take this young man to visit Suffolk in the Beauchamp Tower. Give them fifteen minutes." His eyes flashed at me. "No more mind."

The guard nodded and led me into the Beauchamp Tower. Compared with the Gentleman Gaoler's House it smelled damp and was freezing cold. We climbed two flights of stone steps until we reached a heavy oak door covered with iron studs. He looked through the small grille in the door, to ensure his prisoner was visible and not preparing to attack him, then opened it and indicated me to enter.

"I'll be back in fifteen minutes," he began to close the heavy door, then paused, grinning maliciously, "if I remember." The door closed and I could hear him chuckling as he clumped down the stone steps.

Suffolk was crouched on the floor in the corner of the room. His clothing was filthy and covered in straw. There was a huge bruise over his right eye and his hands were cut all over, as if he had been crawling on a stone floor.

"Richard! It's you."

His lips were cut and began to bleed as soon as he spoke. His eyes were bloodshot and had the defeated look of a beaten dog. I stared in dismay and disgust. My once proud, once respected master was reduced to this. A broken man, broken in body and spirit. He tried to rise and I heard him gasp as the pain of his invisible injuries made themselves felt.

"My Lord! You do not look well. Have they beaten you?"

Suffolk coughed. "Not here, no. At my capture – that was

none too gentle. Huntingdon seemed to think he had a score to settle. I shall be alright. How is my daughter?"

"She is better housed than you sir, and I'll warrant better fed also. We are not far away – in Master Partridge's house beneath the wall to your left. If you look from this window you may be able to see her walking on yonder wall some days, but she will not be able to see you – we have tried – it's too dark in here to see in from down there."

Suffolk nodded absent-mindedly. He didn't seem to be listening.

"Do you want for anything my Lord?"

Suffolk smiled a damaged, cracked, bloody smile. "Perhaps my freedom and the opportunity for a fresh start. I do not seem to have made much of a job of this last one."

He stared at me. It was the crazed stare of a man overcome.

"We could have won you know. We could have pulled it off. We were so close. God was not on our side."

I glared at him. The man I once admired and respected, who had effectively sold his daughter in pursuit of his own power and betterment.

"Is that why you returned to Catholicism? Because God was not on your side?"

Suffolk shrugged. It was a resigned shrug, the shrug of a man who has stopped fighting, who doesn't care anymore.

"Well? It's all the same isn't it? Kings, Queens, Archbishops, Bishops, priests, rules, prayer books, black rubrics. It's all a game, a competition, made by man, not by God."

I looked at him, pityingly, but deep down aware that in this most uncertain of worlds, one day, in the future, it might be me crouching there and some other, younger, man standing over me.

"Will they kill you?"

Suffolk nodded. "Yes, this time Queen Mary's advisors will win the argument. This time they will execute us all, they have to – to encourage the others."

"And Jane?"

A tear ran down Suffolk's face. He seemed genuinely remorseful. "This time she will die. I have killed her. Queen Mary cannot afford to be merciful now. We rolled the dice too many times against her. They will insist now; Arundel, Winchester, Pembroke, Reynard, they all have to protect themselves, to show they were on the right side when the Spanish finally arrive as victors, with their Inquisition."

Painfully he dragged himself up and stood, awkwardly, against the wall. He seemed to have regained a little of his self-esteem by standing. Not much, but a little.

"Privilege. It's a game Richard, based on power and prerogative. A greedy, dirty, brutal little game. And if you want to play it, you have to be greedier, dirtier, and more brutal than the next man. The game is called 'winner takes all and the devil takes the hindmost'."

He began to cough and the pain made him double up. After a couple of minutes, he regained himself and tried to stand upright again.

"Please ask Jane to forgive me. I did not wish this on her. I only wished for the best – the very best – for her. Sadly we played and we lost. Now it's all over."

I heard the guard's boots scraping up the steps outside. The key turned angrily in the lock and the door creaked back.

"Time's up."

I looked, for what I knew was the last time, at my former mentor and master. The man who had made so much difference to my life, but who, in the end, had created the worst outcome I could possibly have imagined. Suffolk stared back at me, eyes dead.

What men do to others in their greed, I thought.

"Time's up."

I nodded. That said it all. That was it. Certainly, absolutely, finally. Time was up. I turned towards the gaoler, then back to Suffolk for the last time. I did not say 'goodbye'. Somehow the word would not come. I just turned and left.

Suffolk nodded and slid back down the wall into his crouching position. I understood, but had no pity left.

CHAPTER 73

8th February 1554 – Tower of London

None of us had slept. Jane appeared early the next morning looking pale and drawn, but still more robust than the ladies, whose sobs had echoed round the house all night.

They had known, as soon as Sir John Bridges had appeared at the door late the night before, that it was bad news.

He had looked distraught, for over the months of her captivity, Sir John had taken a great liking for Jane and begun to treat her as a daughter. She, in turn, had grown to treat him as a friend, for he was always generous in how he performed his duties and a regular and sensitive visitor, who was always willing to tell us the news from outside. We had just been going to bed when there had been a bang at the door. Mistress Partridge had held the door wide, and Sir John had stumbled in, dropping to one knee in front of Jane, who had immediately drawn back in horror.

"My Lady, I am so sorry. Her Majesty has decreed that you and your husband will be executed here the day after tomorrow, at ten o'clock in the morning. Your husband first on Tower Hill and you to follow, on the Green." His eyes had looked like those of a faithful hound as he had looked up at her, begging forgiveness.

Jane's immediate reaction was to ask how she was to die, for in the case of women, the correct sentence for treason was burning at the stake. That was the one thing which terrified her.

Bridges had croaked out his answer, "The axe my Lady" before dropping his head in shame.

Now, next morning, we were trying to come to terms with the fact that Jane had only twenty-four hours to make her arrangements to meet her God in a fitting and composed manner.

As usual, Jane took the lead and began to list the things that needed doing. There was the dress to select – a warm one, that she would not shiver and appear afraid, and of a suitably sombre colour. She must write her final speech, for it was customary to have it copied so that it might be saved for posterity. She wanted to make her farewells to all present and needed time to prepare for that, and she wanted to write to her sister and father. But most of all, she needed time to pray, to write a special prayer, and to prepare herself for the world beyond – a world which she said already beckoned her from the other side of that one, dreadful moment.

None had an appetite for food and by eight o'clock we were being busy, although in the case of the ladies, much of it seemed to be activity for activity's sake. I felt useless and in the way, as the ladies went to and fro, bringing writing materials and making endless little lists, sniffing as they did so.

It was ten o'clock, and the ladies had calmed down and brought some order to their day's work, when the Dean arrived. Dr Richard Feckenham was both Dean of St Paul's and Abbott of Westminster and at thirty-nine a kind, knowledgeable and thoughtful man. He was also well known as a staunch Catholic, who had been sent to the Tower by King Edward for preaching an anti-reformist sermon, and only released when Queen Mary came to the throne. Jane did not want to see him, but agreed out of good manners.

"Madam, I lament your heavy case," he began, "yet I doubt not that you bear out this sorrow with a constant and patient mind."

Jane inclined her head to him. "You are welcome to me sir, if your coming be to give Christian exhortation." She led him to the fire where they sat in comfort and spoke for over an hour.

Suddenly, he rose to his feet and left, a look of enthusiasm on his face, and I and the ladies looked at each other, wondering what gave him such apparent energy on so sad a day.

❧　❦

By early afternoon, Feckenham was back, arriving as we were just finishing our dinner. After an empty start, the morning's orderly progress had revived our spirits and with them our appetites had also returned.

The Dean wasted no time returning to his conversation with Jane.

"Since we spoke this morning, my Lady, I have spoken with the Queen herself. I have her commitment that your date of execution has been put back – to the 12th of February. In that time I am instructed by her Majesty to do all in my power to bring you to acceptance of the true Catholic faith, and if I am successful, she has promised that you will be reprieved."

He sat back, as if awaiting applause, or at least thanks. I watched from the corner of the room. *I fear this good man is going to be disappointed*, I thought.

I was right. Jane smiled at the Dean and put a hand upon his.

"Alas, sir, it was not my desire to prolong my days. As for death, I utterly despise it, and her Majesty's pleasure being such, I willingly undergo it. You are much deceived if you think I have any desire for longer life, for I assure you, since the time you went from me the time hath been so odious to me that I long for nothing so much as death; neither did I wish the Queen to be solicited for such a purpose."

Feckenham stood his ground, confident, it appeared, that he could save this good Lady in both senses of the word.

"I beg you Lady, indulge me a little longer, for these issues are of such import and the value of life so high, it must not easily be thrown away. I ask you to join me in the Chapel yonder, tomorrow morning, to debate this matter further."

At first Jane refused.

"This disputation may be fit for the living," she said, "but not for the dying. Leave me to make my peace with God."

However, the Dean's manner was so light and friendly, and his arguments so easy and natural, that she eventually agreed to meet the following morning, not in the Chapel of St Peter ad Vincula, as he had suggested, but in the more austere Chapel of St John the Evangelist in the White Tower.

ஒ ௸

Next day they met again. Jane insisted on being accompanied, by me, Mrs Jacob and Mrs Tilney, but Nurse Ellen said she found the whole thing too much and begged to be excused.

I approved of the choice. The Chapel of St John, often referred to as the White Chapel, lay deep in the first floor of the huge White Tower, its austere white stone walls hardly changed since they had been built by the Normans over 500 years before. The simplicity of the chapel seemed to calm Jane and she looked forward to her continuing discussions with the Dean with a degree of pleasure.

"I am strangely taken by this man," she admitted, as my namesake arrived and removed his heavy cloak. "I have always considered Catholics to be ungodly heretics, full of bigotry, but Feckenham reminds me of my dear John Aylmer – a plain country man with plain and honest speaking. What chance, you think, that I can convert him to the truth, even as he tries to lead me to the Queen's ways?" I thought it was highly unlikely that either of them would let go of their deep-set beliefs, but shared with Jane the pleasure that the debate was at least conducted in a civilized manner.

Feckenham began with the formalities, a scribe sat to his side, taking notes.

"I am here come to you at this present, sent from the Queen and her Council, to instruct you in the true doctrine of the right faith; although I have so great confidence in you, that I shall have, I trust, little need to travail with you much therein."

Jane warmed to the debate.

"Forsooth I heartily thank the Queen's Highness which is not unmindful of her humble subject; and I hope, likewise, that you no less will do your duty therein both truly and faithfully, according to that you were sent for."

I watched and listened in awe as they debated to and fro for over two hours. Each point Feckenham made seemed eminently reasonable, and every time, Jane responded with an opposite view, argued with equal conviction and with matching precision of argument and supporting evidence. In the end, I thought, it simply comes down to faith – what you believe in, deep down, and for that reason, the likelihood of either being swayed by the arguments of the other was remote indeed.

391

Finally, as might have been predicted, their argument focused on the sacraments and specifically on the issues of transubstantiation. I had heard Jane on this subject many times and knew how personally she took the repellent idea that at the moment of the sacrament the physical body and blood of Christ were present. I remembered her quoting the small rhyme written by King Edward and knew that on this issue, above all, Feckenham would make no progress with her.

Finally, he acknowledged that he was beaten, that the challenge was too much, and that the condition of the Queen's offer of mercy would not be achieved.

"I am sorry for you, for I am sure that we two shall never meet," he said, sadly, as they parted.

Jane nodded, thoughtfully. She had clearly grown to like and respect the Dean; perhaps the first strongly committed Catholic whose sincerity and reason she had ever accepted.

"True it is that we shall never meet, except God turn your heart; for I am assured, unless you repent and turn to God, you are in evil case."

Feckenham nodded sagely, his eyes on hers. They were like-minded in so many ways; each convinced and committed to their beliefs. He smiled sadly as Jane continued.

"And I pray God, in the bowels of His mercy, to send you His Holy Spirit, for He hath given you His great gift of utterance, if it pleased Him also to open the eyes of your heart."

It was time to leave. They began to descend the steep stone steps of the White Tower. As they came out of the main door, they looked down together, across the Tower Green, where both knew, Jane would meet her end in three days time. Feckenham paused and turned again to Jane.

"May it please you that I should accompany you to the scaffold, Lady?"

Jane looked down at the spot where she was soon to die. She smiled, a slow, private smile, her mind already on that morning in the future.

"Yes that would be a kindness, and it would, indeed, please me."

They parted on the steps to the White Tower, Jane walking slowly back to the Gentleman Gaoler's House, possibly for the last time, followed by the ladies and me and a single guard, who remained at a discreet distance

ᕘ ᕚ

The following morning I watched Jane as she wrote her letters. She had asked me to be present, 'for company', as she did so, and from time to time she would look up and smile at me, as if my presence gave her strength.

She was writing to Catherine. As she finished the letter she powdered the ink and blew across it gently.

"I don't expect she will take my advice, but I have offered it anyway." She passed the letter across to me. I soon found the section she was referring to.

Live still to die, deny the world, deny the Devil and despise the flesh. Take up your Cross. As touching my death, rejoice, as I do, and adsist that I shall be delivered from corruption and put on incorruption.
Farewell, dear sister. Put your only trust in God, who only must uphold you.

Your loving sister,
Jane Dudley

Tears filled my eyes as I read it. Jane was right, Catherine would not follow the advice; certainly not with the committed piety that her sister intended. I could see her now, tears flowing down her cheeks as she read the letter in her room at Sheen, or perhaps even at Whitehall, for she and her mother seemed to be back in favour with the Queen, despite her father and sister's imprisonment.

What a strange mechanical world the royal Court was. How could Catherine continue her day-to-day ways, dressing up, feasting, curtsying, smiling, knowing her sister and her father were shortly to die brutal deaths at the hand of the Queen they curtseyed to? But perhaps they had no choice. Life did go on, and if you were of royal blood, it was the Court life you continued with. The Queen would salve her conscience (if she had one) with the thought that she had done her very best – sent Feckenham with a passport to survival.

As for Catherine and Frances, what else would they do? They could hardly hide themselves away in a nunnery – most of them had been closed down. No, the truth was that life did go on. People steeled themselves to the brutality of royal politics, stepped past the bodies as quickly as possible, and continued with their own lives. I thought about my own position. What would I do after, when it was all over? I had no idea, and while Jane was here, beside me, still alive, still warm, I would not, could not, address it.

I looked up. Jane was watching me, a sad smile on her face.

"She will find a life after this. She will smile and laugh again. And so will you Richard. You must, for I shall be released from the pain of this life and happy with my Maker."

A tear started to run down my cheek and I sniffed, embarrassed that she had seen into my thoughts. I tried to reply, but no words would come. I pushed my fist into my face, trying to push the emotions back down my throat, but they would not subside.

"Do not cry for me Richard. For I have told you, there is nothing to cry for. Rather rejoice with me that I can be at peace. I shall meet, and debate with, all those whose writings have given me so much pleasure this many years. Imagine, Richard, I shall speak to Socrates, Plato, all of them. Can you imagine, I may yet understand mathematics?"

I looked at her uncertainly. I did not think my faith extended that far. I tried to smile at her, but my sadness prevented it from forming.

"And if you do not cry for me, Richard, rather should you not cry for yourself either, except in the knowledge that you still have life's burdens ahead of you. But remember this, that I shall watch over you, and I shall pray for you daily, as I shall for my family."

She put a reassuring hand on my arm.

"Rest assured Richard, you should face your future with as much confidence as I face mine. Put your trust in God, act honestly to all men and be courageous."

I wiped my hand across my face as Lady Tilney fussed into the room. What a useless fool I must look. We were supposed to be here helping and supporting Jane in her hour of need, and instead she was comforting me.

Gently, she took the letter back from me and folded it.

"Now I must write to my father."

ஒ CHAPTER 74 ௸

11th February 1554 – Tower of London

In response to the horror of the coming events, and perhaps like the survivors at Court, we were clinging to a routine. Jane insisted that we took our meals on time. "Would you have me starve to death?" she asked Mrs Jacob, but the joke was too much for poor Nurse Ellen, who ran from the room in floods or tears.

Then came another disturbance to our constancy. Jane was sitting in the better light in the window seat, writing her speech from the scaffold, when Sir John Bridges arrived with the news that Guilford Dudley had asked if he could see his wife once more before he died and the Queen had granted his request, if Jane wanted to see him.

Jane put down her pen and turned to Sir John.

"How is my husband?"

"He fares badly my Lady. He has not come to terms with his fate as you have, and does not, I fear, share your faith in the Lord. He is in a state of collapse, falling to the ground and crying at the unfairness of his fate."

Jane's face hardened. I could tell by her face that the request had broken into the cocoon of self-control she had been building progressively day by day.

"Poor Guilford. He has little to thank his mother for."

She looked up at Sir John Bridges, waiting quietly for her instruction.

"Thank you Sir John, and I thank her Majesty for her kindness, but I do not think such a meeting would benefit either of us now. Please ask my husband kindly to omit these moments of grief, and tell him that we shall shortly behold each other in a better place."

Jane smiled at him, to indicate that the discussion was at an end, and returned to her writing. Bridges coughed nervously, and Jane looked up at him again, raising her eyebrows in enquiry.

"I am sorry to disturb you further my Lady, but I wonder if I might crave a request – a small item to remember you by?" He shuffled awkwardly from foot to foot as he spoke.

Jane's mood softened. "Of course, Sir John, I thank you for the thought and the request."

She looked round the room and reached across to a miniature prayer book, bound in velvet. She opened it at the back and on a blank page wrote

Forasmuch as you have desired so simple a woman to write in so worthy a book, good Master Lieutenant, therefore shall I, as a friend, desire you, and as a Christian require you, to call upon God, to incline your heart to His laws and not to take the word of truth utterly out of your mouth. Live still to die, that by death you may purchase eternal life.

For as the preacher sayeth, there is a time to be born and a time to die, and the day of death is better than the day of our birth.

Yours,

As the Lord knoweth, as a friend
Jane Dudley

"You shall have this when I am gone."

Sir John bowed deeply, then, hesitantly, embraced her. "You are in our prayers, my Lady."

Awkwardly, he made his way out and Jane returned to her writing.

> If justice is done with my body, my soul will find mercy with God. Death will give pain to my body for its sins, but the soul will be justified before God. If my faults deserve punishment, my youth at least, and my imprudence were worthy of excuse. God and posterity will show me more favour.

She looked at it and nodded in satisfaction, powdering and blowing it carefully. Then she looked up at me and smiled, content, as if her work were done.

"Did you write to your father?"

In reply she lifted a piece of letter paper from the table before her, and passed it over to me. "It's a rough copy. I have already sent him the fair copy."

> Father,
>
> Although it hath pleased God to hasten my death by you, by whom my life should have been lengthened, yet can I so patiently take it that I yield God hearty thanks for shortening my woeful days. Herein I may count myself blessed that, washing my hands with my innocency, my guiltless blood may cry before the Lord.
>
> The Lord continue to keep you, that at the last we may meet in Heaven.
>
> Your obedient daughter till death,
>
> Jane

I read the words and looked up at her.

"How do you think he will take it?" she asked.

"Hard."

Jane nodded. "I thought so, that is why I shall also send him this, when I am gone." She passed across her prayer book, the one she intended to carry to the scaffold.

The Lord comfort your Grace. Though it hath pleased God to take away two of your children, think not that you have lost them, but trust that we, by losing this mortal life, have won an immortal life; and I, for my part, as I have honoured your Grace in this life, will pray for you in another life.

I closed the book and returned it to her.

"Yes, that is fitting, and will comfort him in what will, no doubt, be his own adversity. Have you written to your mother?"

Jane shook her head. "Only to my father."

She sat for a moment, thinking.

"I do not blame him for any of this, I blame my mother. She is a woman of appetites, for wealth, for respect, for influence and for power over others. She has an exaggerated awareness of her royal blood, which, when unfulfilled, makes her resentful, greedy and selfish. Poor Father. A weak man and a strong woman make an unhappy combination in a man's world, especially when it is the woman who has the royal connection."

We sat silently for a few moments. Jane seemed to have written all she wanted to, and to be composed. Finally, as if rousing herself to face another challenge, she stood up and walked towards me.

Instinctively, I went to stand, but she waved me down and sat on my lap in the large chair.

"It is time to say goodbye Richard. Tomorrow will be the most difficult day of my life.

"Mrs Tilney and Mrs Jacob will accompany me to the scaffold. I fear for them, for it will be harder for them than it will for me. Each of us has his or her own way of handling adversity, and, as you have seen many times before, mine is to withdraw into myself and handle it alone. I have therefore decided to say goodbye to you and to Ellen this evening. Ellen will find tomorrow particularly difficult, for she has known me since childhood. It is better done this way.

"As for you Richard, you have been a good and loyal servant and friend these many days. In all the world, only you and John

Aylmer have consistently told me the truth, even when I did not want to hear it. And you and you alone, have treated me like a person and not like a pawn of opportunity in the chess game of life. I wish I had been able, through position and personality, to respond to you as fully as I would have liked, but circumstances have not allowed it."

I put my arms round her and held her.

"You know I love you Jane, in my own way."

She smiled a distant smile, as if life itself was already a memory.

"I know it, Richard. In the last year, you have showed me more love than my father or my husband ever could. I in return, love you also, not as a husband, not as a father, but as a dear, dear friend."

She leaned towards me and I held her tightly, not wanting to let go, her very smallness and vulnerability pulling me like a magnet. For five minutes we clung to each other, her heart beat slowing down and her muscles relaxing. Then I felt her heart begin to speed up and I knew she was about to leave me. She sat back and looked at me carefully, as one would look at a view for the last time in order to capture it, then she kissed me gently, on the lips.

"Please leave me now, for tomorrow I must meet my Maker. Death is the one thing we must all do alone, but as I cross that bridge, I shall have my God beckoning me from the other side, and that will give me all the courage I need to make the crossing. If you are present tomorrow morning on the Green, please stand where I cannot see you, for I want to remember you as we are here, now, not as an anguished face in the crowd."

She stood up and, automatically, I did the same. Once again, she leaned forward and, reaching up, gently kissed me.

"Do not grieve for me, for I welcome the place to which I am going and am able to step away from this life without sorrow. Remember me as I am now. Go forward and make an honest life. Always be true to yourself and do not shrink in the face of adversity, for your soul is yours and yours alone, save for God himself. Go now, and send Ellen to me, for I am at peace."

CHAPTER 75

12th February 1554 – Tower of London

It was early when they came. But already she was waiting for them.

In accordance with Jane's wishes, I was trying to keep out of her way. We had said our farewells and I knew that Jane would now have withdrawn into herself, acting out, step by step, the events that the day required with the courage and self-control that was expected.

Now the first clumsy step in the process had begun, as the panel of matrons arrived to verify that the Lady was not pregnant, for had she been so, her fate would by law have been delayed until after the birth.

It was not easy to remain invisible in so small a house, and I was soon joined by Mrs Jacob, who was faced with the same challenge.

"Oh Richard. What a dreadful day this is. She is doing wonderfully well. I hope she maintains her composure to the end."

I smiled a small, wry smile. "She will. They will not beat her in this. Jane has already risen above all of them. In her mind she has already left us, and is standing on the bridge to heaven waiting for the Lord to receive her. If only I had such faith."

Mrs Jacob nodded. "Amen to that."

"I thought you were going to accompany her today – with Mrs Tilney?"

"I was, but early this morning Ellen begged me to allow her to do so instead. She and Elizabeth Tilney are, after all, her closest servants and have been with her since she was a child. Elizabeth will do what has to be done and Ellen will cry most wonderfully when it is all over. Lady Jane has said her farewells to me and asked me to remain with you until it is all over."

I smiled my understanding. "I thought of going onto the walls – to be out of the way, as she requested, but then I thought, 'What if she calls for me? I must be available.'"

Mrs Jacob agreed. "I went through the same thoughts myself.

I decided to remain here, in the back room, until I heard her leave for the Green, then slip out quietly."

"Do you intend to see her die?"

She nodded, a tear in the corner of her eye. "I feel I must – to be with her in spirit. I could not live with myself if I turned my back on her at that final moment. The Lord knows I do not wish to witness so awful a thing, but somehow I feel I must."

I took her hand. "I feel exactly the same. I lay awake all night, trying to decide what was the right thing to do. In the end I decided I had to be with her, to share her pain."

We sat, as the matrons left and the three ladies upstairs prepared themselves. Jane had chosen the black velvet gown she wore at her trial and she would be putting it on, now that the examination was over. Master Partridge and his wife had thoughtfully left the small house early that morning, and the lower house was quiet. I fiddled with the buttons of my jerkin and Mrs Jacob flicked her eyes across at me.

"Go to the wall Richard. You can watch her husband pass by from there and if she does need you, I can call from the steps."

"Are you sure?" Relieved, I opened the door quietly and, seeing no one there, slipped quietly across the front room and out of the door.

It was cold, but thankfully windless, with a clear blue sky and wintery sunshine; the sort of winter's day you remember long afterwards. Thank God it was not one of those damp cold days with a wind to cut into your bones.

Quickly I climbed the steps onto the wall above and looked outward, across to Tower Hill, where a crowd had assembled around the scaffold. I heard a noise behind me, and turned to see Guilford Dudley, walking from the Beauchamp Tower toward the main gate. He was accompanied by Sir Anthony Browne, John Throckmorton, and a number of other gentlemen who had rallied to his support in the face of Queen Mary's refusal to let him have a Reformist priest. Slowly and quietly, they walked the few hundred yards up Tower Hill and climbed the scaffold, Guilford crying pitifully the whole time.

From where I was standing, I could not hear the words, but I saw the executioner – a huge man dressed in dramatic scarlet – step forward and receive his fee. Guilford made a very short speech; he seemed to be holding up better in the final stage of his ordeal. He was bandaged, led to the block and knelt forward. The axeman took position, legs apart, wielding the shining axe to his right. As soon as Guilford's arms were outstretched, he swung, backward and down, and the head fell at first strike. The crowd cheered as the executioner stepped forward, lifting the head high for all to see, then callously dropping it into the straw filled basket.

I took a number of deep breaths. Although it had been distant from me, and I had no element of liking – even compassion – for Guilford Dudley, it was still a shock to see how suddenly a man could be reduced from a Lord of the realm to a basket of meat, still oozing blood.

The executioner wiped the axe and began to walk back toward the Tower. The gentlemen fell in behind him and the solemn procession was followed by a cart, carrying Guilford's body, and the head, wrapped in a sheet, in the blood-soaked basket beside it. Slowly they entered the gate to the Tower and turned left, past the Beauchamp Tower where Guilford had spent the last months of his life.

The cart continued up the slope, past Tower Green, and stopped outside the door of the chapel of St Peter ad Vincula, the accompanying gentlemen and the executioner stopping a few yards short, at the small, temporary scaffold which had been erected a few days before, on Tower Green.

I wondered where Jane was now. Something, I didn't know what, told me she was standing at the upstairs window of the house as the cart went past, and had watched Guilford's body make the last few yards of its journey to the burial place. Now it was time for her to do the same. My heart started beating faster and I felt dizzy as I waited for her to appear.

She left the house below me, accompanied by Sir John Bridges and Dr Richard Feckenham, and began the short walk across the Green. It was only a few paces, but even in that short distance, two things were clearly evident. The first was how small she was – surrounded by large gentlemen, she looked diminutive, simply a child. But if the dimensions of the person walking to her own execution were those of a child, the stature of that person was, indeed, that of a great Lady.

She did not hurry, to keep pace with the men, but walked with measured steps, at her own pace, so that all those around her had to chop their strides to remain with her. Looking down, I thought she did not look like a prisoner, being led forward by a band of strong men, but more like a Queen, walking confidently at her own pace, surrounded by followers, each eager to match his pace with hers.

As she reached the scaffold, two servant butchers – I could not describe their callous inhumanity otherwise – dragged Guilford's body from the cart and began to take it into the chapel. Jane saw the movement and turned, seeing, for a brief moment, her husband's still warm body being carried unceremoniously into the church. It was the one thing she had not prepared for, and she gave a gasp of horror.

"Oh Guilford, Guilford! The antepast that you have tasted and I shall soon taste, is not so bitter as to make my flesh tremble; for all this is nothing to the feast that you and I shall partake this day in Paradise."

Standing a short distance away on the wall above them, I heard it all clearly. I felt so proud of her bravery and self-control. At the same time, her words put a pang of sorrow in my heart, for as she addressed her husband in this intimate way, I realized, now and for ever, once and for all, that I was out of her life; that wherever she went after this terrible episode, I would not be part of it. The thought hit me like a blow, and for a moment I felt sorry for myself. Then, just as suddenly, I realized how self-centred I was being, and watched as Jane embraced Dr Feckenham and bade him leave, perhaps to spare him the sight of what was to follow, but more probably, I thought, to allow her to focus on her final responsibilities in this life.

Jane mounted the scaffold and faced the scarlet-clad executioner who stood, block and axe behind his back. She turned to Sir John Bridges and asked, "Can I speak what is in my mind?"

"Yes ma'am" he replied, pale faced, and she approached the rail.

"Good people. I am come hither to die, and by a law I am condemned to the same. My offence against the Queen's Highness was only in consent to the devices of others, which is now deemed treason; but it was never of my seeking, but by counsel of those who should seem to have further understanding of things than I, which knew little of the law, and much less of the titles of the Crown. But touching the procurement and the desire thereof by me, or on my behalf, I do wash my hands in innocency thereof before God, and in the face of all you good Christian people this day."

She wrung her hands, and held her prayer book tightly, perhaps for support.

"I pray you all, good Christian people, to bear me witness that I die a true Christian woman, and that I look to be saved by none other means but only by the mercy of God, in the blood of His only Son, Jesus Christ. And I confess that when I did know the world of God, I neglected the same and loved myself and the world, and therefore this plague and punishment is justly and worthily happened unto me and my sins; and yet I thank God of His goodness, that He hath given me a time and respite to repent."

She lifted her head and addressed the very back row of the small crowd who had been allowed to enter the Tower to see her die.

"And now, good people, while I am alive, I pray you to assist me with your prayers."

She turned to Feckenham, who had remained by her side.

"Shall I say this psalm?"

After clearing his throat, Feckenham replied, "Yea."

Lady Jane knelt and, in a strong voice, recited all nineteen verses of the Fifty-First Psalm in English, whilst Feckenham, kneeling beside her, followed in Latin.

At the end they both rose and Jane said, "God I beseech Him abundantly reward you for your kindness towards me. Although I must needs say, it was more unwelcome to me than my instant death is terrible."

Feckenham could not summon a reply and Jane leaned forward and kissed him. She then said goodbye to Sir John Bridges and gave him her prayer book, then signalled Nurse Ellen, to whom she gave her handkerchief and gloves.

Jane began to undo her gown and the executioner, assuming he would take it as part of his fee, as was customary, stepped forward.

"Let me alone!" cried Jane and the huge man stood back, uncertainly. Ellen, who had controlled herself better than Jane had expected until the prayers were complete, was now in a state of total agitation, and Elizabeth Tilney had to remove the gown. Even she was overcome, however, and the two of them sobbed together as Jane was left, holding the handkerchief to form her blindfold in her hand.

The headsman came forward again and knelt. "Do you forgive me madam?" he asked.

"Most willingly," replied Jane, managing to give him a comforting smile.

Gently he led her forward. "Stand on the straw madam, if you please."

Jane moved forward and, kneeling, for the first time, saw the block. The headsman stood over her. "Will you take it off before I lay me down?" she asked, her voice now suddenly smaller.

"No madam," he replied, reassuringly.

Kneeling alone in the straw, she tied her own blindfold and then felt forward for the block. Her hands were inches short of it and she began to feel around, suddenly uncertain. "Where is it? Where is it?"

Everyone stood, immobile, uncertain.

"What shall I do?" she cried, now sounding frightened for the first time.

Someone in the crowd climbed up the scaffold and led her

cold hands onto the block. She moved her knees forward a few inches and placed her head on the block.

"Lord into Thy hands I commend my spirit," she said, her voice stronger again.

The axe fell cleanly and buried itself deep in the block. The small head jumped forward and fell, spurting blood into the straw.

The executioner let go of the axe, which remained embedded in the block, and stepped forward, lifting Jane's head by the hair. He held it high.

"So perish all the Queen's enemies! Behold the head of a traitor."

There was a moan of anguish and resignation from the crowd. Some of them stepped back, disturbed, as they realized that her blood had spattered their clothing. Slowly the crowd and the Tower officials began to disperse, leaving Jane's body lying there in the cold. Mrs Tilney and Nurse Ellen were left with the body of their mistress, and friend.

I knelt on the wall and prayed for Jane, for the ladies below, for myself and for a world which could act so unfairly in the interests of self- preservation. The two butchers emerged from the church and began to walk toward Jane's body. Seeing them coming, Nurse Ellen screamed, "No! Leave her alone! Haven't you done enough?"

I ran down the steps and across the Green, pushing the butchers back as I arrived.

"Leave her," I shouted. "We will do it. Just show us where to go. Just show us. Don't touch her! Don't you dare touch her."

I wrapped the small body in my cloak and lifted it gently. She weighed nothing. Then, shocked, I realized that her head still lay where the headsman had put it down. Mrs Tilney and Nurse Ellen were staring at it, their hands over their mouths. I screamed at one of the butchers.

"You!"

The servant stared at me, catatonic with fear.

"Wrap her head. Carefully mind, and bring it with you. You,

the other, lead the way into the church. And show due reverence to the body of this Lady or by God I will smash your heads to pulp on the very flagstones and lay you alongside her."

I carried her into the church, where a small coffin stood on trestles, ready to receive her. I tried to put her in it, but the bulk of my cloak prevented it. The leading servant turned to me, pleading.

"Please sir, let us do it. It is our job and we know what to do. We will honour her sir, ladies, have no fear. You may pray here if you wish, for you will be left in peace, but please let us do what we have to do."

I looked into the man's eyes. He was not a callous butcher, just a poorly paid servant, trying to do a grisly job. Gently I let go of the little body and stepped back.

"I am sorry. You are right. Here!" I reached into my jerkin and took two gold coins from my purse. I handed one to each of the body-servants.

"Treat her gently. Please treat her gently."

Slowly, holding each other for support, I led Nurse Ellen and Mrs Tilney towards the back of the church, where we might pray in peace. Mrs Tilney, ever practical, shook me off as we reached the doorway.

"I will fetch Mrs Jacob. She was watching from the house and will be wondering what has happened to us. She will want to pray with us, I am sure."

❧ ❦

We returned to the house just after twelve o'clock and found Mrs Partridge had laid dinner for us.

"I didn't know if you could face anything, but it seemed the right thing to do. We all have to continue, somehow."

We thanked her and sat at table, thinking more than eating.

"Where will you go now?" asked Mrs Partridge. "Not that I am trying to throw you out, you understand. You are welcome to stay if you wish. I just thought you might want to ..."

Nobody knew the answer. We had all focused our thinking

407

on this day and this day alone. Mrs Tilney, as usual, was the practical one.

"We will collect her Ladyship's possessions and our own bits and pieces, and take them to Suffolk Place. Edmund Tucker will know what to do. You go ahead when we have eaten Richard and tell them we are coming. Tidying up here is ladies' work."

ॐ   ॐ

It was mid-afternoon when I was ready to leave. Now it felt strange. After months of being cooped up here – how long was it? Seven months Lady Jane had been held in the Tower and with the exception of the very occasional trip outside, we had remained with her throughout.

It would be strange to be out there again, free of this place which had dominated our lives for so long. As I began to walk toward the gates of the Tower, I was thinking of the few occasions I had been able to go outside – almost all of them to visit the Earl of Devon, for his riding lessons.

As I reached the gate the yeomen held me back with their halberds. For a moment I panicked. Were they going to hold me here?

"I am free to leave. I was Lady Jane's servant and now am returning to the Duke's house."

"That's alright young man," grinned the older of the two, "we are just keeping the gate open for Sir Robert Southwell. He'll be here any minute to interrogate the new prisoner."

"Oh, what new prisoner is that?" I asked, conversationally. The yeoman jerked his head toward the Bell Tower above us.

"Edward Courtenay, Earl of Devon. Brought in here this morning he was, arrested for treasonable negligence, just after the Lady lost her head. Friend of yours is he?"

I stood in the gateway to the Tower of London and looked round the cobbled lanes and the small patch of grass which formed Tower Green.

"No," I said, "I don't know him at all. I'm just a servant."

As I spoke, three of the ravens began cawing noisily across the

Green. I looked at the halberdiers, frightened that they would have the same thought that was flooding into my head.

Judas Iscariot! I am no better than Judas Iscariot!

But my instinct for survival gave me strength and, avoiding their eyes, for it seemed they had not noticed the ravens, I hurried past the halberdiers and away from the Tower, wanting only to lose myself in the crowds on London Bridge.

I stumbled forward, eyes full of tears, clumsily bumping into people as I went, unwilling to look at anyone, wanting only to be alone with my grief, grimly focusing on the only useful thing I could do; to tell Edmund that they had finally destroyed the fine, honest lady we both knew and loved, and to ask him to prepare to help the ladies, for they would surely need support from both of us.

❧ CHAPTER 76 ❧

12th–13th February 1554 – Suffolk Place

I blundered on towards London Bridge, walked away from the Tower without once looking back. I could not face the memory of what I had just left behind. Inside I was torn apart. Part of me wanted to get as far away as possible from the horror of seeing dear Jane so bloodily mutilated. At the same time, another part of me wanted to turn back, to kneel by her grave and try to say to her all the things I should have said but failed to say when she was alive.

How could I have failed her so badly, done so little to protect and support her?

Yet as my heart grieved that I had not done more while she was alive, a cold, isolating realization came into my mind, that in the end, there was nothing any of us could have done, for her demise had had its roots in Northumberland's eternal greed for power, a greed almost matched by Lady Frances' own obsession with recovering her family's place in history and Suffolk's spineless acceptance of both, at the expense of his own child's life.

At the turn in Thames Street, halfway to the north end of London Bridge, and a safe distance from the Tower, I paused. This, I knew, was the point at which the Tower would disappear from view, and I could not think of Jane watching me leave her without so much as a backward look. It felt like a rejection, a betrayal, of someone who had become closer to me than any other over the last six months and to whom I owed much of my learning and perhaps most of my attitudes. I turned and looked at the Tower, walls shining in the late afternoon sun.

Was she in there still? Or had she already left for a better place? I found myself taking off my cap and looking again at the Tower and then up to the sky. I raised my cap to her and began to cry. Passers by glared at me as I stood, sobbing, on the road's edge, following my upward gaze as if wondering what I was looking at.

The remainder of the walk from the Tower to Suffolk Place was not far – no more than a mile – but as I put away the memories of Jane to be retrieved again on less public occasions, and began to look about me at the world in which I remained, seemingly alone, it came as a shock to me now. In particular, having pushed my way southward across London Bridge, past the stallholders and northbound travellers, I was shocked to see the number of gibbets on the Southwark side, containing the stinking bodies of the newly condemned rioters. The Queen's mercy to the rank and file of Wyatt's army clearly did not extend to their leaders. It was here, for the first, but by no means the last time, that I heard the Queen described as "Bloody Mary", a title which gave me the shivers when I remembered how close I myself had been to involvement with Edward Courtenay and his fellow conspirators.

~ ~

It was strange, arriving at Suffolk Place. It had been seven months since I had last slept here and, although physically the building remained unchanged, its atmosphere had transformed completely. Gone was the crowded energy of the headquarters of a scheming high-born family. Gone, too, was the terrible echo of Jane's arguments with her parents about the marriage they had arranged for her. Now the house was quiet and still, as if getting its own breath back, after being surrounded by the throng of Wyatt's army only two weeks before.

One constant in my life was there, however.

Edmund Tucker had returned only that morning from Sheen, where he was currently spending most of his time, to collect some items required by Lady Frances. Ever with an eye on her own and her family's future, she had, he explained, been working hard to cement her relationship with Queen Mary, in the face of her daughter's impending execution and her husband's imprisonment and spending most of her time at Whitehall. Edmund was due to return to Sheen the following day, after sending the items in question upriver with 'a reliable boatman'.

"Do you still employ the Barley brothers?" I asked, as we sat overlooking the Thames and catching up on old times.

"John and Dick? Yes of course. Best boatmen on the river. And reliably the rudest too."

He laughed, awkwardly, and I laughed with him. It was good to laugh again, if only for a moment. At the beginning of the conversation, I had tried to stop myself, feeling it was disrespectful to the broken body I had seen interred not six hours before, under the floor in St Peter ad Vincula, but then I had remembered again Jane's words, and at the same time realized that Edmund was using humour to mask his own pain. For he, too, had loved Jane, not least because she had always treated him as a friend, and never teased him about his feminine mannerisms.

For some time we discussed the impending return of Mrs Tilney and Nurse Ellen. It appeared that Mrs Jacob had other plans and would not be returning to Suffolk Place.

"We will go to Sheen together, but you will not be able to see both the girls. Mary is not there – she is with her mother at Whitehall, but Catherine is still at Sheen."

Edmund slipped it into the conversation as if it were a small matter and of no import.

"Catherine? Is she? How does she fare?"

"Not well Richard. This last six months she has been playing

411

a role more like Jane's, dancing and smiling at Court, having been thrown out of her husband's household, and with her sister in prison and under threat of death. She will take Jane's death very badly I fear. It would be much preferable if you were to accompany me and break the news yourself. You were with Jane at the end and you can answer all Catherine's questions and soften the blow."

I thought for a while. I had precious little else to do, except wait to see what happened to my employer, and I had Suffolk's own view that his future was a short one indeed.

"Very well Edmund. I agree. We will ride to Sheen together in the morning, but I must talk to the Barleys again before we leave. It's so long since I was at the butt end of their jokes."

❧ CHAPTER 77 ❧

14th–22nd February 1554 – Suffolk Place

By the time Edmund had given the Barleys their instructions and we had together waited for the morning tide, it was ten o'clock. We watched them depart upstream and gathered our things from the house.

"You will have to ride slowly Edmund. I am out of practice."

"I don't believe what I am hearing. The great horseman asks me to wait for him?"

"Not only have my muscles grown weak in the Tower, but so have my horses.' It will take me weeks to get Jack back into condition. How fat he has been allowed to become, and Ventura and Vixen too!"

Edmund looked chastened. "I am truly sorry if your horses are out of condition Richard, but I manage great houses not great horses. Apart from ensuring they are clean, fed and watered, I cannot keep on top of the grooms' work as you would have done. You will just have to get fit together."

It didn't seem too bad a prospect. My head felt too full of

thoughts and only now did I realize how much my body had wasted away during my months of enforced inactivity. The question which was starting to worry me now was how I would find employment if, as I myself expected, Suffolk was found guilty of treason. For it was almost certain that he would not only lose his life, but his estates would be attained – effectively taken back by the Crown which had probably granted most of them in the first place.

"Edmund? Can I ask you a difficult question?"

"Yes Richard, what is it?"

"When I last visited his Lordship he told me he expected to be executed for his part in the uprising against the Queen's marriage. If that happens, and the remains of Wyatt's army on the Southwark gibbets make it seem probable, he is likely to be attained isn't he?"

"Yes. And if that happens, you are wondering what will happen to us and where will we find employment?" Edmund had clearly been worrying about the same thing. "Well my view is that I am good at what I do, and my skill attaches to the houses I manage, not to the people I work for. So if someone else is gifted one or more of the houses, I am hopeful that they will need someone to run it for them, and will employ me in that capacity. Why do you ask? Are you concerned for yourself?"

"Certainly I am. The problem is, I do not have an established trade and I don't know a lot of powerful people. Furthermore, the ones I did know well are all former followers of Northumberland and somehow I don't think they will be in the ascendancy under this Queen, do you?"

Edmund smirked. "You have the truth of it there alright Richard. Perhaps you should start working on your contacts. What happened to that nice Irish boy, for example. Wasn't he at Court?"

"Fergal? Yes he was, but not for much longer I think. He is still hanging around the Court, waiting to see what will happen, but somehow I cannot see him securing a position of authority as Master of the Queen's bedchamber can you?"

Edmund nodded his agreement. "You could, of course, escape the Court and return to your roots. From what you were saying last night, you might be safer out of it with this Queen in power. There must be people you know back in Devon. What about that Doctor something you were always talking about?"

"Thomas Marwood? Yes I could write to him, it's true. I was hoping to travel home this spring with the Earl, but now he's in the Tower, that visit looks less likely."

"You do choose well, don't you Richard? Why must you fly so close to the sun? It's dangerous, and the rewards, though sometimes large, are sporadic and uncertain. I should forget Earls and Dukes if I were you and settle for life amongst the merchants, or the men of learning. Be measured by your own talents, and not carried by the uncertain patronage of others."

I rode my horse close to Edmund's and laughed. "Someone else gave me that advice on his deathbed."

Edmund turned his head. "Who was that?"

"The late King. King Edward. He told me the same thing, less than a week before he died."

Edmund leaned over and took my reign, bringing both our horses, and those of the followers behind, to a stop.

"Those were prophetic words then Richard. Don't you see – he saw it all coming: the battle for power, the likelihood that his sister (whom he knew in his heart of hearts was his true successor, much as he disliked what she stood for); he could see a battle looming which Mary would eventually win. He was warning you off, Richard! The King was warning you against fixing your colours too publicly to the wrong mast."

We rode on into Sheen in silence. I was going over and over in my head what the King had said to me and why, without realizing it, I had not followed his advice. Edmund, on the other hand, having glibly given me the benefit of his advice, now appeared to be questioning whether he should take more note of that advice for his own future. It was all so uncertain these days.

          ∾ ∾

We came to the house in the darkness of a winter's evening, the temperature dropping fast and a cold mist beginning to drift in from the nearby River Thames.

I could feel the house jump into life as we clattered into the cobbled courtyard. Edmund had that effect on all the houses he visited. Effeminate he might be, but the staff knew and trusted him, and his sheer energy and enthusiasm gave him qualities of comfortable leadership which I envied.

We sat together in the Great Hall. Prior to the dissolution the building had been an abbey and this its refectory, and the long tables remained. Hot supper was brought and I was enjoying my soup and good fresh bread and looking forward to the meat and vegetables which had just been brought to us when I noticed a strange expression on Edmund's face, as if he was trying overly hard to remain expressionless.

"Why are you pulling that strange face Edmund?"

"What strange face?" It was the face of a small baby immediately before it soils itself; a look of intense concentration.

Small, cool hands closed over my eyes and I smelled the perfume on her hair. So that was it. Edmund had seen her creeping up behind me and had been trying – perhaps overly hard – not to give the game away.

"Catherine!"

She climbed over the bench and sat next to me.

"Hello Richard. How are you?"

Her voice had grown huskier – no girl now, this woman exuded an aura of animal femininity.

She squeezed my leg, exactly as her mother had done on the first occasion we had met, beside the fireplace at Shute. "You are getting scrawny. You need more exercise to build up your muscles."

The way she said it seemed to suggest that horses were not a necessary part of the bargain.

"I have not had much opportunity. Seven months is a long time even in an open prison."

Her eyes dropped. "I am sorry. That was inappropriate. I was just trying to tease you."

415

I took her hand and squeezed it gently. "Nothing you say will upset me tonight, for after seeing the death of your dear sister, there can be no more evil in this world; life can only get better."

She went pale and gripped my hand tightly. "I did not know how to raise the subject. Can you tell me about it? Was it awful?"

I looked across at Edmund. I had already been through the whole story of Jane's last days, hour by hour, pain by pain, with him.

He responded immediately. "I shall leave you two alone. Thus is a private conversation and I shall not intrude." Edmund took a large platter of bread and meat and stepped away from the table.

Steadily, I finished my meal and began my story, describing the months of certainty that Jane would eventually be freed, and then the slow realization that Wyatt's rebellion was turning the tables against her. Without being aware of it, I began drinking the strong red wine that sat before us on the table and with each glass I took, she refilled her own. Eventually I reached the final hours; the countdown to that last, terrible morning.

"Not here." She took my hand. "Don't tell me here. The subject is too private for a hall like this. Please come upstairs, where no servants can interrupt us."

She took my hand and led me upstairs, to her room. It was sparsely furnished, as befitted a former abbey, but there was a large bed in the centre of the room, and she led me there.

"Come. This room is freezing, but we will be warm in here."

Beside the bed was a small table and on it three bottles of wine. One was already open and half finished and she refilled our pewter tankards and brought them to the bed.

She kicked off her slippers and climbed in. "Come on. Take your boots and jerkin off. We'll be warm, safe and comfortable here. Just the two of us."

I joined her in the huge bed and she pulled the heavy winter cover around us. I put my arm around her, and we sat, leaning against the carved bed-head, in our own private world. Slowly, quietly, truthfully, but in as kindly a way as I could, I told her what had happened, step by step, as she clung to me.

Catherine wanted to know every detail. Knowing the reality, however awful, was, she said, easier than allowing your imagination to create its own nightmares. Whilst remaining scrupulously honest, I was careful to emphasize the kinder moments; Feckenham's compassion and Jane's words of thanks, Sir John Bridges's steadfast support and Jane's gift of the prayer book. Throughout, I emphasized how Jane had remained composed and, for effect as well as truth, juxtaposed this with Guilford's inability to come to terms with his fate. Jane was, I assured her, wholly confident of what awaited her on the other side and faced the moment of death, if not with equanimity, then at least with confidence that her God was holding her hand all the way through.

As the story unfolded, Catherine became calmer. "She is happy now, isn't she?" she asked. I assured her it was true.

"You have no idea Richard, how hard it has been to play the Court Lady when my sister is awaiting death. I have lain in bed, wanting to scream at the unfairness, the brutality and the selfishness of it all. I have seen the ambassadors scheming, whispering and plotting. They care nothing for people. All they care about is their precious power-politics and the rewards which will likely be theirs if their plan is brought to fruition."

I agreed and pulled her closer to me. We reached to the table and took more wine. Somehow, it seemed to be having no effect.

"Patronage may be a natural consequence of one man's power over many others, but it is a sinful manipulation of man's greed and pride's weakness. Kings and Queens should be above such things, they have enough — no need for further greed."

Catherine slid lower against my chest and put her hand inside my shirt, feeling my heart beating and seeming to gain comfort from its regularity.

"You don't see it from their position." Her voice came from somewhere under my chin.

"They don't see it as wanting more. Their great fear is of losing everything they have. Think about the two Princesses, Mary and Elizabeth. What one gains the other loses — including, possibly, life itself. That is why the ambassadors will now turn their bile against Elizabeth – to protect their investment in Queen Mary. It's disgusting, but it's reality."

"If that is the world of the Court, I, for one, want no more part of it."

I heard myself speak the words and realized as I did so, I had made a decision.

"Nor I. But I may find it more difficult to escape from than you, for I was born into it. But for tonight I am here with you and here I shall remain, safe, warm and – wanting you. Tonight, all we have is each other. Somehow I don't think Jane would disapprove."

The candles were growing dim and guttering. I felt her moving beneath the heavy covers and realized she was undressing. She threw her clothes out of the bed and her nakedness glowed against me. In return, I too, removed my clothes and threw them wildly into the dark. Finally, we clung together in our own private world, safe at last, protected from the world outside, if only for this night, by our unwillingness to think any more about it or even to acknowledge its existence.

❧ ❧

For the next week we remained in our dream, recognizing every morning that it had to end soon, but unwilling to hasten the moment. Indulged by Edmund and the house staff, we rose late, dined privately, walked and rode together beside the river and went to bed early.

With each day, the fear and urgency subsided; fear of losing each other and urgency to consummate the relationship before that happened. We talked of the future and agreed we did not have one, beyond, perhaps, a few more days.

I now knew I would return to Devon and rebuild my life outside the Royal Court, which I had learned to despise.

Catherine, on the other hand, accepted that she was born into that world and, when, in a few days, the spell broke, she would return to it, and, no doubt, be reabsorbed into its ways.

Together, we also looked back, at childhood, and, in particular, at Jane, who both of us had loved, in our different ways. Now we knew for certainty that with her death, our own childhoods had finally been put behind us and that from now on we must try to face the reality of the present with as much enthusiasm as we had our early, childish, dreams for the future.

Hiding there, deep in the covers of this huge bed, we made a pact; that while this stolen moment lasted, we would make the most of it we possibly could. Catherine called it "creating memories" and every day (and every night) we created moments which we knew we would remember all their lives; moments we would look back on with comfort and pleasure, without regret, with no feeling of loss, simply fleeting moments when the good in the world came together and we were able to enjoy it – and each other – to the full.

❧ ❦

Late in the evening of the 17th of February, the spell was broken. A messenger came for Edmund to tell him that the Duke of Suffolk had been tried, condemned and attained. His execution was arranged for February 23rd.

Edmund read the words of the attainder. Suffolk Place, Dorset House and Bradgate Park ... All were clearly included, and all to be returned to the Crown forthwith, but the Chapterhouse at Sheen seemed to have been omitted.

"That may be because Sheen was originally granted to Lady Frances, not to Suffolk himself. The Queen may have decided to leave her friend somewhere to live."

"Are the Manor of Shute in Devon and Shute House mentioned there?" I asked.

Edmund read the document carefully. "Shute. Yes it is here, together with its grounds and hunting park."

I looked at Catherine and saw in her expression that she was thinking the same as I was.

"This may be our last night together. Tomorrow I must ride to Suffolk Place with Edmund to recover the family's movable possessions. We will go to the Tower and see our master, your father, executed. He would expect us to do that. Then we will return here. After that, who knows?"

Catherine nodded and took my hand.

"I shall have to join Mother at Court. But before that, we still have tonight."

❧ CHAPTER 78 ❧

22nd February 1554 – The Chapterhouse, Sheen

I took my example from Jane. Catherine and I said our good-byes in bed, lost in each other's arms. This was how we wanted to remember each other; together, alone, in privacy, and in love. As we lay there, Catherine did not want to be reminded that I was soon to ride to Devon, to start a new life who knew where. And beside her, the last thing I wanted to think about at this precious moment was that Catherine would soon be back at Court, flirting with young Lords, measuring Earls and Dukes as potential husbands, and generally being offered around in the royal cattle market. If it had to end, then at least it could end here, on our own terms.

Before we parted we made each other a promise: no tears, no regrets and no silly dreams that "If only it had been otherwise". We had met, we had fallen in love and, after being kept apart for so long, we had, if only for a short while, been able to declare our love openly to each other and to enjoy its heady warmth, unfettered by family or by politics.

"Think of what we have had, not what we may miss in the future. I love you and always shall. And even if, in some future time, I may love another, I shall never forget you." I had chosen my parting words carefully.

"You were my first love, and I shall always remember you, too," Catherine had replied, equally carefully, for although her short marriage to William, Lord Herbert, had not been seen as a political success by her family, for her and for William it had apparently been a loving and successful marriage at a personal level and she had never pretended to me that it had been anything otherwise.

I left her there, in the bed we had shared for our last, almost idyllic week. We had not forgotten Jane; quite the reverse. Somehow our shared love for her had acted as an additional bond between us, and, conscious that she had sanctioned our relationship, we were able to be happy together, knowing that she would not have wanted us to grieve on her account.

It had turned colder; one of those raw February days when the wind cuts into you and no amount of clothing keeps you entirely warm.

"It's what we call in Devon 'a lazy wind'," I said to Edmund, "goes right through you because it's too lazy to go round you."

Edmund shook the ice off his fur riding coat and grimaced.

"I hope it's not like this tomorrow. Lord Henry may have been a weak man, misled by that dreadful wife of his, and responsible for his daughter's death, but I would not wish such a day on any man for his last on earth."

"Amen to that," I replied, forehead down against the wind to prevent my hat from being torn from my head.

All day we struggled against the wind and the snow and both we and our horses were exhausted by the time we reached Suffolk Place and a hot meal.

❧   ☙

Edmund's prayers seemed partially to have been answered the following morning, for although it remained cold, and snow still fell intermittently, the wind had dropped, and we were able to ride across London Bridge and the short mile to Tower Hill without mishap.

There was only a small crowd to see poor Suffolk off; nothing like the throng which had gathered to see the end of Northumberland's hated life. The crowd stood around us, stamping their feet for warmth, and cheered when the prisoner was at

421

last seen being brought from the Tower up the short slope of Tower Hill. Suffolk acknowledged the crowd, perhaps thinking that their cheers represented some sort of support, but standing at the rear, we could hear the undertone of mutters and realized the crowd were simply wanting the thing to be over and done with, so they could get about their business in the city and get warm.

As with Guilford Dudley's execution, the Queen had insisted that a Catholic priest be present, but in Suffolk's final speech to the crowd he had declared that he would "be saved by none other but only by almighty God, through the passion of His son, Jesus Christ."

He went to the block bravely enough, refusing to shiver in the cold morning air as his coat was removed and his shirt collar folded down to expose his neck. Many in the crowd had expected the heavy ice which lay everywhere to intervene in the event – some said the executioner's feet would slip all over the place and he would "have to take two or three goes at him" but in the event, fresh pine sawdust was spread heavily all over the scaffold and even half-filled the basket into which, with God's blessing, Suffolk's head fell at first blow of the axe.

The crowd dispersed rapidly as Edmund, solicitous on our master's behalf even after his death, moved forward to enquire of the officials where our master was to be buried. "St Peter's Chapel, in the Tower," was the terse and uninterested reply, but it satisfied Edmund who turned to me with a gentle smile on his face.

"Let us hope that he is laid beside his daughter and that, as a result, they can be reconciled in heaven, for what he did to her here on earth was a most heinous thing."

He was right. Forgive and move on.

We retrieved our horses and rode slowly down Tower Hill, past the gates of the Tower of London and on toward London Bridge. Somehow the morning's events did not seem enough. It seemed an insignificant, almost trivial ending for a man who had always treated me with fairness and kindness, and, like others before me (John Aylmer and Adrian Stokes in particular), had given me the opportunity to rise in society and to exercise those talents I had to the full.

Even after a year or more in London, much of it in the Tower, and with the recent aftermath of Wyatt's rebellion clear in my mind, I still found the callous brutality of executions shocking. Looking back over my shoulder at the now-deserted Tower Hill scaffold, I realized that it wasn't the actions of those on the scaffold which I found hard to accept – they had a job to do and a political point to make in order (theoretically) to deter others. No, the really shocking element was the callous response of the crowd, who regularly turned out in their hundreds and sometimes thousands, to see men's heads severed brutally with an axe, or even worse, men hanged and retrieved before death, only to be castrated, disembowelled and finally hacked into quarters.

However serious one man's crime against another, it seemed to me that to degrade him to that extent upon death simply signalled the festering rottenness of society itself, and the brutal selfishness of those who negotiated for such sentences to be passed, and those who carried them out with such obvious relish.

Edmund and I reached the end of London Bridge and paused, watching the throng which daily used the bridge as a passageway over the river and as a market and meeting place. Our thoughts seemed to coincide. Beyond lay an empty Suffolk Place, but with Suffolk attained before his execution, it would shortly be taken into the Queen's power and lost to the family. Already what had, for some time, felt like a warm and grand home, just beyond the worst stench of the city, now seemed part of our past and had no role in our future.

"Let's get drunk!" shouted Edmund decisively.

"In a tavern?" I replied, looking round for a convenient watering hole in the mass of inns and drinking dens which surrounded the end of this, the main thoroughfare to Kent and the south.

"No. Let's go back to the house and toast poor Suffolk in his own wine and brandy. We will have a feast prepared and eat and drink the lot, for if we do not do so, it will either go to waste or some other rich bugger will come and inherit it all."

For the first time in all my conversations with 'Celestial' Edmund, I could hear the hard edge of resentment in his voice, the normally angelic shape of his face contorted by frustrated anger. I had known Edmund for some three years – since July 1551 in fact, when I had first arrived, wide-eyed at the gates of Dorset House. How long ago that seemed now. Yet in all that time, Edmund had always been the master of discretion and self-control; this was the first time I had seen such an outburst, and somehow I liked Edmund the more for it.

"Agreed. Come on Jack, walk on." I squeezed my horse with my heels and felt the crowd melt away as Jack nudged his way forward, Edmund's horse following close behind.

ঞ ঙ

We did not have to rummage around to find what we wanted. Edmund's encyclopaedic memory meant he knew where the best of everything was hidden away.

"If we take it away from here, it's stealing, but if we eat it, or drink it, while we are here, it's only consumption," hiccoughed Edmund, opening another bottle.

We began soon after noon, and continued all afternoon. By five o'clock we were full, and drunk.

"What are you going to do now Richard? Are you coming back to Sheen with me?"

"I shall have to, my other horses and possessions are all there. Besides, I have nowhere else to go.

"Who was your best friend, or advisor, before you met the Grey family?"

"Before I met the Grey family I didn't know many powerful people at all – not well that is. As a young boy I used to turn for advice to Dr Thomas Marwood."

"The physician? The one who went all the way to Italy to learn medicine? Well surely he could help and advise you? You said you wanted to get away from Court and I think you are right. Dear Lady Jane left you with an unfortunate legacy for these times under Queen Mary."

I looked at him enquiringly, eyebrow raised.

"Your faith, and your commitment to reformation of the Church. You underestimate the influence she had on you. I noticed it when you came back from your months in the Tower. Although you were shocked by her death and brought down in a way I have never seen before, you had also gained a faith and with it a new inner confidence – in yourself and your own judgements. You will be much less easily led (and misled) in the future, I'll wager."

"And you Edmund? What does the future hold for you?"

"Oh I shall continue doing what I do best – running a great house somewhere. I have been fortunate to meet a number of influential men along the way. I am confident I shall find somewhere."

"Is that all? Is that all that life offers for you – work, responsibility, a great house to run? Is there nothing else?"

"Do you mean companionship? Yes, I wish it could be possible. There have been situations, but they never came to anything."

"You mean you nearly got married? I didn't know that."

Edmund poured each of us another glass of Suffolk's best Bordeaux wine and grinned at my simplicity.

"Married? Me? Hardly. When I talk of companionship I mean a man, a strong one to look after me and to be my true friend." His long eyelashes lifted provocatively. "I am a natural servant. I am not like you, I do not want to lead – in my work, yes, but not in my private life."

Drunkenly he put his hand on my arm.

"I want to be led, guided, instructed … perhaps even dominated."

I looked into my friend's expressive, almost womanly face.

"Do you mean you are …"

Disappointed, Edmund withdrew his hand.

"Please don't use any of those words Richard. I hate them.

They fail entirely to understand anything. But yes, I have taken pleasure in the physical company of men, and will do again, if the opportunity arises. I should never have said anything. It's the drink. I am sorry."

For a moment I looked at my friend, always so reliable and in control, but now suddenly looking immensely lonely. I reached out and took his hand.

"Don't be sad Edmund. You will find that companionship, I am sure, but you know it will not be with me."

Edmund snatched his hand away.

"No Richard, no. You misunderstand!" he shouted vehemently. "I did not think for one minute – not after seeing you and Lady Catherine. I only wanted you to know – to understand, as a friend. Forgive me."

I shook my head.

"There is nothing to forgive. You are my friend and I do understand. Let us seal our continuing friendship with another bottle." I walked across the room and opened the one bottle remaining on the board, turning back to him as I did so.

"Is that why you joined Suffolk?"

Edmund ran his finger round the rim of his glass, seemingly lost in his memories.

"Yes, in part. It was a good house, and a good opportunity. But in addition, Dorset, as he then was, seemed lonely, as if looking for the same companionship I was searching for. Obviously he was married and had children, but he and Lady Frances seemed distant and I thought, well ... we can all dream."

"And the dream did not become a reality?"

Edmund laughed. "Not in the sense you mean it, and I may have hoped for. I don't think he would have had the courage – or the imagination. No he just wanted someone to play the son he never had. It worked well for a long time – he was a kind and generous master and I was an attentive and loyal servant. We did become friends," he drained his glass in one gulp, "but not lovers. And then you came along."

I looked at him, doubly shocked.

"Did I usurp your position? Did I spoil your friendship with our master? If so, it was never my intention to do so. I swear it."

Edmund poured us both another glass.

"No. No. Not at all. It's just that Suffolk's focus turned to you as far as the substitute son was concerned. In all other respects our relationship continued, and I have no complaints. I wasn't the first. John Aylmer and Adrian Stokes also played that role for a time. John became totally committed to Lady Jane and as for Adrian – well you know that he and Lady Frances were – and still are – what shall I say? Energetic together?"

"Even now? I thought Adrian had been sent packing?"

"Don't you believe a word of it. After you gave him the beating of a lifetime, he was sent to Bradgate, but Lady Frances wrote to him every week and whenever the opportunity has arisen (which I admit has been little, this past year) they have wasted no opportunity in getting together. I am sure he has already been sent an instruction to return to Sheen – she would not dare declare him at Court, the Queen would forbid it and in any event, she would be a laughing stock. In fact, Richard, you ought to be on your guard, for he is likely to arrive at Sheen shortly after we do."

I climbed unsteadily to my feet.

"Which reminds me. We have a long and cold ride in the morning."

Edmund stood opposite me, equally unsteady. He gave me a slow, enticing smile.

"If only I could say as Lady Catherine did."

I gripped the edge of the table and leaned toward him.

"What was that?"

Edmund rolled his head, in the action of a lady throwing her long hair behind her.

"We still have tonight!"

I burst out laughing, and Edmund joined me, giggling drunkenly.

"Go to bed Edmund. And in your own room! I'll see you in the morning."

CHAPTER 79

24th February 1554 – The Chapterhouse, Sheen

We felt like death when we left Suffolk Place the next morning, and, after many hours buffeting against an icy wind, even worse when we arrived at Sheen. After a cold day, we received an even colder welcome, for Lady Frances was in one of her nastier moods. Edmund, with his subtle guile, soon wheedled the reason from one of the servants.

It appeared that even Lady Frances, with her thick skin, had found life at Court intolerable at the time her husband was to be executed, and so soon after the demise of her daughter, and had decided to hide away at Sheen until the focus of attention had died down. Having escaped the Court and hidden herself away from her husband's final days, she took our attendance at his execution as an implied criticism of herself and received us very coldly.

It was typical of Lady Frances's spiteful nature that, not having seen me for seven months while I accompanied her daughter in the Tower, she took pleasure in telling me, first, that Catherine had departed and was now attending again at Court, and second, that Adrian had been summoned from Bradgate park and would be joining her here at Sheen in the very near future.

"I don't know what you will do here Richard, to be sure, for Adrian and Edmund will have everything under control and in any event, having switched your allegiance to Lady Jane, now deceased, I hardly think we have any function you could usefully perform for us. Perhaps Adrian will be able to think of something when he arrives."

I was sure he could. So that was the lie of the land. Lady Frances ruled the roost, Adrian was back in her good books and, no doubt, her bed (if he had ever left either of them) and any association with, or loyalty from, the past was lost.

It was three hours before a nervous-looking maid named May crept up to me whilst Lady Frances was elsewhere and gave me a note.

"This is from Lady Catherine sir. She said to give it direct to you and not to let Lady Frances see it, for she would surely burn it before you heard about it."

I thanked her and found a quiet corner in which to read.

Dearest Richard,

Thank you for a week I shall always remember. I have been called to Court by the Queen, and since, as I understand, my mother is shortly to leave the Court to rest at Sheen (she being unwell after all the events of recent weeks), I must attend to the Queen's wishes.

We both knew this would happen soon. Now it has, and we each shall depart and go our separate ways.

Go forward into your future with hope and courage, as I know you will, always carrying the memory of my love. I for my part, shall always remember you, until my dying day. Jane said in one of her dear letters to me that we would all meet again in heaven and I trust she is right – she usually was.

Until then, may life serve you well, with the health and happiness you truly deserve.

Your ever loving
Cat

Carefully, I folded the letter. This was it; the end of one life but, hopefully, the beginning of a new one.

There was nothing left for me here. My relationship with the Grey family was over, and it was time to move on.

But where?

❧ CHAPTER 80 ❧

1st March 1554 – The Chapterhouse, Sheen

It was peculiar – like watching my own life unfold in front of me.

On the evening of the 1st March, just as it was growing dark, and in the middle of yet another snowstorm, Adrian arrived, frozen stiff. He was leading a party of about ten, with horses, carts and what appeared to be all the family's possessions.

No sooner had the party arrived than Lady Frances welcomed Adrian with hot drinks and ushered him to her room, where their food was served privately. For the next week the former pattern repeated itself.

While the lovers enjoyed their privacy, the rest of the house went steadily about its own business, managed, as always, by Edmund. Slowly, and in his usual methodical manner, he pieced the story together.

It appeared the instruction had come direct by Queen's messenger: Bradgate Park was attained and anything remaining after the 1st of March would be considered the property of the Crown. At the same time, Adrian had been tasked by Lady Frances with bringing everything which might be useful down south to Sheen. It was clear that Lady Frances had already given up Bradgate; it was now part of her past. Adrian had understood the situation and ransacked the house, bringing everything which might have any value whatsoever. There was nothing left, and James Ulverscroft and the remaining staff were left to fend for themselves until a new occupier appeared on the scene.

ð̀ð   ð̀s

The morning of the 9th March was bright and sunny but still with a crisp frost, which burned off quickly as the sun rose.

The lovers appeared, dressed in all their finery, and were shortly attended by a local priest. They were married quietly in the chapel and after an afternoon out riding, disappeared upstairs once again.

I watched them go. In the week since Adrian had arrived at Sheen, we had not spoken once, and somehow I did not relish our first conversation.

Edmund called me into the Great Hall.

"Richard! Come and meet Jonathan Bolitho. Jonathan is a merchant, a Cornishman from Falmouth, and is travelling home by road through Exeter. He tells me his route will take him through Honiton and for the price of a night's board and lodging when he gets there for himself and his three followers, he will carry messages for you to your friends there."

It was a heaven-sent opportunity. Immediately I jumped into action and wrote, one letter to Dr Marwood and one to my father. Bolitho joined me and Edmund for supper and accepted Edmund's offer to stay the night at Sheen, before setting off in the morning.

I took an immediate liking to Jonathan. He was short and strong as an ox, with short dark hair and a sailor's earring. Like many in the West Country he did a bit of everything. In addition to being a merchant, he had a small farm, which his wife and son now ran. He had a fishing boat, which two of his other sons worked around Falmouth Bay and out past the Manacles, and he also traded horses. I showed him Ventura, Vixen and Jack and the saddle the King had given me. He took a great interest in Ventura, for he occasionally traded Spanish horses from Bilbao, and rated him the finest he had ever seen.

"Sell him up here," was his advice, "you won't find anyone in the West Country who can pay the right price for a horse like that, especially with his background."

In the end I decided to keep Jack and Vixen and to sell Ventura and the King's saddle before moving back west. Jonathan told me how much I should expect to get for the two – it was three or four times what I had expected – and even suggested some possible buyers. The following morning we departed the best of friends.

"Come and see me if you're in Falmouth area. We will make you a real Cornish welcome – a 'proper job' as we call it. Stay for a week, fish, ride, we will always be pleased to see you."

In the morning, I watched him go, carrying not only my two letters, but my hopes for the future. Somehow, I felt confident that both were in good hands.

❧ CHAPTER 81 ❧

14th March 1554 – The Chapterhouse, Sheen

"Richard – a letter for you."

It seemed impossible – not a reply from Dr Marwood already – Jonathan would not have reached Honiton yet.

As soon as I saw the letter I recognized Catherine's flowery but slightly erratic handwriting.

Dear Richard,

Once again, our world is turned upside down. The Queen has heard of our mother's marriage to Adrian Stokes and she is furious. Mary and I are forbidden to live under the roof of "such a couple" as the Queen calls them, and we have been sent here to Hanworth, to live with the Dowager Duchess of Somerset. She is something of a dragon, but means well, although the house has a strangely Catholic influence and her priest is strongly of that conviction.

Anyway, anything for an easy life I say, so Mary and I have decided not to argue if the issue becomes important. At least we have some company of nearer our own age, for her son, Lord Hertford, is living at home with his sister, Lady Jane Seymour, and both have made us very welcome.

I cannot complain, for the Queen has voted me a pension of £80 a year in my own right. I think she is still upset at the way she was goaded into treating poor Jane and now regrets her decision, which she says she was forced into. In part, I am sure she blames mother for stepping aside from what she calls the "false succession" and putting Jane in the position she finally could not escape from. Mary is also treated very kindly by the Queen. Of course, as you will remember well, the Queen has almost been a family member since we were very small. Mary asks me to tell you she is well, but not grown much!

On 27th February I received official notice that my marriage to poor William Herbert has finally been annulled, so I am officially unmarried and still a virgin (Please don't tell anybody!). At least that allows me to be looked upon at the Court as a person and not as a headless goat. Nobody knew how to address me or approach me until now.

Dearest Richard, I still remember with great fondness the many wonderful times we spent together and I hope you fulfil your dreams. I shall, no doubt, remain at Court and at Hanworth until some noble Lord makes the Queen a proposal she finds fitting for me. I only hope it will be an Englishman – you know how bad my languages are.

Fondest memories,

Catherine Grey

I looked at the end of the letter. Already 'ever loving' had been reduced to 'fondest memories'. It appeared that love didn't take long to fade when there were new interests around. I wondered if Catherine's interest in Lord Hertford had been revived. Looking back, she had often mentioned his name in wistful terms when he was betrothed to Jane. What did it matter? She was gone.

They were both gone, and I missed them terribly. So much, it hurt.

❧ CHAPTER 82 ❧

April 1554 – The Chapterhouse, Sheen

As the days wore on, my confidence in Jonathan Bolitho began to fade. Had my letter reached Dr Marwood? I was sure that if he had received it, Thomas would have replied quickly – it was his manner to do so. And with each day, my position became more intolerable.

First came the reminders that I was remaining at Sheen on suf-ferance – "purely on the basis of my generosity", was the phrase Adrian liked to use, for already he was strutting around as master of the house, indulged by Lady Frances, who seemed to have been reduced to the role of simpering maiden by her new lover.

Then came the sexual innuendo. "She may have played with you once, Richard, but it takes a man to make a woman with child and that is what I am, and that is what she is." It seemed to me it was Adrian's way of getting even for the beating I had given him.

Somehow, though, I could not rise to the bait. The harsh truth was that just as Lady Frances had already obliterated Bradgate Park from her memory, so I had put the Grey family into the past in my mind; I merely needed Thomas Marwood's letter to open the door to the future.

Finally, halfway through April, the ultimatum was issued.

"Lady Frances and I have decided to return to Leicestershire. The air suits us better and we have a small manor house, more to our liking, at Beaumanor, by the village of Woodhouse. Of course, Lady Frances will occasionally visit the Court, as her daughters are Maids of Honour to the Queen, and we shall keep Sheen as a convenient resting place when she does so. However, we shall not maintain a permanent staff here, so you and your friend 'Celestial' Edmund will not be required. Perhaps you could start some little enterprise together – open a flower shop perhaps? Alternatively, you might re-apply for your old post at Shute House. I understand the Queen has given the estate to her Principal Secretary of State, Sir William Petre. You never know, he might need a man of letters?" The words were spoken in a sneering, mocking tone, which then became steely. "In any event, we will want you out of here by the end of next month, as the house will then be locked up. You had better start packing."

I had seethed. I had considered giving Adrian another beating, to remind him of the first, but there was really no point. And as Edmund unkindly (but accurately) reminded me, I did need somewhere to live until Thomas Marwood's letter arrived.

"Hold your breath Richard. The letter will come. And anyway, I like the idea of a flower shop!"

It was strange how often Edmund managed to get the last word.

23rd May 1554 – The Chapterhouse, Sheen

"Richard – a letter for you." Edmund came running down the path from the house, carrying the package.

Years later I would remember that letter arriving. It always took me back to the end of my last meeting with Lord Henry, in the Beauchamp Tower, when I had heard the gaoler's footsteps and the scrape of the key. I remembered how, for a few seconds, I had panicked, thinking the gaoler would tell me I had to remain there, rather than opening the door wide to let me out.

Now, opening the letter, I felt the same mixture of apprehension and excitement. Would the contents of this letter (as I hoped and prayed) contain the key to my escape from the Court and the disintegrating Grey family, or would it merely confirm the continuation of my imprisonment here, under the domineering, hateful rule of Adrian Stokes?

The letter was certainly from Thomas Marwood – the Doctor's handwriting was easily recognizable and Edmund confirmed that it had been delivered by a messenger boy who had been given it personally by the Doctor in London. In London? Why was Thomas Marwood there? Feverishly, I opened the letter.

Dear Richard,

First thanks for your letter, which I read with great pleasure (if tinged with sadness), and which brought back so many memories. It hardly seems three years since you set out on your great adventure; how the world has changed since then.

Second, please accept my apologies for my slowness in replying. It was not the fault of the good Bolitho, who delivered your letter safely to me in Honiton with his own hand, not a week after you had written it. However, I must, in my own defence, plead good reason for the delay, as your letter arrived immediately after a summons from Stephen Gardiner, Bishop of Winchester and Lord Chancellor, to join a medical panel, in London. Indeed, had it arrived a day later, I should already have departed on my own journey.

As you see, I am now in London, a member of the Lord Chancellor's Panel. The panel includes two royal physicians, Dr Thomas Wendy and Dr George Owen, both of whom recently examined the Princess Elizabeth at Ashridge, and who are most eminent and highly regarded. We are required to examine the condition of Edward Courtenay, Earl of Devon, who has been charged with complicity in the Wyatt uprising. He is a good Catholic who has spent the majority of his poor life in prison, and the Queen has insisted on a report as to his medical condition before further decisions are made about his future.

As a result of the Chancellor's summons, I had to rearrange my life with some rapidity and after an eventful journey (which I shall have pleasure in recounting to you when we meet), now find myself in London, waiting to be called to see the Earl. We expect this to be within days – certainly before the end of the week.

I was distressed to hear how badly events have turned out for you. Dorset was regarded as a sound man when you joined him; none of us could have predicted that his alliance with Warwick would have raised either of them so high, or that the late King's death would have thrown the country into such turmoil.

I have pondered long and hard about the thoughts you expressed in your letter, and should be honoured to accompany you back to Devon. The journey will give us ample opportunity to discuss the future. Should you wish it, I would be delighted to have you work with me, helping the sick of Honiton and the surrounding valleys, and would do all in my power to teach you the little skills I have brought back from Padua or learned since then, by (sometimes bitter) experience.

However, let us discuss it when we meet. Knowing you as I do, I expect the idea of remaining in your home country will soon be replaced by a desire for further adventures. Who knows? You have the ability and, it would appear, the financial security to attend at the University of

Oxford, or Cambridge and study the law. I am sure there are many paths which you could pursue and we shall discuss them when we meet. In the meantime, a period of relative tranquillity back home will not come amiss, and I look forward to your company on the journey.

We are likely to be accompanied by a friend of yours – Fergal Fitzpatrick, who will probably ride with us part of the way to Devon before finding a ship from Bristol or Exeter to his native Ireland. He sends his prayers and best wishes for your good health, and says he, too, is looking forward to seeing you again.

Until the pleasure of our journey home together, I remain,

Your good friend
Thomas Marwood

I read the letter twice. A feeling of warmth spread through me. I wanted to shout, to run, to cry. I looked up at the sky, then turned, slowly, taking in every detail of the view. I looked at the old monastery building, now turned into a great house, but even now, perhaps, beginning its decline. I absorbed the meadows leading down to the river, that great artery of activity which made these houses so valuable, with their easy access by boat to London. The heat of a strong May sun soaked into my muscles and the very bones beneath.

This was another of those days – days I would remember for the whole of my life, days when my life changed. I felt a great surge of energy, but at the same time, a comfortable tranquillity. It was like the first day of real strength after a debilitating illness; the removal of shackles and the opening of doors.

Slowly, smiling, I walked toward the house. I was free. I was my own man. The future was mine, and mine alone.

CHAPTER 84

28th May 1554 – The Chapterhouse, Sheen

It was settled. I had received word from Thomas that we were to depart for Devon in two days' time. I looked around the small room which I had been allowed to maintain until my departure.

With the exception of Jack, my honest stallion, and Vixen, the ever-reliable mare, both of which remained with their tack in the stables below, everything I owned in the world was cluttered around me in this room. I lay on the truckle bed, back against the wall, and surveyed the results of my life so far. In a week I would be nineteen and, God willing, back in Devon with my family and friends. What had I to show for those years?

The large box of gold – the proceeds from selling Ventura and the King's saddle to Robert Treate, meant that I was financially secure. There was certainly enough to buy a good farm, with a dry house, a reliable water supply and a view over my own land.

The sword and dagger lying at the foot of my bed were proof of my progress up the social ladder. Or were they? Perhaps all they really represented was my temporary relationship with Lord Henry Grey and his family, a relationship which was at an end.

Now they had all gone their separate ways. Catherine and little Mary were at Hanworth, no doubt already immersed in their new life there. Catherine was probably making cow eyes at Lord Hertford already – or worse. By the way she had described him, she seemed receptive enough. I would probably never find out. Very little of the Court tittle-tattle would reach me down in Devon, and my chances of returning to Court life were remote indeed. Perhaps I should follow John Aylmer's example and spend a year or two in Switzerland until, God willing, Princess Elizabeth should replace her sister on the throne of England and bring some sanity back to our country?

There was nothing left for me here. Even at this moment, Lady Frances and the newly elevated Adrian Stokes were contemplating her child-to-be and closing down this great house in preparation for their retreat to Beaumanor – for however brave a face they tried to put on it, the reality was that they were financially ruined, and socially ostracized.

Adrian would resent it; for years he had schemed his way toward what he regarded as the higher echelons of society and the prime source of the fountain of wealth. Now they had fallen off the ladder and the fountain had (by Lady Frances's demanding standards) dried up.

And Lady Frances? No doubt she would find fault in everyone else: her daughter's failure to make good the most wonderful opportunity anyone could have given to them; her husband's inability to talk the other Councillors around; and Northumberland's failure to beat Queen Mary militarily.

And then there were the dead.

I remembered with deep sadness my last visit to Lord Henry. How quickly that proud and handsome man had become diminished by the events around him. He had always treated me more than fairly and never made unreasonable demands upon me. But looking back at events with the perfect focus of hindsight, I realized that, though honest, the Duke of Suffolk was a weak man of very limited abilities, who, had he married a less ambitious woman, would probably have lived out his days on some small estate, raising his family, hunting and gambling, but making little real dent in the world outside.

Then there was Jane. My mind went back to the first time I had met her. How false were the conclusions I had drawn about her at that time. I reached across to the heavy chest at the foot of my bed and carefully lifted the book. It was all I had – that is to say, the only physical thing I had to remember her by: Bullinger's "Of Christian Perfection". Her father had told her to keep it during her long incarceration in the Tower, and on her last morning – long after she had taken her farewell from me – she had asked Nurse Ellen to make sure I had it, to remember our conversations and the principles we shared.

Carefully I turned the pages, reading a word here, a word

there, but all the time thinking of Jane. Slowly a thought developed in my mind. I had not been wrong about her on the day we had first met. By the standards of the Devon boy standing in the fireplace she was cold, she was withdrawn and she was pious. The fact that, three years later, I held this book as a memento of the woman I admired, respected and – yes – loved more than any other person in the world, was an indication not of how much she had changed, but how far I had come in understanding her.

Slowly I kissed the book and wrapped it in a spare shirt, before putting it into the chest. I walked to the small window and looked out across the meadows toward the Thames.

The question now was how easily, if at all, I would settle back into the world of my childhood. Only time would tell. I was so looking forward to that journey west, not only for the expected pleasure of the transition back to 'my own world', but for the opportunity to discuss all these issues with the two men who might be able to help me come to terms with it all.

That evening, I saw Adrian Stokes walking towards me, a smirk on his face. We approached, each smiling and stopped, face to face.

"Still here Richard? No home to go to? No friends left? I thought you would have gone by now. One more week and you'll be out on your ear!"

I inclined my head and smiled back.

"Indeed Adrian. And such pleasure at the prospect you could not imagine. My friends arrive in a few days and we will travel west together. I am looking forward to the journey and to returning to my true home."

The smirk on Adrian's face had begun to slip.

"And you Adrian? I trust Beaumanor will be to your liking. More manageable than Bradgate, no doubt. How fares Lady Frances? Well I hope, and the child to be. I wish you all well for the future."

I bowed low and walked on, slowly, and with considerable satisfaction. Tomorrow I would ride to London and deliver Ventura and the King's saddle to Robert Treate, the rich goldsmith who had bought them, and return to Sheen by river. It would be my last tie with this life finally severed; then I would be free to begin the next.

❧ CHAPTER 85 ❦

1st June 1554 – Wiltshire, near Stonehenge

"He is a good friend isn't he?" Dr Thomas Marwood watched as I waved my final farewell to Fergal Fitzpatrick.

After much discussion when we had met at Sheen, three days ago, Fergal had decided to make his way home via Bristol – there were many more ships travelling between there and the Irish coast, and as a result, we had avoided Salisbury and taken the more northerly route, through Andover and Amesbury. Fergal had sensed my sombre mood and used his Irish charm to jolly me out of it. Once started, we had laughed the whole way from Surrey to Wiltshire, until it was time for our paths to separate.

Now, on the windswept chalk uplands of Salisbury Plain, Thomas and I gave one last wave, as Fergal and his party led their pack mules and carts northwest, along the Shrewton road, towards Devizes, Bath, and the docks at Bristol.

❧   ❦

Thomas and I left the ancient stones of Stonehenge behind us and breasted the hill near Yarnbury Castle. Now, stretched before us was the way home, down across the green Wylye valley, back up over the northern shoulder of Cranbourne Chase and out into the wide flatlands of the Blackmoor Vale.

Already the character of the land was changing, and I could feel the pull of Devon, still over the horizon ahead of us. Once on the down slope of Cranbourne Chase, at Mere, I knew we would be able to see all the way past Yeovil and Illminster to the Blackdown Hills – and home country I could almost smell it already.

It was strange how quickly the memories faded as they were replaced by the images of what lay ahead.

I remembered what Adrian had said to me: "You have seen greatness and you have touched it. But remember – in all of this, you have been on the edge of that greatness and that is where you will remain – on the edge."

Was it true? Yes of course it was, as far as the past went, but as to Adrian's prediction for the future, I was not so sure. Did it matter? Right now, all I wanted to do was to find my family and re-gather my thoughts.

What had the King made me promise?

"Don't say 'Suffolk's man' ... Be your own man."

They were good words, and I would follow them; but most important of all were the last words Jane had spoken to me, the night before she died.

"Do not grieve for me, for I welcome the place to which I am going and am able to step away from this life without sorrow. Remember me as I am now. Go forward and make an honest life. Always be true to yourself and do not shrink in the face of adversity, for your soul is yours and yours alone, save for God himself."

I looked back over my shoulder, imagining, for a moment, that I might see them all behind me, waving goodbye. The low-lying mist which had shrouded the valley was burning off rapidly as the June sun rose higher in the sky and gained in strength. It was going to be a beautiful day.